... you,

without him they won't get their han...
They're going to have to reassess the situation, and
that can only work in our favour.'

'And how do you work that one out? Because the
way I see it, we're still going to have to get the disk
for them.'

'But it gives us time,' Beth pointed out.

'To do *what*?'

'I don't know that yet.'

'We give them the disk, Beth. We don't start playing heroes with these people. They're professionals.'

'They also murdered my husband in cold blood,'
Beth retorted, her eyes blazing. 'He died for that
disk. And if they get hold of it now they've won.
Don't you see that? I owe it to Ian to do everything
in my power to try to bring them to justice.'

'Not if it means putting my son's life on the line.
You play by their rules, Beth,' Novak levelled a
warning finger at her, 'because if you don't, and
something happens to John, I'll be the one coming
after you. Not them. You just remember that.'

Also by Alastair MacNeill in paperback

MOONBLOOD
DOUBLE-BLIND

Soon to be available in hardcover

COUNTERPLOT

ALASTAIR MACNEILL

DAMAGE
CONTROL

ORION

An Orion Paperback
First published in Great Britain in 1998
by Victor Gollancz
This paperback edition published in 1999 by
Orion Books Ltd,
Orion House, 5 Upper St Martin's Lane,
London WC2H 9EA

A CIP catalogue record for this book
is available from the British Library.

ISBN: 0 75282 729 4

Printed and bound in Great Britain by
Clays Ltd, St Ives plc

PREFACE

All he had to do was squeeze the trigger. Dressed in black, his face streaked with camouflage cream, he lay motionless on the lip of the ridge, his body concealed by the dense foliage around him. The powerful night scope, attached to a TRG 21 sniper rifle, was focused on the man in the white towelling robe crouched at the edge of the illuminated swimming-pool below, talking to a woman who was treading water a few feet away from him. He was in his late thirties with a pale complexion and a wispy beard. The woman climbed out of the pool and he tossed a towel in her direction then crossed to a set of cheap plastic pool furniture and sat down. The woman, in an ill-fitting one-piece costume that accentuated her plump figure, towelled her wet hair as she continued to talk to him. He seemed uninterested in what she was saying and glanced impatiently towards the house. He shouted in exasperation and, on receiving no reply, threw up his hands in disgust and reached for the bottle of wine on the table beside him. The sniper tweaked the night scope fractionally to focus the man's forehead between the fine cross hairs. All he had to do was squeeze the trigger . . .

Suddenly a female voice called out. The man looked round in his chair, his mouth curled in a salacious grin. The sniper instinctively tilted the night scope to follow his gaze until he picked out the woman who had emerged from the house. She was beautiful. Probably still in her late teens, with an exquisite figure and black hair cascading down on to slender, tanned shoulders. She took the bottle from the man and, putting it to her lips, drank greedily until the wine seeped from the corners of her mouth, down her neck and across her small breasts. The man pulled her roughly down on to his lap and she giggled as he licked the wine from her skin. She jumped to her feet and deftly evaded his hand when he tried to grab her arm to pull her back towards him. The other woman moved behind him and slid her hands down his chest, underneath his towelling robe, but he shrugged her off. When she tried to kiss his neck he turned round in his chair and slapped her viciously across the face. She stumbled backwards, her hand clutched to her bleeding lip. The teenager scoffed at her then straddled the man on the chair and made no attempt to stop him when he reached behind her to unfasten the top half of her bikini.

The sniper felt no sympathy for the spurned older woman. No disdain for the dissolute teenager. No compassion for the man he was about to kill. This was a contract and he prided himself on his professionalism. He waited patiently for a clear shot while the man caressed the teenager's breasts as she sat astride him, her head thrown back in rapture as his hands explored her skin. The moment came when she climbed off him then knelt down in front of his chair and eased down the front of his swimming trunks.

The sniper squeezed the trigger. The bullet took the man in the centre of the forehead, propelling him backwards in the chair. He landed face down on the patio, a gaping hole in the back of his head where the soft-nosed bullet had exited his skull. The older woman looked down slowly, almost as if in a trance, at the blood and gristle that had sprayed across her bare legs. She began to scream. The teenager, in a state of shock, instinctively reached for the discarded top of her bikini and clutched it to her naked breasts. Only then did she force herself to look at the dead man. She, too, began to scream.

But by then the sniper had already ghosted away into the night.

ONE

Wednesday

'I know you said you didn't want to be disturbed, Beth, but there's a policeman here to see you.'

'Not again!' Elizabeth Grant rasped into the telephone. 'Show him into my office,' she instructed her secretary, 'tell him I'll be along shortly.' She replaced the handset then looked across the table at Emma Kendry, her partner in Kendry Grant Associates, an élite London-based recruitment agency, which specialized in head-hunting senior executives, mainly from within the thriving financial sector of the city. 'We'll have to reschedule the meeting,' she said, then gathered up the loose sheets of paper on the desk, slipped them back into the folder she had brought with her for the weekly conference in Emma's office, and got to her feet. 'The Fraud Squad are back . . . again. I honestly thought I'd seen the last of them after Mark went to jail.'

'I'll call you when I get back from lunch and arrange a time to reschedule the meeting,' Emma called after Beth, as she headed for the door. 'We got most of it done today anyway.'

Beth acknowledged Emma with a wave over her shoulder as she left the office. She closed the door behind her. It wasn't just the Fraud Squad that she'd hoped to have seen the last of after the trial five years earlier. If there was to be another trial – and she was called as a witness – she would encounter Mark Lee again. With hindsight, she couldn't believe just how infatuated

7

she had been with him at the time. But, then, it was always easy to be wise after the event. *Love is blind*, she thought contemptuously. She had been so blinkered that she'd been incapable of seeing the devious character he had hidden so well behind his good looks and acute financial mind. He had caused her so much anguish, especially when he had tried to implicate her in his insider deals shortly after his arrest. It had been a desperate, and cowardly, attempt to shift the blame away from himself. The police weren't taken in, and no charges were ever brought against her. But that was in the past. She had a new life now. A husband whom she adored. A partner in business whom she trusted implicitly and who also happened to be her best friend. She was godmother to Emma's two-year-old daughter. Life was treating her well. She didn't need to have her past mistakes dredged up all over again . . .

Beth was thirty-four, and kept in shape by attending aerobics classes with Emma three times a week at a health studio a couple of blocks away from their plush offices in Kensington. She had strong, attractive features and shoulder-length natural blonde hair, which she usually wore in a ponytail. Although she never consciously played on her looks, they gave her a self-assured confidence which, at times, could be said to border on arrogance. She was the first to admit as much. But, then, she knew she was beautiful. She'd never had a problem with that.

She entered her outer office and her secretary nodded when she gestured to the closed door. She strode briskly across the deep-pile carpet, pushed open the door and swept into her office. The man, who had been sitting in the leather armchair against the adjacent wall, got to his feet. It wasn't the same officer who had questioned her earlier in the week. She put him in his mid-forties. He was wearing an off-the-peg suit. Not particularly fashionable.

'I'm Detective Inspector David Aldrich,' he said, producing his warrant card. 'Are you Mrs Elizabeth Grant?'

'Yes,' Beth said indignantly, tossing the folder on to her desk.

Then she swung round to face him, anger in her eyes. 'As I told your colleague on Tuesday, Mark didn't confide anything to me about his little scam. It's all there in the transcripts of the trial, if one of you had bothered to read them. Maybe then you'd stop harassing me and let me get on with my life.'

'I'm afraid I don't know what you're talking about, Mrs Grant,' came the puzzled reply.

'You are from the Fraud Squad, aren't you?' Beth said uncertainly.

'No, I'm with the Metropolitan CID.'

'So this has got nothing to do with Mark Lee?'

'No. I'm afraid I've got some bad news for you.' He indicated the padded leather swivel chair behind the desk. 'I think it would be best if you were to sit down.'

'Don't patronize me,' Beth countered, but there was now an unease in her voice that she couldn't hide. 'Just tell me why you're here.'

'Please, Mrs Grant,' Aldrich said, gesturing to the chair again.

She sat down slowly. 'Is it Ian? Has something happened to him?'

'I'm afraid so,' Aldrich said, holding her stare. 'Your husband was shot last night.'

'Oh, my God.' Beth swallowed, then said, 'How serious is it?'

'I'm afraid he's dead, Mrs Grant. I'm very sorry.'

'Dead?' She shook her head as if trying to ward off what he had just told her. 'That's impossible. We spoke on the phone last night. Just last night. He's not even in the country. He hasn't been for the past few days. You must be mistaken. It can't be him.'

'It happened in Zürich around eleven o'clock last night,' Aldrich replied, then paused to check his notebook. 'He was shot outside a jazz club called Straight Street.'

'Ian doesn't even like jazz. He would never have gone there.

Not a jazz club. Not Ian. No, not Ian.' She was talking rapidly, almost incoherently, as if trying to convince herself that none of what she had been told was true.

'Mrs Grant—'

'Ian doesn't like jazz, don't you understand that?' she said, getting to her feet and moving to the window. She stared down absently into the busy street below, but there was no recognition in her eyes at what she saw. 'He likes classical music,' she told Aldrich, without looking at him. 'Brahms. Beethoven. Mozart. Not jazz. Never jazz.'

Aldrich put a hand lightly on her arm. 'Please, Mrs Grant, sit down.'

'Not jazz,' she said, as tears trickled down her cheeks. 'Not . . . jazz . . .'

Aldrich tightened his grip on her arm when her legs buckled and he helped her back to the chair. Having noted earlier the crystal decanters on the sideboard, he quickly poured a measure of brandy and returned to where she was sitting with the tumbler. Her hands were trembling and, unsure whether she might drop it were he to let go, he put the tumbler to her lips. She took a sip then pushed away the glass. He tried to get her to drink a little more but she buried her face in her hands and sobbed uncontrollably.

The telephone rang. Aldrich was quick to answer it. 'Could I speak to Beth Grant please?' a female voice inquired.

'I'm afraid she's unavailable right now,' Aldrich said.

'This is her partner, Emma Kendry. Why can't she come to the phone?'

'Mrs Kendry, my name's Detective Inspector Aldrich. I've just had to break some very distressing news to Mrs Grant. I think it would be best if you were to come to her office. She could certainly do with your support right now.'

Aldrich remained discreetly in the background as Emma comforted Beth by the window. He noticed that she had shed tears of her own as she hugged Beth, but he wasn't sure whether she was crying for her friend's loss or for the death of Ian Grant.

When Beth eased herself from her friend's embrace her eyes were red and her cheeks smeared with mascara. She wiped her palms across her face but only succeeded in further smudging the mascara. Emma took a paper tissue from the box on the desk and wet a section but Beth stopped her when she tried to wipe away the mascara.

She turned to Aldrich. 'Would you excuse me, please? I'll be back shortly.' Her voice was calm and, without waiting for a reply, she crossed to the adjoining bathroom and closed the door behind her. When she re-emerged a few minutes later she had washed her face and applied fresh makeup. 'I apologize for breaking down in front of you like that,' she said, matter-of-factly, to Aldrich before sitting down behind her desk again. The earlier vulnerability had gone. Now there was a determined edge to her voice, which caught him by surprise.

'You really have nothing to apologize for, Mrs Grant,' Aldrich said.

'Please, won't you sit down, Detective Inspector?' Beth said, gesturing to the sofa against the wall behind him. 'Would you care for something to drink?' she added, clasping her hands together on the desk in front of her. 'Tea? Coffee? Something stronger, perhaps.' She laughed fleetingly. 'Sorry, I forgot. You can't drink on duty, can you?'

'No, nothing, thank you.' Aldrich had seen relatives in denial before when trying to come to terms with the death of a loved one. Beth Grant had displayed those signs when he had first broken the news to her that her husband was dead. He could understand that. But he'd never seen a transformation like this. One minute she was openly grieving. The next she appeared to be in total control. Almost as if she'd flicked some internal switch while she had been in the bathroom. It unnerved him. He shot an uneasy glance in Emma's direction and noticed that she was watching Beth closely. Unlike Aldrich, she understood exactly what Beth was doing. Beth had displayed a vulnerability, which she would regard as weakness, especially in front of a stranger. Now she was taking control of the situation once more. *Control.* Beth always had to be in control. Now more than ever. Ian was dead. Beth had to be hurting inside more than she could ever imagine. Yet the barriers were up again. She was single-minded, hard-headed, cold-hearted. *No, not cold-hearted.* It just sometimes seemed that way with Beth . . .

'Sit, Emma,' Beth said sharply, as if she were ordering a dog to heel.

Emma bit back a retort and sat down. For a moment she thought Beth's obstinacy was going to break when she lowered her eyes and stared at her clenched hands but, after several deep breaths, she raised her head again and focused on Aldrich. 'I'd appreciate it if you would tell me exactly what happened at this club last night.'

'I don't have all the details as yet, just what was passed on to me by the Swiss authorities earlier this morning,' Aldrich replied, almost apologetically.

'Then tell me what you know.'

'It would seem that your husband was at Straight Street with an American woman – Amy Michaels.' Aldrich paused to gauge any reaction to the name. There was none. 'Do you know her, Mrs Grant?'

'No. Should I?' Beth brushed a loose strand of hair away from her face. 'I don't know anyone in Zürich, Detective Inspector. I've never even been there. It's where Ian conducted a lot of his business. Perhaps Amy Michaels was a business associate that he'd gone out there to meet.'

'No, she wasn't,' Aldrich replied. 'The Swiss authorities have checked that out already. In fact, she seems to be something of a mystery. All they know about her is that she checked into the same hotel on the day your husband arrived in Zürich. They were seen together several times after that. But nobody knows who she is.'

'Did she kill Ian?' Beth asked bluntly.

Again, her apparent coldness caught Aldrich off guard. 'Several witnesses saw your husband leave the club shortly after eleven last night. He exited through a side door leading into an alley. She went after him. The Swiss authorities don't know as yet whether he knew she was following him. A short time later a member of staff heard a noise in the alley. When he went to investigate he saw Amy Michaels crouched over your husband's body. She was holding a gun in her hand. She saw the man and fled. She hasn't been seen since but all airports and border posts have been alerted. The local police are confident that she's still in the country. It's only a matter of time before they find her.'

'Who's handling the arrangements to return Ian's body to London?' Beth asked. 'The British or American embassy? Ian was an American.'

'I believe the American consulate in Zürich are dealing with it.'

'Then that's who I'll contact when I get out there,' Beth said.

'There's really no reason for you to go to Zürich, Mrs Grant. The consulate will see to everything.'

'On the contrary, I think there's every reason for me to go to Zürich,' Beth said. 'My husband's dead, Detective Inspector. Shot outside a jazz club by some mysterious woman who's now on the run. Ian hated jazz. So what was he doing there in the first place? That alone makes no sense unless he was meeting someone at the club. If so, whom? Was it Amy Michaels? Who is she? Why did she kill him? I want answers. And the only way I'm going to get them is to fly to Zürich.'

'The Swiss police will be investigating every aspect of the case. I have every confidence that they'll have Amy Michaels in custody before too long.'

'You'll forgive me if I reserve judgement until I get there.' Beth picked up her phone and rang her secretary in the outer office. 'Karen, book me on the next available flight to Zürich –

and a room at the Zum Storchen Hotel. It's where Ian always stayed when he was there on business. Call me back as soon as you've confirmed the bookings.' She replaced the receiver then got to her feet. 'I appreciate you coming here in person, Detective Inspector. I know it would have been a lot easier for you to have broken the news to me over the phone.'

'Mrs Grant, I would still advise you against going to Zürich,' Aldrich told her. 'The local police won't appreciate you interfering with their investigation.'

'I have no intention of interfering with their investigation,' Beth replied, surprised. 'I knew Ian better than anyone. I believe that puts me in a unique position to be able to help them with their inquiries. Surely that can't be a bad thing.'

Aldrich handed her his card. 'That's my number at the Yard should you need me. Please feel free to call me at any time. Again, may I say how sorry I am for your loss.'

Beth looked down. 'Thank you,' she said.

Emma saw Aldrich to the door and closed it again behind him. 'What he said made a lot of sense, Beth. You don't need to go to Zürich. Let the local police handle the investigation.'

Beth wiped her eyes. 'Ian was one of this country's leading human rights lawyers. And that meant he had a lot of enemies. Powerful enemies with money behind them. He was always the first to admit that. How do I know that the Swiss government aren't involved in some way with his death?'

'Come on, Beth, you sound just like Ian with one of his conspiracy theories,' Emma said, before she could check herself. She immediately regretted her tactless outburst but made no move to comfort Beth when she turned away from her. It wouldn't have been appreciated. She noticed Beth brush her hand across her cheeks. 'I'm sorry, Beth. That was totally insensitive of me. I know the hell you must be going through right now.'

'Do you?' Beth swung round. She made no attempt to stem the fresh tears which streamed down her cheeks. 'I don't think you have the faintest idea of just how I'm feeling right now. Ian's dead, Emma. My Ian . . .'

'Sit down,' Emma said softly, and eased her into the nearest chair. 'You cry all you want. Let it out, Beth. Let it out.' She cursed silently when the telephone rang and crossed to the desk to answer it. Beth's flight and hotel room had been booked.

'When's the flight?' Beth asked, after Emma had hung up. The tears had stopped.

'Six thirty-five tonight. From Heathrow. You can pick up your ticket at the flight desk.'

'Aren't you going to try to stop me?' Beth challenged. 'You seemed to agree with Aldrich's reservations about me going to Zürich. Do you think I should play the grieving widow and sit dutifully by the telephone waiting for news to filter through from Scotland Yard?'

'I know quite well that once you've set your mind on a course of action, nothing's going to stop you.'

'I have to go, Emma,' Beth faltered, 'if only for my own peace of mind. You do understand that, don't you?'

'Yes,' Emma replied.

Beth got to her feet and pulled on her coat. 'I'd better get back to the house. I've still got a few things to do before I leave for Zürich.'

'I'll give you a lift home,' Emma offered.

'I can drive myself,' Beth assured her, 'and, anyway, you're taking a client out to lunch today.'

'I can cancel that.'

'No!' Beth snapped. 'That's an important account, Emma. We need to keep them sweet.'

'I think, given the circumstances, he'd understand,' Emma said.

'I'll be fine,' Beth smiled. 'Honestly. But I wouldn't say no to a lift to the airport this afternoon. Say three thirty?'

'I'll be there.'

'You always are, and that's what makes you so special to me.

Don't you ever forget that.' Beth hugged her friend, then left the room.

It was only when she got home that the full impact of Ian's death hit her. At the office she had still been able to distance herself from the reality of the situation. There had been nothing personal to remind her of him. No photographs of him on her desk. No mementoes of his endless travels on the walls. She had never been one for that kind of sentimentality.

Yet the moment she opened the front door she was swamped by a deluge of memories that engulfed her. Wherever she looked, whatever she saw, she was reminded of Ian. Jumbled recollections emerged from her subconscious. She stumbled down the hallway, kicking off her shoes as she went, and into the lounge, where she headed for the drinks cabinet. Her hands were trembling as she poured herself a whisky, which she downed in a single gulp. At that moment she would have drunk herself unconscious if she thought it would have helped. But she knew it wouldn't bring Ian back. And neither would it douse the pain burning deep inside her. She suddenly felt angry with him. How could he leave her like this? Now, when she desperately needed the security of his love, he wasn't there for her. *Let it out, Beth. Let it out.* She was crying uncontrollably, hurting inside more than she could ever have imagined.

Her eyes went to the bottle of whisky. She wanted another drink, which was so unlike her. She had never been drunk in her life. Well, she did get a little tipsy at Emma's wedding. She found herself smiling through the tears as memories of the reception came back to her. She had managed to haul Ian on to the dance floor, which in itself was a feat worthy of a mention in the Queen's Honours List. Ian *never* danced, apart from once at their own wedding five years earlier, after the service at the small church in Dornoch, deep in the Scottish Highlands. He had refused to wear a kilt or even Grant tartan trousers. But, then, that was Ian. Shy. Taciturn. Even remote at times.

But, in his own quiet way, just as self-confident as her. She realized that her anger had dissipated. Acceptance? Maybe she was jumping the gun. She crossed to the drinks cabinet, screwed the top back on the whisky bottle. She wouldn't be needing any more to drink. She was past the self-pity, the anger, the bitterness. She looked at the clock on the mantelpiece. She still had a couple of hours before Emma was due to pick her up. She decided to take a bath. Then she would pack. She walked through to the bathroom, turned on the water, and as she began to undress another thought came to mind.

Who was Amy Michaels?

TWO

The flying time from London to Zürich was an hour and forty minutes but, with the Continent being an hour ahead of GMT, it was 9.15 p.m. when the Boeing 757 touched down at Kloten Airport and taxied to a berth close to the terminal building. Beth had travelled first class as those had been the only seats still available at such short notice. Normally she would never have indulged in such extravagance, but she had to admit that she'd enjoyed being pampered by the flight attendants. The attention had helped her. And that had been important. It had allowed her to concentrate on Amy Michaels. How had Ian met her? Why had they met at the jazz club? Had she duped him into going there? Had he gone there willingly? Were they friends? More than friends? *Had he slept with her?*

How many times had she tortured herself with *that* question? And each time she had dismissed the idea as absurd. Ian with another woman? Preposterous. So why did the question keep returning to haunt her? She had always trusted him implicitly and hated herself for even thinking that he could have been unfaithful to her.

She was one of the last passengers to disembark and after clearing Passport Control she made her way to the baggage collection area. A battered canvas backpack from an earlier flight was the only piece of luggage on the carousel. She watched it revolving slowly and found herself wondering to whom it belonged. Had it been forgotten? She pushed the thought from her mind when the first pieces of luggage from her flight emerged into view. She didn't have to wait long for her suitcase and, placing it on a trolley along with her overnight bag, she walked unchallenged through the green zone and out into the concourse. She remembered Ian telling her on more than one occasion that, much as he enjoyed his trips to Switzerland, he could never get over just how expensive it was compared to the rest of Europe. Taxi fares, in particular, were exorbitant. He always used the feeder train to travel the ten minutes from the airport to the city's main railway station then completed the remainder of his journey to the hotel in a taxi. It was cheaper and quicker than taking a taxi in from the airport. She was about to make for the escalator leading down to the station when she heard her name announced over the public-address system. She was asked to report to the information desk. She was puzzled, and not a little unnerved. She hadn't expected to be met off the plane. It was with trepidation that she crossed to the information desk and identified herself to the assistant behind the counter. She was directed to a man standing a short distance away. He had short blond hair and a firm, well-toned physique but what caught her eye was his too-tight grey suit.

'Mrs Grant?' he asked, when she approached him.

'Yes,' she replied warily.

'Richard Kerwin, I'm with the American consulate here in Zürich.' He held out his ID card for her to see. 'May I express my deepest sympathies to you over your tragic loss.'

'Thank you, but to be perfectly honest I wasn't expecting a welcoming party,' she said.

'The British consulate rang us earlier today to say that you were on your way out here. They told us which flight you would be on, and as we're handling the arrangements to have your husband's body returned to London, we thought it only right to meet you at the airport and offer you any assistance we can while you're here in Zürich.'

'Has Amy Michaels been arrested yet?' Beth asked.

'Not as yet, no, but I'm told that the Swiss police have several important leads. I'm sure it will only be a matter of time before she's taken into custody.'

'I'll believe that when it happens,' Beth said shortly.

'I have a car outside to take you to your hotel. Allow me,' he said, and picked up her suitcase and overnight bag before leading the way to the main doors.

'Did you know my husband?' Beth asked, as the automatic doors slid open and they stepped out into the cool night air.

'I'm afraid not. I've only been out here the past week.'

'And as the newest kid on the block, you get the thankless task of chaperoning the grieving widow around Zürich,' she said.

'I can assure you it's not like that at all, Mrs Grant.'

Beth stopped abruptly. 'It's really not necessary, Mr Kerwin. I don't need a chaperon. I can look after myself.'

'As I said, Mrs Grant, I'm merely here as a contact should you need any assistance from the American consulate while you're in Zürich.'

Beth managed a weak smile. 'I'm sorry. It's just that it's been . . . a really long day.'

'I can believe that,' he replied, then handed her luggage to the driver who had got out of the stationary black Mercedes and hurried towards them. The cases were deposited in the boot then the driver opened the back door for them.

'Where to, sir?' the driver asked after getting back behind the wheel.

'Where are you staying, Mrs Grant?' Kerwin asked.

'The Zum Storchen Hotel,' she replied.

The driver activated the soundproof panel between the front

and back seats then started up the vehicle and drove towards the exit.

'Do you know why your husband was here in Zürich, Mrs Grant?'

The question caught Beth by surprise. She gave a quick shrug. 'I assumed it had something to do with his work as a human rights lawyer. Ian often came to Zürich. Why do you ask?'

'From what we can gather from the local police, we have reason to believe that your husband's recent visits to Zürich had nothing to do with his work. At least, not directly.'

'Then what *was* he doing here?' Beth asked when Kerwin fell silent.

'We don't know exactly,' Kerwin replied. 'He rang the consulate two days ago and spoke to the chargé d'affaires. He seemed agitated. He said that he had some information that he wanted to pass on personally to our ambassador in Bern.'

'What kind of information?'

'We don't know that either, other than it was contained on a floppy disk. That's all he would reveal at the time. But he did say that he would contact the consulate again today with more information.'

'Are you suggesting that he was murdered because of this disk?'

'I'm not suggesting anything, Mrs Grant. There was no disk on the body. And neither was it in his hotel room. Of course, the assassin could have taken it . . . last night.'

'You mean Amy Michaels?' Beth said bluntly.

'We won't know that until she's been apprehended. I realize that this may appear insensitive at a time like this, but I have to ask you whether you've received any packages from your husband in the last couple of days.'

'No, I haven't.'

'I had to ask, you understand. If he was killed because of the disk, it's imperative that we locate it. And quickly.' Kerwin peered out of the window when the Mercedes drew to a halt in the cobbled courtyard in front of the hotel. 'Ah, here we are. I'll call you in the morning and let you know if there've been any new developments.'

'Why don't you just give me your card? That way I can call you at my discretion.'

Kerwin felt in his pockets then gave her a sheepish grin. 'I don't have a card on me, but I'll give you the number of the consulate as well as my direct line. If you can't get through to me, just leave a message with the switchboard operator and I'll get back to you as soon as I can.' He jotted down two numbers in his notepad, tore off the sheet and handed it to her. 'Again, my deepest sympathies.'

'Thank you,' Beth said, then got out of the car. The driver handed her luggage to a porter and Beth followed him into the lobby and announced herself to the receptionist. She was asked to complete the registration card then the receptionist withdrew into the back office to make a phone call. Beth had already guessed that she was calling her superior and a short time later a bespectacled man in a black jacket and pinstriped trousers emerged from the lift and crossed to the desk. He introduced himself as the general manager of the hotel and offered her his condolences, adding that if there was anything she needed she must contact either him or any member of his management team. All the relevant numbers had been typed up on a sheet of paper and left beside the telephone in her room.

'I appreciate the offer, but I'd just as soon be treated like any other guest,' Beth told him. 'I neither expect, nor want, preferential treatment while I'm staying here. But thank you all the same.'

'As you wish,' the manager replied, then watched as the receptionist handed a key to the porter. 'We have reserved a river-facing room for you. It has a magnificent view of the Limmat. Quite breathtaking at night.'

'I look forward to seeing it, but right now I'd like you to call a taxi for me. I want to go to the jazz club Straight Street. Is it far from here?'

'You won't need a taxi. It's only a few minutes' walk from here. On the other side of the river. In the Old Town. Let me show you where it is.' He told the porter to take her luggage up to the room then led her across to the concierge's desk to get a tourist map of the city. He unfolded it, indicated the hotel with a cross and drew a circle to represent the location of Straight Street. 'The Rathaus Bridge is right next to the hotel. Cross it and you are in the Niederdorf, part of the Old Town. It is the hub of Zürich's night life, but perfectly safe to walk around at night, even for a woman on her own.'

'Do you know who owns the club?' Beth asked.

'Mike Novak.'

'He doesn't sound Swiss,' Beth said.

'He's an American. He was married to Christina Baumann. You may have heard of her.'

'Can't say I have,' Beth replied.

'She was a model in the eighties. She came from Zürich. I believe she met him while she was in America. They settled over here after they got married.'

'You talk about her in the past tense. Is she dead?'

'Yes.'

'Did you know my husband?' Beth asked. 'He always stayed here whenever he was in Zürich.'

'Yes, I knew him. We occasionally had a drink together. Charming man, I liked him.'

'And did you know Amy Michaels?' Beth asked.

'No, I never met her,' he said brusquely. 'I believe this was her first stay here. She kept very much to herself. Even the staff were hard pressed to give the police a description of her.'

'Do you know what she did?'

The manager was clearly embarrassed by Beth's questions. 'Something to do with computers. A programmer, I believe it

23

is called. At least that is what she put down on the registration card. But, then, she could just as easily have made that up, not so?' He held out his hand towards her. 'Again, my condolences to you on your loss.'

'Thank you,' Beth said. The manager headed for the elevator and stepped inside. The doors closed behind him.

She found the club without much difficulty but it wasn't as she had imagined it. You've been watching too many old Hollywood movies, she thought ruefully. There was no garish neon sign in the shape of a musical instrument on the outside wall, no bouncers at the door. Instead she found herself looking at a bland, whitewashed exterior with the words *Straight Street* painted in italics above the entrance. A single window, with pale blue curtains drawn across it, faced out on to the cobbled side-street where she was standing. An oblong-shaped box, with a glass façade, was fixed to the wall close to the door. Inside was a schedule of gigs for the following months. It also contained a colour photograph of the resident band, Martinique.

She went inside but was stopped by a youth seated behind a wooden table in the foyer. She was asked to pay a nominal cover charge, then given a ticket and directed to the open double doors further down the corridor. She paused in the doorway to look around her. This was more as she had envisaged it: a spacious, smoke-filled room with a bar running the length of one wall and the stage directly ahead. A tape was playing through the loudspeakers at either end of the stage. Three men were on stage, the word Martinique displayed prominently across the face of the bass drum. A fourth man climbed up the stairs at the side of the stage and called out something to his colleagues. There was a ripple of laughter from the occupants of the tables in front of the stage. The man grinned when the guitarist, who was crouched down beside one of the speakers, waved him away.

The club was packed and Beth had to negotiate a route

through the tables to reach the bar. One of the barmen said something to her in German that she didn't understand. 'I'm looking for Mike Novak,' she told him.

The barman scanned the room then pointed to a table directly in front of the stage. He asked her if she wanted a drink and when she declined he went to serve another customer at the far end of the counter. She was about to call out to him and ask him which of the three men at the table was Novak when the band began to play. She made her way to the table where the three men were sitting with a woman, not much older than herself. She put her hand lightly on the shoulder of the man nearest her to get his attention. 'I'm looking for Mike Novak,' she said close to his ear.

He indicated the man seated beside him, wearing an open-necked white shirt and a pair of jeans and, patting him on the knee, indicated Beth standing behind them. 'Are you Mike Novak?' she asked. He nodded. 'I'm Beth Grant. Ian Grant was my husband.'

Novak stared at her for a moment, then excused himself from the table and beckoned her to follow him. He led her to a side door, then down a corridor to a black-painted door. Pushing it open, he switched on the light then gestured her to enter. The walls were lined with framed photographs of inter-nationally renowned jazz musicians, many of the photographs taken at the club, and all with an accompanying dedication written across them. She noticed that Novak didn't appear in any of them. He moved a pile of invoices from a chair and dumped them on top of yet more invoices on his desk. He indicated for her to sit down and eased himself into the padded leather swivel chair behind the desk.

It was the first time that she had seen him properly. She estimated him to be in his late thirties, and he was good-looking, tanned, with tousled collar-length black hair streaked with flecks of grey. 'I'm sorry about Ian,' he said, breaking the silence.

'You make it sound as if you knew him?' she asked, surprised that Novak referred to him by his first name.

'Yeah, I knew Ian,' Novak replied with a quick shrug. 'He always came here whenever he was in Zürich. What I didn't know was that he was married. He certainly never mentioned that to me.'

'You must have seen the wedding ring,' Beth said.

Novak was about to say something, paused, then sat back in his chair and propped the sole of his shoe against the side of the desk. 'I guess I didn't see it.'

'You mean you never saw him wearing it,' she said. 'Please don't patronize me, Mr Novak. I'm beginning to realize that there was more to Ian than met the eye. I always thought he hated jazz. Not only was he in a jazz club on the night he was murdered, but now I discover that he used to come here whenever he was in Zürich.'

'I think it's best if you speak to Inspector Stefan Kessler. He's in charge of the case. I've already given him a statement.'

'I'm sure I'll speak to him in due course,' she said, 'but right now I want you to tell me what you knew about Ian. You have to understand, this is a side of him I never knew. That's why I have to know, Mr Novak.' She saw the uncertainty in his eyes. 'Please, if only for my own peace of mind.'

'I don't think Ian particularly liked jazz,' Novak said after a thoughtful silence. 'We certainly never discussed it. He used to come here . . . well, because it's discreet.'

'Discreet?' Beth said uncertainly. 'What exactly are you saying?'

'I don't think this is—'

'What exactly are you saying?' she cut in angrily, this time stressing each word forcefully. He held her stare, but said nothing. 'If you're worried about having to deal with a grieving widow weeping hysterically in your office, forget it. I did my crying back home. And to be perfectly honest, if you're implying what I think you are, tears will be the last thing on my mind.'

'Ian used to bring women to the club,' Novak admitted. 'As I said, it's discreet. We have several secluded booths on the second floor where ... well, you know. Let's just say they're very private.'

'Women? Plural?' Beth hissed, her eyes blazing. 'Who exactly were these *women*?'

'I didn't know any of them,' he said, purposely avoiding eye contact. 'Ian would introduce them to me when I went to have a drink with him, but the names never meant anything to me. They were all locals, or at least they were Swiss. That much I do know.'

'Let's try that again, shall we? Only this time tell me the truth.'

Novak let his foot drop to the floor then he sat forward, his arms resting on the desk. 'I was telling you the truth when I said I didn't know any of them. At least not personally. But there was one ... Well, I'd seen her in here before. Just by sight, you understand. She was quite a looker. That's why I remembered her face. She charged by the hour. Very expensive. Very classy, if you get my meaning.'

'In other words, she was a prostitute,' Beth concluded.

'We're not talking about some stepper here. You'd never catch her on the streets. I was surprised that Ian could ...' Novak's voice trailed off uncomfortably.

'Afford her – is that what you were going to say? That makes two of us. I did all of Ian's accounts. He was hopeless with his finances. If he'd been paying for the services of prostitutes while he was out of the country then I think I'd have noticed some discrepancy in his expenses, don't you? So it begs the question, who was footing the bill?'

'I don't want to appear insensitive, Mrs Grant, but this really has nothing to do with me. With hindsight I realize now that I shouldn't have said anything to you about it in the first place.'

'I'm glad you did. Admittedly it throws up more questions than answers, but that's been the case right from the start, hasn't it? What do you know about Amy Michaels?'

'Nothing. I didn't even meet her. In fact, I never spoke to Ian last night. We were so busy I ended up working as a stand-in barman.'

'So where does she fit into all this? She's not local, which would imply that she probably wasn't one of his whores. So why bring her here?'

'As I said just now, the best thing for you to do is speak to Kessler. From what I understand, he's got the best clear-up rate of any detective in Zürich. Not only will he be able to bring you up to speed on any developments, but he'll certainly know a lot more about the case than I do. The first I knew about the shooting was when the alarm was raised. I was behind the bar when it happened.'

'Did Kessler say anything about a disk that Ian may have had with him last night?' she asked.

'No. Why do you ask?'

'The man from the American consulate mentioned it in the car on the way to the hotel. What was his name again? Kerwin. That's right. Richard Kerwin.' Beth noticed the look of doubt flash across Novak's face. 'What is it?' she asked anxiously.

'You've obviously got the wrong name. I know all the consulate staff well. They often come here to kick back and have a few drinks. There's no Richard Kerwin at the consulate.'

'That was definitely the name. He even showed me his consulate pass. He did say that he'd only been here for a week,' she replied uneasily.

'I would have heard about him even if I hadn't met him. But let me check anyway.' Novak opened the diary on his desk, found the number he wanted, then reached for the telephone and dialled out. He got through to the duty officer at the American consulate. 'Hey, Dan, it's Mike Novak. How you doing?' He chuckled at the reply, his eyes never leaving Beth's face. 'Dan, have you got a new guy working there? Name of Richard Kerwin.' His face remained impassive as he listened to the reply. 'Yeah, that's what I thought. No, it's nothing. Just a rumour I heard. Thought I'd better check it out anyway just in case you guys were holding out on me.' He chuckled again. 'Thanks, Dan. See you at the weekend, eh? 'Bye.' He replaced the receiver. 'Just as I thought. Nobody by that name at the consulate.'

Beth shuddered. 'Then who was he, and how did he know I'd be on that particular flight? The airline wouldn't have given out those details. He must have had inside information.'

'There's obviously a lot more to this than first meets the eye. That's why it's essential that you talk to Kessler as soon as possible. Tell him everything.'

'I will,' she said softly, then got to her feet and extended her hand towards Novak. 'Thank you for your time, and for being so honest with me. I appreciate it.'

'Not at all,' Novak replied, gripping her hand gently, but firmly.

'I'll see myself out,' Beth told him, and left his office. She made her way back to the club where the band were still playing. Not that she took any notice of them. She had to get out. She desperately needed some fresh air. Clear her thoughts. She emerged into the foyer and wiped a trembling hand across her clammy forehead. Her body heaved and she clamped her hand over her mouth before hurrying towards the wash room. Shoving open the door, she crossed to an empty cubicle, secured the door behind her, then threw up violently until there was nothing left to expel. Then she straightened up and leaned back against the door. Her legs were shaking. She was sweating. Loose strands of hair were plastered to her face. She brushed them back over her head then flushed the lavatory before lowering the lid and sitting down.

She wanted to cry, but found she couldn't. There was now only anger where there had once been grief. How could she grieve for a man who had deceived her so cruelly? She felt betrayed and disgusted – but more than anything else, she felt dirty. This was the man who had shared her bed. How many times had he been unfaithful to her during the course of their marriage? Not that the number mattered. The very fact that he had was hurt enough. It was as if she had been married to a stranger for the past five years because the Ian Grant she had loved so deeply as a friend, confidant and husband certainly hadn't been the man she thought she knew. Yet part of her anger was aimed at herself. She was no fool: why had she never suspected it?

It was several minutes before she felt ready to leave the cubicle. A couple of women were applying fresh makeup, and both glanced at Beth's reflection in the mirror. Their eyes lingered on her and she knew she looked a mess. Splashing cold water over her face, she used a sheet of paper towel to dry herself but decided against putting on any fresh makeup. She left the wash room and walked towards the exit.

'Your ticket is valid for the rest of the night,' the youth behind the table told her. 'Word is Mr Novak's going to jam on stage with Martinique later tonight. He doesn't play much these days, which is a pity. He's really good, you know.'

'Thanks, but I think I've had more than enough excitement for one day,' Beth replied caustically, and walked out into the night.

Beth returned to the hotel and took the elevator to her floor. Her mind was still in turmoil and, although she was physically exhausted, she doubted whether she would get much sleep that night. But she knew it was essential that she had a clear head when she met with Kessler the following morning. Which meant rest. A hot bath always helped her to relax after a hectic day at the office, and she had already decided on a long soak even before she emerged from the elevator and walked the short distance to her room. She used the key to activate the magnetic lock but as she opened the door she sensed someone behind her. Before she could react she felt something sharp press into the small of her back. She instinctively raised her hands to chest level. It was a gesture more of uncertainty than of fear.

'Put your hands down, for Christ's sake! Get inside.' It was a woman's voice. Soft. Threatening.

Beth did as she was told and the door was closed quietly behind her. Only then did she look round. The woman was roughly her own age: short black hair, attractive, no makeup, tight-fitting jeans, white blouse, a loose-fitting brown leather jacket. 'You're Amy Michaels, aren't you?' Beth said.

'Who else would I be?'

Beth's eyes went to the woman's hands. She didn't appear to be armed. 'Where's the gun?'

Amy smiled faintly and raised her forefinger. 'A little bit of improvisation, that's all. I had to get you into the room.'

'And what's to stop me ringing the police and having you arrested?' Beth said, glancing at the telephone beside the bed.

'Nothing.' Amy sat down on the edge of the bed then picked up the phone and held it out to her. 'Go ahead, call them, if that's what you want.'

'You're very sure of yourself, aren't you?' Beth said, but made no move to take the receiver.

'Don't mistake confidence for bravado,' Amy replied softly, then hung up. When she looked up again at Beth the self-assurance was gone. There was now only fear and uncertainty in her eyes. 'I didn't kill Ian. You've got to believe that. I've been set up. But I didn't do it, Beth.'

'Then who did?' Beth asked, making no attempt to conceal her scepticism.

'There was a man talking to Ian in the club last night, only I don't know who he was. I'd never seen him before.' Amy got to her feet and crossed to the window, where she looked out across the tranquil waters of the Limmat river which lapped at the foundations of the hotel. 'It's beautiful, isn't it? So serene. So peaceful.' When she turned round there were tears in her eyes. 'I'm scared, Beth.'

All Beth's instincts were screaming at her not to be taken in by any of this. It was a charade. Amy Michaels had killed Ian and should be turned over to the police. *What if she's innocent?* The question caught her unawares. The evidence was overwhelming. Amy Michaels had been seen at the crime scene with the murder weapon in her hand. She had run away when challenged. Any jury would convict her on that evidence alone. Yet the question lingered in her mind. *What if she's innocent?*

'This man you saw talking to Ian at the club last night. What did he look like?'

'Early forties. Short blond hair. Well-built. And he was wearing a grey suit that was obviously too small for him. It looked real uncomfortable.'

'Kerwin!' Beth gasped, ashen-faced.

'Who?'

Beth sat down slowly. Her mind was racing. But she couldn't think straight. She desperately tried to clear her head. It was pointless. All it did was throw up even more questions and she wanted answers. Amy Michaels was the one person who may have some of those answers. It was a chance she had to take. 'Did you hear what they were saying?'

'No. They were out of earshot. Ian seemed anxious and preoccupied all night, but he dismissed my concerns when I confronted him about it. He said it was just my imagination. It wasn't. I know that.'

'Did you know he was going to meet this man at the club?'

'No. Why do you keep calling him "this man"? You obviously know who he is, judging by your reaction when I described him to you. Who is he, Beth?'

'I don't know,' Beth replied truthfully.

'But you've obviously seen him before.'

'The man you described met me off the plane tonight. He called himself Richard Kerwin, and claimed to be from the American consulate here in Zürich. But when I spoke to Mike Novak earlier tonight, he said there was no such person at the consulate. He even rang the consulate to confirm it.'

'What did he want?' Amy asked.

Beth didn't know how much she should tell Amy. She certainly didn't trust her. But at the same time she also knew that Amy was her one link to what had happened to Ian. She wanted answers from Amy. And that meant *quid pro quo*. It was only fair. 'This man – Kerwin – asked me whether Ian had sent me a computer disk in the past couple of days. He seemed to think that Ian's visit to Zürich had something to do with this disk.'

'It did,' Amy replied bluntly.

'You know about the disk?' Beth asked excitedly.

'Of it.' Amy gestured to the mini-bar. 'May I?'

'Help yourself,' Beth said. 'Tell me about the disk.'

'There's nothing to tell.' Amy crouched in front of the fridge and selected an orange juice. Unscrewing the cap, she took a long quaff then turned back to Beth. 'You don't know anything about me, do you?'

'Apart from the fact that you're a computer programmer. At least, that's what you claimed to be on your registration card. I don't even know whether that's true.'

'It sounds more respectable than calling myself a professional hacker,' Amy said, with a wry smile. 'That's how I first met Ian. He hired me to hack into certain files which couldn't be . . . accessed legally.'

'Were they related to his work?' Beth asked.

'No idea. He never told me what he wanted them for. I never asked. It was better that way.'

'Why were you in Zürich?'

'Ian rang me last week and asked me to meet up with him here. He said he would pay my airfare as well as all my expenses. No explanation other than that. I'd never been to Europe before so naturally I jumped at the chance. It was only when I got here that he told me about the disk. He wanted me to access certain documents that were mentioned on it. I told him that I could just as easily have done it from my own computer back home but he said the contents of the disk were of a highly sensitive nature and that he wanted to be on hand when I downloaded the information. That's all he told me. I never saw the disk.'

'So you never accessed any of the data he wanted?' Beth said.

Amy shook her head. 'We were due to start accessing it within the next couple of days. I don't know why he delayed doing it for so long. And I didn't ask. Why should I? I was being well paid for my time.'

'Why did you go to the club with him last night?'

'Because he invited me. I don't know why. As I said just now, he was clearly agitated about something. He hardly said anything all night. Then, around ten forty-five, he met this man you call Kerwin. They talked for a while then . . . Kerwin took Ian by the arm and appeared to escort him from the club. They left through a side entrance. Ian didn't struggle, but it was obvious that he didn't want to go. I sensed that something was wrong. That's why I went after them. I heard them having a heated argument in the alley at the back of the club. Kerwin wanted the disk. Ian refused to give it to him. Kerwin drew an automatic from a holster clipped to the back of his trousers. It had a silencer attached to it. He shot Ian in the chest. No warning. It was only then that I saw he was wearing gloves. Then he dropped the gun and ran away. I hurried over to where Ian was lying . . . but it was obvious that . . . well, he was dead. I guess I was in a state of shock because the next thing I know I'm holding the gun. I don't even remember picking it up. That's when the barman came out into the alley and saw me crouched over Ian with the gun in my hand. What else would he think under the circumstances? I panicked. I dropped the gun and ran away. That's the truth, Beth. I know how I'd feel if I was in your place listening to this, but I didn't kill Ian. I swear I didn't kill him.'

'How did you know I was coming to Zürich? Or which flight I'd be on? Or, for that matter, that I would be staying here?' Beth challenged.

'I didn't know for sure that you *would* be coming here until I confirmed it on the passenger manifest. As for your staying here, all it took was a phone call. This was the first hotel I rang. I asked to speak to you and was told you hadn't checked in as yet. That's how I knew where you were staying.'

'The airlines don't give out names on their passenger manifest,' Beth said suspiciously.

'I got the information from their database. All I needed was an on-line computer. I used one at the library. It really wasn't that difficult to get in. Any firewall can be breached with the right know-how.'

'Why did you come here? What do you want from me?'

'To help me clear my name.'

'What can I possibly do? Your only chance is to tell the police what you told—'

'Tell them what?' Amy cut in incredulously. 'Obviously nobody saw Kerwin with Ian at the club last night otherwise it would have been in the papers this morning. The Swiss authorities are thorough if nothing else. No, I'm regarded as the only suspect, Beth. All the police want is to clear this case up as quickly and cleanly as possible. That's why I came here tonight. You're my only chance now. You've got to help me find Kerwin. He's the key to it all.'

Beth said nothing. She knew that Amy had taken a great risk by coming back to the hotel. It was the one place where she could have been recognized. Why take that risk if this was all an elaborate act to save her own skin? And then there was Kerwin. Had she not encountered him earlier that night at the airport she could have easily dismissed Amy's story and had no qualms about handing her over to the police. But it was too much of a coincidence for them both to have encountered him within twenty-four hours. Amy was right. He was the key. Now all they had to do was find him. What was she getting herself into here?

There was a knock on the door. She saw the terror in Amy's eyes and found herself wanting to help her. Another knock. She grabbed Amy's arm, propelled her into the bathroom and closed the door. Then she peered through the spy-hole. She didn't recognize the man standing in the corridor. Average height. Nondescript features. Mid-to-late thirties. Thinning black hair. Wire-framed glasses.

'Mrs Grant?' The man knocked again on the door.

'Who is it?' Beth blurted out, and cursed herself silently for sounding so apprehensive.

'Inspector Stefan Kessler.' A warrant card was held up to the spy-hole. 'May I speak with you, please?'

Beth glanced towards the bathroom door. What if Kessler were to discover Amy Michaels? How could she explain harbouring a fugitive in her room? Would it make her an accessory to the murder of her own husband? It was a ridiculous idea, she knew, yet frighteningly feasible all the same. Let him in, Beth, she told herself. You have to, otherwise it'll look even more suspicious. She opened the door.

'I'm sorry to disturb you at this late hour, Mrs Grant, but I only learned within the last half an hour that you were in Zürich. May I come in?'

'Yes, of course,' Beth replied. 'I was just about to take a bath. It's been a very long day for me.'

'I can assure you that I won't take up any more of your time than is absolutely necessary. My sympathies to you on your bereavement.' He sounded indifferent, as if he was merely going through the motions.

Kessler crossed to the window and looked across at Nieder-dorf where he had spent much of the previous night investigating the homicide. He didn't look at her when he spoke. 'I know an officer from Scotland Yard came to see you earlier today, but I would like to ask you some questions myself. Do you know Amy Michaels?'

'No.'

'Did your husband ever mention her name to you?'

'No.'

'So you have no idea why he was at Straight Street with her last night?'

'No.'

'Do you know why he was in Zürich?'

'He was out here on business. He often came to Zürich. It's the headquarters of Freedom In Europe, one of the human rights organizations he often represented in court.'

'Whatever his business was out here, it had nothing to do with Freedom In Europe.' Kessler turned away from the window. 'I spoke to the director personally this morning. He didn't even know your husband was here. And neither did any of his staff.'

'I had no idea,' Beth said.

'Mrs Grant, did you and your husband have any . . . marital problems?'

Anger flashed in Beth's eyes. 'Why don't you just come out and say it, Inspector? Was Ian unfaithful to me? That is what you're asking, isn't it?'

'Was he?' Kessler replied coldly.

'Not that I was ever aware of, but he did spend a lot of time away from home. He would have had every opportunity, and I would have been none the wiser. As for whether he was banging Amy Michaels, you tell me. You're the detective.'

'They were seen together several times here at the hotel, but that in itself doesn't prove anything. That's why I was hoping you could have shed some light on the matter.'

'The only person who can do that is Amy Michaels. I assume you still have no leads as to her current whereabouts?'

'We have several leads, which are being followed up as we speak,' Kessler told her. 'I have every confidence that Amy Michaels will be in custody within the next twenty-four hours.'

'You will let me know when she's apprehended?'

'Of course.' Kessler moved to the door, then paused outside the bathroom to look round at her. 'Thank you for your time, Mrs Grant. I'll be in touch.' Beth's heart missed a beat when he appeared to peer through the narrow aperture between the bathroom door and the jamb. The corners of his mouth tugged in a forced smile. 'I'll leave you to your bath. Goodnight.'

She waited until Kessler had gone then crossed to the bathroom door and slid it open. Amy was pressed up against the wall adjacent to the door. Beth knew that Kessler couldn't have seen her from where he had been standing. 'Thanks for not giving me away,' Amy said, and put a hand lightly on Beth's arm.

'I didn't do it for you,' Beth shot back, jerking her arm away. 'If Kerwin did kill Ian, I want to know why. And if Kessler arrests you, I'll never get to the truth.'

'So you do believe me, then,' Amy said, with obvious relief.

'Did I say that?' Beth took a miniature of whisky from the mini-bar and poured it into a tumbler. She took a sip, then looked across at Amy hovering uncertainly at the door. 'You can't possibly stay here. Not even tonight.'

'But I don't have anywhere else to go,' Amy replied.

'I've got an idea, but whether it'll work is another matter.' Beth sank the rest of the whisky in the tumbler then pulled on her jacket. 'Wait for me here. I won't be long.'

'Where are you going?' Amy asked.

'Just wait here.' Beth saw the apprehension in the other woman's face. 'You're going to have to trust me on this.'

'I'm coming with you,' Amy announced defiantly, and raised a hand before Beth could answer. 'Right now I trust you about as much as you trust me. At least this way I'll have a chance of getting away if it is a trap.'

'I had every opportunity to turn you in when Kessler was here. I didn't. Doesn't that tell you anything? Just wait here for me. Otherwise you're on your own.'

'Beth?' Amy called out softly after her. 'I didn't sleep with Ian. It was strictly business. You have to believe that.'

Beth was about to reply, thought better of it, and had to force herself not to slam the door behind her. She took the lift to the foyer, handed in her key at reception, and left the hotel. She paused in the entrance to look around her. A young couple were locked in a passionate embrace a short distance away. Other than that the square appeared to be deserted. She headed off in the direction of the Rathaus Bridge. Moments later, a figure slipped from the shadows on the opposite side of the square and began to follow her at a discreet distance.

THREE

'Forget it!'

'It'll just be until—'

'No.' Novak was quick to cut across Beth's protests. 'If you want to protect Amy Michaels, that's your choice. But don't bring me in on it. I don't want to know.'

They were seated in Novak's private office at the club. Beth had explained to him what Amy had told her at the hotel. She had asked if he would harbour Amy, at least until Kerwin was found. His response was hardly surprising. She knew that, had the roles been reversed, she would have reacted in exactly the same way. But there was nobody else to whom she could turn for help.

'I can't believe that you've been taken in by her,' Novak said. 'She murdered your husband. You've got to turn her over to the police. Let them deal with it.'

'And what if she's telling the truth?' Beth asked.

'C'mon, you only have to look at the evidence against her to see that she's guilty as hell.' Novak snorted disdainfully.

'Then explain how she knew about Kerwin.'

'I can't,' Novak replied, shifting uncomfortably in his chair. 'But that still doesn't mean I want to get involved in any of this. Harbouring a fugitive is a crime in any country. If the police were to find her on the premises, not only would I be arrested but I'd also lose my licence and the club would be shut down. I'm damned if I'm going to take that kind of risk for someone I don't even know.'

'Why should the police find her here? It's the last place they'd look.'

'I said no. And that's an end to it. For your sake, I'm prepared to forget this conversation ever took place.' Novak looked at his watch then got to his feet. 'If you'll excuse me, I'm due on stage shortly. I'll show you out.'

'I think I can find my own way,' Beth said, brushing past him and opening the door. She stopped sharply as she was about to step out into the corridor. A heavy-set man was standing directly in front of her, early fifties, balding grey hair, day-old growth, glasses, crumpled cream linen suit.

'Can I help you?' Novak said from behind her. 'This part of the club isn't open to the public. Where exactly do you want to be?'

'Right here.' The accent was clipped, German. The man removed a leather wallet from the inside pocket of his jacket and extended it towards Novak. 'My name's Ralf Jago. I'm with Interpol.'

'Interpol?' Novak echoed, looking at the warrant card.

'Do you know that if you stand close enough to the door you can hear everything that's being said in the room?' Jago said, tapping the door with his knuckle as if to make his point. 'The conversation about Amy Michaels was illuminating, to say the least.'

'I don't fucking believe this!' Novak snapped.

Beth's eyes were focused on Jago. 'Then you'll know that Mr Novak wanted nothing to do with any of it right from the start. So if anyone has to answer for their actions, it's me. Not him.'

'You don't have to answer for your actions, Mrs Grant, at least not to me. I think you'll find that we're on the same side. I don't believe Amy Michaels murdered your husband either.'

Beth glanced at Novak and felt the same uncertainty that she saw in his eyes. 'I don't follow,' she said to Jago. 'Aren't you part of the team investigating Ian's death?'

'I'm not working with the local police if that's what you mean,' Jago told her. 'In fact, I don't believe they even know I'm here. Why don't we go inside and talk?'

'This doesn't concern me, so I'll leave you to it,' Novak said, moving towards the door.

'Mike, please stay,' Beth said, and she placed a hand on his arm when he tried to slip past her.

'I don't want to get involved,' Novak replied, pulling his arm away.

'You're already involved, Mr Novak,' Jago said.

'Mike, please, sit down,' Beth said softly.

'I don't want to!' Novak shot back. 'I'm due on stage shortly. Now, if you'll both excuse me.'

'I could have this club closed down with one phone call, Mr Novak,' Jago called after him. It had the desired effect. Novak stopped. 'I have connections at Interpol who have a lot of influential friends at the highest levels of almost every government in the world. Switzerland's no exception. I promise I'll be brief. Then you can go on stage and play. I really can't say fairer than that, can I?'

'You've got five minutes, Jago,' Novak said, then returned to the chair behind his desk and sat down.

'Five minutes is all I'll need,' Jago assured him, with a placating smile, then eased himself into the leather armchair against the wall. 'Mmm, this is very comfortable,' he said, patting the arms. 'I could do with a chair like this in my office.'

'How did you know I was here?' Beth demanded. 'Did you follow me from the hotel?'

'Yes,' Jago replied apologetically. 'It was all a bit cloak-and-dagger, I'm afraid. Not really my forte. Actually, I've had you under observation ever since you first arrived in Zürich.'

'Then you saw Kerwin at the airport,' she said.

'Richard Kerwin. That's one of the aliases he uses. Can't say I thought much of his suit, though.'

'So who is he?' Beth asked.

'His real name's Robert Kilgarry,' Jago said.

'What does he do? He's obviously not with the American consulate. Mike found that out soon enough.'

Jago laughed as he unwrapped the Cellophane from the cigar he'd removed from his jacket pocket. 'No, I wouldn't say he was the consulate type, Mrs Grant. Bob Kilgarry's an assassin. And very good at his work, so I'm told.'

Beth shuddered. 'Did he kill Ian?' she asked, shakily.

'According to Amy Michaels he did.' Jago lit his cigar. He waited until the tip was glowing before snapping shut the lighter and pocketing it again. 'And if they know she saw him kill your husband, as she claims, then she'll be the next target. They don't take prisoners.'

'Who the hell are "they"?' Novak snapped.

'That will become apparent in due course,' Jago told him.

'So what's on this disk Kilgarry was after?' Beth pressed.

'We're jumping the gun here,' Jago replied. 'I'll try to explain the situation as best I can. Four months ago your husband contacted the director of Interpol at our headquarters in Lyon. He told him that he'd been approached by someone offering to sell him sensitive information about a covert organization known as the Cabal. His contact claimed to have access to inside information that could blow the organization wide open. The director put him in touch with me as I'd been investigating it, without success, for the last year. I became Ian's liaison at Interpol. But his contact was cagy. He would only deal with Ian. Nobody else. Over the ensuing months his contact passed him valuable information about the internal workings of the Cabal, which he, in turn, forwarded to Interpol. Information that we could never have got ourselves.'

'So what exactly is the Cabal?' Novak asked.

Jago took a long drag on his cigar and blew the smoke up

towards the ceiling. 'I don't know exactly when it was formed, my guess would be some time within the last five years. It was the brainchild of the previous director of the CIA. He chaired a top-secret meeting at a CIA safe-house in the States, which was attended by the directors of several of the more influential European intelligence agencies. The agenda was quite simple – he wanted to set up a team of assassins to execute those international criminals who were regarded as beyond the reach of the law. And as the organization had no formal ties to any one country, there could be no comebacks on any of those attending the meeting. My guess is that he was probably looking to take out senior figures in some of the more omnipotent drug cartels in South and Central America, and several have been killed in mysterious circumstances in the last few years. Murders that have never been satisfactorily explained.' He looked across at Beth. 'The British, by all accounts, were also receptive to the idea. It was a perfect opportunity for them to target members of the IRA whom they knew to have carried out atrocities on the British mainland but couldn't be prosecuted through lack of evidence. A covert shoot-to-kill policy made to look like just another sectarian murder. It was the perfect cover story as far as they were concerned.

'There were, however, certain rules. No government was to be told about the organization's existence. Each intelligence agency would pay a fixed amount into a slush fund, managed by the CIA, which would help to finance it. And to ensure that no agency misused it, a dossier on any intended target had to be forwarded to the other members, who would then vote on whether the target merited assassination. A majority verdict would carry the motion. And, lastly, it was agreed that the director of the CIA would select a candidate to head the organization, to be known as the Cabal. But the candidate would only be known to the other intelligence agencies by a pseudonym. The motion was carried unanimously and that was how—'

A knock on the door interrupted him. 'Yes, what is it?' Novak called out irritably.

The door opened and the band's drummer peered into the room. He nodded in acknowledgement to Beth and Jago, then looked at Novak. 'We're about to go on. Are you ready?'

Novak's eyes flickered to Beth then back to the musician. 'Go on without me. I've got some business to attend to first. I'll join you as soon as I'm finished.'

'You're not having second thoughts, are you? I know it's been a while since you last jammed with us—'

'I said I'll join you as soon as I'm finished,' Novak interrupted angrily.

'Sure,' the musician said, with a quick smile, then closed the door quietly behind him.

'And I thought you were in such a hurry to get on stage,' Jago said, with a hint of sarcasm.

'Just get on with it,' Novak said wearily.

'The person chosen to head up the Cabal was a Langley spook with several years' experience in the field. He speaks several European languages fluently but, to this day, I still don't know his real name. Only his pseudonym – Sammy Kahn. He was told to review hundreds of files, then pick three assassins to work exclusively for the Cabal on the type of salary that would ensure total loyalty. All three still work for it.' Jago tapped the end of his cigar into the ashtray on Novak's desk. 'From what Ian's contact told him, the Cabal worked perfectly for the first few years. Then last year the former director of the CIA collapsed and died of a heart-attack on a golf course in Washington. The other intelligence chiefs weren't unduly worried about the future of the Cabal, until they discovered that nobody else at Langley had any idea that it even existed. The director had been running it by himself, so when he died, all contact was broken. That's when the Cabal began to take on an identity of its own. Kahn went freelance, hiring out its services to the highest bidder. No questions asked if the money was paid up front. It all came to a head when one of the outgoing intelligence chiefs got a rush of conscience and told his government about the Cabal's existence. He wouldn't implicate any of his partners, other than to say that the former director of the CIA had been the ringleader. The US President ordered the FBI to undertake an inquiry into its activities with orders to shut it down with immediate effect and bring those responsible to justice. The CIA were justifiably upset that they weren't given the chance to put their own house in order, but the President was determined to use a neutral organization to head up the investigation. That's when I was drafted in to work alongside the FBI as their European liaison. And, as I said, we'd come up with very little until Ian approached us.'

Jago removed an envelope from his pocket and spilled out the contents on to the desk. Three photographs. 'These are the three assassins who work for the Cabal.' He separated one from the pack and pushed it across to Beth. 'You already know of Bob Kilgarry. Ex-Marine. Divorced. Currently lives in Fort Lauderdale. Regarded as the best sniper of the trio. Possibly the weak link. He's been known, on occasion, to question the validity of taking out his intended target. But having said that, he's always carried out his orders to the letter.' He tapped the second photograph. 'Alain Racine. Former Legionnaire. Also worked as a mercenary. Ian used to call him Pretty Boy. He's as charming as he's good-looking. He's also totally without conscience. Lives in Paris. Unmarried.' He handed the third photograph to Beth. 'He's the pick of the bunch and is always given the more perilous assignments. His name's Petr Voskov. A former officer in Spetznaz, the élite Russian Special Forces. Married, with one child. A strict disciplinarian. Like Kahn, he's fluent in several languages.'

'If you know where they live, why not just move in and arrest them?'

'Because we don't have enough evidence against them. At the moment we only have the word of Ian's contact,' Jago told her.

'And now that Ian's dead . . . well, we've lost our one link to the Cabal. We're back to square one again.'

'Why not just take out the three assassins?' Novak said. 'Give them a dose of their own medicine.'

'That's not how we operate, Mr Novak, contrary to what you may see in the movies. And even if such a drastic step were to be contemplated, Kahn would rebuild from the inside and start again. It's Kahn we're after. He's the linch-pin. Without him, the Cabal can't operate.'

'Do you have a picture of him?' Novak asked.

'If I did, I could probably find out who he is. Kahn's a complete enigma. Even the three assassins have never seen him. He's only a voice on the phone to them. That way if an operation was compromised, there would be no comeback on Kahn. Those four make up the Cabal.'

'Only the four of them?' Beth said, in surprise. 'The way you talked about it, I imagined it to be a lot bigger than that.'

'Those are the core personnel, but it does have on its payroll senior people within the government, military, and law-enforcement agencies of almost every country in the world. Only we don't know who they are. And that's what's on the disk. The names of their contacts. With that kind of information we could break the Cabal. Only it's encrypted, all the Cabal's documents are. But they have a decryption code built into the mainframe of their computer network. Ian's contact told him how to access it once he was inside the program. First he would have to bypass all the firewalls built in to protect the system. And his contact didn't know how to do that.'

'Cue Amy Michaels,' Beth said.

'Precisely. From what Ian told me about her, she'd helped him access case documents in the past. Only they'd never met before. Her choice, I believe. She's a bit of a loner. Prefers computers to people.'

'Did Ian ever give you any clue as to the identity of his contact?'

'No. He was always very protective. But having said that, it has to be someone with access to the mainframe. That narrows it down to the four core members of the Cabal. And I certainly don't think it's Kahn. Which only leaves these three.' Jago tapped each photograph in turn.

'You said that Kilgarry had doubts about killing some of his intended targets,' Beth pointed out.

'It doesn't prove anything. And if we were to pull in the wrong man, Kahn would go to ground and we'll never get him. As I keep saying, Mrs Grant, Kahn is the key figure to the overall success of this whole operation. It's the only way we can shut down the Cabal for ever.'

'OK, so you've told us about the Cabal,' Novak said. 'Now tell us why? And don't give us that spiel about Beth having the right to know because of what happened to Ian. I don't buy it. And I'm quite sure she doesn't either.'

Jago smiled. 'There are actually two reasons why I told you. One is that you're both already involved and there's nobody else I can realistically turn to for help while I'm out here. I certainly can't trust the local police. I'm not saying that Kessler's on the Cabal's payroll, but we do know that there are senior officers in the Swiss police who have already been bought. And they could influence the direction of Kessler's investigation. Second, I need you to shield Amy Michaels until I can recover the disk. I know that Kessler's under a lot of pressure from his superiors to get a result. That means finding her as quickly as possible and bringing her to trial. They're not interested in conspiracy theories, only in a conviction. I also believe that her life would be in danger if she were taken into custody. The Cabal can't afford to let her stand trial.'

'As I said to Beth, I can't take that kind of risk. I would lose my licence and the club—'

'You wouldn't lose anything.' Jago was quick to reassure him. 'This is the last place the police would think to look for her. And even in the unlikely event that she was discovered, I would clear up any misunderstanding with the relevant authorities. Also, you're both now known to the Cabal. You'll be on their lists.' He paused to let it sink in then repeated, 'You wouldn't lose your licence or your club, Mr Novak. You have my word on that. So what do you say? Will you help?'

Novak looked from Jago to Beth. 'OK, I'll do it,' he said, resignedly. 'There's a room above the club that I sometimes use when I don't feel like driving home late at night. It's very basic, though – single bed, table and chair, sink, toilet in the adjoining room. It's the best I can do.'

'I think, after what she's been through in the past twenty-four hours, it'll be like a suite at the Ritz,' Jago said, stubbing out his cigar.

'The club closes at two in the morning. Bring her to the back entrance about three. I'll be waiting for you.' Novak got to his feet. 'Now, if you'll excuse me, I have to make an appearance on stage.'

'You play the saxophone, don't you?' Jago said, as Novak crossed to the door.

'Yeah, that's right, although not much these days, since the accident.' Novak opened the door. 'Three o'clock. Make sure you're on time. I won't wait for you.'

'What accident?' Beth asked, after Novak had left the room.

'I know only what Ian told me. Novak was a session musician back in the States but before he could cut his own album he was involved in a car crash and severed the tendons on his right wrist. They never healed properly so he's not able to play for more than a few minutes before his wrist begins to ache. Then he has to stop. I've never heard him play. Not that it would mean anything to me, though. I'm not a fan of jazz.'

'Neither was Ian, or at least that's what he always led me to believe,' Beth said.

'His passion was classical music. We talked about it endlessly, although our tastes weren't always the same. I liked Ian. He was a good man.'

49

'So if he didn't like jazz why did he keep coming here with a succession of prostitutes?' Beth demanded.

'How did you know about that?' Jago said, surprised.

'Novak said he recognized one of the girls Ian was with at the club,' Beth replied, then furrowed her brow. 'You knew about it, didn't you?'

Jago nodded. 'But it's not what you think, Mrs Grant.'

'No, of course not,' she said sarcastically. 'Ian paid them for their sparkling conversation.'

'Ian didn't pay for their services. His contact did. He used them as couriers, nothing more. And he paid them handsomely for their time. These weren't street hookers, they were high-class call-girls, very discreet. He would give them an envelope with encrypted information for Ian with instructions when to deliver it to him at the club. He varied the girls so as not to arouse suspicion. Ian would meet the girl at a prearranged time in a secluded booth here at the club and she would hand over the envelope. They would have a drink together, then he would leave.' Jago chuckled to himself. 'I can't believe that you could ever suspect Ian of sleeping with them. He would never have cheated on you. And I think you know that, don't you?'

Beth realized she was crying when Jago extended his handkerchief towards her, but she felt as if a great weight had been lifted from her shoulders. How could she have ever doubted him? She wiped her eyes then handed back the handkerchief.

'You loved him very much, didn't you?' Jago pocketed the handkerchief.

'I know what you're thinking,' Beth said. 'You can't imagine the two of us together. We're chalk and cheese. Am I right?' Jago conceded the point with a rueful nod. 'Everybody thought that. But opposites attract. My best friend, Emma, called us the Magnets. And that's exactly what we were.' More tears. 'I'm sorry,' she muttered self-consciously, and reached for the box of tissues on Novak's desk.

'You have nothing to apologize for. In fact, you're bearing up remarkably well.'

'I think the mask's beginning to crack,' Beth replied, with a grim smile. She wiped her cheeks then pushed the tissue under her cuff. 'There's just one thing I still don't understand. Why was Ian approached in the first place? Why didn't his contact just take the story to a newspaper?'

'Your husband was one of the most respected human rights lawyers in Europe. He was also incorruptible. His name would have carried a lot of weight once the truth came out. And it will. I wouldn't have confided in you if I had any doubts on that score.' He gathered together the photographs and returned them to the envelope, which he then slipped back into his pocket. 'I think we should go. I still need to talk to Miss Michaels. That could take some time.'

Beth got to her feet. 'It would be best if we didn't go into the hotel together. We don't want to arouse suspicion.'

'Agreed. I'll let you go first so that you can explain the situation to her. I know the number of your room. I'll be along in due course.'

Beth paused at the door to look back at Jago. 'What about Kessler? He came to my room earlier tonight. What if he's got the hotel under surveillance?'

'Why should he? He's after Amy Michaels, not you. You're the last person he would expect her to turn to for sanctuary. But, having said that, don't take any unnecessary risks. Kessler's a dangerous adversary. Remember that.'

'I knew there was something I forgot to bring with me,' he said, screwing up his eyes when the clouds broke and the sun appeared over the mountainous horizon.

'You always forget something, Daddy,' his son replied.

He shot a mock-disapproving look at the youth seated beside him in the front of the car. Andreas was seven. It was his birthday, and as part of his son's present, he was taking him to the ski resort at Amden to try out the new skis he and his wife had bought for him. Only Marthe couldn't go with them. She had a backlog of homework to mark that weekend. He knew Andreas was disappointed that she wasn't with them, but that couldn't be helped. He was determined to make up for it with a weekend of skiing Andreas would never forget. The family were all good skiers. Marthe was the best, although he never liked to admit that, especially not to her. Andreas had already shown great potential and an instructor had suggested that he might even make the professional circuit one day. He felt proud, although he knew that Marthe was less convinced. Her brother was an exceptional skier, who had been far better than Andreas at his age – or, at least, according to Marthe – and had been a junior slalom champion at the age of twelve, yet he had never had the same success at senior level. He just hadn't been good enough. Only time would tell for Andreas . . .

'Daddy, there's a petrol station,' Andreas said, interrupting his thoughts. 'You can buy some sunglasses in there. Can I have some chocolate?'

'At nine fifteen in the morning?'

'But it's my birthday,' Andreas said.

'Don't push it,' he replied sternly, but he was smiling. He turned off the road and parked the car at the back of the pumps. He knew he could easily make Amden on a single tank of petrol, and he had filled up before they left Zürich that morning. At least he hadn't forgotten that! They crossed the forecourt together and, holding open the door, he ushered his son inside. He smiled to himself as Andreas headed straight for the confectionery stand. Then he looked across at the counter. A young couple were standing with their backs to him. Their clothes were dirty and unkempt. It was then he noticed the look of terror on the assistant's face behind the counter. Something was wrong. He was still moving towards the couple when the woman noticed him. She called out a warning to her partner who swung round, revealing a SIG 220 automatic. He lunged at the youth, at the same time using his forearm to deflect the gun hand. A shot rang *out. He chopped down hard on the youth's wrist, forcing him to drop the weapon. The woman grabbed him from behind. She was yelling obscenities as she clawed at his face. He lashed out with his fist and heard the crack of breaking bones as he caught her flush on the nose. She screamed and stumbled backwards, knocking over a magazine stand, her hands clutched to her shattered nose as blood streamed down her face. The youth caught him with a jarring punch to the midriff, winding him and forcing him down on one knee. The automatic was within range. The youth read his intentions and kicked it away. It disappeared under a freezer. The man grabbed his girlfriend's arm and they ran from the shop.*

He struggled to his feet, his breathing still ragged, but before he could go after them a piercing shriek tore the silence. He looked round sharply at the assistant behind the counter, whose face was frozen in horror. Slowly, reluctantly, he followed her stare.

Andreas lay motionless on the floor, the front of his shirt soaked in blood. He rushed across to his son and pressed a finger against the carotid artery, but the small tear in the child's shirt where the bullet had ripped through the fabric was directly over the heart. Tears streamed down his cheeks as he cradled his son's lifeless body to his chest. The anguished howl that echoed across the stillness materialized from the depths of his soul . . .

Stefan Kessler awoke with a start. He was soaked in sweat. His breathing was ragged and uneven. It took several seconds for his eyes to become acclimatized to the darkened room. He turned his head to look at the illuminated dial of the alarm clock on the table beside the bed: 3.17 a.m. He threw back the duvet and sat on the edge of the bed, his head in his hands. Had he screamed aloud in his dream, just as he had at the petrol station the previous year as he held his dead son in his arms? It wouldn't have been the first time. Marthe would always comfort him when it happened, stroking his hair and soothing him.

That had been before the marriage began to disintegrate. Now they slept in separate rooms. Separate rooms for separate lives. There had been times when they had come together as husband and wife but that hadn't happened for some months now. Not since Marthe had discovered she was pregnant. She had believed that it would bring them closer again. She had been wrong. He had told her bluntly that he didn't want a substitute for Andreas. Yet she had stayed with him, hoping that the gradual swell of her belly would change his mind. It hadn't. And it wouldn't.

Despite this, he knew that she wanted to salvage their marriage, otherwise she would have already filed for divorce. And she certainly had grounds for it – his unreasonable behaviour, his violent temper, his unpredictable mood swings. It all stemmed from the guilt, eating away inside him like some insidious cancerous growth. Stefan Kessler blamed himself for the death of his son and nothing would ever change that. Twice in the last month he had got as far as pushing the barrel of his Walther P88 into his mouth. Yet he couldn't bring himself to pull the trigger. How could he face Andreas in the afterlife, knowing that his actions at the petrol station had cost the life of his only child? That made him a coward. It was a brutal realization that only added to his mounting guilt.

He slipped on his dressing gown, tied the belt around his waist, and left the spare bedroom. He moved silently down the dark corridor and paused outside the master bedroom, eased open the door and peered inside. His eyes settled on the silhouette of his sleeping wife. The duvet only partially covered her naked body – she never wore anything in bed. There was a time when he could get aroused just thinking about her beside him but not any more. Now she was little more than a stranger living in his house. He tolerated her, no more, no less. Closing the door again, he made his way downstairs to the kitchen. He helped himself to a chicken drumstick and a glass of milk from the fridge then went through to the lounge and sat down in his favourite armchair in front of the bay window, overlooking the garden illuminated by the pale rays of the crescent moon.

His eyes went to the folder on the coffee table beside him.

The Amy Michaels folder he had brought home from the station that night. How many times had he read through the witness statements? How many times had he studied the photographs of the crime scene? How many times had he been forced to tell his superior that he was no closer to finding Amy Michaels than he had been at the outset of the investigation? What didn't help was that he had no photograph of her. When he had searched her room at the Zum Storchen there were no documents of any kind to be found. And as it was unlikely that she would have taken them with her to the club, the only alternative was that she had returned to the hotel after killing Ian Grant and removed all forms of identification. It was a calculated move on her part, further pointing to her guilt. Prints had been lifted from her suitcase and forwarded to Interpol. They drew a blank. She had no record. Neither did she have a face, other than the photofit that one of the receptionists had put together at the station. The barman who had seen her crouched over the body had identified her from the photofit but even that had been after some deliberation. Kessler needed a photograph. He needed to know something about her. Anything. She was a mystery. He hated mysteries. That was for the movies. He wanted results. That meant finding her and getting a confession out of her. The photofit had been passed on to all his informers, together with the offer of a handsome reward for any information leading to an arrest and conviction. It had also been shown on the local news programmes. But it wasn't enough. Viewers would be far more receptive to a photograph. That gave the suspect a face, which would invariably jog a lot more memories. He knew that Interpol had circulated the photofit to all law-enforcement agencies in Europe and the United States. He knew his best shot was the States. She was American. She lived there – although not at the address she had put down on the registration card at the hotel. That had been checked out early on in the investigation and found to be false.

Someone *had* to recognize the photofit. Which would mean an address. And an address would mean access to a photograph. Everybody had photographs of themselves at home. All he could do was wait ... and hope the FBI came up with something positive.

He drank the milk in one gulp then, chewing at the drumstick, he went back to bed.

FOUR

Thursday

'More coffee?'

Petr Voskov shook his head but didn't look up from the morning paper he was reading at the kitchen table. His wife refilled her own cup and took a sip, then studied her husband seated across the table from her. He couldn't be described as handsome in the conventional sense, even she would admit that, but there was something charismatic about his rugged, weatherbeaten features that she found both comforting and attractive. His hair had been flecked with grey when she had first met him at his twenty-first birthday party. Now he was completely grey. She thought it made him look distinguished, even though he wore it cropped close to his skull. When she thought about it, she realized that she had never seen his hair any other way. He had been a soldier all his life. It was all he knew. A former officer with Spetznaz, he had fought with distinction in Afghanistan and had been decorated for bravery in 1984 by the then Soviet premier, Konstantin Chernenko.

After the fall of Communism, the backbone of the once-proud military had been ripped out by those seeking to take the country down the new road of democracy. Although a card-carrying Communist, he had never been influenced by politics: his loyalty had always been to his unit. And with each cutback the military had lost that little bit more of its self-esteem. Soldiers weren't paid. Rations weren't forthcoming. Weapons weren't upgraded. And this affected Spetznaz just as it did any other arm of the military. Morale reached crisis level. Discontent was rife among the men. They began to search for other means to support their families. Many turned to crime as a lucrative alternative. Anarchy became a real threat. Officers who tried to prevent the widespread corruption from spreading further within the ranks were killed by the same men who had once aspired to be like them. That was when her husband had turned his back on the military. She knew it had been the hardest decision of his life. And it had cut deep. Not that he had shown it – he never showed his emotions, not even to her. It was his way. And nothing would ever change that.

Yet conflict raged inside her, which she knew she would have to bear alone. She knew that he had been recruited as a freelance assassin by some clandestine agency soon after he left Spetznaz. He had allowed her to know that much. Nothing more. She told their seven-year-old daughter that her father's regular trips abroad were all part of his new job. But she never elaborated. It soon became apparent that he was being well paid for his services and they now lived in a beautiful mansion with a magnificent garden on the outskirts of Moscow. Two expensive Japanese cars were parked in the double garage at the side of the house. Their daughter attended one of the top junior schools in the country. This when many in the new, democratic Russia were living well below the poverty line. But it was a lifestyle that had been paid for with blood money – and that was something with which she had been finding it increasingly difficult to reconcile herself.

'Daddy! Daddy!'

The excited voice broke her train of thought and she smiled as their daughter hurried into the room, still in her pyjamas, clutching an exercise book. She hadn't seen her father for three days – he had only arrived back at the house late the previous evening – and, wrapping her small arms around his muscular waist, hugged him tightly.

'How was your trip, Daddy?' she asked.

'It went very well,' he replied, almost formally. He indicated the school book she was carrying. 'Is that the maths test you did while I was away?'

She nodded, opened the book at the relevant page and placed it in front of him. 'I only got one wrong,' she said proudly. 'I came second in the class.'

'Not good enough,' he said, and focused only on the single cross on the page. He checked the problem then shook his head in disapproval at what he regarded as a basic mistake. 'There's no prizes for second best. You know you can do better.'

'I will, Daddy!'

'Good. Now go and get dressed. I'll take you to school.'

She beamed at him – he rarely took her to school – then scurried from the room to get ready. 'She got one answer wrong, Petr. I think that merits some kind of praise, don't you?'

'Which I'm sure you've already heaped on her.' He looked across the table at his wife. 'But you like to cosset her, don't you?'

'She's only seven years old. She's not some recruit that you have to keep putting down on the parade ground. You can be a real cold-hearted bastard at times. Do you know that?'

'So you keep telling me.'

'One day you're going to come back from one of your little trips abroad and find us gone,' she told him. 'I've got more than enough money salted away to start a new life for us away from here.'

'I'd never let you take my daughter away from me,' he replied, then picked up the bread-knife off the table and ran the tip of his thumb lightly down the serrated blade without taking his eyes off her face. 'Believe it.' He tossed the knife back on the table then went upstairs to his daughter's bedroom. She was putting on her school uniform. He sat down on her bed. 'Would you like to see a movie this afternoon?'

59

'Which one?' she asked excitedly.

'Your choice.'

'Thank you, Daddy,' she said, and kissed him.

'Just finish getting dressed, will you? You don't want to be late for school. I'll wait for you downstairs.' He left the room and was about to descend the stairs when he heard his cellular phone ringing in the master bedroom further down the corridor. Only one person ever called him on his cellphone. Sammy Kahn.

'I was about to hang up, you took so long to answer.'

'I didn't hear it at first,' Voskov replied. 'I was with my daughter.'

'How is she?'

'She's fine, thank you. I'm treating her to a movie this afternoon.'

There was a pause. 'Sorry, Petr, but you're going to have to take a raincheck on that. I need you right away.'

'I only got back from Bosnia late last night,' Voskov reminded Kahn curtly.

'Yes, I heard. It was a good hit by all accounts. Well done. One less Bosnian war criminal for the toothless UN to worry about in the future. The Croats paid handsomely to have that contract carried out. Were there any problems?'

'No, he was too busy drooling over some bit of teenage jailbait to even know I was there. What's so important that you need me right away?'

'I assume you know Ian Grant's dead?'

'I read about it in the paper this morning. But what's it got to do with us?'

'Everything. He'd been receiving sensitive information about the Cabal for the past few months. He knew too much. He had to be killed to ensure his silence. But he was supposed to have had a disk on him when he was shot. Only it wasn't on the body and neither was it in his hotel room. That disk could destroy the Cabal, were it to fall into the wrong hands. Which is why I've decided to bring in the other cleaners as well. The three of you will work as a team to recover the disk.'

'But that's unprecedented,' Voskov said, in amazement. 'The whole idea was that we would always work as individuals to minimize the damage to the Cabal if any of us was compromised.'

'Then that should give you an idea of just how important this disk is to the Cabal.'

'I don't even know their names.'

'Bob Kilgarry and Alain Racine. I've already contacted them. In fact, Kilgarry's already here. He met Grant's widow at the airport yesterday, posing as an embassy official, to find out whether Grant had forwarded the disk to her. She knew nothing about it. He said he believed her.'

'Are you in Zürich?' Voskov asked.

'I've been here since the beginning of the week. There's a flight leaving Moscow for Zürich later this morning. You're already booked on it. All the necessary documentation is waiting for you in the usual place at the airport. There're also detailed dossiers on both Kilgarry and Racine for you to read on the plane. You'll link up with them out here. You'll be the team leader.'

'Do Kilgarry and Racine know that?'

'They've been told.'

'And how did they take it?' Voskov pressed.

'They're professionals. They know how to take orders. To be fair, though, I should warn you that Kilgarry wasn't enamoured at the idea. He wanted to know why he couldn't be the leader. That's Kilgarry for you. Arrogant to the last. But damn good all the same. Don't push them, Petr. Give them some leeway. The last thing we need is for the three of you to be at each other's throats.'

'There's more to this than just the recovery of the disk, isn't there?' Voskov said. 'If that's all it was, we could have still worked individually without damaging each other's confidentiality.'

'You're quick, Petr,' Kahn said, after a thoughtful pause. 'The information Grant was receiving had to have come from someone inside the Cabal. I've done some checking with dates and times and you're the only one whose movements put you in the clear.'

'What are you saying? That either Kilgarry or Racine have been passing inside information to Grant? It doesn't make any sense, Sammy.'

'All I know is that it wasn't me, and it wasn't you. So that leaves the two of them as the prime suspects. Which is another reason why I want the three of you to work together. That way you can keep an eye on them. Obviously they don't know that I suspect one of them but other than that I've given them the same briefing as you.'

'Am I supposed to play detective and find out which one it was?' Voskov inquired.

'All I want you to do is recover the disk. Leave the rest to me.'

'What about this woman, Amy Michaels? Does she know what's on the disk?'

'It's encrypted. She wouldn't understand the code. It's what she saw at the club that could be cause for concern. She could ID Grant's killer in a line-up. But at the moment she's no real threat. I know where she is anyway. And when the disk has been recovered she'll be terminated as a precaution. I'll let you deal with it personally.'

'Who did kill Grant?'

'You've got a plane to catch, Petr.' Kahn ignored the question. 'I'll speak to you again once you reach Zürich. Have a good flight. Sorry about your plans for this afternoon. I'm sure your daughter will understand.'

Voskov switched off the cellphone and got to his feet. Only

then did he see his wife standing in the doorway, her arms folded across her chest. Her eyes were cold. 'Duty calls?' she asked tersely.

'I leave at midday,' was all he told her.

Their daughter appeared behind her, immaculately dressed in her school uniform. Her eyes went to the cellphone in her father's hand. 'You're going away again, aren't you?' she said. All she knew was that any call he received on his cellphone invariably meant him having to leave the house within a few hours.

'It's business,' he replied. 'We'll go to the movies another time.'

'I understand, Daddy,' she said, with a brave smile, even though her disappointment was obvious. 'I'm ready to go to school now.'

'Your mother will take you. I've got to pack. I'll see you when I get back.'

'Goodbye, Daddy,' she whispered, then hurried down the stairs to wait for her mother in the kitchen.

'You could have at least taken her to school,' his wife said angrily.

'Just take her,' he said. 'And don't worry, I'll be gone before you get back.'

His wife glared at him, then spun round and stalked off. He stared at the empty doorway, sadness in his eyes, then retrieved his overnight bag from the cupboard and began to pack.

Jedediah Olsen was a bigot, a homophobe, a racist and a misogynist, yet like so many of his type he chose to believe he was devoutly religious and never missed church on Sundays. He was foul-mouthed, even in front of his three children, especially after he had put away a few extra-strength beers while sitting in front of the television set. He was several stone overweight and sweated profusely. He was the sheriff of Livingstone Point (pop. 537), a small, unremarkable town, which slumbered on the banks of the Yazoo river in the heartland of Mississippi. Crime was virtually non-existent – the occasional fender-bender in the high street, a drunk-and-disorderly charge on a Friday night. It was always on a Friday night, after the men had been paid their weekly wages, in cash, from the paper mill on the outskirts of the town. The mill was all that kept Livingstone Point alive. It was the kind of town where the scuttlebutt abounded behind closed doors, especially at the hair salon in the high street. There, gossip knew no bounds . . .

Jed Olsen dropped his wife off at the salon, as he did every Friday morning, then drove the short distance to his office and parked the town's only patrol car in his official space directly in front of the entrance. He climbed from the vehicle, touched his hat respectfully to one of the town elders as she shuffled along the dusty sidewalk, then pushed open the front door and entered the building.

'Morning, Jed.'

'Morning, Phyllis.' Olsen acknowledged the middle-aged woman seated behind the counter. Phyllis Kastner had been working at the sheriff's office for as long as he could remember, certainly before he was elected sheriff. Her husband worked at the mill. She was the typist, telephonist and coffee-maker. His customary mug of steaming black coffee was already on his desk when he sat down.

'Thought you might be interested in this.' She placed two sheets of paper on the desk in front of him. 'Came through on the fax machine last night. It's from the FBI in Washington.'

He hated it when she interfered with his work. Her place was behind the counter, not poking about in his official business. Not that he said anything. He knew better than to upset Phyllis. The last time he had bad-mouthed her she had walked out of the office in tears and he had been forced to give her a small pay rise as an incentive to come back. The annual budget couldn't stretch to another. Best to keep his mouth shut. He scrutinized the top sheet of paper. A photofit of a woman in her mid-thirties. Short black hair. Pretty. 'I got no idea who she is,' Olsen said, in exasperation.

'Look at the second page.'

Olsen read through the accompanying text. 'Amy Michaels? That girl who moved into the old Hemmings mansion a couple of years back? Lives there like a hermit. What the hell would she be doing in Switzerland?" He studied the photofit again, then shook his head. 'Same age. But the hair's different. And the face . . . Nah, that ain't her.'

'These photofits never look realistic, Jed, you should know that,' she replied, making it sound like an accusation. 'It says in the fax that she's a computer programmer. And I've heard that Amy Michaels has got a lot of computer equipment out at the house. It could be her, Jed.'

Olsen wasn't convinced. He took a sip of coffee then replaced the mug on his desk. 'I still say it ain't her, Phyllis. Sure, she could have cut her hair. But the face.'

'How many times have you seen Amy Michaels face to face?' Phyllis asked, arms akimbo.

'I've seen her around,' was the defensive reply. 'I drove out there just after she first moved in to welcome her to Livingstone Point. She was real abrupt. Didn't want to know me. Hell, I didn't push it.' Another sip of coffee. 'I still say it ain't her but I'll check all the same. We wouldn't want to upset the Feds in DC, now, would we?'

'I can get you her number if you want to call her,' Phyllis offered.

'Nah, I'll take a drive out to the house. If she ain't there, I'll take a look around, see what I can find.'

'Well?' Phyllis asked when Olsen returned to the office an hour later, dabbing his sweating face with an already damp handkerchief.

'No sign of Amy Michaels.' He slumped into the battered chair behind his desk. 'The house is all locked up. She ain't there.'

'Then you'd better call the FBI and tell them.' Phyllis grinned at him. 'They might even send one of their agents down here to investigate. We've never had the FBI in Livingstone Point before. It's sure to get the tongues wagging around town.'

'I can believe that,' Olsen muttered.

'You want me to call them for you?'

'It's OK, I've got the number here.' Olsen scanned his desk for the fax.

'No, I've got it.' She held it up. 'I'll put the call through to you once I've got them on the line.'

Olsen bit back his anger. The fax had been lying on his desk when he had left the office. She had taken it while he was out. He just hated it when she helped herself to things off his desk. It undermined his authority.

'I'm through to FBI headquarters in Washington,' she announced, her hand over the mouthpiece. 'I've asked to be put through to the agent in charge.'

'I'll take it from here, Phyllis. Transfer the call to my phone.'

She removed her hand from the mouthpiece and put on her best telephone voice when she spoke. 'Hello, is that Special Agent Frank Dawson?' Pause. 'Oh, good. This is the sheriff's office at Livingstone Point. I'm calling about the fax you sent out last night. I think we may have something for you.'

'Phyllis!' Olsen stabbed a finger at the telephone on his desk.

'I'm putting you through to Sheriff Olsen. One moment, please.'

Olsen waited until the call had been transferred from the switchboard, then picked up the handset and sat back in his chair. 'Special Agent Dawson, this is Sheriff Jed Olsen. Livingstone Point, Mississippi.'

'Morning, Sheriff. I believe you have some information for me about Amy Michaels.'

'We got an Amy Michaels living down here. She's about the same age as the suspect you're looking for, but I'm not convinced that she's the face in the photofit. And she has long hair.'

'Hair can be cut. And as for the photofit, it's merely a composite made up by a witness in Zürich.'

'I checked out her house earlier this morning. It's all locked up. She ain't there. But what did catch my eye was all the computer stuff she had in her study. I could see it through the window.'

'Now you've got me interested, Sheriff,' Dawson said. 'Tell me more about her.'

'There really ain't much to tell,' Olsen replied, apologetically. 'She moved down here a couple of years ago. From what I remember, she came from one of the big cities up north. Her folks died and left her a shitload of money. Why she chose to move down here, God knows. Maybe she just wanted the solitude. She keeps very much to herself. She ain't married. She don't socialize. Hell, it ain't natural.'

'To each their own, Sheriff. How well did you know her?'

'I spoke to her when she first arrived and I've seen her around town a few times, but that's as far as it goes. Like I said, she keeps to herself. She ain't broken the law, so I got no reason to talk to her.'

'Tell me about these computers you saw at the house,' Dawson said.

'What the hell do I know about computers?' Olsen snorted. 'One looks just like another to me. I wouldn't have a clue how to use them.'

'Which answers my next question. You wouldn't be able to access any information that might be stored on them.'

'You got *that* right,' Olsen told him. 'You want to know

what's on those computers, you're going to have to send one of your people down from Washington to do it.'

'I'll be coming down personally to check them out. It's by far the best lead I've got up to now. I should be there by late afternoon. What I want you to do meantime is to find out who knew Amy Michaels. She may have been a recluse, but she still had to eat. Did she have her groceries delivered to the house? Who delivered them? Where did she get the computers from? Who serviced them? Did she order computer accessories through the mail? If so, did the mailman know her? Where did she bank? Did the manager know her? Did any of the tellers know her? I want to try and build up a profile of her because right now we've got jack shit to work on. Do some canvassing, Sheriff, find out what you can before I get there.'

'I'll get on to it right away,' Olsen promised.

'One more thing. Is there anywhere a small plane could put down in your neck of the woods?'

'Almost any place. It ain't exactly a built-up metropolis around here.'

'Excellent. Now all you have to do is tell me where Livingstone Point is.'

It was mid-afternoon when the Swissair flight from Moscow touched down at Zürich's Kloten International Airport. Voskov was one of the first to disembark and after clearing Passport Control and collecting his suitcase he took a taxi to the small, nondescript hotel in the centre of the city where Kilgarry and Racine were already booked in under false names. The three would remain there until further notice. He had memorized the dossiers on the flight and had already singled out Kilgarry as a potential troublemaker. Kahn had been right to call him arrogant. Admittedly he was a damn good sniper – probably even better than himself, judging by his impressive military CV – but he also had a violent temper, which had got him into trouble with his superiors while he had been in the Marines. It had ultimately cost him a future in the military. Voskov knew he would have to watch Kilgarry carefully. He had come across men like him before in Spetznaz. He knew how to deal with them. He was confident he could deal with Kilgarry. If not, he'd have him removed to safeguard the operation.

After checking into the hotel, under the assumed name in the false passport he had used to travel from Moscow, he got the room numbers of Kilgarry and Racine from the receptionist then went up to his own room where he unpacked his suitcase before taking a shower and changing into fresh clothes. Then he rang the two men and asked to meet with them in his room.

Kilgarry was the first to arrive. 'Peter, good to meet you,' he said, in his strong Texan drawl, shaking Voskov's hand.

'It's Petr. There's no second E. It's the Russian spelling.'

'I'll be sure to remember that,' Kilgarry said.

Voskov wasn't sure whether there had been a touch of irony in Kilgarry's voice. He let it pass. 'I assume you've been briefed in full about the operation?'

'Only what Kahn told me, but I'm sure there's more to it than that. There always is. You only get told what you need to know. The rest gets filled in later.'

'That's what makes Kahn such a good handler,' Voskov said.

'I guess,' Kilgarry said, without conviction. 'I read your CV on the plane. You've got a fucking impressive military record with Spetznaz. I hear you guys have to go through all kinds of psychological shit as part of your training.'

'It helps to focus the mind. That's what made Spetznaz the best of all the Special Forces units during the Cold War.'

'Yeah, you guys did well in Afghanistan, didn't you? The Mujaheddin kicked your sorry asses all the way back to Moscow.'

'Spetznaz had an overall success rate of eighty per cent during the conflict in Afghanistan. I can't speak for the other units. And as for having our "sorry asses" kicked all the way back to Moscow, I'd prefer to call it an expedient withdrawal.

In fact, when you think about it, there's a lot of similarities to what happened to your sorry asses in Vietnam.'

There was a knock at the door before Kilgarry could mount a suitable riposte. Voskov answered the door and as he shook Racine's hand he found himself thinking that the photograph in the dossier hadn't done the Frenchman justice. Racine was exceptionally good-looking: a rich tan, shoulder-length sun-bleached blond hair, a gold earring, vivid white teeth. Yet Voskov knew that appearances could be deceptive. Behind the looks and the genial personality lay the cold, calculating mind of a pathological killer, whose dedication to the job could, at times, border on the psychopathic. According to his dossier, he had tortured several of his targets before executing them, then justified his actions to Kahn by claiming that he had only been giving them a taste of their own medicine. Of the two men, Racine was certainly the more dangerous. But he was also the one Voskov knew he could count on to back him up if the need arose. Racine wasn't interested in leadership, which was a comfort.

'Well, here we are together at last, the Three Musketeers,' Racine announced. His English was impeccable, despite the intrusive Parisian accent.

'OK, so now we've all met. What's next?' Kilgarry asked, from the window, as he looked down into the street below.

'We wait,' Voskov told him. 'Kahn will contact me with further instructions when the need arises.'

'Fucking brilliant,' Kilgarry muttered.

'I'm in charge of this operation,' Voskov told Kilgarry. 'If you don't like it, take it up with Kahn. Otherwise, we do it my way. OK?'

Kilgarry said nothing. Racine lay down on the double bed, clasped his hands behind his head, then looked at Voskov. 'So, Petr, tell us about Spetznaz.'

'What do you want to know?' Voskov eased himself into the armchair at the foot of the bed.

'Everything, my friend,' Racine replied, with a broad grin. 'Absolutely everything.'

'Mike?'

Novak spun round as he was about to unlock the front door to the club. 'Beth! You startled me! What are you doing here?'

'I had to get out of my hotel room,' she replied. 'All I've been doing is lying on my bed thinking about Ian. Good times. Bad times. They're all the same to me right now. Just painful memories. And all they were doing was making me increasingly depressed. That's why I came here, but the club was closed. I've been waiting outside for the past forty-five minutes.'

'You're lucky. Normally I'd only come in around six. But I thought I'd better look in on Amy and make sure she's all right before the staff arrive.' Novak unlocked the door and held it open for her. He followed her inside and locked it again behind him. He opened a box on the wall and activated several switches. Moments later the foyer was bathed in light. 'That's better. Come on, I'll take you up to the room.'

'I'm sorry I had to drag you into this, Mike,' she said, as she followed him up a flight of stairs.

'I can't say I'm too thrilled about it either, but if she's innocent then it's only right that she gets a chance to prove it. And if this is the only way, so be it. I just hope Jago finds this disk quickly. I've got nothing personal against Amy but having her here makes me real uncomfortable. I know Jago said he could straighten out any misunderstandings with the authorities if she was discovered here, but I could lose my licence for harbouring a wanted felon. This club's my life, Beth. I can't imagine doing anything else.'

'I understand how you feel,' Beth said. 'I hardly slept a wink last night. All I could think about was whether I'd done the right thing. That's when I wasn't having guilt trips about doubting Ian's fidelity in the first place.'

'I know where you're coming from,' Novak said, as they

walked the length of the corridor together. 'I did the same with my wife. Only it was the other way round with me. I could never bring myself to believe that she could have been unfaithful. More fool me, eh?' He paused outside the door at the end of the corridor and knocked twice, paused, then three times more. The door was unlocked from the inside then opened.

'Am I glad to see you two!' Amy said.

'Why, is something wrong?' Novak asked anxiously.

'No, but you can only talk to yourself for so long before you start to question your own sanity.'

Beth looked around the room. It was small with a single bed beneath the only window. The curtains were drawn. She crossed to the table and picked up a photograph. 'Is this your wife?' she asked Novak, without taking her eyes off the woman's face.

'Yeah. That's Christina.'

'She was very beautiful,' Beth said, replacing the photograph on the table before picking up the one beside it. 'Who's this?'

'That's my son, John. He's ten. That photo was taken at Interlaken. We spent a weekend there earlier this year.'

'I didn't know you had a son. Is he your only child?'

'Yeah,' Novak replied. 'He's a good kid. He's had to put up with a lot, considering the anti-social hours I work. I don't get to see him as much as I'd like. I keep saying I'm going to change that, but running the club takes up so much of my time.'

'Any news from Jago?' Amy asked, after Beth had put down the photograph.

'I spoke to him earlier this afternoon,' Beth said. 'He said he was working on some leads, but he wouldn't tell me what they were. He's supposed to ring me at the hotel tonight around eight. Whether he will is another matter. He seems to be lost in his own little world right now.'

'I don't care, just as long as he gets that disk and exposes Kilgarry as the murderer,' Amy said grimly. 'That's all that matters right now. Because if he doesn't, I don't have to tell you that I'm looking at a bleak future in a Swiss jail.'

'I rang my partner in London earlier today,' Beth said. 'I asked her to open all my mail, both at home and at work, in case Ian sent the disk directly to me – or even if he just sent me a letter with instructions to tell me where I can find it. I didn't tell her about the contents of the disk. What she doesn't know can't hurt her. She promised to call me at the hotel the moment she found anything.'

'You hungry?' Novak asked Amy, breaking the uneasy silence that had descended on the room.

'I haven't eaten since that snack you brought up last night.'

'I've got a few microwave meals in my office. It's all I eat when I'm here. I'll get you one.'

'Thanks, I'd appreciate that.' Amy watched Novak leave the room. 'I like Mike. He's dependable. And, let's face it, there aren't many guys like that around these days.'

'What turned you so cynical against men?' Beth asked, sitting on the edge of the bed.

'I've been around.'

'I don't know anything about you except that you're into computers. I don't know where you're from, whether you're married.'

'And I intend to keep it that way,' Amy told her. 'I'm a private person. I keep myself to myself. That way there can be no misunderstandings.'

'You really are defensive, aren't you? It almost sounds as if you've got something to hide.'

'Maybe I have.' Amy held Beth's intense stare. She pulled out the chair and sat down. 'I've learned the hard way not to venture anything up front about myself. Don't get me wrong, I appreciate what you and Mike are doing for me. More than you can ever imagine. But that doesn't mean I want to start swapping personal experiences with you. I won't pry into your life. All I ask is the same courtesy in return. I'm sorry if that sounds ungrateful but that's just the way I am. I always keep my distance. Always have – ever since I was a kid. My father taught me that. There, I've just given you an insight into my childhood. Not very exciting, now, was it?'

'Someone you trusted must have hurt you to make you like this,' Beth said.

'Don't try to analyse me, Beth,' Amy shot back. 'It doesn't become you.'

'What's going on here – claws at five paces?' Novak was in the doorway, a tray in his hands.

'A misunderstanding, that's all,' Amy said, smiling at Beth, then she gestured to the tray Novak was holding. 'What have you got there? It smells delicious.'

'Ravioli.' Novak placed the tray on the table.

'I'll leave you to eat in peace,' Beth said, getting to her feet. 'I know just how much you like to be alone.'

'What the hell's going on between the two of you?' Novak asked, after Beth had left the room.

'As I said, a misunderstanding. But, then, Beth's the type of person who likes to get her own way. And when she doesn't, she takes it personally.'

'Considering what she's been through these past two days, not to mention the fact that she's gone out on a limb to help you when she could just as easily have handed you over to Kessler, I think you could be a little more understanding, don't you?'

'I speak my mind, Mike, that's the way I am. I'm sorry if she can't accept that.' Amy gestured to the plate in front of her. 'Do you mind if I eat this while it's still hot?'

'Help yourself – and don't forget to lock the door behind me.' Novak left the room and went downstairs, where he found Beth standing in the foyer, her back pressed against the wall, her arms across her chest. 'Are you OK?' he asked, as he approached her.

Beth turned her head to look at him. 'She's spirited, if

nothing else. Maybe I *am* too intrusive, I don't know. I guess it goes with the job.'

'I don't even know what you do,' Novak said, sheepishly.

'Buy me a coffee and I'll tell you.'

'There's a little bistro at the end of the street, which makes the best damn coffee in Zürich. But, then, I would say that – I'm a silent partner in the business.'

'You're full of surprises!' she said, as they walked to the door.

Sheriff Jed Olsen shielded his eyes from the dying sun as he watched the shimmering twin-seater Cessna approach the landing strip in a field on the outskirts of town. It touched down and bounced along the makeshift runway before coming to a halt close to the sheriff's car. Olsen spat out the gum he had been chewing, then advanced towards the plane but stopped abruptly when the passenger door opened and a well-dressed African-American in his late thirties got out. He took an attaché case and battered canvas suitcase from behind the seat then gave the pilot a wave, slammed the door shut and crossed to where Olsen was still rooted to the spot. 'I'm Special Agent Frank Dawson,' he shouted, above the deafening roar of the Cessna's engine, and extended a hand in greeting. 'You must be Sheriff Jed Olsen?'

'You're Dawson?' Olsen made no attempt to conceal the contempt that filtered into his voice.

Dawson wasn't surprised by the reaction. He'd met Olsen's type before. Jerkwater town. Jerkwater mentality. Not that it bothered him. He was there to do a job, and he was also smart enough to be able to rise above that kind of petty discrimination. But not without getting in a little dig first. 'Is something wrong, Sheriff? You look a bit . . . off-colour.'

'No, I'm fine.' Olsen managed a quick smile that didn't quite reach his eyes. He reluctantly shook Dawson's outstretched hand. 'Welcome to Livingstone Point,' he added, as an afterthought.

'Thank you,' Dawson said, taking in his surroundings. Not a building in sight. Just a vast wilderness of trees and lush vegetation as far as the eye could see. He could easily get used to that kind of environment. The Cessna turned round, built up speed as it headed back down the field, then lifted off into the amber skyline. 'It's beautiful out here,' he said, after the Cessna banked away into the distance.

'You're right. Hell, you can keep Washington as far as I'm concerned. I've never been there, and I don't intend to if I can help it. This is my territory, and I wouldn't give it up for anything.'

'Can't say I blame you.' Dawson followed Olsen to the rear of the patrol car.

'You're the first Federal agent we've ever had down here,' Olsen said, opening the trunk.

'I'm honoured,' Dawson said, placing his cases inside. 'Tell me, is there anywhere in Livingstone Point for me to stay? Hotel? Guesthouse?'

'Well . . .' Olsen gave an uncomfortable shrug. 'You have to realize, this is a small town. We don't get many tourists round here.'

'Maybe I can stay with you, then?' Dawson said, poker-faced. 'You'd be fully remunerated, of course. I do have an accommodation allowance.'

Olsen's hand froze on the lid of the trunk as he was about to slam it shut. 'There is a hotel in town,' he said. 'There's sure to be a room available. I'll have Phyllis make a reservation for you. She's the telephonist at my office.'

'Thank you, I'd appreciate that,' Dawson said, smiling faintly as Olsen shut the trunk.

'You'll find that we're a real friendly town,' Olsen said, opening the back door of the patrol car.

'I'd rather sit up front with you, Sheriff,' Dawson said, knowing full well the discomfort it would cause Olsen, especially within the town. 'Assuming you don't mind, that is?'

Olsen forced a fleeting smile. 'No, not at all.' With that he closed the back door and climbed in behind the wheel. 'You want to go straight to the hotel?'

'I'm more interested in going to Amy Michaels's house. Did you find out anything about her?'

'Matter of fact I did,' Olsen said, putting the car into gear and heading off down the narrow dirt track towards the main road.

'So?' Dawson asked, when Olsen failed to elaborate.

'Best person to talk to is Lester, Dave Burman's son. Dave runs the grocery store in the high street. It seems she has her groceries delivered to the house twice a week. Lester always takes them out to her. I also spoke to Floyd this afternoon – he's the mailman who's been working this area for the last thirty years. Said he'd spoken to her a few times since she moved in, but only to say hello. So far I haven't figured out who serviced her computers, or where she bought them.'

'We might find that out when we get to the house. I also want to speak to this Lester. As soon as possible.'

'The Burmans' house is on the way to the Hemmings place. We can stop off there.'

'Why's it called the Hemmings place?'

'That house had been in the Hemmings family for generations. It's probably about a hundred and fifty years old. Maybe older. Been modernized, though. Albert and Ruth Hemmings were the last of the line to live there. Their boy was killed in Vietnam. They didn't have any other children. Albert's been dead twenty years now. Ruth died a few years back. That's when the house went on the market. Amy Michaels met the asking price. As far as I know, nobody else even put in a bid.'

'You don't like her, do you?' Dawson said bluntly.

'I don't know her well enough to be able to form an opinion one way or another,' Olsen replied, without taking his eyes off the road. 'Like I said, we don't get many visitors around these parts. And even fewer come to live here. You got to understand, this is a very small, tightly knit community. So when an outsider settles here, the locals kind of expect them to get involved in some of the town's activities. God knows, there ain't that many things to do in Livingstone Point. But she made no effort to make friends or to become part of the community. That upset a lot of the townsfolk.'

'Including you?'

'I think she could have made more of an effort to be sociable.' Olsen cast a sidelong glance at Dawson. 'I take it these questions are all part of this profiling you mentioned earlier over the phone?'

'Correct.'

'That's the Burman place up ahead.' Olsen gestured to a gloomy, isolated farmstead, partially concealed from view behind some trees. He turned the patrol car off the main road on to what was little more than a narrow, bumpy dirt track. 'There's Lester, tinkering with that damn banger of his.' A gangly youth in dungarees was bent over the open hood of a rusting red Cadillac. 'With the amount of time he spends working on it, you'd think he'd at least have got it going by now. Not a chance. It just sits there. Never moved an inch since he bought it last year. But that's Lester for you. Means well, but he ain't too bright.'

Lester straightened up on hearing the sound of the engine. He was in his early twenties with straggly shoulder-length hair. He gave Olsen a lopsided grin then wiped his greasy hands on an oily rag hanging from the pocket of his dungarees. Olsen parked the car then got out and looked across the roof at him. 'This is the man I was telling you about, Lester. Special Agent Dawson. He's flown down from Washington.'

'Are you a real Fed?' Lester asked in awe.

'I was when I left Washington,' Dawson replied, with a friendly smile. He sensed that Lester was comfortable with him. Maybe there was hope for Livingstone Point, after all. He held out his laminated warrant card and saw the young man look from the leather wallet to his own hands. 'Take it. A bit of grease won't hurt it.'

'I'm going up to the house to get a drink,' Olsen announced, to nobody in particular, although Dawson assumed it had been for his benefit.

'You want to know about Amy, don't you?' Lester said, handing the wallet back to Dawson after Olsen had driven off in the direction of the house.

'That's right. The sheriff says you deliver the groceries to her house.'

'Twice a week, Mondays and Thursdays, without fail. She calls her order through to the store and I deliver it that same afternoon. Pa told her she could have credit but she didn't want to know. Always pays COD. And she always gives me a tip.'

'How well do you know her, Lester?'

Lester's cheeks reddened and he looked down at his scuffed shoes.

'You like her, don't you?' Dawson said.

'I once asked her out – you know, on a date. There was this country and western evening at Hennessey's about a year back. That's the main bar in town. She said no. But she did say that if she were to have gone, I'd have been the only guy in town she'd have wanted to go with. That kind of made me feel . . . well, you know . . . that maybe she does like me a bit.'

'I'm sure she does, Lester,' Dawson said.

'Where is she?' Lester blurted out suddenly. 'She didn't put in an order this week. First time since she arrived here that she's done that. She . . . she ain't in any kind of trouble, is she? I'd hate it if she were in any trouble. She's a real nice lady. I know the townsfolk don't speak too good about her, but she's always treated me real well. She is all right, isn't she?'

'To the best of my knowledge she is.' Dawson took a copy of the photofit from his pocket and showed it to Lester. 'Is that her?'

'No.'

'You seem very sure of that.'

'That ain't her. That ain't Amy Michaels.'

'Why do you say that?' Dawson asked.

'Amy's got long hair. And a thinner face. And her eyes . . .'

'What about her eyes?' Dawson asked, using a black pen to change the features in the photofit.

'Bigger. They made her look – kind of cute.'

'Cute eyes,' Dawson muttered to himself, without looking up from the photofit. 'What else?'

'It's hard to explain,' Lester was shifting uneasily on his feet, 'but she got photos of herself in the house. I seen them before.'

'I'm going there next anyway so I'll be sure to look out for them.' Dawson glanced past Lester when Olsen emerged from the house, a half-eaten bread roll in one hand and a can of soda in the other. He devoured the remnants of the roll on the way back to the patrol car, wiped his hands on the back of his trousers, then climbed behind the wheel. 'Thanks for your help, Lester,' Dawson said, extending a hand towards the youth.

Lester gave his hands another wipe on the rag. His face lit up in a broad grin. 'Wait until I tell the guys down at Hennessey's tonight that I met a real-life Fed. They won't believe it. We only ever get to see you guys on TV.'

'Any luck?' Olsen asked, after Dawson had climbed into the passenger seat beside him.

'He told me a few things,' Dawson replied evasively, 'but what I really need to see is the house. If there are any clues to be found, that's where they'll be.'

'Then let's go.'

Peaceful. Tranquil. Serene. Those were the words that came to mind when Frank Dawson first saw the house, with its pretty whitewashed walls, black shutters, dusty red-tiled roof, overlooking a little river that wound its way past the foot of the garden. The overhanging branches of an old willow tree, its trunk twisted and gnarled with age, trailed languidly across the surface of the rippling water. He almost expected – even hoped – to see an artist with an easel and canvas, sitting pensively on the riverbank, attempting to capture the moment for posterity. He snapped out of his reverie. Olsen had stopped the car, killed the engine and was watching him. 'It's beautiful, isn't it?' Dawson said.

'I guess it is, now that you mention it,' Olsen said, without sounding particularly enthusiastic, 'although to be honest, I never really gave it much thought. Robbie Hemmings and I were childhood buddies. This place was like a second home to me. I just took it for granted. Always have. Good memories.'

'Come on, let's take a closer look.' Dawson got out of the car and went to the door. He knocked several times. No reply. 'Is there an alarm system?' he asked, stepping back from the door.

'Are you kidding? Hell, this ain't Washington. You can still go to sleep with your back door unlocked in Livingstone Point. The last burglary we had was a hungry raccoon who scared the bejasus out of old Mrs Clemson over on Union Street.' Olsen laughed and patted his ample stomach. 'That was some day, I tell you. Most excitement I've had in years.' The smile died on his lips when Dawson removed a bunch of keys from his pocket and approached the front door. 'What you got there?' he asked, hurrying after him.

'Skeleton keys.' Dawson tried one in the lock. 'I've yet to find a lock that one of these won't open.'

'That's illegal . . . isn't it?' Olsen asked uncertainly.

'Sure, but what's the alternative? Break a window to get inside?' After several attempts he found the right key, unlocked the door and stepped inside. The hall was sparsely furnished. No pictures or photographs on the walls. The house had an aura of loneliness about it. Yet when he found her workplace it was almost as if he had been magically transported into another world. The walls were brightly papered. An expensive hi-fi system was positioned against one wall. Framed film posters covered another wall. Mostly French *film noir* by the look of it. A single framed print, at least ten foot high, filled the wall adjacent to the door. It was a photograph of a white computer keyboard and a mouse set against a black background. It did nothing for him. But he could understand her fixation with the image when he took in the computer equipment lined up on two trestle tables positioned directly in front of the wide bay window overlooking the river. Four VDUs, with accompanying keyboards, and two laser printers positioned on either end of the tables. Dozens of folders were stacked up against the walls underneath the tables, several so bulky that they had overflowed, spilling their contents across the bare wooden floorboards.

'Holy mother!' Olsen exclaimed from the doorway. 'This is some real serious shit she's got here.'

'State of the art.' Dawson retrieved one of the folders from under the nearest table. 'Have you checked the rest of the house?' He was leafing absently through the printouts.

'Yeah. She ain't here.' Olsen entered the room, cast a questioning look at the enlarged print of the keyboard and mouse, scratched his head in bewilderment, then crossed to where Dawson was standing. 'What you got there?'

'It looks like stuff she's downloaded off the Internet.' Dawson replaced the dossier under the table. He got to his feet but when he turned to Olsen his eyes went to the figure standing in the doorway. 'What are you doing here?'

'I – I just thought – I could – maybe, you know – help you,' Lester stammered. 'I didn't mean no harm.'

'How did you get here?' Dawson asked.

'I came in the truck,' Lester told him. 'It's my daddy's truck, really, but I always use it for deliveries.'

'This ain't no place for you, Lester,' Olsen said angrily. 'This is official police business. You go on home now.'

'It's not right in here, you know,' Lester said, directing his comment at Dawson.

'What are you talking about?' Dawson asked.

'The rug's missing,' Lester replied, becoming increasingly confident, knowing that he had something positive to contribute. He pointed to the centre of the floor. 'There was a rug – right there. It's always been there, ever since I've been delivering stuff to the house.' He glanced at Olsen. 'She never keeps the back door locked, not when she's expecting me. I always put the groceries in the kitchen then come through here to say hello to her. Sometimes she offers me a coffee – but only if she ain't too busy. She tried to show me how the computers work, but I don't understand them. She's real clever, you know.'

'Describe the carpet,' Dawson said.

'It was pale blue. She always keeps it real clean. Like the rest of the house.'

'Size?' Dawson prompted.

'I dunno . . . about six feet long. Maybe seven. Something like that. I never really looked at it. I just know it was there.'

'Can you see whether there's anything else missing?'

'I wouldn't know about that,' he said defensively. 'I never came in here to nose around. Amy always invited—'

'Just take a look around, Lester!' Olsen cut in sharply.

Lester walked the length of the two trestle tables. 'There was a photograph right here,' he said, pointing to a space on the table between two computer terminals. 'Definitely. I remember it.'

'Of her?' Dawson asked when Lester fell silent.

'Yes. It was a real pretty picture too.'

'What about other photos? Parents? Ex-boyfriends? Anything like that?'

'I never saw any,' Lester replied. 'She never spoke about her parents, except the one time when she told me they were dead. I don't know how it happened, though. She never said. She doesn't have any other relatives, far as I know. Her parents left her a lot of money. That's how she could afford to buy this place.'

'Did she ever have people staying with her?' Dawson said.

'No. She liked to be on her own.' Lester looked accusingly at Olsen. 'I know the townsfolk thought she was weird. I even heard some of them say that she was . . . you know, gay. But what do they know about her anyway? They're just full of small-town gossip.'

Dawson saw the look of discomfort on the sheriff's face. The words had obviously been directed as much at him as at others in the town. He had to admit to taking a certain pleasure in Olsen's discomfiture. 'Thanks, Lester, you've been a great help. Now you must let us get on with our work.'

'Sheriff, Ma said to tell you that there's more than enough stew to go round if you want to stop in for dinner on your way home,' Lester told Olsen. 'She knows it's the night your wife goes ten-pin bowling with her friends in Jackson.'

'You tell your ma that I'd—'

'The sheriff's got quite enough on his plate here as it is,' Dawson intervened.

'Tell your ma I appreciate the offer, but I'm gonna be working late,' Olsen said, reluctantly. He waited until Lester had left then turned to Dawson. 'What do you make of what he said about the rug?'

'I'm not jumping to any conclusions at this point. I'm going to bring in a forensics team to check the house thoroughly.'

'There's a lab down in Jackson. That's the nearest one. I can call them tonight. They'd be here by morning.'

'No, this is a Federal case. I'll be bringing in my own people from Washington.' Dawson sat down and activated the first computer. 'You've got a lot of files to get through, Sheriff. I suggest you make a start if you want to get home tonight.'

FIVE

Friday

'Beth?'

 'Uh-huh.'

 'Beth, it's Emma!'

She opened her eyes and looked at her watch: 8.48 a.m. – an hour ahead of London. She knew that Emma would have been up since five, have gone for her daily run, had a bath and eaten a light breakfast, while *she* was still lying in bed. She felt a pang of guilt, even though she had had very little sleep for the second night in a row. She struggled to come awake, rubbing her eyes groggily.

'Beth, are you still there?' Emma asked.

'I'm here.' Beth sat up and pulled the pillow from underneath her to cushion her back against the wooden headboard. 'Sorry, I'm still half asleep.'

'Then you'd better wake up. I'm at your house. There's a letter here from Ian. I recognize his handwriting on the envelope.'

Beth was instantly awake. Part of her was excited at the prospect of solving the mystery of the missing disk. Yet another part of her was fearful that it would only draw her deeper into an already dangerous situation. But she knew there was no turning back. 'Read it out to me, Emma,' she said.

There was a pause at the other end of the line as Emma opened the envelope. 'Oh, my God,' she gasped.

'What is it?' Beth demanded.

'I can't read this to you.'

'Emma, I have to know what's in the letter,' Beth implored her. 'Read it to me. Please.'

'"My darling Beth,"' Emma began, the discomfort apparent in her voice. '"If you receive this letter then you'll already know . . ."'

'Emma!' Beth said in frustration when her friend's voice trailed off. 'Just read it. Please.'

'I'm sorry,' Emma replied softly. '"If you receive this letter then you'll already know I'm dead. I gave the letter to a trusted colleague of mine here in Zürich with strict instructions to forward it to you, should anything happen to me. I've been working with Interpol on an under-cover investigation these past few months – it had nothing to do with my work as a lawyer – but recently my position has become ever more dangerous as those we're investigating now know that I'm on to them. These are ruthless people, Beth, and they will stop at nothing to ensure that they are never publicly exposed. I realize that none of this will make any sense to you but I don't want to tell you any more than is absolutely necessary to safeguard you from reprisals. But with your help they can finally be brought to justice. Then the truth will come out into the open and they wouldn't dare harm you in the full glare of world publicity without further implicating themselves.

'"The evidence I have accumulated against them over the months is stored on a floppy disk, which I put in an envelope and left for safekeeping with a lawyer based here in Zürich. His name is Dietmar Strohmaier. His offices are in Beethoven-strasse, next to the Mövenpick restaurant. He knows nothing about the investigation, or what's contained on the disk. In fact, he thinks the envelope contains documents relating to one of my cases. I gave him specific instructions to give you the envelope should you request it in person (but only in person, not over the telephone). You must take your passport with you as a means of identification. I know it sounds like a load of nonsense but, as I mentioned earlier, these people will stop at nothing to protect themselves. Once you have the disk it's essential that you contact a man called Ralf Jago at Interpol headquarters in France. Don't tell anyone else, not even the local police. Jago will know what to do and he'll make arrangements to meet you as soon as possible to take the disk off your hands. I can't stress this enough, Beth, don't give the disk to anyone other than Ralf Jago. I'm sure that you're even more confused now than ever, but I can't tell you any more than I already have. You must understand that. It will all become apparent after the truth comes out.

'"Beth, you know I was never very good at expressing my emotions at the best of times. And now is no different. In fact, if anything, it's even harder. I don't know what to write right now, other than to say that I love you more than life itself. God, what a cliché, but it's true. Just remember that wherever you go – whatever you do – I'll be watching over you. Always and for ever. Ian."'

'Thanks, Emma,' Beth said, as the tears streamed down her cheeks. She had begun to cry almost as soon as Emma started to read the letter but had made no attempt to stop herself. Now she reached for a tissue and wiped her wet cheeks.

'Are you OK?' Emma asked.

'Yes. Really.'

'Does the letter make any sense to you?'

'Not really, no,' Beth lied. She was determined not to involve Emma any more than she already had. 'Maybe it'll make more sense after I've got the disk from the lawyer and met with this Ralf Jago that Ian mentioned in the letter.'

'Whatever you do, Beth, be careful. From what Ian said in the letter, the people he was investigating won't stop at anything to get their hands on the disk. They've proved that already. And you're an obvious target for them. It's natural for them to assume that Ian would have turned to you for help, particularly with something as sensitive as this. You're the one person he knew he could trust. You must contact Jago right away and tell him about the letter. That way he can meet you in Zürich and maybe go with you to see the lawyer, Strohmaier.'

'Yes, that makes sense,' Beth agreed.

'Do you want me to send Ian's letter to you?' Emma asked.

'No. Keep it until I get back. All being well, I should be at work on Monday.'

'It's too quick, Beth. You need time to grieve. There aren't many meetings scheduled for next week anyway. I can handle them. That's not a problem.'

'It would be for me,' Beth said. 'I want to get back to work as quickly as possible. It's the only way I'm going to get over Ian's death, not moping about the house feeling sorry for myself.'

'We'll talk about it when you get back to London,' Emma said, diplomatically.

'There's nothing to talk about. I'll be back at work next week. End of discussion.'

'I know you only too well when you're in this mood. There's no reasoning with you. I'll speak to you again over the weekend. Take care of yourself, Beth.'

'I will. And, Emma, thanks.' Beth replaced the receiver, found the number of the hotel where Jago was staying, and asked to be put through to his room. There was no answer. She hung up, then got out of bed and went to take a shower.

Voskov picked up the handset after the first ring. 'Yes?'

'It's Kahn. I've found out the location of the disk. Grant left it with a lawyer here in Zürich for safekeeping. Only we can't get to it – at least, not without Beth Grant's help. Are Kilgarry and Racine with you?'

'No.'

'Are they up yet?'

'Yes, we had breakfast together earlier this morning.'

'Good. Now, listen carefully, this is what I want you to do.'

Mike Novak rarely surfaced before midday. He had no telephone in his bedroom – any morning calls were met by a cordial message on his answering-machine and could be returned in the afternoon.

The door of his darkened bedroom opened shortly after seven o'clock that morning and his son, John, entered the room. He crossed to the double bed and pulled back the top of the duvet to reveal his father's dishevelled hair. He eased it back a little more and an unshaven face and a bare shoulder came into view. He shook his father's arm. 'Dad, wake up,' he said. No response. He shook him harder. 'Dad, wake up!' he repeated, louder this time. Novak muttered something under his breath, which John knew was an expletive, then rolled away from him. The shaking continued until Novak turned on to his back and peered irritably at his son through slitted eyes. 'Dad, wake up,' John urged.

'What is it? Jesus, I only got in at four this morning.'

'It's important. There's a guy on the phone who says he has to speak to you right away. His name's Ralf Jago.'

'Oh, I don't believe it.' Novak groaned and struggled into a sitting position. 'Where's the phone?'

'I left it in the hall.' John giggled. 'I thought he better not hear your waking-up noises.'

'Just get the phone, will you?' Novak said, swinging a playful punch at his son's arm but John evaded it and disappeared into the hall. He returned a moment later with the cordless phone and gave it to his father.

'Jago, what the fu—' Novak checked himself. 'What d'you want? I'm tired.'

'I've just received a call from Amy Michaels. She was almost hysterical. She said that someone was trying to break into the club. Then the line went dead, as if it had been cut. I'm calling you on my cellphone. I'm on my way over there now. How soon can you be at the club?'

'Twenty minutes. Have you called the cops?'

'You're obviously still half asleep, Novak. How can I call the cops? What would I tell them? That someone broke into your club and snatched a wanted criminal that we've been harbouring for the past two days? I'm sure they'd understand.'

'I'm on my way,' Novak said, cut the connection and scrambled out of bed.

'What's happening, Dad?' John asked, as his father picked up his jeans from the floor and pulled them on. 'You said something about calling the cops. What's going on?'

'It's nothing,' Novak replied, then pulled on a clean T-shirt before disappearing into the bathroom. When he emerged he slipped on a pair of canvas plimsolls, grabbed his car keys off the dresser and left the room. John hurried after him.

'Dad? Dad, what's going on?'

'I'll tell you when I get back, OK?' Novak went into the kitchen where the au pair was busy unloading the crockery from the dish-washer. He left through the side door, which led directly into the garage. Getting behind the wheel, he used a remote control to activate the garage door, then started the engine and reversed down the driveway. He swung the car out into the street but failed to notice the two men seated in a van parked a short distance away as he drove off.

Voskov watched impassively as Novak drove past them, then looked across at the house again. It was bordered on three sides by rows of towering poplar trees and the nearest neighbour was fifty yards down the road. Perfect. He nodded to Kilgarry in the passenger seat beside him. Kilgarry took a last draw on his cigarette, flicked the butt through the open window. Then they slipped on black balaclavas before checking their SIG-Sauer automatics and returning them to the holsters clipped to the back of their belts. Voskov started up the van and drove to the house.

Novak drove the short distance from his home, on the outskirts of Horgen – a picturesque village spread across the banks of Lake Zürich – to the ferry port. Luck was with him and the car ferry, which traversed the lake every fifteen minutes, was just coming in to dock. Ten minutes later he was on the opposite side in Herrliberg and he drove along the lakeside, through the affluent villages of Kusnacht and Zollikon, before arriving in Zürich itself. He parked the car, as normal, on the waterfront beside the Limmat river – the myriad side-streets in the Niederdorf only accessible to pedestrians. He went the last couple of hundred yards to the club on foot.

To his surprise he found Beth standing outside it. 'What are you doing here?' he asked, taking the keys from his pocket.

'I got a call from Jago to say that someone was trying to break in,' Beth replied. 'He said he'd meet me here. There's no sign of him, though.'

'I got the same call,' Novak said warily. 'I came over straight away.'

'I've already taken a look around. All the windows appear to be undamaged and the front door's locked. I've been knocking for the past few minutes, but if Amy's inside she's not answering. But that's hardly surprising, is it?'

'There's only one way to find out if she's all right,' Novak said, then unlocked the door and followed Beth inside. They went upstairs and he tried the door to Amy's room. It was locked from the inside. That gave him hope. He used the coded knock, and a sense of unease swept through him when there was no reply. He knocked again. 'Amy, it's Mike Novak.' Nothing. 'Amy, are you in there?'

Then the door was unlocked from the inside. 'Thank God it's you,' Amy said, with relief.

'Jago rang us both as soon as you'd called him at his hotel,' Beth told Amy.

Amy gave them a questioning look. 'What are you talking about? I never called Jago. I don't even know where he's staying.'

'You never called Jago to say that someone was trying to break into the club?' Novak said.

'I never called Jago period,' Amy insisted. 'And to the best of my knowledge, nobody tried to break into the club either. But how would I know, locked away in here?'

'So why were you so relieved to see us when you opened the door?' Beth queried.

'Someone's been knocking on the front door for the past ten minutes,' Amy replied. 'I could hear it in here. I thought it might be the cops.'

'That was me,' Beth said ruefully. 'I got here before Mike. I was worried that something had happened to you.'

'Well, you can see for yourself I'm fine,' Amy said.

'We've obviously been set up,' Novak concluded. 'Question is, why?'

'It could have something to do with the letter,' Beth replied, then looked slowly from Amy to Novak. 'I haven't told you about that, have I?' She recounted what she had heard from Emma earlier that morning.

'Did you tell Jago about it when he called you at the hotel?' Amy asked, once she had finished.

'Naturally . . .' Beth trailed off when she realized what Amy was implying. 'If that wasn't Jago who rang me earlier this morning, then whoever it was now knows that Ian left the disk with Strohmaier.'

'If it wasn't Jago, the caller already knew,' Novak said. 'Why else would he have sent us both here on a wild-goose chase?'

'But how *could* he have known?' Beth asked incredulously.

'I don't know. And neither do I know why they want us here.

I'm going downstairs to call Jago. I left the number on the desk in my office.'

'Do you think the caller was someone from . . . the Cabal?' Beth asked as she followed Novak from the room.

'Right now it would seem the most likely explanation, wouldn't it?' Novak led the way down to his office. Unlocking the door, he found the number and dialled out. He asked to be put through to Jago's room. He let the phone ring for some time then replaced the receiver. 'Maybe he's been sent off on some wild-goose chase too, so that we can't get hold of him.'

The phone rang.

Novak looked from Beth to Amy then reached out a hand to pick it up. 'Hello?' he said tentatively.

'Am I speaking to Michael Novak?' The accent was Russian.

'Yes,' he said hesitantly. 'Who is this?'

'Please put the call on to your speaker-phone so that everyone can hear our conversation.'

'How did you know that I've got a speaker-phone in my office?' Novak demanded.

'Just do it, Mr Novak.'

Novak did as he was told then placed the handset on the table. 'I asked who you were?'

'I heard you the first time. Names are unimportant. What is important as far as you're concerned, however, is that I'm calling from the phone in your lounge. Your son and the au pair, Mademoiselle Perrault, are in the kitchen. My colleague is with them. Don't worry, they're both quite safe. And they'll remain that way as long as you co-operate with us.'

'What do you want with my son?' Novak blurted out, his eyes riveted on the speaker.

'He's a means to an end. Nothing more. And as long as you do as you're told, you should be reunited with him again within the next couple of hours.'

'You so much as touch—'

'Let's not reduce this to a melodrama, Mr Novak,' the Russian cut across him. 'As I said, co-operate with us and your son and the girl won't come to any harm.'

'I want to speak to John.' Novak's mind was in turmoil and all he wanted was to hear his son's voice, to know that he was safe. That was all that mattered.

'Bring the boy in here,' he heard the Russian call. The voice was muffled, as if there was a hand over the mouthpiece.

'John? John?' Novak shouted frantically. 'John, are you there?'

'Dad?'

'Are you all right? Have they hurt you?'

'I'm OK, but I'm scared. They've both got guns. And masks—'

'That's enough!' the Russian grated. Again the hand was put over the mouthpiece. 'Take him back into the kitchen. Close the door behind you.' There was a moment's delay before he spoke into the handset again. 'At least now you know that there are two of us. We're armed with handguns as well as sub-machine-guns. So should any attempt be made by the police to storm the house I'll execute both hostages without a moment's hesitation. Believe it, Novak.'

'I've no doubt you would,' Novak replied bitterly, but there was no fight left in his voice.

'I can understand now why you sent Mike here,' said Beth, 'to get him out the way so that you could get into the house and take John hostage – but why me?'

'Ah, Mrs Grant,' Voskov said. 'I needed you both together for my plan to work. And before I forget, my condolences to you on your loss. Your husband was a good man. Foolish, perhaps, but a good man all the same.'

'Screw your condolences, you bastard,' Beth shot back, and glanced sharply at Amy when she put a hand on her arm. 'You want the disk, don't you?'

'The disk for the two hostages. A straight swap.'

'You must have known about the disk before you called me at the hotel. How did you find out so quickly?'

'Your phones back in London, both at home and at work, have been tapped for the past few days. As were your business partner's. And while we're on the subject of Emma Kendry, I realize that you might be thinking right now that you have no real incentive to hand over the disk. After all, you don't even know Novak's boy. That's why I took the precaution earlier of putting out a contract on Mrs Kendry's daughter, which would be carried out should you be foolish enough to go to the authorities. How old is Jessica now? Two, isn't she? And such a pretty little girl. It would be a tragedy if anything were to happen to her. And her parents would be even more devastated by her loss when they found out that you could have prevented it, if you had just chosen to co-operate with us in the first place.' There was a moment's pause. 'I don't make empty threats, Mrs Grant. Be sure to bear that in mind.'

'What do you want us to do?' Novak asked.

'It's really quite simple. You and Mrs Grant will go to Strohmaier's office and get the disk. Once you have it, wait by the public telephone on the other side of the street, directly opposite the Mövenpick restaurant. You'll get a call giving you further instructions.' The line went dead.

'That was Voskov, wasn't it?' Beth said at length, breaking the silence that had descended over the room.

'Russian accent. Who else?' Novak switched off the speaker and sat back in his chair, staring at the ceiling. The full impact of his helplessness was only now beginning to set in. He knew that Voskov would have no hesitation in killing John and Marie, should it not go according to plan. And who was to say he wouldn't kill them anyway after he had taken possession of the disk? This was a man devoid of conscience. Or feeling. Or, at least, that was how he read Voskov from what Jago had said about him. And this was the demon who was holding his son hostage. His initial anger was gone. Now he was more scared than he had ever felt in his life.

'Mike, I'm sorry,' Beth said. 'I had no idea it would come to this.'

'Damn you for what you've done,' he said, in a venomous tone. 'Damn you!'

'John will be fine as long as we do as they say.' Beth knew her words sounded empty and hollow.

'Yeah?' came the sceptical riposte.

'They wouldn't be wearing balaclavas unless they intended to let him and your au pair go once they have the disk. It stands to reason that if it was their intention to kill them, they wouldn't have bothered to hide their faces, would they?'

'I'm glad you're so sure about that.' Novak pushed back the chair and got to his feet.

'What happens to me after you've given them the disk?'

Beth and Novak looked round at Amy, who was sitting in a corner of the room. They had momentarily forgotten she was there.

'That disk represents the only realistic chance I have of clearing my name,' Amy continued. 'Without it, I'm looking at the next twenty years in a Swiss jail.'

'My son's life is at stake,' Novak replied. 'You're going to have to take your chances.'

'Jago said he would intervene on your behalf,' Beth reminded her.

'Sure, when he had the disk safely in his possession. Not before. And if he doesn't have the disk, what's to stop him throwing me to the wolves?'

'Why would he do that?' Beth asked.

'Because to back me up he would have to divulge publicly what information he already has on the Cabal. It's obviously not enough to get a conviction – maybe not even an arrest – otherwise he wouldn't need the disk so badly, and it would only push the organization even further underground. He would never get Sammy Kahn after that.'

'I'm not putting my son's life on the line for you, or anyone else, and that's an end to it,' Novak told her. 'So if you don't like it you'd better start running now. Because, as of now, you're on your own.'

'He's right, Amy,' Beth said. 'We don't have any choice but to do exactly as Voskov says. At least for now. There are three lives at stake here. I'm Jessica's godmother. I know I could never live with myself if anything were to happen to her.'

'I just hope you can live with yourself while I'm rotting in some Swiss jail for a crime I didn't commit.' Amy strode from the room.

They heard her footsteps on the stairs, followed, moments later, by the sound of a door being slammed shut. 'What am I supposed to do about her?' Novak asked, turning to Beth. 'I'm damned if I'm going to leave the club unlocked while we're out so that she can leave, if that's what she decides to do.'

'She's not going anywhere,' Beth said calmly.

'How do you know?'

'Call it female intuition.' Beth crossed to the door where she paused to look round at him. 'Come on, let's go.'

'I'm afraid Mr Strohmaier's not in.'

'When do you expect him back?' Beth asked the receptionist seated behind the spacious semi-circular mahogany desk, which overlooked the tastefully decorated waiting room.

'He'll be in the office on Monday morning. He's been working on a complicated fraud case for the last three months. It ended yesterday and all he wanted to do was to get away for a few days.'

'Is there any way we can contact him?' Novak asked.

'He didn't say where he was going. The whole idea was that he wouldn't be disturbed while he was away. He didn't even leave a contact number. I'm sorry.' The receptionist looked from Beth to Novak. 'May I ask what this is about? Perhaps I could get one of the other partners to see you if it's a matter of some urgency. Otherwise I can make an appointment for you to see Mr Strohmaier next week.'

'My husband, Ian Grant, left a computer disk with Mr Strohmaier earlier this week. He also left instructions that I could collect it from Mr Strohmaier if I came here in person. It's imperative that I get the disk today.'

'Ian Grant, the lawyer?' the receptionist asked. Beth nodded. 'I'm so sorry for your loss.'

'Thank you,' Beth said.

'Mr Strohmaier didn't mention anything about the disk to me before he left, but maybe he left instructions with one of the other partners. If you'll bear with me, I'll ask them if they know anything about it. Would you care to take a seat while you wait?'

They sat down out of earshot of two other clients in the waiting room. 'This just gets better and better,' Novak hissed to Beth. 'What if the partners don't know anything about the disk? Where the hell will that leave us?'

'Let's just wait and see, shall we?' Beth tried to inject some much-needed composure into her voice, but her heart was racing as a mixture of apprehension and fear jangled every nerve in her body. She had no idea how Voskov would react if they didn't deliver the disk. In theory, this was a situation beyond their control. But whether Voskov would see it that way would be another matter altogether. And that's what really scared her . . .

'Mrs Grant?'

She looked over at the receptionist, then got to her feet and crossed to the desk, Novak right behind her. 'Well?' she inquired. 'Do they know about the disk?'

'I'm afraid not.'

'Chances are it's in his safe,' Novak said. 'Surely someone here has the combination in case of an emergency.'

The receptionist shook her head. 'Mr Strohmaier's the only one who knows it. It's company policy. I'm sorry.'

'So there's no way we can get the disk before Monday morning?' Novak said.

'I'm afraid not.' The receptionist smiled regretfully. 'I'm sorry I can't be of more help. If it's urgent, I would suggest that you get in touch with the police. I'm sure they will make every effort to try and locate him for you. Our police are generally very helpful in such cases.' Her eyes went to Beth. 'And I'm sure they would be particularly sympathetic to your circumstances. Other than that, there's really not much else I can do to help you.'

'Thank you for your time,' Beth said, with a brief smile, then followed Novak from the office.

'Now what?' he asked, pressing the button for the elevator.

'We tell Voskov the truth. It's all we can do. He's not going to do anything to John. After all, he needs the disk. And John's his insurance that we get it for him. It's just going to take that bit longer.'

'I wish I could share your optimism,' he said, entering the elevator after her.

She said nothing. She only hoped she was right. Because if she wasn't . . . it didn't bear thinking about. They left the building together and crossed the street to the public telephone. Beth looked around her slowly. Were they being watched? It seemed the most likely explanation. How else would Voskov know when they were in position to receive the call? She scanned the length of parked cars on either side of the road. All appeared to be empty.

The telephone rang. They exchanged glances, then she picked up the handset and raised it to her ear.

'Do you have the disk?' The accent was French. Racine.

'No.'

'Why not? You were told what would happen—'

'Why don't you just shut up and hear me out?' Beth cut in

furiously, all her pent-up emotion bursting to the surface before she could check herself. She knew that it could have been a mistake to antagonize him, but she seemed to have got away with it – there was silence on the other end of the line. She then went on to explain the situation to him.

'And there's no way that you can contact Strohmaier until he gets back to Zürich?' Racine asked, when she had finished. He wasn't rattled, but she could hear in his voice that he had been caught off-guard. She felt as if she had the upper hand, even if it was only for a short time. She took a certain pleasure in that brief sense of power.

'That's what we were told,' she replied. 'What do you want us to do now?'

'Wait by the phone.' The line went dead.

She replaced the handset and allowed herself a faint smile of satisfaction. 'That was Racine. He's going to call me back. He obviously needs to consult with Voskov now that their original plan has been thrown off course. Let them sweat for a change.'

'You're actually enjoying this, aren't you?' Novak said, in disbelief.

'I'm enjoying the fact that they're having to back-pedal.'

'And when they do, it's my son that they'll be pulling back with them,' Novak countered. 'Just remember that, Beth.'

'I told you, Mike, they won't touch John. They're going to need him now more than ever. Because without him they won't get their hands on the disk. And that's what this is all about. They're going to have to reassess the situation, and that can only work in our favour.'

'And how do you work that one out? Because the way I see it, we're still going to have to get the disk for them.'

'But it gives us time,' Beth pointed out.

'To do *what*?'

'I don't know that yet.'

'We give them the disk, Beth. We don't start playing fucking heroes with these people. They're professionals.'

'They also murdered my husband in cold blood,' Beth retorted, her eyes blazing. 'He died for that disk. And if they get hold of it now they've won. Don't you see that? I owe it to Ian to do everything in my power to try to bring them to justice.'

'Not if it means putting my son's life on the line. You play by their rules, Beth,' Novak levelled a warning finger at her, 'because if you don't, and something happens to John, I'll be the one coming after you. Not them. You just remember that.'

The telephone rang before she could respond. She picked up the receiver.

'Go back to Novak's house. Park the car in the garage as normal. You'll be given further instructions once you get there. And it goes without saying that you don't attempt to make contact with anyone on the way. If you do, the deal's off and the hostages will be executed. Do I make myself clear?'

'Perfectly,' Beth replied, through clenched teeth. The line went dead. She hung up and recounted Racine's orders to Novak. He said nothing, then walked off in the direction of his car.

Stefan Kessler always kept a framed photograph of his son displayed prominently on his desk. It was the last one taken of him before his death. He knew that his wife kept an identical, albeit smaller, copy in her purse. His eyes lingered on the freckled face beaming out at him as he thought about the incident at breakfast earlier that morning. It had started out like any other morning in the last six months. Barely any words spoken. A tacit acknowledgement of each other. Nothing more. Marthe had started it. To be fair to her, he knew that she had only been attempting to bridge the ever-widening chasm between them before it was too late. Except he felt that way already. There was no going back, as far as he was concerned. How could there be without Andreas? The marriage had died with his son. She meant nothing to him without Andreas.

As had always been Marthe's way, she had come straight to the point. Did he still love her? A single yes or no would have sufficed. Only that had been too difficult for him. Instead he had launched into a vitriolic attack on her and lost his temper, which ended with him grabbing the edge of the table and upturning it, spilling the contents across the kitchen floor. The table had missed her by a matter of inches. A sliver of broken crockery had sliced a gash in her leg, not deep, but it had bled profusely. What still haunted him was the look of fear in her eyes – not for herself, but for the safety of her unborn baby. Nothing, and nobody, was worth that risk. She had reached the crossroads and realized there was no way back for either of them. The marriage was finally over.

She had contacted her best friend, Bettina Lehmann, a fellow teacher, and arranged to stay with her and her husband for the next few days until she could find accommodation. His own friendship with Manfred Lehmann, who had been best man at their wedding, went back to their childhood. While he had joined the police force on completing his military service, Manfred had decided to remain in the Swiss Army and was now a senior officer with the Special Forces parachute unit.

He touched the face in the photograph. *I'm sorry, kid, but it's for the best.*

'What did you say, Stefan?' a detective asked from an adjoining desk.

Kessler gave him a puzzled frown, then realized he must have been thinking aloud. 'Nothing,' he replied, then looked at the figure approaching his desk. 'What have you got for me, Sergeant? It better be something good.'

Sergeant Hans Matzke handed him a folder. 'That's the man we believe tailed Beth Grant to Novak's club on Wednesday night.'

'Finally!' Kessler opened the folder. 'Ralf Jago . . . Interpol?' he said. 'What the hell's their interest in this case?'

'I don't know, sir, but it could explain why it's taken us so long to identify him,' Matzke suggested. 'He must be working independently of the local police, otherwise he'd have checked in with us when he first arrived in Zürich.'

'I can assure you that's going to stop very quickly once I've had a word with him. If he's got something constructive to contribute to the investigation, I want to know about it. I'm under enough fucking pressure as it is without having Interpol adding to my problems.'

'You've always maintained that you thought Beth Grant was hiding something from you when you went to see her at the hotel,' Matzke said. 'This could be it.'

'Possibly, but why would he tail her if they'd already met? Why not just go with her to the club? No, I think there's more to it than that. Only I don't have anything on her – at least, not yet. But she's being watched around the clock.' Kessler picked up the telephone, dialled the number of Jago's hotel, and asked to be put through to his room. There was no reply. He left a message with the switchboard operator to have Jago call him as soon as he got in, then replaced the receiver and sat back in his chair, his hands clasped behind his head. 'I got a call this morning from the FBI. A Special Agent Frank Dawson. They've found out where Amy Michaels lives. A small town in rural Mississippi. He's at the house now, sifting through the data on her computers.'

'Computers? Plural?'

Kessler nodded. 'By all accounts she's got several. I just hope one of them throws up something useful to the investigation. Dawson said he'll keep me posted on any new developments.'

The telephone rang. Matzke answered it, then extended the receiver to his superior.

'It's Schneider, sir. Sergeant Dannhauser and I tailed Beth Grant and Novak to a firm of lawyers in Beethovenstrasse. When they came out they went to a public phone on the opposite side of the street. They got two calls. Then they left in his car. Sergeant Dannhauser's following them. I've just had a word with the receptionist at the law firm. She said that they wanted to collect a computer disk from one of the partners – a Dietmar Strohmaier. It seems that Ian Grant left the disk with him earlier in the week with instructions for his wife to pick it up. Only problem is, the lawyer's gone away for a few days and she's got no contact number for him. He's due back in Zürich on Sunday night.'

'Did the receptionist know what was on the disk?' Kessler asked.

'No, sir. But she did say that they both seemed pretty upset when they found out that they would have to wait until Strohmaier returned before they could get it.'

'Tell Dannhauser I want to know exactly where they go,' Kessler said, then replaced the receiver. He explained briefly to Matzke what Schneider had said then wrote Strohmaier's name on a sheet of paper and gave it to him. 'Find out everything you can about him. And put out a nationwide alert for him. I want him found as soon as possible.'

'Do you think the disk is the breakthrough you're looking for to crack the case?' Matzke reached for the telephone on Kessler's desk.

'We'll only know that when we get it, won't we?' Kessler gestured to the receiver in Matzke's hand. 'Start dialling, Sergeant.'

SIX

Neither of them spoke during the drive back to Novak's house. Both were caught up in their own private thoughts. As always Beth found herself thinking about Ian. She knew that with everything that had been going on since she arrived in Zürich, she hadn't been able to concentrate fully on his memory. Which was probably for the best. It had helped to make the pain of her loss more bearable. Admittedly, she knew she wasn't confronting her emotions head on – that would come in time, when all this was over. And time was what she needed to come to terms with her loss. Or was she just using that as an excuse? It was a question she'd asked herself repeatedly over the past couple of days, and one which still had no satisfactory answer.

She glanced at Novak. His eyes remained fixed on the road. She decided against trying to initiate conversation. She knew it wouldn't have been appreciated. She focused her mind on the events of the day. She had been horrified when Voskov had called the club and told her that he had put out a contract on little Jessica. She would do anything to protect her god-daughter.

Yet there was another side to the equation. Ian had died to ensure that the disk was passed to the proper authorities. If Voskov had his way, he would get the disk and all Ian's work would have been in vain. She desperately wanted to find a way to complete it for him, but there could be no compromise without more bloodshed. She had considered the idea that Voskov was bluffing about the contract on Jessica but she had quickly dismissed it with an overwhelming sense of guilt. How could she even think of risking a child's life? Which put her back at square one. No solution. At least, not yet . . .

Novak swung the car into the driveway, used the remote control to activate the garage door and drove inside. He closed the door behind him. Only then did he look at Beth. There was fear in his eyes. She squeezed his arm in an attempt to reassure him. Which was crazy, when she thought about it – she knew his eyes only mirrored her own feelings. He managed a taut smile, then got out of the car and moved towards the door that led into the kitchen. It was ajar. He pushed it open and found himself face to face with a man in camouflage trousers and a white vest, stretched across his muscular torso. His face was concealed under a black balaclava and he held a lightweight Mini-Uzi in one hand, aimed at Novak. A Swiss SIG-Sauer P-225 automatic was tucked into a holster on his belt.

The man took a step back from the door then gestured Novak inside. Then he noticed Beth, hovering in the doorway. 'You too, inside!' he snapped.

She recognized the voice as the man who had met her at the airport, passing himself off as an official of the American embassy. Bob Kilgarry. Not that she said anything. If any of them suspected for a moment that she and Novak knew their real identities, it could put all their lives in danger. Yet she still felt a surge of fury pulse through her as she stared at the American. If Amy was to be believed, and she had no reason to doubt her word any more, this was the man who had murdered Ian. She had never hated anyone as much as she did Kilgarry at that moment. If the tables had been turned, and she was the one holding the gun, she wouldn't have hesitated to pump the whole magazine into him. No hesitation whatsoever.

'Where's John?' Novak took a step towards Kilgarry.

The stumpy submachine-gun tightened in Kilgarry's hand.

'You don't fucking move without my permission, Novak. Now back off!'

'You're pretty jumpy for someone holding a gun,' Novak said.

Beth, her initial rage now replaced by contempt for the gunman, found herself watching Novak. She was far more interested in his apparent transformation than in any threat made by Kilgarry. Gone was his earlier defensive concern for John's safety. Now he was on the attack, getting at Kilgarry, pushing him, refusing to show any fear in front of their captors. He was obviously playing a role – for his son.

Then she heard the sound of a car and, looking round, saw a silver Volvo hatchback through the kitchen window. It pulled up outside the back door. She couldn't see the driver's face but as the door swung open she was shoved roughly in the small of the back, and it was only Novak's quick reflexes that prevented her from falling. By the time she had regained her footing the driver had entered the kitchen through the back door, carrying a hold-all and wearing a balaclava. She realized then that by distracting her, Kilgarry had been protecting the identity of his colleague, making sure that she did not see his face, but ragged edges of blond hair protruded from under the edges of the helmet. It was Racine. Voskov would be in the lounge, guarding the hostages.

'Next time put the fucking balaclava on before you get out of the car,' Kilgarry snarled at Racine.

'*Oui, mon père.*' Racine opened the holdall and removed a submachine-gun identical to Kilgarry's.

'Go through to the lounge,' Kilgarry growled at Novak. 'Your boy's in there. You, too, Mrs Grant.'

Novak and Beth hurried down the hall, followed closely by Kilgarry and Racine, and burst in. Voskov was seated in the armchair directly opposite the door, the submachine-gun trained on the two figures on the sofa. John leaped to his feet and ran across to his father, who crouched down to take him in his arms.

'Who are these men, Dad? Why are they here? What do they want?'

'I'll explain it all to you later. But don't worry, they won't hurt you.'

'Will they hurt *you*?' John drew away from his father, his eyes wide and apprehensive.

'No.' Novak smiled reassuringly and touched the boy's cheek. 'No, they just want me to get something for them. Then they'll leave.'

'What do they want you to get for them?'

'As I said, I'll tell you later. Right now, all that matters is that you're OK.' Novak looked across at Marie. 'They haven't hurt you, have they?'

'*Non, monsieur*,' she said, but he could see the fear in her face.

'Take her and the boy into the kitchen,' Voskov told Racine. 'I want to speak to Novak and Mrs Grant alone.'

'You want me to stay?' Kilgarry asked.

'Did I ask you to stay?' Voskov retorted sharply. 'Take them into the kitchen!'

Kilgarry grabbed John roughly by the arm and the boy cried out in pain as he was yanked towards the door. He saw a movement out of the corner of his eye and was still turning when Novak's hammering punch caught him on the side of the face, knocking him back against the wall. The submachine-gun fell from his hand and landed inches away from where Novak was standing. Novak's eyes flickered towards the fallen weapon but he made no attempt to grab it, not with Racine aiming at his stomach.

'You're gonna pay for that,' Kilgarry snarled, advancing on him.

'Leave him!' Voskov ordered.

'Nobody does that to me—'

'I said, *leave him*,' Voskov repeated.

Kilgarry glared at him then said, 'This isn't over yet. Just remember that.'

Racine handed the gun back to Kilgarry and the two men followed John and Marie from the room. Voskov closed the door behind them and gestured Beth and Novak to sit on the sofa. He remained by the door. 'We're all a little on edge right now. Your son won't be manhandled again as long as you continue to co-operate with us. You have my word on that.'

'And that's supposed to reassure me?' Novak shot back.

'I never go back on my word.'

'So what happens now?' Beth asked. 'I won't be able to retrieve the disk before Monday at the earliest.'

'Then we wait.' His cellphone rang and he cursed under his breath before unclipping it from his belt to answer it.

'It's Sammy Kahn.'

Voskov glanced at Novak and Beth, then put his hand lightly over the mouthpiece. 'Excuse me,' he said politely, then stepped out into the hall and closed the door again behind him. 'Sorry, Novak and Grant were in the room. We can talk freely now.'

'Have you got the disk?'

'We've got problems,' Voskov replied, then went on to detail the events of the morning.

'And you've checked that they're on the level?' Kahn asked, when he had finished.

'They're on the level.'

'I'll make some inquiries about Strohmaier from this end. Call in some favours from the local police. The sooner we find him, the sooner we can get the disk and pull out. I don't want you in that house any longer than is absolutely necessary. The longer you stay there, the more chance there is of something going wrong.'

'Tempers are already beginning to fray,' Voskov said.

'Kilgarry?'

'Who else?'

'Keep him sweet. We need him.'

'What about Novak and the woman? Do we hold them here with us until we've got the disk?'

'It's essential that Novak keeps to his normal routine. He still has to go to his club over the weekend. He's not going to step out of line as long as you're holding his boy hostage at the house. As for Beth Grant, have her check out of the hotel as soon as possible and move into the house.'

'Jago knows that she's staying at the hotel,' Voskov pointed out. 'He's going to be suspicious when he finds her gone.'

'You let me worry about Jago.'

'What are you going to do?'

'You concentrate on Grant and Novak and leave Jago to me. Now, is there anything else you need to tell me?'

'No, I don't think so,' Voskov replied, after a thoughtful pause.

'I'll call you again this afternoon for an update on any further developments. By then I'll have an APB put out on Strohmaier. I've got some good connections in the local police force. I've every confidence that he'll be found within the next twenty-four hours.'

Voskov switched off the cellphone, clipped it back on to his belt, and was about to return to the lounge when Racine emerged from Novak's bedroom further down the hall. 'What were you doing in there?' he asked.

Racine beckoned to him and went back into the bedroom. The Venetian blinds were drawn at a sharp angle, which allowed them to see out but would have made it almost impossible for them to be spotted. 'There's a car parked a short distance from the house. The white Toyota. Single occupant. You can see it through the trees.'

Voskov nodded. 'What of it?'

'It wasn't there when I arrived,' Racine told him.

'Were you followed?'

'No!'

'Then what are you worried about?'

'What if the cops are tailing the Englishwoman, as a precaution?' Racine said.

'Then you would have spotted the car earlier, wouldn't you?'

'Yes, sure.'

'What are you saying here, Racine? That some local cop could have followed you all the way out here without you even knowing it?'

'It's a busy road,' Racine replied defensively.

'So you *could* have been followed from town? Is that it?' Racine didn't reply. 'There's one way to find out if he's been following the woman.'

'How?'

'You'll be told soon enough,' was all Voskov said before leaving the room.

'I want to see Stefan Kessler! Now!'

Kessler recognized the voice even before he looked up from his paperwork. He acknowledged the detective who was blocking the man's passage into the squad room. 'It's OK, let him through.'

The policeman stepped aside. 'We need to talk,' the man said, approaching Kessler's desk.

'This isn't the time or the place, Manny. I got a shitload of work to get through here. We'll talk later.'

Manfred Lehmann placed his large hands on the desk and leaned towards Kessler. 'I'm not leaving until I've said my piece. We can either talk here in front of your colleagues, or we can talk in private. It's your choice, Stefan.'

Kessler looked around him slowly: several detectives were watching them. He closed the folder he had been working on and got to his feet. Lehmann followed him out into the corridor. He was several inches taller than Kessler, sturdier in build, and looked more like an ageing skinhead with his cropped black hair than a senior officer in the élite Swiss

Special Forces. Kessler found an empty interview room and gestured for Lehmann to enter.

He closed the door behind them but as he turned round Lehmann grabbed him by the lapels and slammed him up against the wall. 'What the hell do you think you were doing this morning? Bettina's got Marthe in tears at home. Another few inches and that table would have landed on top of her. You could have killed your own baby.'

'It's *her* baby, not mine,' Kessler snarled, breaking free and smoothing down the front of his jacket.

'It's as much your baby as it is hers, and you know it!' Lehmann's fists were balled at his sides. 'It's about time you stopped brooding about the past and started to take some responsibility for Marthe and your child.'

'It was a mistake, conceived in a moment of weakness. And I'm as much to blame as she is in that respect. But she knew right from the start that I didn't want the baby. I don't want a substitute for Andreas. She had every opportunity to terminate the pregnancy in those first few weeks, but she chose to keep it. That was her decision. That makes it *her* baby.'

Lehmann punched the wall in frustration then stalked over to the caged window where he stood motionless as he struggled to regain his composure. Only when he had did he turn back to Kessler. 'You know what gets me most about all this, Stefan? The fact that Marthe still loves you. She always has. She's always lived in the hope that the two of you could still save the marriage. Why else would she have put up with your petulance and petty tantrums when anyone else would have walked out on you long ago? She feels the pain just as much as you do. Only you've always been too busy feeling sorry for yourself to notice it. And you know something? Unlike you, she's dealt with her grief constructively by looking to the future. That's why she chose to have another child. Not to replace Andreas. Nobody can ever do that. All she's ever wanted to do was try to bring some happiness back into both your lives. She sure as hell deserves it after what you've put her through these past few months.'

Lehmann crossed to the door where he paused to look at Kessler. 'I came here angry. I wanted to take a swing at you for what you did to Marthe this morning. But not any more. Now I just pity you. You've lost your self-esteem. You've lost your dignity. And now you've lost your best friend. I don't know you any more. And, to be honest, I don't want to, not if this is what you've become. You're a fool, Stefan. Maybe one day you'll come to your senses and realize that. I just hope for your sake that when that day comes Marthe's still prepared to take you back because you don't deserve someone like her. You really don't.' With that he wrenched open the door and disappeared into the corridor.

Kessler stared at the open door then swung round and kicked furiously at the desk in the centre of the room, knocking it over. The two chairs on either side of it clattered noisily to the floor as well. Moments later Sergeant Hans Matzke hurried into the room, followed by two others. They took in the scene, exchanged glances, then left.

'Are you all right, sir?' Matzke asked.

'Why shouldn't I be?' Kessler replied coldly.

'I just thought that ... well ... perhaps ...' Matzke trailed off uncomfortably.

'You just thought that I'd finally cracked under the pressure. Is that what you were going to say?' Kessler could see he was right, even though Matzke remained silent. 'Oh, don't worry, Sergeant. Half the detectives in here think I should be quickly – and quietly – pensioned off. The other half think I'm certifiable. None of them want to work with me any more. Yet I still have the best clear-up rate of anyone in the squad room. Why else do you think I was assigned the Grant case? They want a quick result upstairs, and they know I'm the one capable of getting it for them.'

'Yes, sir.' Matzke did not sound convinced.

'Is there any other reason why you're here, Sergeant, other than your concern over my well-being?'

'Yes, sir. The *juge d'instruction* is here. He wants to see you.'

'Oh, that's all I need.' Kessler groaned. 'Where is he?'

'Interview room three, sir. I told him you were questioning a suspect in here. He said he'd wait there for you until you'd finished.'

'Then I'd better not keep him waiting any longer than is necessary. Sergeant, tidy up the room, will you? We wouldn't want *him* thinking I was cracking under the pressure, now would we?'

Criminal investigations in Switzerland are normally handled by the local police in each of the country's twenty-six state cantons. The cantons are independent with their own constitution, legislation and judiciary. Homicides are rarely investigated without the direct intervention of either a *procureur*, a general attorney, or a *juge d'instruction*, a magistrate who oversees the case before it can be brought to trial. Many police officers find the intervention of these bureaucratic administrators an unwelcome interference as they have the federal right to overrule a particular line of inquiry, although few exercise such an extreme measure.

Kessler's methods of investigation had often brought him into direct conflict with his superiors and several times he had been hauled up in front of a *juge d'instruction* or a *procureur* to explain himself. It only added to the hostility he already felt for them. Reaching the closed door, he took a deep breath then pushed it open and stepped inside. The *juge d'instruction*, a balding man in his mid-fifties, looked up from the document he was reading and pointed to the empty chair on the opposite side of the table. Kessler sat down.

The *juge d'instruction* removed his reading glasses, slipped them into his jacket pocket, then returned the document to the battered briefcase at his elbow before folding his hands together on the table. 'What's your interest in Ralf Jago?'

The question caught Kessler by surprise. He took a moment to answer. 'Jago's been nosing around the Grant investigation. I want to know why.'

'No, you don't.'

'I don't understand,' Kessler said, bewildered.

'It's really quite simple, Kessler. Jago doesn't concern you.'

'He does if he knows something about the investigation. And his presence here in Zürich would suggest that.'

'Let me put it another way,' the *juge d'instruction* said, his eyes never leaving Kessler's face. 'Stay away from Ralf Jago. That's an order.'

'Then you tell me why Interpol are so interested in Ian Grant's death.' Silence. 'Has it got something to do with this disk he left with Strohmaier before he was murdered?' Silence. 'What's on the disk? At least tell me that.'

'Your job is to find Amy Michaels and charge her with the murder of Ian Grant. You've certainly got enough evidence against her. So far you seem to have failed in your task. Or do you have any more leads since we last spoke on the phone?'

'The disk is a lead,' Kessler replied tersely.

'Perhaps.'

'Do you want me to find the disk or not?' Kessler asked, unable to keep the rising anger from his voice.

'It would certainly reflect well on your record if you did. And if you do, you're to call me immediately. Day or night. It doesn't matter. I'll come to the station personally and take it off your hands.'

'And what will you do with it?' Kessler challenged.

The *juge d'instruction* pushed back his chair and got to his feet. 'Remember what I said, Kessler. Leave Jago alone. If I hear that you've gone anywhere near him while he's here in Zürich you'll be taken off the case immediately. I hope I make myself understood.'

Kessler pushed back his chair so hard that it clattered noisily against the wall behind him. 'I don't like being played for a fool. I have a right to know what's on that disk and how it could affect the outcome of the investigation. This is still my case.'

'You weren't assigned to this case because of your brilliant detective work, Kessler,' the *juge d'instruction* said facetiously. 'Maybe once, but not any more. You're one foul-up away from an indefinite suspension. And I know that if you were suspended, you've made enough enemies over the years who would see to it that you never got your badge back. So don't go presuming that you can still throw your weight around like you did in the old days. You got away with it then because you were a damn fine detective. But those days are long gone. Now you just do as you're told. And if you don't like it, as I said I'll put you on suspension. Is that what you want?'

'This is my whole life,' Kessler said. 'It's all that's kept me sane since my son died. Don't take it away from me.'

'I'd say that was up to you, wouldn't you?' The *juge d'instruction* picked up his briefcase. 'And it goes without saying, of course, that we never had this conversation. Careless talk costs careers. And it wouldn't just be yours either. Don't drag anyone else down with you, Kessler. It wouldn't be worth it anyway because ultimately it would be your word against mine. And who do you think would be believed?'

'You've got it all worked out, haven't you?'

'We like to think so.' The *juge d'instruction* was about to turn away when a sudden thought came to him. 'Have you heard any more from the FBI? What was that special agent's name again? Dawson, was it?'

'Frank Dawson,' Kessler replied. 'And no, I haven't heard any more from him, not since he rang to say that he's located Amy Michaels's house.'

'Then perhaps you should call him. I've got a feeling that you're going to need all the help you can get.'

*

'Morning.'

'May I help you?' Phyllis Kastner asked, when Dawson entered the sheriff's office.

'I'm Special Agent Frank Dawson. You must be Phyllis. I believe I've got you to thank for booking me in at the hotel last night. That was very kind of you. Thank you.'

'Well, it was no problem at all,' she said, her voice softening. 'I'm sorry, I didn't realize who you were. I thought you were just another ... well ...' She smiled awkwardly to try to hide her embarrassment.

'You thought I was just another what?' Dawson asked, in a mock-innocent voice.

'Just get the man some coffee, will you, Phyllis?' Sheriff Olsen barked from behind his desk.

'Yes, of course.' Phyllis, cheeks flushed, hurried across to the percolator in the corner of the room.

'An Inspector Kessler called you from Zürich a few minutes ago,' Olsen told Dawson. 'I said that you'd call him back when you got in.'

Dawson nodded then smiled politely at Phyllis when she handed him a mug of freshly brewed coffee.

'Did you sleep well at the hotel last night, Mr Dawson?' she asked, hovering beside him.

'What little sleep I got.' Dawson moved several dog-eared folders from the chair in front of Olsen's desk before he sat down.

'What time did you get back to the hotel?' Olsen asked. 'I only got home around two this morning. You said before I left Amy Michaels's house that you were going to work some more on those computers before you turned in for the night.'

'I got a couple of hours' sleep. That's enough for me.'

'I couldn't handle that. Hell, I had about six and I'm still half asleep this morning,' Olsen said, and rubbed his bloodshot eyes for added effect. 'So what time are you expecting your crew to get in from Washington? You said it would probably be some time this morning.'

'Should be. They're flying into Jackson. Charter plane. They could even be there already. They'll pick up cars then drive on here.'

'Did you find anything useful on the computers after I'd gone home?'

'No, but, then, I just scratched the surface. There's so much information stored in them. That's why I'm bringing in a team of experts.' Dawson took a sip of coffee before continuing, 'You remember Lester telling us about that missing photograph last night? The one she kept on the table beside the computers?'

'Yeah,' Olsen said. 'Did you find it?'

'No. In fact, I couldn't find a single photograph of her in the whole house. Admittedly I didn't carry out a thorough search, but I had a pretty good look all the same. No photographs anywhere.'

'Not a one?' Olsen responded in surprise.

Dawson shook his head. 'I'll have a couple of my men go through the house again, make sure I didn't miss anything.'

'You thinking what I'm thinking?' Olsen said, with a curious frown.

'As I said last night, I'm not jumping to any conclusions until I've had Forensics go through that house with a fine-tooth comb. As far as I'm concerned, Amy Michaels is on the run in Switzerland, wanted for the murder of Ian Grant. Nothing I've seen so far makes me change my mind.'

'What about the missing photo? And the missing rug? And the fact that you couldn't find any photos of her anywhere in the house. It's suspicious, you've got to admit that.'

'She could have taken the photo with her. She could have soiled the rug and tossed it in the garbage. Maybe she didn't keep any other photos of herself, I don't know. It's all specu-lation at the moment, Sheriff. And that's something I intend to avoid at all costs as long as I'm in charge of this investigation. Is that clear?'

Olsen's eyes flicked past Dawson to the scruffily dressed figure who entered the office. He was in his mid-sixties, wearing a pair of faded dungarees over a white shirt, scuffed sandals and a sweat-stained baseball cap. 'What brings you here at this time of the morning, Henry?'

'Him.' The man pointed at Dawson. 'You're that Fed from Washington, aren't you?'

'That's right,' Dawson agreed.

'Yeah, I thought as much. They said I couldn't miss you,' he added. 'Black face. Well dressed. Good manners. That's a rarity around here, I tell you.'

'As is tact, obviously,' Dawson said, but there was no malice in his voice.

'This is Henry Monroe. He's got a hog farm a few miles out of town,' Olsen told Dawson, then lowered his voice. 'Been a widower for a few years now. Drinks a lot. Always has. And I swear he's been in debt from the day he was born.'

'What's that you say, Jed?' Monroe shuffled towards them.

'I was just telling Special Agent Dawson who you were,' Olsen replied.

'That coffee sure smells good, Phyllis,' Monroe said in passing.

Olsen nodded absently at Phyllis when she glanced at him. 'So what do you want to see Special Agent Dawson about, Henry?' he asked.

'You're looking for Amy Michaels, ain't ya?' Monroe asked Dawson.

'That's correct,' Dawson answered. 'Why? Do you know something that might be of some help in finding her?'

'Maybe,' Monroe replied, taking the mug from Phyllis, who returned to her desk.

'Henry, we ain't got time for games,' Olsen chided Monroe.

'If you know something, spit it out. Otherwise don't come here wasting our time.'

'I live out at Drummond Creek,' Monroe said, addressing Dawson. 'Miss Amy is my nearest neighbour, by a couple of miles. I got a coupla dogs and when I take them for a walk down by the river I always pass her house. I see her around. Not often, you understand, but from time to time. Now some of the locals, they think she's kind of stuck up on account she don't socialize with them. But she ain't like that, mister. At least not with me. She's always real friendly.'

'Henry, will you just get to the point?' Olsen said, in frustration.

'Last weekend – Saturday, I think it was – I was walking the dogs down by the river. It would have been around six o'clock in the evening. I saw a vehicle parked outside Miss Amy's house. Had an out-of-state licence plate. Red Hyundai. It was a hired car. Had a Hertz sticker on the window. I thought it kind of strange 'cause Miss Amy don't like people visiting her. But, then, I guess Jed's told you that already. I didn't nose about none, I just kept on walking like I always do. None of my business anyway. Well, I come back past the house about twenty minutes later and I see this guy. He never saw me, though. I was on the other side of the river. He was putting something in the trunk. I didn't think nothing of it at the time. Not until I spoke to Lester this morning. He brought some groceries out to the farm. Told me about the Feds being in town. First time I knew anything about it. He tells me he was helping you out at Miss Amy's house yesterday. Checking things out for you.'

'Aw, please, Lester wasn't helping us none.' Olsen snorted indignantly.

Dawson raised a hand to silence him. 'Go on, Mr Monroe. Lester told you he was helping us with our inquiries. Then what happened?'

'Then he says about this rug that's missing from the house.

It ain't missing, well, not as such, on account as I saw the man put it in the trunk of the hired car. All rolled up it was. As I said, at the time I thought nothing of it. Why should I? It wasn't none of my business. But now Lester says that Miss Amy's gone missing. That's why I came into town straight away to tell you. I seen it on the TV before where they kill someone, roll up the body in a carpet, and put it in the trunk of a car then bury it somewhere. You don't … think that's what happened, do you? I sure hope not. I like Miss Amy.'

'I'm sure there's a logical explanation to what you saw, Mr Monroe,' Dawson forced a smile, 'but obviously we'll have to check it out all the same. You said that the red Hyundai had an out-of-state licence plate. Do you remember which state it was from?'

'Florida,' Monroe replied, without hesitation. 'But I don't remember the number. I didn't write it down or nothing. And my memory, well, it ain't what it used to be.'

'What about the man? Did you get a proper look at him?'

'I'd sure know him if I saw him again. Looked kind of like a … soldier, I guess. Short blond hair. Good build.'

'I've got a team coming in from Washington later this morning, Mr Monroe. If you don't mind, I'd like you to put together a photofit with one of them this afternoon.'

'What's a photofit?' Monroe queried.

'A face that's put together on a computer,' Dawson replied.

'Like you sometimes see on America's Most Wanted?' Monroe said, with a nicotine-stained grin.

'Exactly,' Dawson said. 'Would you mind if one of my men drove out to your farm this afternoon to see you?'

'Not at all. Like I said, Miss Amy was a real nice lady. If something bad has happened to her, I want to help in any way I can.'

'Thank you for taking the time to come in this morning, Mr Monroe,' Dawson said. 'I appreciate it.'

Monroe finished the coffee then placed the empty mug on

Olsen's desk. 'Mighty fine coffee, Phyllis,' he muttered, before he disappeared into the street.

'You still think there's nothing suspicious about her disappearance?' Olsen asked, breaking the silence.

'To be honest, that's not what I was thinking.' Dawson looked slowly around the room before his eyes settled on Olsen again. 'If that isn't Amy Michaels on the run in Switzerland, then who is it?'

SEVEN

Stefan Kessler was hurt, angry, bitter and confused. Hurt that his best friend of thirty years had turned his back on him when he had needed him most. Not that he could have ever told Manny that. He was far too proud to ask for help. Marthe had always predicted that his obstinacy would be his downfall. He was angry that the *juge d'instruction* had told him that unless he investigated the case *his* way, even if that meant ignoring vital clues, he would be suspended and probably never allowed back on the force. He was bitter about the accusations the man had levelled at him – he still regarded himself as a damn good detective. And he was determined to prove it. *His* way. But, most of all, he was confused. For the first time since he took charge of the investigation, he found himself beginning to question whether Amy Michaels had murdered Ian Grant. She had been seen with him at the club. Fact. She had been seen following him into the alleyway at the side of the club. Fact. She had been seen with the murder weapon in her hand. Fact. Did that make her a murderer? He'd certainly thought so at the time. Now he wasn't so sure.

Why had the *juge d'instruction* been so adamant that Jago be left out of the investigation? Why did he want the disk so badly? What was on the disk? Was he trying to suppress evidence? If so, on whose orders? And was Amy Michaels being set up to take the fall for a crime she didn't commit merely to tie up all the loose ends? The more he thought about it, the more he realized that there was more to the investigation than first met the eye. And if the *juge d'instruction* thought he was going to use him as a puppet, pulling his strings to make him dance to *his* tune, he was in for a big surprise. His career meant more to him than anything else, yet he had always prided himself on being ethical when it came to investigative techniques. Sure, he'd bend the rules as much as the next detective if it meant getting a result, but he was never dishonest. He never took bribes. He never looked the other way. And he never suppressed evidence. It was his own code of honour – and he would never break it. Even if it meant losing his job. The *juge d'instruction* had picked the wrong man to manipulate to his own corrupt ends. He would find Amy Michaels. He would find the disk. He would find the truth—

The telephone rang. He was quick to answer it. 'Kessler,' he barked sharply.

'It's Sergeant Dannhauser, sir. I followed Novak and Grant to the Zum Storchen Hotel. He remained in the car while she went inside. She reappeared about ten minutes later, with her suitcase and overnight bag. Then they called at his Club, and after that they visited a TV rental shop and took a set back to the Club. Now it looks like he's going back to his house in Horgen. I rang the hotel on the car phone and I was told she'd checked out and hadn't left a forwarding address.'

'Did they say why she'd checked out in such a hurry?'

'No, sir. Do you want me to question her when they reach Novak's house?'

'Assuming they're returning to the house,' Kessler mused. 'No, just keep it under surveillance and make sure you inform me of any developments.'

'Yes, sir.'

Kessler sat back in his chair, clasped his hands behind his

head, and stared thoughtfully at the telephone. Something was wrong. Only he didn't know what. At least, not yet . . .

'They're back.'

Voskov crossed to the bedroom window, where Racine was standing in front of the partially drawn Venetian blinds. He wasn't interested in Novak's car when it pulled into the driveway and drove the short distance to the garage. His eyes were focused on the road, waiting to see whether the car had been followed to the house. Moments later he had his answer when the car that had been parked out front earlier, and which had tailed Novak and Grant from the house, pulled up within sight of the window. Although the vehicle was visible through the trees, the driver's face was obscured by a low-hanging branch.

'You think it's the cops?' Racine asked.

'Who else can it be?' Voskov turned away from the window.

'You think they know we're in here?'

Voskov sighed. 'If they did, they'd have either made a move against us, or at least made themselves known in an attempt to negotiate the release of the hostages. No, it's my guess they've got Mrs Grant under surveillance. But that doesn't mean our problems are over. When they find out she's checked out of the hotel, they're going to want to know why. And that means someone's going to come here before long to ask some awkward questions.'

'How are you going to play it?' Racine asked.

'First I want you to park the van and the car in the woods behind the house. You won't be seen from the road. Then cover them up.'

Racine shouldered his submachine-gun and left the room.

Voskov took a last look at the car parked in the street, then followed him out. He entered the kitchen as Novak and Beth came in from the garage. 'Well?' he said, after Racine had closed the back door behind him on his way out.

'I checked out of the hotel,' Beth said.

'Good. You know that you were followed to and from the hotel, don't you?' Voskov could see by the look of surprise on their faces that they had not spotted the tail. 'I'm moving the vehicles in case anyone comes snooping around here. We don't want to advertise our presence, do we?'

'Who tailed us? Do you know?' Novak asked.

'Probably the local police.' Voskov looked at Beth. 'They've obviously decided to keep you under surveillance as long as you remain here in Zürich.'

'Why would they do that?'

'I don't know – maybe you've aroused their suspicion in some way. But don't worry, they don't know about us. Of that I'm certain.'

'And what if someone comes to the house asking questions?' Novak wanted to know.

'Then you'll just have to answer them, won't you?' Voskov said. 'We'll all be in the next room. Say the wrong thing and the hostages will be executed. Starting with your son. Believe it.'

'I believe it.' Novak was tight-lipped.

'When do you normally start work?' Voskov asked.

'About six o'clock on weekdays. Saturdays I try to be there by five. Why d'you ask?'

'Because you're going to the club as usual tonight. It's imperative that you stick to your usual routine so as not to arouse suspicion. Of course, Mrs Grant and your son will remain here with us.' Voskov opened the kitchen door, stepped out into the hall, then beckoned for them to follow him. 'I have something to show you. I think it might be of interest to both of you.'

Kilgarry was guarding John and Marie in the lounge. He was sitting in the armchair in front of the window, with the curtains drawn. John jumped to his feet when his father entered the room and hurried over to him. Kilgarry made no move to stop him. 'You OK?' Novak asked, crouching down in front of his son. John nodded. 'How's Marie?'

'She's OK . . . I think,' John glanced across at her. She smiled at him. His eyes went to Kilgarry. 'He keeps whispering to her. I don't know what he's saying but he always laughs. She looks scared of him.'

'You're the head of the house when I'm not here. That means you've got to look out for her when the two of you are alone. The next time he does that you tell this man here.' Novak pointed to Voskov. He saw the unease on John's face as he followed the direction of his father's finger. 'It's OK, he's the leader. He'll tell the man to stop bothering Marie.'

'He won't hurt me, will he?'

'No, I promise he won't.' Novak explained the situation to Voskov, who nodded, then looked across at Kilgarry.

'Is it working?'

'Yeah.' Kilgarry indicated the electronic device on the coffee table beside his chair.

'While the two of you were out – conveniently taking your tail with you – we placed minute cameras and infrared sensors at the main access points into the grounds of your property,' Voskov told Novak. 'We've also concealed them around the perimeter of the house, beside doors and windows. If an infrared beam is broken, it'll activate one of the lights on the receiver. It's not so much to keep you in the house as to keep unwelcome visitors out. We'll know exactly which sensor is triggered, and take appropriate action.'

'Meaning?' Novak asked.

'Meaning that if it's a periphery sensor, we'd go on a low key alert until we found out who or what had set it off. But if any of the sensors around the windows or doors were triggered then we would automatically assume that the house was being stormed and go on a red alert.'

'Meaning that you'd kill the hostages?' Beth said, having ensured that John was out of earshot.

'Meaning I'd assess the situation and react accordingly,' Voskov corrected her.

'It amounts to the same thing,' Beth said.

'Please, why don't you sit down?' Voskov gestured to the couch.

Beth let John sit with his father on the vacant couch and she sat next to Marie. She introduced herself. 'I'm sorry that you had to get caught up in all of this,' she said, hoping she sounded sincere.

'It has happened, *n'est-ce pas?*' Marie gave a philosophical shrug. 'I heard about your husband. I am sorry.'

'You two, shut up!' Kilgarry snapped at them.

Marie spoke to him in French and there was burst of laughter from the doorway. Kilgarry looked up to see Racine standing there. 'What the fuck did she say to me?'

'I really don't think you want to know.' Racine was still chuckling.

Kilgarry scowled at Marie. 'You want to say something, you say it in English. Understand, bitch?'

'And spoil my only fun?' Marie replied scornfully. 'I don't think so.'

'*You* don't think so,' he retorted angrily.

'I want to see you outside,' Voskov said, snapping his fingers at Kilgarry. The American stood his ground. 'That means now!'

Kilgarry followed him from the room. Voskov led him into the kitchen then grabbed him by the front of his white vest and pushed him up against the wall. 'Leave the girl alone. That means no more offensive comments to her when Racine and I are out of the room. In fact, don't even talk to her unless it's directly related to a particular aspect of the operation. Do I make myself clear?'

'How did you know about that?' Kilgarry paused. 'Of course, the fucking kid.'

'Stay away from her. That's an order.'

'Fuck your orders,' Kilgarry snarled, breaking Voskov's grip on his vest.

Voskov slammed the butt of his submachine-gun into Kilgarry's midriff, winding him, then grabbed the American's balaclava, forcing him to look up at him. 'Kahn put me in charge of this operation. Racine doesn't seem to have a problem with it. If you do, you can walk away now. I'm not going to stop you. We've got enough problems as it is without you adding to them. You're either in or out. What's it going to be?'

'Kahn would have me marked the moment I walked out the door,' Kilgarry hissed, as he struggled to catch his breath.

'That's not my problem,' Voskov said. 'In or out? Your choice.'

'You know damn well I'm in – my ass is just as much on the line as yours if that disk were to fall into the wrong hands.'

Voskov grabbed Kilgarry's arm and yanked him to his feet. 'Then start acting like a member of this team. Now, get back into the lounge. And *don't* rile the girl.'

Kilgarry glared at him then strode from the room and shoved past Racine, who was still standing in the doorway of the lounge. He resumed his seat by the window. He felt Marie's eyes on him, but didn't look at her. That was the second time now that Voskov had humiliated him. He'd bite his tongue, and bide his time – until the right moment. Then he would kill him.

Kessler despised informers. He had to admit that many of his cases in the past had been solved by them but that still didn't mean he had to like them. They were invariably greedy, shallow, weak, and with no scruples when it came to exposing a fellow criminal.

Willie Meine was more odious than any other informer he had on his payroll. He was the only man Kessler knew who had, quite literally, sold his mother for financial gain. She had shielded her other two sons from the authorities after they had pulled off a daring heist on one of the city's top diamond merchants. All three were subsequently sent down without ever knowing who had tipped off the police. That was what made him so invaluable as an informer – his ability to disguise his life of betrayal and deception even from his own kin. Meine had called him a short time ago at the station, telling him he had some information for him.

Kessler parked the unmarked police car outside a small, nondescript bar on Graugasse – in the Niederdorf – a known haunt of some of the city's felons. The building broke many of the canton's stringent health regulations, but the authorities turned a blind eye to its unhygienic shortcomings: shutting it down would only scatter the patrons to other bars, which would make it that much harder to keep tabs on them. He pushed open the door, took a step inside, then paused to look around him. He recognized a lot of the faces. Some he had put away. Some he would still put away. Some met his gaze defiantly. Some looked away. He scanned the room until his eyes settled on the dishevelled figure of Willie Meine. Not surprisingly, Meine was sitting alone in one of the booths that lined the wall opposite the bar. He had few friends and the only way he could find temporary companionship was by ingratiating himself with a group of cons and buying them drinks. It was also the way he sniffed out the information he passed on to the police.

Meine smiled nervously at Kessler as he approached the booth. 'Inspector Kessler, what a pleasant surprise—'

The rest of the sentence was torn from Meine's lips when Kessler grabbed him by the scruff of his collar, wrenched him out of the booth and let him fall heavily to the floor. Meine was still trying to wrap his arms protectively around his head when Kessler twisted one arm painfully behind his back and snapped a handcuff over his wrist. He did the same with the other arm then jerked him to his feet and, grabbing a handful of his long, unwashed hair, flung him face down on the table, spilling the remnants of the beer over the upholstered bench. He heard mutters behind him as he searched Meine and, after satisfying himself that he was clean, kept Meine's face pressed down on the table as he looked at the row of drinkers at the bar. The muttering ceased. Most of them turned away, not wanting to get involved, but one man stared back defiantly. Kessler's evidence had helped put him away on a charge of armed robbery, and Kessler hadn't known he was out. Probably on parole. If he could bait the bastard, force him to violate his licence conditions, he'd have him back inside within the hour. That would be a satisfying afternoon's work.

'You got a problem?' Kessler asked, without taking his eyes off the man.

'You're either brave or stupid, coming in here without any back-up,' came the insolent reply.

'I'm here to make an arrest. That's all. I'm not looking for trouble. But if you so much as step out of line, you'll be back inside quicker than you can draw breath. Is that what you want?'

'Don't be a fucking idiot.' The barman grabbed the con's arm as he was about to climb off his stool. 'You only got out this morning. You touch him and you'll be drawing your pension by the time they let you out again.'

'He's the one who put me away in the first place.' The con shrugged off the barman's hand.

'Can't you see he wants you to have a go at him?' the barman said. 'He's not worth it. Just let it go.'

'It would be self-defence. His word against ours.'

'And who do you think a judge would believe?'

Kessler smiled triumphantly when the man reluctantly resumed his seat. 'I'd buy the landlord a drink if I were you,' he said to the con. 'He's just saved you from another stretch inside.'

'Just get out, and take your garbage with you,' the barman told Kessler.

'My pleasure.' Kessler pulled Meine upright, marched him out of the bar and shoved him into the back of the unmarked police car. He got in behind the wheel, and drove the short distance to the bottom of the lane before turning out into the main road, which ran parallel to the Limmat river.

'You didn't have to be so rough back there, Inspector,' Meine whined.

'I had to make it look realistic,' Kessler replied. 'Or would you have preferred me to have a drink with you in there while we talked?'

'You know what I mean,' Meine said. 'You can take off the handcuffs now. They're cutting into my wrists.'

'You'll survive. Now, tell me what you've found out.'

'Not until you take off these handcuffs.'

'I'm going to keep driving round until you tell me why you called me. The longer you hold out, the more those cuffs are going to hurt. So start talking, Willie.'

'I heard something from a reliable source but I don't know whether it's got anything to do with your investigation into the Grant murder.' Meine winced as he struggled to get comfortable with his hands manacled behind his back.

'If you stop fidgeting, the cuffs won't hurt so much,' Kessler said, eyeing Meine distastefully in the rear-view mirror. 'What did you hear?'

'Word on the street is that a couple of hitters flew into town earlier this week. Both ex-military. Very professional by all accounts.'

'Names?'

'I'm working on it. All I know is that one's French, the other's American. I should have the names for you by morning.'

'Who's the contract?'

'That's the strange thing about it. I've heard nothing about any contract. And I've been making quite a few inquiries in that direction. I don't know what they're doing here.'

'Then find out.'

'I'm doing my best,' Meine replied tetchily.

'I doubt that, otherwise you'd have all the facts by now and not the bits and pieces you're giving me. Right now you're just wasting my time. Get me all the info, then we'll talk again. And make it soon.' Kessler swung the car into a side-street, stopped and climbed out. He opened the back door, unlocked the handcuffs, then hauled Meine out into the street. 'I want names put to these two killers, Willie, and I want to know what they're doing here in Zürich.'

'You'll get the information, Inspector, you know that.' Meine massaged his wrists. 'Now give me my money.'

'You'll get your money when you give me all the information. Not before.'

'We've always had an understanding—'

'Which has just changed,' Kessler cut in. 'So far you've given me shit. You're going to have to do a lot better than that before you get your money.'

'That's not fair, Inspector, I've levelled with you. I've told you everything I know. I've incurred expenses—'

'I know, by sitting on your ass in a bar. Call me when you've got something worth my time.'

'You owe me.' Meine grabbed Kessler's arm as he reached to open the driver's door.

Kessler rammed his fist into the man's belly. Meine grunted and slid down the wall until he was on his haunches, his arms clasped tightly around his stomach as he gasped for breath. 'You ever touch me again, Willie, and you'll have to be fed intravenously for the next six months. Do I make myself clear?'

'You didn't need to do that,' Meine muttered, his face twisted in agony.

Kessler crouched in front of him, grasped his unshaven chin and forced him to meet his eyes. 'You used to be a good source of information for me. Now you're just a waste of time. I'll give you until eleven o'clock tomorrow morning to get those names for me. If I haven't heard from you by then, I'll put out the word that you're a grass. And I'll start with your own family. I'm sure they'd love to know who sent them down. Jail hasn't mellowed your brothers, by all accounts. Imagine what they'd do to you if they ever found out that you were the one who grassed them up for your thirty bits of silver.'

'You wouldn't – do that, Inspector – please,' Meine stammered, the pain forgotten.

'Eleven o'clock, Willie.' Kessler climbed back into the car and drove away.

'We've got company,' Racine called out to Voskov from the lounge when a light flashed on the receiver. The sensor attached to the main gate had been activated.

Voskov, who had been in the kitchen, hurried through and looked at the portable monitor on the table. He cursed under his breath when the miniature camera mounted at the side of the garage door picked up the figure behind the wheel of the car. 'It's Kessler. Take everyone into the master bedroom, and keep them there. I'll be along shortly. Novak, you stay here.' He waited until his two colleagues had hustled Beth, Marie and John from the room before continuing, 'Get rid of him. There's a microphone in every room in the house, so I'll be able to hear every word you say. I'll also be able to see everything on the monitor so don't even think about passing any notes to him.'

'I don't give a shit about you, or the disk. All I'm concerned about is John's safety. So don't worry, I'm not about to rock the boat. Not with my son's life at stake.'

'That's very wise.' Voskov picked up the receiver and the portable monitor and moved to the door. 'Open the curtains. He won't have seen the window from the driveway. This place has to look as normal as possible.'

Novak was alone when the doorbell rang. He sucked in several lungfuls of air to calm himself, then left the room and walked to the front door. He was surprised to find that his hand wasn't trembling when he reached out to unlatch it. It belied how he was feeling inside. But he had to remain calm. If only outwardly. If only for John.

'Good afternoon, Mr Novak,' Kessler said, in his Swiss-accented English. 'I hope I didn't disturb your sleep. I know you get in late from your club.'

'I was up.' Novak cursed himself silently for his abruptness. *Calm down, for Christ's sake. Just calm down.* 'What brings you out here, Inspector? I gave you a statement at the club on the night of the murder.'

'And a very thorough one at that. I have a few questions, that's all. May I come in?'

'I guess.' Novak stepped aside for him to enter the hall and closed the door behind him.

'Is Mrs Grant here?'

Novak paused before answering. If he said yes, would Kessler ask to see her? Would Voskov release her if he did? If he said no, Kessler might call his bluff. After all, he knew that they had been tailed to and from the hotel. That really left him with no option but to tell the truth. 'Yes, she's here,' he admitted.

'I assumed as much. She checked out of the hotel this morning. Was there any reason for this?'

'I offered to put her up here until she returns to London next week. It seemed the right thing to do after what she's been through these past few days.'

'That's very kind of you, considering you hardly know her.' Kessler smiled, but his eyes were cold as he studied Novak's face.

'I knew Ian. He always came to the club when he was in town.'

'Yes, I recall you mentioning that in your statement. But if I remember correctly, you also said that you didn't know him *that* well. Or am I mistaken?'

'Well enough,' Novak riposted. 'And, anyway, I lost my wife some years back. I know exactly what she's going through right now.'

'I'm sorry, Mr Novak, I don't mean to question your motives in allowing Mrs Grant to stay with you. I was just curious as to why she'd checked out of the hotel so suddenly.'

'Because Mike thought that if I was with him and his son I would be better off than sitting alone in my hotel room while I waited for the phone to ring,' Beth said, from the end of the hall, 'which, incidentally, was remarkably quiet all the time I was there. Do you have any new leads in the case, Inspector? Is that why you're here?'

Kessler found himself on the back foot. 'We have certain leads that are being followed up. I can assure you that you'll be the first to know when we do apprehend Amy Michaels.'

'In other words, Inspector, you're still floundering about in the dark and no nearer to catching her,' Beth said, pushing further on to the offensive. 'I would have thought that a simple phone call would have cleared up the reason why I left the hotel. That way you could have remained at your desk in case any of your men made a startling breakthrough and needed to contact you urgently.'

Kessler held her stare for several seconds before asking, 'Why did the two of you go to the offices of Dietmar Strohmaier today?'

Beth knew it was imperative that she remain on the offensive. It was all she had going for her. Yet inside she felt naked and vulnerable, and those feelings weren't helped by Novak's apparent reluctance to back her up. 'How did you know about that?' she demanded. 'Have you been following me?'

'I've had you followed, yes,' Kessler said bluntly.

'How dare you? You have no right—'

'I have every right, Mrs Grant, make no mistake about that,' Kessler interrupted quickly. 'I can have you watched twenty-four hours a day if I think it will be beneficial to the investigation.'

'What are you saying? That I'm a suspect?' Her voice was laced with contempt. 'You must be really desperate if you're having to resort to such tactics.'

'I have my reasons,' Kessler replied calmly. 'You never answered my question. Why did you two go to Strohmaier's office today?'

'To pick up something that my husband left with him.'

'What?'

'A computer disk.' She knew it was pointless to lie. Whoever had followed them would have spoken to the receptionist after they had gone.

'And did you get it?'

'No. Strohmaier wasn't there. And he won't be back at work until Monday. But, then, I'm sure you know all that already, don't you?'

Kessler nodded. 'What I don't know is what's on the disk.'

'That makes two of us, Inspector. My husband sent a letter to me in London telling me where to pick up the disk, should anything happen to him. He didn't say what was on it.'

'Do you have the letter with you?' Kessler asked.

'No. It arrived after I was already here. My partner called me when she found it and I had her read it to me over the phone.'

'Does she still have the letter?'

'I have no idea,' Beth said truthfully.

'I'd like to see a copy of it if possible. I'll ask an officer from Scotland Yard to contact her about it. Assuming you have no objection, that is?'

'Would it really matter if I did?'

'Well, thank you both for your time.' Kessler ignored the sarcasm. 'Naturally I'll be in touch, should there be any new developments.'

'I won't hold my breath,' Beth said, as Kessler opened the front door. After he had gone she let out a deep sigh and rubbed her hands over her face. 'I've got knots in the pit of my stomach,' she said. 'I had to choose every word carefully in case I ended up incriminating myself.'

'You handled it well,' Novak told her.

She wanted to say 'and with no help from you' when he touched her hand briefly. An insignificant gesture under any other circumstances, but at that moment it meant everything to her. It helped to defuse the tension that had been building up steadily inside her even though she usually preferred to keep her distance from others. 'I'm going to have to call Emma and tell her to destroy the letter before someone from Scotland Yard contacts her.'

'Call her on my cellphone,' Voskov said, emerging from the master bedroom. 'Kessler may already have Novak's phone tapped. We can't take any chances.'

'He's got you rattled, hasn't he?' Novak said, with evident satisfaction.

'It'll take a lot more than some burned-out cop like Kessler to rattle me, Novak.' Voskov handed the phone to Beth. 'Make the call, Mrs Grant. Now.'

Novak was worried about the effect the siege was having on his son. He wasn't thinking about long-term psychological repercussions, just whether John could handle the increasing strain. It had been weighing heavily on his mind but John seemed to be coping well. At least outwardly. And that gave him some comfort.

He left Beth and Voskov in the hall and returned to the lounge. Marie and John had been taken back there after Kessler had left. The curtains were once again drawn across the window. He crossed to the sofa where they were sitting and squatted beside his son.

'Who was that man at the door?' John asked. 'A cop?'

'Yeah, he's in charge of the investigation into Ian Grant's murder. That's the guy who was killed outside the club. You remember I told you about that?'

'Yes,' John replied.

'These guys aren't going to hurt us, John. All they want is a disk that he left with a lawyer before he was murdered but the lawyer's out of town right now. Beth will collect it as soon as he gets back. And when they've got it, they'll go. We've just got to stick it out until then.'

'How do you know they won't kill us after they've got the disk?' John asked.

'They won't.' Novak was horrified that a child could ask such a question. 'Trust me, they won't.'

'He's right, John,' Racine said, from the armchair opposite them. He had heard the whole conversation. 'If it had been our intention to kill you after we got the disk, we wouldn't have bothered to wear these.' He touched the balaclava. 'This way none of you can identify us to the police after we have gone. We're just voices to you.'

Novak found himself nodding in agreement, as if grateful that Racine was trying to put John at his ease. Then, his son asked, 'You'll kill me if I try to run away, though, won't you?'

'No, I wouldn't kill *you*,' Racine said, his eyes moving to Novak.

'Then I promise I won't run away,' John assured him.

'I know that already.' Racine winked at him. 'You're an intelligent kid. Why would you do something stupid like that?'

'So that he wouldn't have to listen to your patronizing bullshit.' Kilgarry snorted from the adjacent armchair.

'There's no need to use that kind of language in front of my son,' Novak said angrily.

'Fuck you,' Kilgarry shot back. It was then that Beth entered the room and he noticed Voskov standing in the doorway. He slumped back in the chair and clasped the submachine-gun in his lap as Voskov approached.

'No more.' Voskov tapped Kilgarry's shoulder as he passed behind his chair. He stopped in front of the window. 'Mrs Grant has asked her partner in London to destroy the letter. We won't have to worry about that now.' He looked at his watch. 'Novak, it's gone four o'clock. How long will it take you to get to your club? You said you're normally there by five.'

'It depends on the ferry. Half an hour at the most.' Novak stood up. 'I'll need to have a shave and a bath first. I assume I can do that without having one of your gorillas watching over me?'

'Go,' Voskov said, 'and leave the bathroom door unlocked.'

Novak moved to the door then paused when a thought came to mind. 'Don't tell me, you've got a camera in the bathroom. That's why you're letting me have a bath in peace.'

'There's no camera in there. Credit us with a little decorum, Novak.' Voskov snapped his fingers at Kilgarry. 'Wait outside for him. He's got exactly fifteen minutes to get ready. If he's not finished by then, go in and pull him out.'

'My pleasure.' Kilgarry got to his feet and followed Novak out.

Kessler had sensed that something wasn't right while he had been at Novak's house. Only he didn't know what it was. And that was what made it so frustrating. It was similar to the feeling he'd experienced when he had first visited Beth in her hotel room shortly after her arrival in Zürich. Nothing specific. Just a hunch. Yet he knew he would never be granted a search warrant for the house on the strength of a hunch. Especially as he would have to go through the *juge d'instruction* to get it. They weren't even on the same side. Or, at least, that's the way it seemed to him. No, he would have to solve the case by himself, without the help – or hindrance – of the *juge d'instruction*.

His first thought had been to contact Sergeant Dannhauser, who was watching the house from the street, and ask him to take a closer look, using the woods directly behind it as additional cover. But he had dismissed the idea as impractical. What if Dannhauser had already been spotted? It meant that his every move would be monitored. And it was essential that the reconnaissance be carried out as discreetly as possible. No, leave Dannhauser where he was. He would do it himself.

Approach from the woods, so as not to be seen from the house, allowing him to carry out a detailed surveillance without raising any suspicion. Not that he had any idea what he would find once he got there. But it had to be done.

He was about to leave his desk when the telephone rang. He cursed angrily and scooped up the receiver. It was the *juge d'instruction*. He wanted to see him right away in his office for a further update on the investigation. Kessler was about to fob him off with some excuse when Sergeant Hans Matzke entered the squad room. The perfect replacement. He beckoned Matzke towards him, then assured the *juge d'instruction* that he would be at his office within the hour.

'You wanted to see me, sir?' Matzke asked, once Kessler had hung up.

'Tell me, Sergeant, how good are you at surveillance?'

Henry Monroe was up to his ankles in mud, a bucket of food scraps in each hand, as he stood among the lively hogs at his isolated farm in Drummond Creek. They were squealing excitedly as they huddled around him, nudging and prodding him with their wet snouts, knowing it was feeding time. A few of the more audacious ones were trying to get their snouts into the buckets and he shoved them away roughly with the sole of a muddy boot. He tilted the malodorous contents of one bucket into the nearest trough. There was a stampede to get to the food and he almost lost his balance when a couple knocked against him in their desperation to reach the trough first. He cursed them, then crossed to the second trough, the mud sucking at his boots with every laborious step, followed devotedly by the stragglers who had been too slow the first time round. He had just emptied the second bucket when he saw the dust thrown up by an approaching car on the dirt road leading up to the farm. He tossed the empty buckets over the wooden fence then clambered out of the pen and watched the car until it came to a halt a few feet away from where he was standing.

It was a black BMW. Looked pretty new to him. The windows were tinted and it wasn't until the door opened that he was able to see the driver for the first time – handsome, mid-thirties, rich tan, expensive designer suit. Typical Ivy Leaguer, he thought.

'Afternoon, sir.' The man beamed. 'Are you Henry Monroe?'

'Sure,' Monroe replied.

The man took a leather wallet from his jacket pocket and held it up in front of Monroe. 'Special Agent Jim Ellis, sir. I'm part of Special Agent Dawson's team. We flew in from Washington today. I believe he told you that someone would be coming out to see you today?'

'Yeah, he told me.'

'Special Agent Dawson said that you could provide us with a photofit of the man you saw at Amy Michaels's house. The one driving the hired car with the out-of-state licence plates?'

'That's right. I saw him as clear as I see you. I'll be able to give you a real good description of him.'

'That really won't be necessary, sir.' Ellis took a small gas gun from his pocket and discharged a vial of lethal hydrocyanic gas directly into Monroe's face. Ellis had swallowed an antidote moments before getting out of the car and would remain unaffected by the deadly gas. Monroe staggered backwards, clutching at his throat as he struggled for breath. Then he dropped to his knees as the gas paralysed his heart. Seconds later he toppled sideways to the ground, his sightless eyes open in death. Ellis checked for a pulse. Nothing. The gas would dissipate and it would appear that Monroe had suffered a fatal heart-attack. He knew from experience that the symptoms would fool even the most experienced pathologist. He removed a cellphone from the glove compartment and punched out a number he had already consigned to memory.

'Sheriff's office, how may I help you?' Phyllis Kastner answered.

'Could I speak to Special Agent Frank Dawson, please?'

'Who shall I say is calling?'

'Special Agent Jim Ellis.'

'One moment.'

There was a pause as the call was transferred, then, 'Jim, have you spoken to Monroe yet?' Dawson asked.

'No, sir. I think you'd better come out to the farm yourself. And you'd better bring the local doctor with you.'

'Why, what's happened?'

Ellis smiled faintly to himself as he looked down at the body sprawled at his feet. 'Henry Monroe's dead, sir.'

'*What?*'

'It looks like he's had a heart-attack, sir. The body's still warm, so he hasn't been dead long.'

'I'm on my way,' Dawson said curtly, and the line went dead.

EIGHT

'We've got a problem.'

'What is it?' Voskov asked.

'It's not what, it's who,' Kahn told him over the phone.

'Go on,' Voskov prompted, when Kahn fell silent.

'From what I hear, Kessler put out the word to all his informers that he's offering a reward for the arrest, and conviction, of Amy Michaels. A pretty big reward by all accounts. So naturally these dirtbags have been ferreting around for the past few days, trying to pick up on something that would lead them to her. They're all way off target. Except one. And he's stumbled on something far more serious. He's been asking questions about two hired guns who recently flew into Zürich. One French. One American.'

'Kilgarry and Racine,' Voskov concluded.

'Who else could it be?'

'And me?'

'No mention of a third, Russian or otherwise. You obviously slipped through the net. He seems to think that they're here to take someone out. From what I can gather from my own sources, Kessler's told him he wants names by the morning otherwise he starts to turn the screw on him. Kessler's career's hanging in the balance as it is so he's desperate to grab on to anything that will help him get back on the right side of his superiors, even if it doesn't appear to have any connection to the case. If he ever found out that it did, it would make the situation that much harder for us to deal with. You said earlier that Kessler has already been to the house. If he'd had any suspicions about the three of you – or even just Racine and Kilgarry – he'd have confronted Novak about it. That's why it's essential that he never gets any closer to the truth. We can't afford any mistakes.'

'I'll deal with it. What's the name of the informer?' Voskov asked.

'Willie Meine,' Kahn replied, then gave him a brief description of the man and an address. 'It's a flat, I believe. He only uses it as a base. Comes and goes at irregular times. Send Racine. It's perfect for him. It shouldn't be difficult for him to get into the flat. Tell him to wait there for Meine. That's his best bet, rather than going out looking for him. The last thing we need is for him to draw attention to himself. It may take some time so tell him to be patient.'

'What if Meine finds out their names and contacts Kessler before going home?' Voskov asked.

'That's what I'm counting on. I've got my main source here in Zürich scouring the streets for him as we speak. He's got specific orders to give him the names that Kilgarry and Racine used to enter the country. You all flew in on forged passports. No one knows where you went from there. Meine won't question the names, he'll just be grateful to get them and keep Kessler off his back. So even if he does decide to contact Kessler tonight, the names will be worthless anyway. Only by the time Kessler's found that out, Meine will be dead.'

'Leave it with me.'

'I'll call you later tonight. Hopefully you'll have an update for me then.'

'I'm sure I will.' Voskov switched off the cellphone and clipped it back on to his belt. He returned to the lounge and beckoned to Racine. 'I've got a little job for you. I've got a feeling you're going to like it.'

It was already beginning to get dark when Sergeant Hans Matzke parked the unmarked police car at the edge of the woods. He got out but couldn't see Novak's house from where he was standing. That meant nobody in the house could see him either. Perfect. He slipped a small flashlight into the sheath attached to his belt then moved cautiously into the undergrowth, careful to tread lightly on the fallen branches that lay across the narrow pathway, which wound its way through the trees.

More and more in the past few months he had found himself contemplating his future as a policeman. He didn't want to end up like Stefan Kessler. He could remember a time when he had hung on Kessler's every word, desperate to learn from the best detective in Zürich. He had been the envy of all his colleagues to have been chosen to partner Kessler after he had left the academy. Now all he saw was the shell of the man he had once admired. None of his colleagues envied him any more. Some pitied him. Others laughed at his misfortune.

He reached the end of the trees and crouched down on the edge of the clearing, using the thick brush as additional cover. The first thing that caught his attention was that the curtains were drawn across the window that faced over the clearing. It wasn't dark so was Novak trying to conceal something inside? Or somebody? The questions flooded his mind, but they were instinctive rather than instructive. He could see a shaft of light spread out across the freshly cut lawn at the back of the house, presumably coming from an unseen window, but the only way he could approach it would be by crossing the clearing. That would leave him exposed. He was already trespassing on private property as it was. No search warrant. No reason for being there, other than to follow up on Kessler's hunch. *Some hunch*, he thought irritably.

Suddenly he heard a door open and a second shaft of light illuminated the lawn, merging with the first. Then the door banged shut and Matzke shrank back into the shadows when a figure appeared from around the side of the house. He had what looked like a black balaclava clutched in one hand and a jacket in the other, draped over his shoulder. He had shoulder-length blond hair. The walk was strong, purposeful – and he was heading directly towards him! Matzke ducked down even further into the undergrowth. His back ached. He didn't move. The man kept to the narrow pathway and only after he had passed within a few feet of Matzke's hiding place did the policeman slowly raise his head and see the holster secured to the belt at the back of the jeans. He waited a few seconds then got to his feet and tiptoed through the foliage until he joined the pathway again. The man was nowhere to be seen. He moved along cautiously, feeling naked without a weapon. Neither he nor Kessler had considered that he might need one. After all, he was only on surveillance duty.

He froze at a rustling sound a short distance ahead. He bent low and edged forward, using his hands to steady himself as he went. He reached a turn in the path and stopped when he saw the blond man, now wearing the jacket, with his back to him, pulling away a succession of branches to reveal a silver Volvo hatchback that had been expertly concealed in the undergrowth. He ducked his head when the man moved round to the front of the car to remove the branches from the bonnet. The movement had been too sudden and he lost his balance. He trod down heavily to steady himself and a twig snapped under-foot. In the silence it sounded more like a peal of thunder, crashing around him. He scrambled back into the undergrowth moments before the man appeared, looking around suspiciously for the source of the noise. The Beretta, which had been on the back of his belt, was now in his hand. Matzke didn't move, didn't dare breathe, as the man scanned the foliage. At last he turned away and disappeared. Still Matzke didn't move, knowing it could be a trap to lure him into the open. Eventually he heard a car engine start up and, moments later, a set of headlights pierced the darkness directly ahead of him. Then the vehicle was reversed away from the trees. Matzke got to his feet, just in time to see the Volvo drive off down the same road that he had used. He ran towards his own car and got in, caught in a dilemma. Follow the Volvo, or continue to keep the house under surveillance? The answer was never in doubt. Starting up the engine, he pulled out into the road and went after the retreating tail-lights.

Novak had never felt less like going to work than he did that afternoon. All he could think about was John, and how he had been forced to leave him at home. Before he had left the house Beth and Marie, independently, had assured him that they would look after him while Novak was gone. He knew they both meant well, but it had been of little comfort. He felt as if he was letting his son down at a time when he needed him most. John was his whole world. He couldn't even begin to imagine how he would cope if anything ever happened to him ...

Pushing the negative thoughts from his mind he parked beside the Limmat then got out of his car and walked the short distance to the club. A familiar, popular figure in the Niederdorf, he paused twice to talk to shop-owners, who greeted him cheerfully from their doorways. Both times he found himself forcing the pace of the conversation. He just wasn't in the mood for small-talk. He was sure they must have sensed this, but they didn't seem to mind and let him go on his way. He reached the club with the keys in his hand. As he unlocked the front door he sensed someone standing behind him.

'We need to talk,' Jago said, when Novak looked round sharply. 'Inside.'

Jago was the last person he had wanted to see but there was no way of brushing him off without arousing suspicion. And he couldn't afford to do that. *Play it cool*, he told himself, as he went in. He followed Jago into the foyer and locked the door again behind them.

'How long before your staff get here?' Jago asked.

'Another hour or so.' Novak pocketed the keys. 'It's Friday night. We're going to be busy and I've got things to do. So let's make this brief, shall we?'

'Why wasn't I told that Beth Grant had checked out of the hotel earlier this afternoon? The first I knew about it was when I tried to phone her room. Where is she now?'

'At my house,' Novak replied. 'You would have been told *if* you were ever around to take our calls.'

'You could have left a message for me to call you,' Jago said.

'Why? You've not bothered to contact either of us since you dumped Amy Michaels on me. It works both ways, Jago.'

'How is she?'

'Why don't you ask her yourself?' Novak jerked a thumb at the roped-off stairs at the end of the foyer. 'Assuming she even wants to see you.'

'I'm sure she will,' Jago said. 'Tell me, has Kessler been to see you again since the night of the murder?'

'He came to the house this afternoon. He also wanted to know why Beth had checked out of the hotel and come to stay with me.'

'What did you tell him?'

'We fobbed him off with some spiel about her not wanting to be alone in her time of grief.'

'Did he buy it?'

'He seemed to.' Novak shrugged. 'You know he's had Beth followed ever since he knew she was in Zürich? There's an unmarked car parked outside my house as we speak.'

'It doesn't surprise me,' was all Jago would say. 'Any word of the disk?'

Novak realized that Jago wouldn't have known about the letter, or about Strohmaier. Beth had tried to contact him after she had spoken to Emma, but Jago hadn't been at the hotel. 'Nothing as yet,' he said, shaking his head. He could only hope he sounded convincing because he certainly didn't feel it inside.

'Me neither,' Jago said. 'I've been following up on several leads today, but every one was a dead end. I just wish I knew what Ian did with that disk. God help us if the Cabal were to get their hands on it first.'

'Maybe they already have,' Novak suggested, going with the flow of the conversation. He didn't know if it was the right tactic but what else could he do without jeopardizing the safety of the hostages? He certainly couldn't tell Jago the truth. He couldn't tell anyone the truth.

'That's not my understanding,' Jago said.

'What do you know?' Novak demanded.

'I can't tell you that – at least, not yet.' There was a hint of apology in Jago's voice. 'It's part of my ongoing investigation. I can't afford to compromise what I already know by discussing it with anyone other than my immediate superior at Interpol. But I will explain everything to you once it's all over. I promise you that. Just bear with me.'

'But we're still expected to share any information we get with you?' Novak retorted, keeping up the pretence. There was no going back now.

'This is my investigation,' Jago reminded him, his tone hardening, 'and that gives me the right to make the rules.'

'As you go along,' Novak added sardonically.

'Let's go and see how Miss Michaels is doing, shall we?' Jago said.

'Let me go up first, OK?' Novak said.

'Why?' Jago asked, surprised.

'Because she might not want to see you. She was pretty much on edge the last time I saw her. She hardly said anything to me, apart from asking me to get her a television to help pass the time. I had to go out and hire one.'

'I think she'd welcome the company,' Jago said.

'I'm not so sure. Let me speak to her.'

Novak went up the stairs and gave the coded knock on the door. The bolt was drawn back and it opened. 'My God, civilization,' she said, then returned to the bed, replaced the pillow against the wall, patted it, then lay down again to continue watching a nature documentary on TV.

'Jago's downstairs. He wants to see you.'

'So send him up,' she replied, without taking her eyes off the screen. 'I could do with a bit of company. Even him.'

'I told him you were on edge the last time I saw you. I know you weren't,' Novak added when she frowned at him, 'but I needed to speak to you alone. He doesn't know anything about Voskov and the others being at the house, or that Beth and I tried to get the disk from Strohmaier. In fact, he doesn't even know about Strohmaier.'

'And you want me to play along, is that it?' She swung her legs off the bed and leaned her elbows on her knees as she stared at him. 'I've got nothing to lose by telling him what I know. In fact, I've everything to gain. As far as I'm concerned, the sooner he gets the disk, the sooner I can clear my name and go home.'

'If he were to get the disk, they would kill John, Beth and Marie. You know that.'

'And if they get the disk, I'll go to jail. I'd say we've got a conflict here, wouldn't you?'

'You know as well as I do that Jago would do everything in his power to clear your name once this is all over. He's got connections. You won't go to jail, Amy.'

'We've been through this before. Jago's not going to bail me out if he doesn't have the disk. He can't afford to make public what he knows about the Cabal.'

'I'm begging you, Amy, please don't tell him. For John's sake. Please.'

Amy was about to reply when she heard the sound of approaching footsteps and a moment later Jago appeared in the doorway. He knocked lightly on the door. 'Good afternoon, Miss Michaels,' he said genially. 'I thought I'd drop by to see how you were doing.'

Her eyes flickered towards Novak. 'I'm doing fine, thank you. But I don't think that Mike's been completely truthful with you, though.'

'What do you mean?' Jago took a step into the room.

She could see the horror on Novak's face. His fists were clenched at his sides. 'He didn't tell you that I don't want visitors. I'm perfectly happy on my own, now that I've got a TV to keep me company. Right now you're both interrupting a programme I was watching.' She lay down again and clasped her hands behind her head. 'And don't forget to close the door on your way out.'

'Yeah, sure.' Novak mouthed an intensely relieved 'thank you' at her as he ushered Jago from the room. Her face remained impassive and she returned her attention to the screen.

Using a map of the city, Racine had little difficulty in finding the address Voskov had given to him at the house. It turned out to be a block of flats in an ill-lit section of the Old Town, situated behind the cosmopolitan Niederdorf, and not listed on any tourist route. He parked the Volvo on the opposite side of the street and got out. A couple of women, prostitutes judging by their clothing, stood in the pale reflection of one of the few working street-lights. Both were smoking. Neither looked at him. A raised voice drifted from an open window further down the street. This was followed by a clattering sound. Then silence. He crossed the road and paused at the foot of the steps leading into the dark foyer. Palming the Beretta from the holster at the back of his jeans, he slipped it into his jacket pocket and pushed open the door leading into the foyer.

He saw the movement out of the corner of his eye and was

still turning when a hand clawed at his arm. 'Cigarette?' a shaky voice asked, then a stray headlight swept across the foyer, momentarily illuminating the old man's dishevelled clothes and dirty, unshaven face. Racine jerked his arm free but the vagrant grabbed at the hem of his jacket as he made for the stairs at the side of the broken lift. Racine pulled the Beretta from his pocket and brought down the barrel savagely. The vagrant cried out in pain and stumbled back into the shadows, clutching at the gash on his temple. He was still trying to steady himself when Racine clubbed him viciously across the back of the head. He crumpled to the floor. Racine used his foot to push him over on to his back. Satisfied that the man was unconscious, he slipped the automatic into his pocket and made his way to the third floor, where he paused to get his bearings before heading down the dimly lit corridor towards Meine's flat. Several of the apartments appeared to be unoccupied, their doors broken open and the bare floorboards littered with the festering debris of a succession of transients.

He reached Meine's flat and, after slipping on a pair of leather gloves, knocked on the unpainted door. No reply. Again. No reply. He was able to pick the lock with relative ease, slipped inside and closed the door behind him. He was instantly assailed by an overpowering stench of excrement, and he screwed up his face in disgust as he picked his way through the squalor to the window, which he pushed open. He identified where the smell was coming from, crossed the room to an adjacent door, which he assumed led into the bathroom, and closed it without bothering to investigate. *How could anyone live like this?* he thought disdainfully as he searched for somewhere to sit while he waited for Meine to return. There was only an armchair by the window, and a single bed pushed up against the wall. He chose to stand. Removing a cellphone from the inside pocket of his jacket, he dialled a number. Voskov answered.

'I'm in the apartment,' Racine said. 'He's not here.'

'Then you're just going to have to wait for him until he gets back.'

'I guess so.' Racine eyed his surroundings with distaste.

'Call me again when the job's done.' The line went dead.

'The sooner, the better.' Racine pocketed the cellphone. He helped himself to a newspaper from the pile in the corner of the room, placed it strategically over the seat of the chair and sat down. Now all he had to do was wait . . .

Matzke had parked the unmarked police car in an adjoining street, within sight of the Volvo, and he waited until Racine entered the block of flats before going after him, careful to keep his distance. He reached the entrance to the building and was about to go inside when he heard a groan from the darkness beyond the open door. He wished again that he was armed. He stepped into the foyer and his attention was drawn to the figure propped against the wall in the shadows at the side of the door.

'My head.' The figure clutched at the side of his face. 'Help me. My head.'

Matzke crouched down before the man and saw the blood on his cheek. 'What happened?'

'I only asked him for a cigarette.' The old man's face was twisted in pain. 'He hit me. Twice. First time here. Then on the back of the head. I blacked out.'

'Who hit you?'

'I don't know. I've never seen him around here before.'

'Where did he go?' Matzke asked.

'How do I know? Like I said, I passed out.'

'Do you live here?'

'No.'

'Then what are you doing here?'

'I was going to doss down in the foyer for the night,' the old man replied, then added defiantly, 'Ain't no crime in that.'

'It's a crime to trespass. Now get out.'

'And if I refuse? What are you going to do? Call the cops?'

'No need.' Matzke held up his badge.

'Hey, I didn't mean no trouble,' the old man said fearfully, and hauled himself up. 'I was only going to sleep here tonight. I'd have been gone by the morning. Honest.'

'Go and find somewhere else.' Matzke propelled the vagrant out into the street.

The man paused at the foot of the steps. 'You don't have a cigarette on you, do you?' He saw the look of anger flash across Matzke's face. 'I was just asking, that's all.' Then he was gone.

Matzke remained in the foyer, looking at the stairs. It would be pointless to try to find the blond man. He could be in any of the apartments. And he was armed. No, best to report the situation first and take it from there. He returned to the car but no sooner had he got back behind the wheel than one of the prostitutes appeared but as she peered through the open driver's window she found herself looking at his badge. She immediately stepped away from the car, hands raised to acknowledge her mistake, already fearing that she was going to be bagged even before her night's work had begun.

'Just get out of here,' Matzke spat, 'and take that other bitch with you while you're at it. I don't want to see either of you around here again tonight. If I do, I'll bust you both and you'll spend the rest of the night in the cells.'

He watched her return to where the other was standing and they disappeared into an adjacent street. Matzke pushed a cigarette between his lips and lit it, exhaling the smoke through the open window. It was time to report in. But not to Kessler. Kessler was just a means to an end. That much had been obvious when the *juge d'instruction* had met with him shortly after he had first been assigned to work the case with Kessler.

The meeting had come as a complete surprise to him but the *juge d'instruction* had quickly put him at his ease before going on to explain why he had asked to see him. Matzke could still remember the conversation: 'To be perfectly honest, Sergeant,

I have serious reservations about Inspector Kessler. He's certainly not the detective he once was. Not since he lost his son. He just hasn't been able to come to terms with his loss and unfortunately he's allowed his personal grief to encroach on his professional life. It's got to the point now where he's become a liability to those around him. He's now only one foul-up away from an indefinite suspension. What worries me is that when he does screw up again – and I say when rather than if, because it's going to happen – it's going to reflect badly on those around him. You've got an excellent service record to date, Sergeant, and I know that you're in line for a promotion within the next year. Don't let Inspector Kessler ruin your prospects by letting him drag you down with him. That's why I wanted to speak to you in private, to give you the chance to distance yourself from him should he be suspended during the course of this investigation. You report everything to me first, no matter how insignificant it may appear to you at the time, before reporting it to Inspector Kessler. That way he can't blame you for any blunder he may make because I'll be able to back you up, should the need arise. I realize that you may not feel comfortable with this and you're perfectly within your rights to refuse my request. It certainly wouldn't be held against you if you did. It's your decision, Sergeant . . .'

It hadn't been a difficult decision to make, not with a promotion in the pipeline. Kessler was on the way out and Matzke was damned if he was going down with him when he toppled over the edge. He had his own future to think about, which was why he had been passing on all relevant information about the case to the *juge d'instruction* ever since their meeting. Removing a cellphone from the glove compartment, he dialled a number already programmed into its memory. When it was answered he explained the events of the evening, culminating in his arrival at the block of flats a few minutes earlier.

'And you're sure that the blond man doesn't know you

followed him from the house?' the *juge d'instruction* asked, when Matzke had finished.

'No, sir, definitely not. I was careful not to be seen.'

'Excellent. It certainly sounds as if something's going on at the house. Question is, what?'

'Sir, I still feel uncomfortable about not being armed.'

'You don't need to be armed, Sergeant, you're not going to confront him. All I want you to do is remain where you are and follow him again when he leaves. Chances are, he'll return to Novak's house anyway. That's when we'll make our move.'

'What will you do, sir?'

'Bring in a specialist firearms unit to deal with the situation. But don't worry, they won't put your life in any danger. All you have to do is keep the man under surveillance.'

'What do I tell Inspector Kessler?' Matzke asked. 'He'll be expecting me to report in within the next few minutes.'

'Tell him you're still at Novak's house. You've had a look round and there doesn't appear to be anything untoward. It's essential that you stall him as long as possible. If he found out where you really were, chances are he'd want to move in on the flats – even though you've admitted that you don't know where the suspect's gone. You know how impetuous Inspector Kessler can be – and the last thing we need is a gunfight in a residential area where innocent people could get hurt. I want the whole thing isolated at Novak's house before the firearms unit moves in.'

'I understand, sir.'

'Make sure you keep me posted on any new developments, Sergeant. I'll be at home for the rest of the night.'

'Yes, sir.' Matzke switched off the cellphone and reached for the radio to report in to Kessler at police headquarters.

Novak kept a bottle of bourbon in the bottom drawer of the filing cabinet in his office. He was the first to admit that it didn't make much sense with a fully stocked bar on the premises. It was for emergencies, he liked to say. The truth was that he always had a shot of bourbon after the club had closed and he was alone in his office counting the night's takings. Just one, mind. Sometimes it was his first drink of the night. He always liked to have a clear head when he was mixing with the customers – and it was even more important if he was called upon to perform an impromptu jam session with the resident band. There was nothing more unprofessional – or unforgivable – than a musician going on stage drunk. Even half cut was unacceptable. You owed it to your audience to play to the best of your ability. He'd believed that from an early age, having witnessed at first hand the intoxicated antics of his late father, a drummer with a jazz band in his hometown of Seattle. How many times had he seen his father drunk on stage – especially in the last years of his life – out of synch with the rest of the band, forcing them to readjust constantly to compensate for his erratic rhythm? Yet what had made it even more galling was that Bill Novak was extraordinarily talented and could have been as successful as the top session drummers of the time like Philly Joe Jones, Billy Higgins or Max Roach. His failure was three-fold: his drinking, his lack of ambition, and his wife.

Novak looked across at the framed black-and-white photograph of his parents on the wall opposite his desk. It was the only one he had of them together, such was the acrimony within their marriage. That they were both smiling within such close proximity of each other made it all the more remarkable. He hated his mother, Ellie, and made it no secret that he blamed her for the death of his father. She had never been able to relate to her husband's obsession with jazz, and to compensate for the void left in their marriage she had embarked on a string of meaningless affairs, which she'd stretched out over a decade. And because Bill Novak was weak, he sought further solace in the bottle to help him come to terms with the humiliation he felt over his wife's infidelity, which was well known among his peers in Seattle. Mike was twelve when she had first become involved with Johnny Barens, a local gangster with a history of violence. She became obsessed with him and asked her husband for a divorce. He refused. The following night Barens confronted him outside the club where he was playing and a scuffle broke out between them. Bill Novak was stabbed in the stomach and died on the way to hospital. Barens told the police that Ellie Novak had put him up to it. She denied it and, although she was arrested, she was acquitted of any involvement in her husband's death. Barens was found guilty and jailed for life. Bill Novak's parents won a bitter court battle against their daughter-in-law to gain custody of Mike. She left Seattle shortly afterwards, hounded out by the persistence of the gossipmongers, and settled in Tacoma where she remarried and found comfort in religion. He had always suspected, somewhat cynically, that she had only turned to God to help her come to terms with her guilt. He had not spoken to her since she left Seattle, always believing that she had got away with murder. It was something he would never forgive – or forget – for the rest of his life. Not that he had ever attempted to hide the truth from John. He had told his son everything, and had tried to be as unbiased as possible despite the animosity he still felt towards his mother. His one concern was that John might have wanted to initiate a correspondence with the grandmother he had never seen, but John had never mentioned his American grandmother again. It was as if he knew, even at that age, the pain it would have caused his father to reopen old wounds.

The thought of his son jolted him from his memories and he was surprised to find the bottle of bourbon sitting on the desk in front of him. He didn't remember taking it out of the filing cabinet. He considered having a shot, just to steady his nerves, but the way he was feeling, he couldn't guarantee that he wouldn't drink the whole damn bottle. And what would that achieve? He returned it to the bottom drawer of the filing cabinet, closed it, then sat back in his chair. His eyes went to the clock on the desk. It had just gone seven. The customers would start to arrive shortly. The band were due on stage at eight. His enthusiasm for the evening ahead was non-existent. He just wanted it to end so that he could get back home. That's where he should be. Not at the club. What use was he there anyway? The only time he'd left his office since he arrived was to unlock the front door to admit the first of his staff, Bernhard, the head barman. He'd given him the keys and told him to issue any liquor required from the cellar. Twice Bernhard had poked his head round the door, obviously worried about him, but he'd dismissed him with the lame assurance that he was tired. Yet Bernhard knew him better than anyone else on the staff. He was, in all but name, his right hand at the club, hard-working, exceptionally loyal, unquestionably honest. He'd covered for Novak before. Why not again? The last thing he needed, or wanted, was to mingle with the customers that evening. He had to go home, if only for a while. He rang the bar and asked Bernhard to come through to his office. A short time later there was a knock on his door.

'Yes?' Novak barked.

The door opened and Bernhard peered into the room. 'You wanted to see me, boss?'

'Come in, Bernhard. Close the door.'

'Something's wrong, isn't it? You've barely set foot outside your office since I got here. Normally you're already out there chatting to the regulars as they arrive. Actually, a couple of them have already asked after you. I just said you were busy.'

'Thanks, I appreciate that.' Novak sat forward. 'I realize I've been acting kind of weird tonight. And I know I said there was nothing wrong when you asked me before. Well, that's not really true. It's John. He's laid up in bed with a bad fever. He was delirious when I left for work this evening. I've called Marie, our au pair, since I got here. His condition hasn't changed. I'm really worried about him.'

'Has a doctor seen him?'

'Yes, he reckons John's got an infection. He's put him on a course of antibiotics. I thought he should go to hospital but the doctor says they'd just give him the same antibiotics and leave him to sweat it out. But if the fever hasn't broken by morning, he'll have him taken into hospital for tests. I know it's not life-threatening – that's the first thing the doctor told me – but I'm still worried about him. John's never been this ill before.'

'Why don't you go home, boss? I can look after the place.'

'That's what I was thinking. It's why I called you in here – to ask you to cover for me tonight.'

'I'll take care of everything, boss,' Bernhard assured him. 'You go on home. Everything will be fine.'

'I know. And, Bernhard, thanks.'

'I'll be thinking of John tonight.' Bernhard was at the door. 'And when his fever breaks, you tell him we're still on for the Grasshoppers match on Wednesday night. It's a European Cup tie. Sure to be another sell-out crowd.'

'That'll cheer him up,' Novak said, with a quick smile. 'You know, I always thought that if I had a son, he'd share my love of baseball. Instead he turns out to be a soccer nut. I blame you for that. You're the one who got him interested.'

'Considering the options, it's the least I could do,' Bernhard said, with a grin, then left the office and closed the door behind him.

Novak stared at the door. He had hated lying to Bernhard like that, but he couldn't have told him the truth. He couldn't confide in anybody outside the house. These were professionals. They wouldn't hesitate to kill their hostages if they thought they had been double-crossed.

He slipped on his jacket, picked up his keys, then left the club discreetly, through a side entrance to avoid being seen, and walked briskly to where he had left his car.

*

'Heart-attack. Looks that way.'

Sam Arbuther had been the local doctor in Livingstone Point for forty years. He had recently taken on a junior partner with the intention of retiring at the end of the year. However, he still regarded himself as the senior medical practitioner in the area and, as such, had responded personally to the sheriff's call to drive out to Henry Monroe's farm at Drummond Creek. Having lived in Livingstone Point all his life, apart from the years he had spent at medical school, he had never taken to outsiders, which quickly became apparent when it came to dealing with the dark-suited Federal agents who were snooping around when he got to the farm. He didn't like them. And, in particular, he didn't like Frank Dawson.

'How soon can we get the results of the autopsy?' Dawson asked.

'Morning, if you're lucky,' Arbuther said briefly, as he bent over Henry Monroe's body.

'Where's the nearest medical examiner's office?' Dawson asked Sheriff Olsen who was standing beside him. 'Jackson?'

'Uh-huh.' Olsen nodded absently.

'How soon can the ME get here?' Dawson pressed.

'Morning, if you're lucky,' Arbuther responded.

'Not good enough!'

Arbuther was startled by Dawson's tone. 'I told you, Henry died of a heart-attack. He was seventy-six. There are no suspicious circumstances here so you can be sure that the ME isn't gonna drop everything at a moment's notice and come all the way up here just to verify a coronary. Hell, I'll sign the death certificate here and now if you want.'

'What I want is the ME here by *tonight*,' Dawson said.

Arbuther took Olsen's extended hand to help him to his feet. There was disdain in his eyes as he looked at Dawson. 'You aren't listening to me, boy. The ME won't be here until the morning. That's the way it works round here. You'd better get used to it.'

'I'll tell you the way it works around here.' Special Agent Jim Ellis had appeared silently beside Arbuther. 'This is a Federal investigation, which means that Special Agent Dawson is in charge. You don't like it, by all means take it up with your local congressman at your next Klan meeting.'

'I resent the insinuation—'

'And I resent your bigotry.' Ellis picked up the medical bag from beside the body and shoved it roughly into Arbuther's stomach.

'Jim, that's enough,' Dawson said. 'Let the doctor go about his business.'

'We'll try and have the ME come up from Jackson later this afternoon.' Olsen gave Arbuther a sharp look. 'Won't we, Sam?'

'If you say so,' Arbuther mumbled, then walked back to his car.

'You think there's more to Henry's death than meets the eye?' Olsen asked Dawson.

'Right now I don't know what to think.' Dawson watched Ellis place a sheet carefully over the body. 'Monroe was the one person who could have given us a description of the man he saw putting the rug into the trunk of his car outside Amy Michaels's house. As I said yesterday, it could have been nothing. But at the same time it was still the only solid lead we had to go on.'

'Sheriff, you got a call coming through on your radio,' one of the Feds called.

'Sweet Jesus, now what?' Olsen strode off towards the patrol car.

'We've got to have a bit of give and take around here, Jim,' Dawson said quietly to Ellis. 'We're in a small town in the Deep South. We both know this is Klan country. How do you expect them to react to me coming down here like this?'

'Yeah, but who's giving and who's taking?' Ellis cast an icy stare at Arbuther as he got into his car.

'Just give them a bit of slack, Jim, that's all I'm asking. After all, I'm the one who's taking the brunt of their attitude and if I can handle it, so can you. We need these people on our side. Being confrontational isn't going to solve anything. In fact, it's only going to make them even more defensive. Diplomacy, that's what's required.'

'I wish I had your patience, Frank,' Ellis said with a half-smile.

'Believe me, it comes from bitter experience. I grew up in a two-bit hick town not too dissimilar from Livingstone Point. You learn to rise above the prejudice around you. You have to. It's the only way forward.'

'Sam?' Olsen shouted as the doctor was about to drive off. No response. He ran in front of Arbuther's car. 'Sam, wait up!'

'Why do I get the feeling this is bad news?' Ellis said, as Olsen spoke to Arbuther through the open driver's window. A moment later Arbuther switched off the engine.

The sheriff crossed to where Dawson and Ellis were standing. 'A couple of local kids were playing in a field on the other side of town when they found the naked body of a woman, partially buried in the undergrowth.'

'And you think it could be Amy Michaels?' Ellis asked.

'I don't know,' Olsen replied. 'The body's been decapitated and there's no sign of the head. At least, not according to the kids. Not that they hung around to look for it. From what I understand they're pretty shaken up. I got to get over there right away.'

'We'll follow you,' Dawson said.

'What about Henry?' Olsen glanced at the body silhouetted underneath the sheet.

'I'll leave one of my men here until you can arrange to have the body taken away,' Dawson told him.

'Well, it looks like you're going to have to call out the ME after all, Sheriff,' Ellis said smugly.

Olsen opened his mouth to reply, thought better of it, then trudged back to his car.

NINE

'Beer.'

'You got the money to pay for it, Willie?' the barman asked suspiciously.

'You know I'm good for it,' Willie Meine whined, as he patted the pockets of his grubby overcoat. 'I'll pay you at the beginning of next week. I promise. Just one beer. That's all.'

'I don't want your promises, Willie. Only your money. Up front. So let's see it.'

'It's on me,' a voice said beside Meine, and a twenty-franc note was pushed across the counter towards the barman. 'And I'll have one too.'

'Two beers.' The barman plucked the note off the counter.

Meine turned to his benefactor and grinned. 'Oliver Strauss. What brings you here, my friend?'

'You can cut the bullshit, Willie. Friends we're not. I've got a business proposition for you. Believe me, I'd rather be anywhere else right now than standing here talking to you.'

'So what's my cut?' Meine asked, the grin still fixed on his unshaven face.

'Still as direct as ever, I see.'

'Business is business.' Meine took the two glasses from the barman. 'Oh, you can keep the change,' he said, affecting a pompous accent.

'He's really generous with other people's money, isn't he?'

The barman handed some coins to Strauss, who grabbed Meine's arm and led him through the crowd to a vacant space next to the entrance to the men's room. He looked around but the nearest group of drinkers were too busy passing salacious comments among themselves about the two women sitting at a nearby table to take any notice of them. Satisfied, he turned back to Meine.

'I hear that Kessler's got you by the balls this time.'

The glass froze at Meine's lips. 'I – I don't know what you're talking about,' he stammered, and managed a weak laugh. It came out as a whimper.

'Then I guess you don't want the names of the two assassins who flew into Zürich earlier this week,' Strauss said. 'And I thought I was doing you a favour. So long, Willie.'

'Wait, wait!' Meine grabbed Strauss's arm as he turned to leave, spilling beer over both of them.

'Fuck it, Willie,' Strauss snarled, wiping his hand down the front of his beer-splattered shirt.

'Are you saying that you know the names of the two assassins?' Meine asked.

'I might do,' came the evasive reply. 'But they won't mean anything to you if you don't know what I'm talking about.'

'OK, so Kessler's on my back,' Meine conceded. 'But how did you know that?'

'I've got my sources, just like you. Now what are these two names worth to you?'

'You know I haven't got any money—'

'Don't fuck with me, Willie. You want the names, they're gonna cost you. It's as simple as that.'

'I told you, I'm broke at the moment,' Meine said desperately, and pulled out a handful of small denomination coins from his overcoat pocket. 'That's all the money I've got in the world.'

'I can believe that. OK, I'll give you the names.'

'You'll *give* me the names?' Meine frowned suspiciously. 'What's the catch?'

'No catch. But you owe me, Willie. And I will collect on that debt.'

'Definitely. You know you can count on me. Now, what about those names?'

'Richard Kane and Albert Ronet.'

'Why are they here? Is there a hit planned?'

'I don't know, Willie, but if I did I sure as hell wouldn't tell you. I'm not some fucking charity, you know.'

'No, of course not. Look, I appreciate you helping me out like this, Oliver. And whenever you want to call in that marker you know I'll be there for you.'

'For your sake, I certainly hope so.' Strauss finished his beer, thrust the empty glass into Meine's hand and left the bar.

He walked the short distance to the nearest public phone and dialled. 'Sammy Kahn told me to ring this number once I'd made contact with Willie Meine. He's taken the bait. He's all yours now.'

'You said on the phone that you've got those two names for me, Willie,' Kessler said, getting out of his car at the pre-arranged rendezvous, away from prying eyes.

'That's right, Inspector,' Meine grinned. 'I wouldn't let you down. I'm always reliable. You know that.'

'I can think of a lot of words to describe you, Willie. Reliable isn't one of them. Now give me the names.'

'Did you bring the money?' Meine said.

'Names.'

Meine took a step backwards when anger flashed across Kessler's face. 'The names for the money. That's the deal we had.'

Kessler removed an envelope from his pocket but pulled his hand back when Meine reached out to snatch it from him. 'The names, Willie.'

'Richard Kane and Albert Ronet,' Meine blurted out, his eyes never leaving the envelope in Kessler's hand.

'Who gave you this information?'

'You know better than to ask me the name of my source, Inspector. I'm like a priest. I can't betray a trust.'

'Then you'd better pray that the names are on the level, Willie.' Kessler slapped the envelope against the other man's chest. 'Because if they're not I'll be making a few phone calls in the morning and you'll be joining your Maker a lot sooner than you might think.'

'He's a very reliable source, he wouldn't see me wrong,' Meine assured him, but there was a degree of uncertainty in his voice, which he tried to disguise with a smile.

'Then you've got nothing to worry about, have you?' Kessler said.

Meine waited until he had driven off then slit open the envelope with his finger and counted the money. It was all there. Kessler was honest, if nothing else. But what if Kessler had been right to be sceptical about the information? What if Strauss had deliberately given him a bum steer? But why? What would he gain by setting him up? It made no sense. Not that there was anything he could do even if he had been tricked. He had nowhere to run. He pushed the thought from his mind then slipped the envelope into his overcoat pocket and headed for the nearest bar.

Novak had been surprised by Voskov's tolerant reaction when he returned to the house earlier that evening. He had expected a verbal lashing at least, even feared a beating, but neither had materialized once he had reassured Voskov that nobody at the club suspected anything was wrong at the house. It was as if Voskov was relieved to have all the hostages back under one roof again. Not that he had said as much. In fact, he had said hardly anything. He had just nodded then told him to go through to the lounge where John had greeted him enthusiastically. That alone had made the decision worthwhile.

That had been three hours ago. Not much had happened since then. John had fallen asleep within the last twenty minutes, his head resting on his father's leg, and Voskov had given Marie permission to get some bedding to put on the lounge floor. Kilgarry had been dispatched to assist her. They had returned with a couple of mattresses, pillows and several folded sheets. She had made up one of the beds then Novak carried his son across the room and placed him gently on the mattress. Shortly after that Marie had lain down on the second mattress beside him, with only a pillow for comfort, as if to shield him from the two armed men seated nearby. The gesture wasn't lost on Novak, who had a perfect view of them from the sofa. He noticed Kilgarry steal several furtive glances at the prostrate figure of Marie, but he knew the American wouldn't dare go near her with Voskov in the room. He had no idea where Racine was. Not that it mattered. All that did was that he was there to watch over his son.

'Is that your wife?'

Novak looked round at Kilgarry, startled by the question. He followed the gunman's eyes to the framed photograph on the mantelpiece. He acknowledged the question with a curt nod.

'What's her name?'

'Christina,' Novak replied, resenting having to talk about her to someone like Kilgarry.

'You divorced?' Kilgarry asked.

'She's dead.'

'Yeah?' Kilgarry said, indifferently. His eyes lingered on the photograph. 'What a waste of a pretty face. I bet you miss screwing a foxy bitch like that.'

Novak was on his feet but Beth was out of her chair equally fast and grabbed his arm before he could take a step towards

169

Kilgarry, who was also on his feet, waiting for him. She looked round desperately for Voskov, who had left the room moments before. 'Let it go, Mike,' she implored him. 'It's not worth it.'

'I'll make it easier for you, Novak,' Kilgarry said, placing his Mini-Uzi on the armchair he had just vacated. 'You got in a lucky punch the last time. Now let's see how good you are, face to face. Come on, or do you need a woman to speak for you?'

'Let go of my arm, Beth,' Novak said, without taking his eyes off Kilgarry.

'Then what?' she replied. 'Do you want John to see you get your head kicked in? Because that's what's going to happen. You're no fighter, and you know it. Just let it go.'

'Wise words,' Voskov said from the doorway. He entered the room and paused in front of Novak. 'Sit down, before you get hurt.' He turned to Kilgarry. 'I want a word with you. In the hall. Now!'

Kilgarry glared at Novak then snatched up his weapon and stalked out of the room. Novak was still on his feet. Voskov pointed to the sofa and Novak reluctantly resumed his seat. Beth sat down beside him. Voskov crossed to where Kilgarry was standing in the hall, beyond the open door, but neither Novak nor Beth could hear what was said as they talked together in hushed tones. 'That's an order!' Voskov barked at Kilgarry. 'Get some sleep. I'll wake you when it's your watch.' He waited until Kilgarry had disappeared into the spare bedroom and closed the door behind him before returning to the lounge. 'What happened?' he demanded of Novak.

'That moron insulted—'

'Nothing happened,' Novak cut across Beth. 'A misunderstanding, that's all.'

'Strange, that's what he said as well,' Voskov remarked. 'I've told him to get some sleep. Let him cool down a bit.'

'I'd be sure to put him on a short leash when he wakes up,' Beth said.

'I can only apologize for his behaviour,' Voskov said, to their mutual surprise. There was genuine remorse in his voice. But then his voice hardened again. 'He's a professional and he should know better, but I guess this kind of claustrophobia affects different people in different ways.'

'Then perhaps you shouldn't have picked him in the first place,' Novak said.

'I didn't,' Voskov said, then sat down again. He glanced at the motionless figure of John on the mattress nearest the door. 'At least you didn't wake your son. That's something, I suppose.'

'I didn't know you cared,' Novak said ironically.

'I don't.'

'Thanks for stepping in when you did,' he said quietly to Beth. 'I was ready to take a swing at him after what he said about Chrissie. But you were right. I would have only got my head kicked in if I'd tried to go one on one with him. I guess I was just blinded by anger.'

'Anger and love,' Beth replied.

'No, just anger,' Novak said, then sat forward and clasped his hands together as he stared at the carpet. 'Chrissie's a closed chapter in my life. I know that sounds heartless, but our marriage was over long before she died. Love? I don't think there was any left at the end, at least not in the sense of a loving relationship between a husband and wife.'

'I'm sorry, I had no idea,' Beth said, wanting to know more yet at the same time aware that she shouldn't.

'I met Chrissie in the States. After my accident.'

'Yes, I heard about that. You damaged the tendons in your wrist in a car crash.' Beth saw the look of surprise on his face. 'Jago told me. Ian must have said something to him about it. But that's all Jago knew.'

'That's all there is to know, really. To be honest, though, I don't remember telling Ian about the crash. Maybe I did, I don't know. Not that it's any secret. Most of the regulars know about it otherwise they'd be constantly harassing me to get up on stage and jam with the band. I can usually play a couple of numbers before my wrist starts to hurt. That, in itself, wouldn't be too much of a handicap but the sustained pressure on the saxophone also affects my fingers. My brain's telling them to play the notes, but they lose all feeling. That's why I tend to err on the side of caution these days and only play a couple of numbers on stage. Then there can be no embarrassing mishaps.'

'I'd like to hear you play some time,' Beth said.

'D'you like jazz?'

'Not really, but I don't know much about it,' Beth admitted ruefully.

'You'll have to come to the club when this is over. As my personal guest. Best table in the house so even if you don't like the music you won't be able to fault the service.'

'Thanks, I'd like that.' Beth glanced across at Voskov. He was staring at the closed curtains, apparently lost in thought. She turned back to Novak. 'Did Christina like jazz?' There was no immediate answer. 'I'm sorry, I didn't mean to be inquisitive.'

'I don't mind talking about her. I was just thinking about your question, that's all. Yeah, she was crazy about jazz. That's how we first met – at a party after a gig I'd done in LA. She was nineteen. I fell in love with her there and then. But she did have one weakness. Cocaine. I've never been into drugs myself, but I've been around enough musicians to see the effect of coke addiction at first hand. I was a bit uneasy about her using it but she assured me that she only did it socially. And, like a fool, I believed her. If only I'd known what I was getting myself into at the time . . .' His eyes went to his son. 'No, actually I wouldn't have changed a thing. Not a thing.

'Well, the relationship just snowballed from there. We were inseparable after that and the following month I flew out here to see her. I fell in love with the city the moment I saw it. It was a world away from the smog and dirt of LA. We got married ten days later and I returned to the States to settle my affairs then came back here. I've never been home since. I moved into Chrissie's apartment and six months later she was pregnant. That's when our marriage began to fall apart.

'She was at the pinnacle of her career, and the last thing she wanted was a baby. She told me that enough times but, as a Catholic, she couldn't have an abortion. She became withdrawn and moody and began to use cocaine regularly towards the end of her pregnancy. Fortunately John was born with no side-effects. By then our marriage was in tatters. She surrounded herself with a group of so-called friends and regularly threw coke parties at the apartment. I dreaded leaving John alone with her while I was at the club. I know she'd never have harmed him, but she often wasn't in any fit state to look after him.'

'Did she continue modelling after he was born?' Beth asked.

'She never modelled again after she became pregnant. And, of course, it was all my fault for getting her pregnant in the first place. I was in a no-win situation. By the time John was a year old I was taking him to the club with me and letting him sleep in the room upstairs. Initially he couldn't sleep because of the noise but once he'd got used to it, he used to fall asleep within minutes of going to bed. Now he could probably sleep through a nuclear holocaust.

'Chrissie died a week before John's second birthday. I came back from the club early one morning and found her lying on the sofa in the lounge. I tried to wake her. No response. I called an ambulance but there was nothing the paramedics could do. The autopsy revealed that she'd taken an overdose of sleeping tablets, and washed them down with a cocktail of vodka and whisky. A verdict of suicide was recorded. Only there was no note. No explanation.'

'You don't believe she meant to kill herself, do you?' Beth said, staring at his bowed head.

'I think it was a cry for help that went terribly wrong,' he said, after a silence. 'In the last couple of months of her life she'd told me on more than one occasion that she wanted to kick the habit, for John's sake. To be honest, even if she *had* cleaned up her act, I don't think the marriage would have survived. We were already too far apart. But at least John would have had a mother to help balance his upbringing. It hasn't been easy raising him on my own.'

Beth looked at John, his tranquil face partially covered by the sheet. 'I'm no expert on children, but I'd say you haven't done a bad job up to now.'

'Up to now,' he said. 'God only knows what kind of psychological damage this weekend's going to do to him in the long term.'

'Or to any of us for that matter,' Beth added. 'Does John know the truth about his mother?'

Novak nodded. 'It was a hell of a decision to have to make, though. He was too young to remember much about her when she was alive and ideally I'd have preferred him to have imagined her as the beautiful, carefree nineteen-year-old I first met back in LA. But to the Swiss, Chrissie was the local girl who made good in the world of international fashion and her death made headline news right across the country. For days afterwards I couldn't move for the paparazzi. They hounded me wherever I went. It was a nightmare at the time. Even now the press still run the occasional story on her. Only it's not the local girl makes good any more. Now it's the self-destruction of a fashion princess, or something equally grotesque. I couldn't have protected John from that. He'd have learned the truth sooner or later. And it was better coming from me than from some schoolyard bully out to torment him.'

'You know you did the right thing, Mike.'

'Yeah?' He sounded unconvinced. 'A kid that age shouldn't need to be told those kind of truths. These are supposed to be his innocent years. Not that there was ever much chance of that. He's had to grow up very quickly. And that's something I regret. I even thought about taking him back to the States after

Chrissie died. At least he would have been shielded over there. But this is his home. He was born out here. Why should he be forced to leave?'

'Your roots are out here as well now,' Beth reminded him. 'I know how much the club means to you.'

'Sure it does, but I'd have sold Straight Street in an instant if I thought it would benefit John to take him back to the States.'

'Why's it called Straight Street?'

'It's the title of a tune by my favourite artist, John Coltrane.'

'And did you name John after him too?' she asked.

Novak nodded. 'At the beginning of Chrissie's pregnancy we agreed that I would name the baby if it was a boy, and she would name it if it was a girl. John was my only choice. Thankfully Chrissie liked it otherwise it could have caused a few problems. We were each as stubborn as the other.' They both fell silent before he spoke again, this time addressing Voskov. 'Do you mind if I go to the john? Or do I need to take a chaperon with me?'

'Go.' Voskov waited until Novak drew abreast of his arm-chair before he added, 'And in case you have any heroic ideas of trying to overpower my colleague while he's asleep, don't bother. All you'd do is trigger an alarm attached to the inside of the door the moment you opened it. I don't know about you, but I'm enjoying the peace and quiet without him around. Let's leave it that way, shall we?'

Novak left the room without answering. He knew that only Voskov and Kilgarry were in the house. The odds had turned slightly in his favour. Not that he had intended to go into the spare bedroom and tackle Kilgarry. Well, at least, not without a weapon. This was his chance. He knew it was one hell of a risk to take, but the more the situation dragged on, the more he feared for their safety. He remembered Beth saying that they wouldn't have bothered to conceal their faces if they weren't going to let them go once they had the disk. Maybe she was right. But he was less convinced, especially as she'd seen Kilgarry's face. And the American's increasingly erratic behaviour was a real cause for concern. He was spoiling for trouble and although Voskov had kept him in check, it didn't bode well for the next twenty-four hours. He had also seen the way Kilgarry looked at Marie. The bastard was long past the stage of undressing her with his eyes, he was already raping her in his mind. He knew that, given the slightest chance, Kilgarry would readily turn his twisted fantasies into reality. And he was damned if he was going to let him anywhere near her. And if that meant killing Kilgarry, so be it. He was a skilled shot with a handgun, having been taught by his grandfather. Admittedly, shooting at a cardboard target at a gun club was a world away from shooting at flesh and bone, but the fact that his own son was now a potential target would make the transition easier for him when the time came to pull the trigger. Assuming, of course, that he got the opportunity. He knew that Voskov was monitoring his every move on the portable screen in the lounge, but he had to take the chance.

He closed the toilet door, to make it appear as if he was inside, then moved silently down the hall to his bedroom, where he paused to look over his shoulder, almost expecting to see Voskov behind him. It was deserted. This raised his hopes: if Voskov had been watching him on the monitor, surely he would have challenged him already? He slipped into the bedroom. It was dark but he didn't switch on the light in case it was seen from the hall. He crossed to the built-in wardrobe and slid back the door. He reached behind a pile of T-shirts and his fingers brushed against the cold steel of the 9mm Sphinx .3AT automatic. He removed it from its hiding place but as he eased the door over again he saw a movement from the corner of his eye. He swung round, the automatic already at arm's length.

Voskov stood in the doorway. 'You want to kill me, pull the trigger,' he said calmly, but made no attempt to raise the Mini-

Uzi held loosely at his side. Novak kept the automatic trained on Voskov. He wanted desperately to squeeze the trigger, but found that he was unable to do it. 'No, I didn't think you could,' Voskov said, then switched on the light and stepped into the room. 'Not that it would have done you much good without these.' He pulled out a handful of bullets. Novak ejected the magazine. It was empty. 'You didn't think we would have left a loaded gun lying around the house, do you?' Voskov said. 'We checked the house thoroughly when we first got here.' He slammed the Mini-Uzi viciously into Novak's abdomen. Novak gasped and dropped to one knee, his hands clutching his stomach. 'You really should credit us with a little intelligence, Novak.' At that moment the telephone rang in the lounge. 'Get up!' he snapped, then hurried from the room and returned to the lounge. He pointed to Marie, who was sitting up on the mattress. 'You, answer it.'

Marie got to her feet and picked up the receiver, listened briefly, then placed her hand over the mouthpiece. 'It's the club for Monsieur Novak.'

The spare bedroom door opened and Kilgarry emerged into the corridor. 'What the hell's going on? Was that the phone?'

'Yes, bring Novak here. He's in the master bedroom.'

Moments later Kilgarry was back, walking behind Novak who was still holding his stomach. Beth got to her feet when Kilgarry shoved him into the lounge and grasped his arm to steady him. 'Mike, what happened?' she asked.

'I'm OK,' Novak replied, through gritted teeth. 'Just winded, that's all. Who's on the phone, Marie?'

'It's the club,' Marie said. 'He says his name's Karl.'

'That's one of the barmen,' Novak said to Voskov, then took the receiver from her. 'Karl, what's going on?'

'We got a problem here, boss.'

'I guessed that much. Where's Bernhard?'

'He's been taken to hospital.'

'What?' Novak winced as a sharp pain shot through him.

There was silence at the other end of the line. 'Karl, tell me what happened.'

'A group of drunks tried to get into the club. When they were refused entry they became abusive. One grabbed the box containing the door takings but when Bernhard tried to intervene he was cut on the arm with a broken bottle then knocked to the ground and kicked. The men fled with the cash when the staff and some of the regulars went to his assistance. He's going to be OK, boss, but the doctor said he wants to keep him in hospital overnight for observation. The police are here now, taking statements. They want to speak to you too.'

'I'm on my way, Karl. Hold the fort until I get there.'

'Sure thing, boss.'

Novak hung up and explained what had happened to Voskov. He saw the look of disquiet in the Russian's eyes when he had finished. 'I can assure you that I'd much rather stay here with my son,' he told Voskov, 'but it's not as if I've got much choice. The police specifically asked to speak to me. If I don't go, they'll get suspicious and send someone out here. And in any case there's nobody senior at the club now. Bernhard was the only member of staff I trusted to run the place in my absence. I have to get my keys back and, if necessary, lock up after the police have left. But if you want me to stay here, then you'd better prepare for another visit from the police. Is that what you want?'

Voskov led Novak into the hall. 'You can go, but if I see any police activity anywhere near this house I won't hesitate to start executing the hostages. Starting with your son. Believe it.'

'What was that you said to me in the bedroom?' Novak hissed. ' "You really should credit us with a little intelligence." Well, it works both ways.'

'I did, until you went looking for the gun,' Voskov said coldly.

'Wouldn't you have done the same if you were in my position?' Novak growled, but when he continued the hostility had drained from his voice. 'It doesn't mean I'm going to shoot my mouth off to the cops the first opportunity I get. I could have done that when I was at the club earlier. The last thing I want is the police storming the house and risking the lives of the hostages. The disk's not worth it.'

'I'm glad to hear it.'

'But you've got to do something for me,' Novak said.

'I don't believe you're in any position to be asking favours.'

'Well, I'm going to anyway.' Novak jabbed a finger towards Kilgarry, who was standing with his back to them in the centre of the lounge. 'We've both seen the way he looks at Marie. Just keep him away from her, because if he does anything to her while I'm gone, I'll kill him. And fuck the consequences.'

'He won't touch her. You have my word on that. Because if he does, *I'll* kill him.'

Novak believed him and, with that worry off his mind, he left for the club.

The house was dark and empty. It was Kessler's first night alone. It felt strange without his wife. Eerie. Subdued. Not that they had said much to each other lately but there had been something reassuring about her presence whenever he got home. He tossed his jacket on to the chair in the hall and went upstairs, making for the spare bedroom. He paused outside the master bedroom and noticed, in the reflection of the landing light, a faint indentation on the bed where she had laid her suitcase to pack. His eyes went to the telephone beside the bed and, for a fleeting moment, he was tempted to pick up the receiver and call her. Just to hear her voice. He dismissed the thought, went through to the spare bedroom and switched on the answering-machine on the bedside table. There was only one message – to call the station. He sat on the edge of the bed and dialled out. When it was answered he asked to be put through to the squad room.

'Inspector Kessler, we've been trying to get hold of you for the past few hours, but you weren't home and you weren't answering your bleeper.'

Kessler glanced at the bleeper beside the answering-machine where he had left it before going to meet Willie Meine. 'I'm back now,' he said. 'What is it?'

'Sergeant Dannhauser's called in twice this evening. The first time at seven twenty-four – two hours ago – to report that Novak returned unexpectedly to the house and put his car away in the garage, as if he weren't intending to return to the club again tonight. Then Dannhauser called again about ten minutes ago to say that Novak had left the house again. He followed him back to the club. But we'd already received word a short time earlier that there had been an incident. One of the staff was taken to hospital. Uniformed police are at the club now.'

'Why would he have gone home on a busy Friday night?' Kessler pondered.

'You'd have to ask him that yourself, sir.'

'That's exactly what I intend to do,' Kessler said, then hung up. Clipping his bleeper to his belt, he hurried downstairs, collected his jacket, then left the house to drive to the club.

Willie Meine wasn't drunk. Well, at least, he didn't think so. Tipsy, perhaps, but definitely not drunk. That he was walking unevenly made no difference to his impaired judgement. He was ready for bed and any thoughts he had had about the validity of the two names he had given Kessler had long since been consigned to the part of his subconscious that had been the first to blur with the onset of intoxication.

He paused at the mouth of the alley at the back of the apartment block where he lived and scanned the fire escape. It would be a quicker means of reaching his apartment than going to the front and taking the stairs. Navigating an uneven path down the alley, he mounted the fire escape and, clutching the railing, climbed the metal rungs to the third floor. Once inside he lit a cigarette, discarded the empty packet, then made his way down the unlit corridor to the apartment. After several failed attempts, he managed to insert the key in the lock, turned it, pushed open the door and staggered inside. Closing the door behind him, he unbuttoned his overcoat and tried to hang it up but it landed on the floor. He cursed but made no attempt to retrieve it.

'Looks like you had a good night.'

Meine swung round, almost losing his balance, and his eyes settled on the shadowy figure in the armchair by the window. The curtains were drawn behind him. 'Who are you?' he blurted out, as Racine got to his feet.

'My name's Alain Racine, but you probably know me better as Albert Ronet. I believe you've been asking after me. Well, here I am, in person. Ask away.'

'I – I don't know what – you're talking about.' Meine shrank back fearfully against the wall as Racine approached him.

'Oh, I think you do. And do you know what, Willie? I'm going to tell you all about myself and exactly why I'm here in Zürich. Then I'm going to kill you.' Racine punched his fist into Meine's stomach as he reached desperately for the door. Meine cried out in pain and dropped to his knees. Racine grabbed him by the collar, twisted it savagely, then dragged Meine into the centre of the room. When he released him, Meine coughed violently, gasping for breath. Racine picked up a soiled dishcloth he had found earlier in the kitchen and tossed it on to the carpet. 'Put it in your mouth, Willie.'

'No fucking way.' Meine choked at the thought.

Racine drew his automatic from its holster at the back of his jeans and pressed the barrel firmly against Meine's forehead. 'I said, put it in your mouth.' Terrified, Meine grabbed the dishcloth and did as he was told. Racine then picked up two steak knives from the table behind him. 'I found these in the kitchen. It's a real health hazard in there. When was the last time you did the dishes, Willie?' He reholstered the automatic. 'I'm sorry, I'm forgetting my manners, expecting you to speak with your mouth full.' He put his foot on Meine's chest, forcing him on to his back, grabbed one wrist and pinned his hand to the floor close to the side of his head. Then, without warning, Racine brought one of the steak knives down into the centre of Meine's palm. Meine's agonized scream was muffled by the dishcloth and even before he had time to react Racine did the same with his other hand. 'Oh don't worry, Willie, I washed the knives. I'd hate you to get an infection.' He crouched down beside the man and forced the spout of a plastic funnel into the side of his mouth then showed him the bottle of bleach that he had found earlier under the kitchen sink. He uncapped it and, gripping the funnel tightly to counter Meine's struggles, he began to trickle the liquid into his mouth. 'You will forgive me if I don't join you, Willie? Now, let me tell you a bit about myself first. I'm sure you'll find it fascinating.'

'What do you think?'

'Difficult to say. She's probably been dead about a week.' Sam Arbuther glanced up at Sheriff Olsen who was standing over him. 'But don't quote me on that, Jed. We'll get a much better idea after the autopsy.'

'Age?' Olsen continued.

'Again, difficult to say. Late twenties. Early thirties.'

'Amy Michaels was twenty-nine,' Dawson said, behind Olsen, having heard the gist of the conversation. Arbuther gave a dismissive shrug.

'Any luck with the search for the head?' Olsen asked Dawson.

'Not as yet. I've got my men combing the immediate vicinity, but this wood's pretty big. I reckon we're going to need to draft in reinforcements to help. Can I leave that with you? You know the sheriff's department in Jackson. Get them to send up some men as soon as possible. Not that I think we'll find the head, though. Whoever killed her cut it off for a reason, probably to stymie any attempt to identify her. He probably disposed of it in another state.'

'Assuming it was a man.' Olsen watched Arbuther replace the sheet over the naked body.

'The head was severed with a single blow, probably with an axe,' Dawson said. 'You would need a lot of strength to deliver a clean strike like that. That would imply a man. And Henry Monroe saw a man putting the missing rug into the trunk of a car outside Amy Michaels's house. No, my guess is the killer's male.'

'Only there's no sign of the rug either,' Olsen reminded him.

'Which is another reason why I want more men drafted in to help with the search,' Dawson told him.

Arbuther got to his feet. 'I'll arrange to have the body removed for the ME. I contacted him earlier.' His eyes went to Dawson, almost as if in accusation. 'He should be here by early evening.'

'Thanks,' Dawson called after Arbuther, as he headed for his car.

'I'm just doing my job,' Arbuther replied.

'There's really only one way to find out whether it is Amy Michaels,' Olsen said. 'Fingerprints.'

'I'm way ahead of you on that one, Sheriff,' Dawson said, but there was no arrogance in his voice. 'I've already sent Special Agent Ellis to the house to lift some prints off the computer keyboards. We should be spoilt for choice. Then all we have to do is take the prints off the body and send off both sets for analysis. We'll know later tonight whether it's Amy Michaels.'

TEN

'I'm sorry, sir, but the club's closed tonight.'

'I'm the owner,' Novak told the uniformed policeman standing at the entrance to Straight Street.

'Let him through,' a voice called from inside the foyer.

The policeman stepped aside to allow Novak to enter. He saw that the wooden table, where the customers paid their entrance fee, lay upturned on the floor, which was dusted with the shattered glass of several broken beer bottles. Behind it a garish splash of blood spattered the white wallpaper. It was then he noticed Kessler. 'I wouldn't have thought a punch-up worthy of your time, Inspector,' Novak said, taking notice of Kessler's dishevelled appearance – unshaven, hair not brushed, crumpled suit, tie loose at the collar, unpolished shoes.

'Normally it wouldn't be,' Kessler agreed, 'but, under the circumstances, I felt I should come down and take a look for myself. Oh, and by the way, I thought you might like to know that your cash box has been recovered intact. The uniforms have also made several arrests. Of course, it's up to you whether you want to press charges.'

'Damn right I do after what they did to Bernhard,' Novak replied indignantly.

'That's something you'll have to discuss with the investigating officer. He's around here somewhere. I'm sure he'll want to speak to you.'

'So what are you doing here?' Novak demanded, unease gnawing at the pit of his stomach. Did Kessler know something? If so, what?

'It's only natural that I should take an interest after the incident here on Tuesday night. But it's got nothing to do with that. Just a bunch of over-boisterous revellers on a stag night. What does surprise me, though, Mr Novak, is that you weren't here when it happened. I would have thought that Friday was one of your busiest nights of the week.'

'I was here earlier, but I went home to be with my son.' Novak was careful to stick to his original cover story. He couldn't afford any slip-ups. 'He's gone down with a fever.'

'Yes, I heard about that.' Kessler nodded sombrely. 'I'm sorry. I hope it's not serious.'

'The doctor was optimistic that the fever would break by morning.'

'That's good news. Only you didn't mention it when I was at your house earlier today. I would have thought it would have been uppermost in your mind.'

'I don't see why I should have mentioned it to you,' Novak said. 'It's got nothing to do with the investigation.'

'True,' Kessler conceded, but he sounded sceptical.

'What exactly are you getting at, Inspector?' Novak knew he had to go on the offensive, if only to conceal his apprehension. 'Are you suggesting I'm lying?'

'I never said a word, Mr Novak,' Kessler replied, hands extended, palms upturned, in a gesture of appeasement.

'If you don't believe me, call the house. Ask Beth. Ask Marie. They'll verify what I've told you. Why would I lie to you about something like that?'

'I'm sure you wouldn't.' Kessler patted Novak's shoulder. 'Well, it doesn't look as if there's anything for me to do around here. I might as well go home.' He moved to the entrance then looked back to Novak. 'I hope your son will be better in the morning. Good night.'

'Meine's dead.'

'Any problems?' Voskov replied over the cellphone.

Racine looked down at the body at his feet and smiled contentedly to himself. 'No problems at all.'

'I spoke to Kahn earlier. Seems that you were tailed from the house.'

'*Why wasn't I told this before?*'

'Because you were in no immediate danger. It's a cop. Name's Matzke. He's a sergeant working with Kessler on the Grant case. But don't worry, he's reporting directly to the *juge d'instruction*.'

'*Don't worry?* The *juge d'instruction* is senior to Kessler.'

'And he's also on the Cabal's payroll. That's how Kahn knew about Matzke. Kessler still thinks he's snooping around the woods at the back of the house.'

'Shit! So it was him I heard in the woods when I was going to the car earlier this evening,' Racine said, snapping his fingers. 'I thought I heard a noise in the bushes but when I went to check I couldn't see anything.'

'That makes sense. He told the *juge d'instruction* he'd seen you, but that you hadn't seen him. And that you were armed. He's not carrying, which is why he didn't follow you into the building.'

'Do you have a description of the car he's driving? The licence plates?'

'No. All I know is that he's parked out front, within sight of the building. Let him tail you. It's the only way you're going to spot him.'

'I didn't spot him on the way over here,' Racine said sharply, but the anger was directed at himself for his oversight. 'What do you want me to do once I've identified the car?'

'I'm sure I don't have to spell it out to you,' Voskov said

bluntly. 'And make sure you do it in an isolated area. That way the body won't be discovered for some time.'

'If I kill him, we're going to have every cop in the city looking for us.'

'Let them, because by the time the body's been found and Kessler has managed to unravel the circumstances behind his death, we'll be long gone. Not only that, but they won't know who to look for either. Don't come back to the house. We're going to have to revert to the back-up plan now that we've been compromised. We'll meet you at the cable car in an hour's time. We'll be taking the hostages with us, so if you're not there we'll go on anyway. The snowmobiles are secured in an outhouse close to the disembarkation point. We'll take two, and leave the third for you. You've got a map to direct you to the chalet.'

'I'll be there. But who'll be operating the cable car?'

'Kahn's had a contact on twenty-four-hour stand-by ever since we arrived in Switzerland in case we needed to use the chalet.'

'See you in an hour.' Racine switched off the cellphone and opened the door. He peered into the corridor. It was deserted. He locked the door behind him and walked briskly down the corridor, but as he turned the corner he almost bumped into a child sitting on the top step. The little girl, whom he estimated to be no more than six, looked round in fright and he gave her a reassuring smile when she scrambled to her feet, dropping her battered plastic doll. His first thought was that a child of that age should have been in bed. His second was that she had seen his face. A potential witness.

He crouched at the top of the stairs, slipped his hand into his pocket and felt the cold steel handle of the switchblade he always carried. His fingers closed around it, then he picked up the doll with his other hand and held it out to her, trying to lure her within range. She stood still, her eyes searching his face. He smiled again to put her at her ease while his fingers caressed the handle of the blade in his pocket. Another couple of steps and she would be within range. A second step. Then a third. She reached out a hand towards the doll. All he had to do was grab her hand, pull her to him, and it would be over. Quickly. Silently. Yet the blade remained unopened in his pocket. Her tiny fingers curled around the arm of the doll. He made no move to grab her hand. No move to open the blade. He let her take the doll and she cuddled it tightly to her chest. Then he sensed someone behind him. He looked round. The woman was in her twenties. Her face was ghostly white, her eyes lifeless, and as she held out her hand towards the child he saw the track marks on her arm. Heroin. He should have guessed. The little girl scampered past him and took her mother's hand. The woman looked down impassively at Racine then led her back to an open door further down the corridor. He waited until they had gone inside then stood up, removed the blade from his pocket, sprang it inches from his leg. In a way he was glad that the mother had appeared when she did. Otherwise he might have let his emotions get the better of him. But, then, he had always liked children. Concealing the switch-blade behind his back, he made his way to the apartment. He knocked at the door then tightened his grip on the blade as he waited for it to be answered.

Matzke had his orders. *Follow the blond man when he leaves the building, but don't attempt to intercept him. Just follow him and report back once he reaches his destination.* That was what the *juge d'instruction* had said the last time he had contacted him at his home. And keep Kessler in the dark, which he had done with relative ease over the past few hours. He was rather proud of that. Kessler was on his way out. Yesterday's hero. Matzke had no more use for him. But the *juge d'instruction* was a different proposition. Keep on his good side and a promotion wouldn't be far off. Of that he was sure. And that was all that mattered . . .

He lit another cigarette, the last in the packet, then glanced at his watch. It had been three hours since the blond man had gone into the apartment building. What was he doing in there? He'd had enough time to speculate while he waited. Not that speculation counted for anything. But at least it had helped to pass the time. Now, though, he was becoming increasingly restless. He wanted to stretch his legs – if only to take a piss in the alleyway across the street. But he couldn't afford to take the chance of leaving the car. What if the man came out of the building while he was relieving himself? He would never forgive himself if he lost him now. And neither would the *juge d'instruction*. He had to sit it out. The discomfort was a small price to pay for a promotion . . .

He sat forward when he noticed a figure emerge from the building. It was *him*. He watched Racine cross to his car, get inside, and moments later the engine started up. He waited until the car had swung out into the road then went after him, careful to remain at a discreet distance. It quickly became apparent that they weren't headed back to Novak's house. Within a few minutes they had reached the outskirts of the city. Where were they going? Was he leaving town? A rendez-vous, perhaps? But with whom? He pushed the unanswered questions from his mind. Shortly before the turn-off to Duben-dorf, a small town eight miles north of Zürich, the car ahead indicated that it was turning right. Matzke was baffled. They were headed into the woods. A thought flashed through his head. It could be an ambush. And he wasn't armed. At that moment the car turned off and disappeared. Matzke was in two minds. Should he follow him? Should he call for assistance? If he hesitated now, he would certainly lose him – *and* his promotion. He turned off on to the narrow dirt road, but there was no sign of the car. He kept his speed low, his headlights on full, and as he turned the first bend in the road he saw the stationary tail-lights ahead. The car was parked at the side of the road, the engine still running. The driver's door was open and he could see from the interior light that nobody was inside. Had the driver fled into the trees, knowing he was being followed? After all, he couldn't know that Matzke wasn't armed. But what if it was a trap? He knew he had to investigate. He pulled up beside the abandoned car and scanned his surroundings. Apart from those areas of the road illuminated by the lights of the two cars, he was enveloped in darkness. Hardly a good omen. His eyes went to the radio. Again the thought of calling for back-up crossed his mind. It made sense. And he knew it. Better safe than sorry. He unclipped the radio from under the dashboard.

The first bullet shattered the side window and embedded itself in the back of the driver's seat inches from his right shoulder. The radio tumbled from his fingers as he ducked down below the dashboard. But he knew he wasn't safe. He had to get away fast. Easing his foot down on to the clutch, his body tensed for the inevitability of the next shot, he slipped the car into reverse. He knew he couldn't sit up. He was going to have to do it blind. At least initially. And that frightened him almost as much as the anticipation of the second bullet – there was a sharp bend in the road behind. Only he couldn't see it from his concealed position below the dashboard. Not even in the rear-view mirror. That gave him an idea and he reached up a hand to tilt the mirror downwards. The second bullet pierced the windscreen and he screamed in agony when the lead tore through his wrist. He dropped his arm to cradle it to his chest but in his confusion he unwittingly lifted his foot off the clutch. The car lurched backward, stalled, and the engine died. Silence. Now frantic with fear, he picked up the fallen radio. It was cold and slippery in his bloodied fingers. But even as he put out an emergency call to police headquarters, he knew that it was too little, too late . . .

'Yes?' Voskov said tersely.

'Matzke's dead,' Racine told him. There was a moment's

pause. 'There could be a problem, though. He was on the police radio when I got to him. I don't know how much he told them before I shot him.'

'Where are you now?'

'I'm in the car, on my way to the rendezvous. Are we still going with the back-up plan?'

'Yes. We'll meet you there.' Voskov beckoned Kilgarry to him. 'We're going to have to move out,' he said, in a hushed voice. 'I'll explain later. We'll take Mrs Grant and the boy with us.'

'What about Novak?'

'Forget Novak. We've got to get out now.'

'And her?' Kilgarry indicated Marie.

'We don't need her.'

'She could still come in useful,' Kilgarry said, with a knowing smile.

'Just keep your mind on the job,' Voskov snapped.

'What's the harm in taking her with us? I'll take responsibility for her.'

'I know what else you'd take, given half a chance,' Voskov said, in disgust. 'It's not going to happen. Believe it. Now go and get the gear. We don't have much time.'

Kilgarry opened his mouth to argue, thought better of it, then strode from the room.

'Mrs Grant, you and the boy will be coming with us,' Voskov said to Beth.

'Where are we going?' Beth asked.

'To another location. But don't worry, you'll both be safe.'

'What about Marie?' Beth asked.

'She'll remain here.' Voskov looked at Marie. 'You will be tied up, but otherwise left unharmed. We have no reason to hurt you. You'll be discovered soon enough and released.'

'And what if I refuse to go with you?' Beth said.

'Then you'll be sedated. One way or another, Mrs Grant, you *will* be coming with us. You're too important to this operation for us to leave you behind.'

'Then why are you taking John too?' Marie entered the conversation for the first time. She looked down at the boy. 'How can he be of any importance to you? He's only a child.'

'And children make the best hostages,' Voskov replied. 'Wake him.' Marie made no move towards John. 'I said, wake him. Or I'll do it myself.'

Marie crossed reluctantly to where John was sleeping, just as Kilgarry returned to the room, having collected the three holdalls from the kitchen. 'You want me to handcuff them?' he asked. Voskov nodded.

'You're not putting those things on me,' Beth said, as she backed away from the advancing Kilgarry.

'Mrs Grant, you are beginning to irritate me,' Voskov said, menacingly, then he grabbed a handful of Marie's hair as she was about to wake John, jerking her head back on to her shoulders, and pressed the barrel of the Mini-Uzi against her temple. 'Now either you turn around and put your hands behind your back or I will pull the trigger. Then my colleague will sedate you, physically if necessary. Believe it.'

'For God's sake, don't hurt her,' Beth begged, seeing the terror in Marie's eyes. 'I'll do as you say. Please, just don't hurt her.'

'Turn round!' Kilgarry snarled, then pulled her arms behind her back, and clicked the handcuffs over her wrists.

Only then did Voskov lower the Mini-Uzi and release Marie. 'Wake the boy,' he ordered, then unzipped one of the holdalls, removed a roll of masking tape, and tossed it to Kilgarry who tore off a strip and secured it across Beth's mouth.

Marie shook John awake. He looked around the room and paused uneasily when he saw the tape over Beth's mouth. 'What's happening? Where's Dad?'

'Your father had to go back to the club,' Marie told him.

'Why didn't he wake me up before he left?'

'He didn't want to disturb you.'

'We don't have time for this,' Voskov barked at Marie. 'Get the boy on his feet. We've got to get out of here.'

'Where are we going?' John said to Marie.

'You and Mrs Grant are going with these men,' she replied. 'I don't know where they're taking you.'

'Aren't you coming?'

'No,' Marie replied, almost in apology.

'Then I'm not going either,' John replied.

'This is bullshit.' Kilgarry yanked John to his feet and shoved him against the wall.

'Don't hurt him,' Marie screamed, lunging at Kilgarry, who lashed the barrel of his Mini-Uzi across the side of her face.

'Marie!' John twisted free of Kilgarry and fell to the floor beside her. She was dazed from the blow and a trickle of blood seeped down her cheek from the cut below her eye.

Voskov grabbed Kilgarry's arm to prevent him from reaching for John again. 'Just get the spike and sedate him,' he ordered. Kilgarry removed a hypodermic from a case in one of the hold-alls and, with Voskov pinning John's arms to his sides, inserted the needle into the crook of the boy's arm and released the liquid into his bloodstream. The anaesthetic took hold within seconds and John slipped into unconsciousness. 'Take them to the van,' Voskov said. Kilgarry lifted John effortlessly in one arm and followed Beth out. Voskov took a second syringe from the case then knelt beside Marie. Before she had time to react he injected the anaesthetic into her bloodstream. He waited until she was unconscious then used the masking tape to bind her ankles and wrists but decided against gagging her in case she had an adverse reaction to the drug and threw up. He turned on the television set to drown her calls for help when she came round, although he knew that if Matzke had radioed through to police headquarters before he died there was every chance she would be found before the effects of the tranquil-lizer wore off. Retrieving the holdalls, he hurried through into the kitchen, switched off the light, then locked the door behind him, discarded the key in a nearby flower-bed, then sprinted across the lawn to the footpath leading into the woods. By the time Voskov reached the van Kilgarry had ordered Beth into the back and placed the unconscious John on the floor beside her. He waited until Kilgarry had got in then closed the door, removed the branches that had camouflaged the vehicle, then got in, fired up the engine and drove through the woods on to a back road. He scanned it and, satisfied that it wasn't under surveillance, drove away at speed.

Kessler slowed the unmarked police car to a halt in front of the barricade that had been erected across the mouth of the slip road leading into the woods. Half a dozen patrol cars were already parked at the side of the road, lights flashing. Several uniformed policemen stood together in a huddle, their sombre faces illuminated by the headlights of the patrol car behind them. One noticed Kessler and brought him to the attention of his colleagues. They stared coldly at him, accusation in their eyes.

He hadn't sent Matzke to his death, but they weren't to know that, and he could understand their resentment. He would have felt the same, were he in their position. He showed his badge to the patrolman on duty at the barricade and was allowed through. He walked the short distance to where a tarpaulin tent had been erected around Matzke's car, which was now illuminated by two powerful overhead spotlights. The *juge d'instruction* beckoned him over to the open driver's door. A sheet had been placed discreetly over Matzke's body, which was still in the car. He nodded to a young policeman, who lifted back the sheet. Matzke had been shot through the head at close range. Kessler gestured for the sheet to be lowered again, then followed the *juge d'instruction* from of the confined space.

'What was he doing out here?' the *juge d'instruction* demanded once they were out of earshot of the nearest policeman.

'I don't know.' Kessler raised a hand before the man could challenge his reply. 'He was supposed to have been keeping a house in Horgen under surveillance. He called in twice tonight. The first time to report that he had done a detailed recce of the area at the back of the house and found nothing untoward. The second time was about an hour later. He said he was still there and that everything was quiet. I never heard from him again after that. So what the hell he was doing out here . . . I'm as much in the dark as you are.'

'I've got a dead policeman back there, Kessler. Executed in cold blood while he was trying to radio through to headquarters for help. A policeman who was supposed to have been working under your command. And now you tell me that he was working independently of your orders. How do you think that's going to look in my report?'

'I can only tell you what I know!' Kessler was exasperated.

'Which is nothing,' the other man replied contemptuously. 'I told you the other day that you were one foul-up away from an indefinite suspension. What happened tonight is way beyond any foul-up. You're going to be crucified once I write up my report. And rightly so. You're finished, Kessler. I'll see to that.'

'You can't hold me accountable for this,' Kessler said. 'Matzke must have had a damn good reason for disregarding his orders without first radioing through to headquarters. Whatever happened here has to be linked to something he witnessed earlier tonight at Novak's house. And I intend to find out what it was.'

'I didn't make myself clear. Not only are you off the case, but you're also suspended with immediate effect. Now go home.'

'Not until I've got to the bottom of this.'

'I already have the situation under control. I dispatched an armed-response unit to the house in Horgen as soon as I heard about Matzke's death. I should be receiving a report from them shortly. Not only that, but Novak has also been picked up at his club and taken in for questioning. So, as you can see, the investigation is already out of your hands. Now, if you'll excuse me, I've got work to do.' The *juge d'instruction* wagged a finger at Kessler. 'If you don't leave now, I'll have a uniform escort you back to your car. Don't humiliate yourself any more than you already have.'

Kessler bit back his rage and returned to his car but as he opened the door he heard a snide comment from one of the uniformed policemen. He looked round but it was impossible to know who was responsible – not that he would have said anything: emotions were high and there was no point in adding to the tension. Anyway, he had more than enough to worry about as it was. Suspended, perhaps indefinitely. Why hadn't Matzke kept him informed of his movements? Had he done so, it might have saved his life. He would never have allowed him to tail an armed suspect, not unless he had a weapon. Was Matzke aware that his killer was armed? Or had he been led into the fatal ambush without knowing the truth? So many questions. No answers. And now that he had been suspended, he might never find out what really happened. He had little faith in the investigative abilities of the *juge d'instruction*. But, then, he was probably biased. At least he agreed with him about sending an armed-response unit to Novak's house as soon as he had heard about Matzke's death . . .

Kessler swung his car off the road and braked. He sat motionless for some time, gripping the steering wheel as he stared ahead, his mind in turmoil. Why hadn't he picked up on that earlier? He turned the car round and sped back in the direction of the crime scene.

'I want to talk to you. Now!'

The *juge d'instruction* spun round. His initial look of surprise changed to anger when he saw Kessler. 'You've got some nerve coming back here. This time I will have you forcibly evicted.'

'What's going on?' a voice demanded, and a moment later the imposing figure of the Chief of Police straightened up from behind the car where a member of the forensics team had been pointing out the spent cartridge that lay beside the open driver's door.

'Good evening, sir,' Kessler said, respectfully. 'I didn't realize you were here.'

'I've just arrived,' the Chief replied. 'You're Kessler, aren't you?'

'Yes, sir.'

'I was led to believe that you'd been suspended after what happened here tonight.'

'Yes, sir, I was, but I'd like to clarify something that the *juge d'instruction* told me before he put me on suspension. I believe it may have a crucial bearing on the investigation. I'd prefer to talk outside. In private. And I'd be grateful if you would bear witness to what I have to ask him.'

'I'm very sorry about this, sir,' the *juge d'instruction* said. 'I'll have Kessler removed—'

'No, let him speak,' the Chief interrupted.

'Sir, whatever he has to say—'

'Are you questioning my authority?'

'No, sir, of course not.'

'Then let's step outside, shall we?' The Chief led the two men away from the tarpaulin tent and paused only when they were out of earshot of the forensics team. 'Very well, Kessler, let's hear what you've got to say. And I warn you now, this better not be a waste of time.'

'I don't believe it is, sir.' Kessler turned to the *juge d'instruction*. 'You told me earlier that you'd sent an armed-response unit to Novak's house in Horgen as soon as you heard about Matzke's death.'

'Yes, what of it?'

'How did you know that Matzke had been keeping Novak's house under surveillance?'

'I was told when headquarters phoned me at home to inform me of Matzke's death,' he replied irritably.

'No, you weren't,' Kessler said. 'I was the only person who knew that Matzke had Novak's house under surveillance. I even checked with headquarters to make sure. He only managed to pinpoint his current position on the radio before he was killed. He never mentioned that he had been in Horgen earlier tonight. So how did you know about it?'

'This is ridiculous.' The *juge d'instruction* looked to the Chief for support.

'I'd like an answer to that as well,' the Chief said.

'Sir, I don't believe I have to—'

'Answer the question!' the Chief thundered.

Kessler's cellphone rang before the man could reply. 'Excuse me, sir,' he said to the Chief and answered it. The conversation was brief and when he slipped the cellphone back in his jacket pocket his eyes were fixed accusingly on the *juge d'instruction*. 'That was headquarters. I also asked them to find out if Matzke had made or received any calls on his cellular phone tonight. He made two. Both to your home.'

'What?' the Chief said in amazement. He looked at the *juge d'instruction*. 'Is this true?'

'Yes, sir, it is. I asked him to keep me posted on his movements. I didn't believe that Kessler was in a fit state of mind to carry out this investigation.'

'Yet you specifically asked for Kessler to head up the investigation in the first place,' the Chief said. 'You can't have it both ways.'

'I admit that I initially thought Kessler was the right man for this case. But I realized that I had made a mistake. His personal life's in turmoil and I believe it's affecting his judgement. I thought it prudent to have Matzke report to me as well.'

'Then why not just have Kessler removed from the case?'

'Because he needed someone he thought he could manipulate, sir,' Kessler answered for him. 'I don't know who he's working for, but whoever it is wants Amy Michaels arrested and charged with the murder of Ian Grant.'

'This is outrageous,' the *juge d'instruction* said testily.

'Ask him about Jago, sir,' Kessler said to the Chief.

'Who?' The Chief was baffled.

'Ralf Jago. He's one of Interpol's top investigators. He's been poking his nose into the Ian Grant investigation ever since he flew in from Lyon a few days ago. When I wanted to question him the *juge d'instruction* gave me specific orders to leave him alone. I was never given a reason why.'

'Is this true?' the Chief asked the *juge d'instruction*.

'No, sir, it's not. This is the first I've heard about this man Jago.'

'I've got the whole conversation on tape,' Kessler said. 'You made the mistake of confronting me in one of the interview rooms at the station. I'd be more than happy to give the original tape to the Chief. I'm sure he'd find it fascinating.'

'There's only one way to resolve this,' the Chief said to Kessler. 'Speak to Jago and find out what he knows. And, should he refuse to co-operate, you have my personal authority to have him arrested and taken in for further questioning.' He shook his head. 'I don't know what's going on here, but I intend to find out. I want you both at the station within the hour. Along with Jago. Then maybe we can get some answers.'

'Where's John? Where have they taken him?'

'Please, Mr Novak, sit down,' the Chief of Police said, and motioned for him to resume his seat in the interview room.

'No, I won't fucking sit down!' Novak's voice was filled with a mixture of anger, fear and frustration, but when he took a step towards the Chief a detective was quick to block his path.

'It's OK,' the Chief assured the man, who returned to his vigil by the door. 'If you think that taking a swing at me will make you feel better, Mr Novak, then by all means go ahead. Only right now I'm not your enemy. You're your own enemy by not agreeing to co-operate with us.'

The Chief's words caught Novak off-guard, and only then did he realize that his fists were clenched. He slumped dejectedly on to the wooden chair behind him. 'I wasn't going to hit you,' he said, hollowly, as he stared at the floor. 'I just feel so helpless in here when I should be out looking for John.'

'And just where would you start to look?' the Chief asked quietly. 'No, it's best if you leave that to us. We have the resources at our disposal to find him. But we're going to need your help. We need to build up a picture of the kidnappers. Your au pair has already given us a statement. Now we need one from you as well. As detailed as possible.'

'The men you're looking for are Petr Voskov, Alain Racine and Bob Kilgarry.'

'You know their names?' The Chief was astonished. 'According to what your au pair has told us, they all wore balaclavas to conceal their faces.'

'They never suspected that I knew their identities,' Novak replied. 'If they did, they would have had to kill us to cover their tracks.'

'You've lost me, Mr Novak. How could you know their identities if they were wearing balaclavas?'

'Ralf Jago told me at the club on Wednesday night. Beth was there as well. Beth Grant, that is.'

'Ralf Jago again,' the Chief murmured. 'I might have guessed.'

'That's right, but I only know what he chose to tell us about the Cabal.'

'The Cabal?' The Chief nodded. 'I've heard about this organization, but I always thought it was more of a myth than anything else.'

'Not according to Jago it isn't. He's the man you should

speak to about it. As I said, he only told us what he thought we should know.'

The telephone rang and the detective answered it. He listened then extended the receiver towards the Chief, who said, 'Would you excuse me, please?' to Novak, and he and the other man left the room. Novak emerged into the corridor and saw Marie sitting forlornly on a bench further down the corridor, her head in her hands. When she raised her head he could see that she had been crying. He sat down beside her and squeezed her hand. She wrapped her arms tightly around his neck.

'Thank God you're safe,' Novak said, stroking her hair as she clung to him.

She was sobbing. 'I'm sorry, Monsieur, I couldn't stop them taking John.'

He eased himself from her embrace then took a handkerchief from his pocket and gave it to her. 'You've got nothing to apologize for, Marie,' he said, as she wiped the tears from her cheeks. 'I'm the one who should be apologizing to you after what you've been forced to endure these past twelve hours. This had nothing to do with you.'

'It had nothing to do with you or John either,' she said, handing back the handkerchief.

'I know, but I allowed myself to get drawn into it. And that put both your lives in danger. Had I known at the time . . .' He trailed off helplessly. 'I guess any fool can be wise with hindsight.'

'You did it to help Mrs Grant. I know that now. What you did wasn't wrong.'

'It was wrong to put innocent lives at risk.' Novak sat back and stared at the opposite wall. 'Marie, I know that this has been a terrifying ordeal for you and . . . well, I'd fully understand if you wanted to return to Paris. Naturally I'd pay your air fare and any other expenses – as well as a bonus on top of your salary. You've been wonderful, especially to John.'

'You want me to leave?' Marie asked, looking hurt.

'Of course not. I just thought that you might want to be with your family after what's happened.'

'I would like to stay here,' she said.

'Believe me, the feeling's mutual,' he said, kissing her cheek lightly.

'Very touching.'

Novak looked up to find Kessler watching them. He hadn't heard him approach. 'What do you want?' he demanded, trying to conceal the discomfort in his voice.

'What I want I won't get,' Kessler said cryptically.

'What's that supposed to mean?' Novak asked.

'I would like to have you arrested for hindering the police in the course of their duties. Had you told me about these men when I came to your house—'

'Then we wouldn't be having this conversation,' Novak interrupted. 'They would have killed us both, after executing Marie, John and Beth. My only concern was to get you out of the house before they got trigger-happy. If it's a crime to protect the people I care about, then go ahead and arrest me because I'm as guilty as hell.'

'If you had told me – or even warned me about the situation – then we could have moved against these men and prevented them from kidnapping Mrs Grant and your son.'

'You have no idea who you're dealing with, do you? These aren't two-bit hoodlums out for a fast buck! They're professional killers. They'd kill you as soon as give you the time of day.'

'And how do you know so much about them?' Kessler asked. 'Did they tell you who they were?'

'Jago told him,' the Chief of Police said from the doorway of the interview room. He had heard the tail end of the conversation. 'Kessler, I want to see you in here now. Mr Novak, if you'll bear with me, I'll be with you shortly.' He looked at Marie and switched to French for her benefit. 'Mademoiselle

Perrault, you have already given us a statement. You are free to leave now if you want. I can arrange to have a patrol car take you home.'

'I will wait for Monsieur Novak,' she replied.

'Go on home, Marie, I don't know how long I'm going to be here,' Novak urged.

The Chief beckoned Kessler into the room, told the other detective to organize a lift for Marie, and closed the door again behind him. 'You're officially back on the case, Kessler.'

'Will I still be working with the *juge d'instruction*?' Kessler asked suspiciously.

'No. I authorized a search of his house after your allegations against him. Certain . . . improprieties, shall we say? . . . came to light during the search. He's been suspended pending a full investigation. From now on you'll report directly to me.'

'Yes, sir.'

'I'm told that Ralf Jago has just been brought in for questioning. I want him to come face to face with Novak. According to Novak, not only did Jago tell him about an organization known as the Cabal, but he also gave him the names of the three men who kidnapped Beth Grant and his son. So let's see Jago talk his way out of that with Novak in the room.'

'Why would Jago confide in Novak, sir?' Kessler was puzzled.

'That's what you're going to find out,' the Chief told him. 'It's still your case, Kessler. Just make sure you keep me informed.'

'You can count on it, sir.'

'I'll send Novak in on my way out.' The Chief paused at the door. 'Give him some space. He must be going through hell right now, not knowing what's happened to his son. He doesn't need you needling him.'

'Sir, if I'd known earlier what was going on at the house we could have brought in an armed-response unit and all three kidnappers would be in custody by now.'

'Novak never wanted to be a hero. All he wanted to do was

protect his son, and the other hostages in the house. For someone who lost his own son in tragic circumstances, you of all people should understand that.'

'I never tried to be a hero, sir.' Kessler hated talking to anyone about his son. The all-consuming guilt was his burden to carry alone.

'I know. You just did what came naturally to you as a policeman when you saw what was happening. That's the difference between you and Novak. Remember that when you're dealing with him.'

Kessler sat down slowly at the table after the Chief had left the room. It was true, he had acted like a policeman that fateful morning. *If only* he hadn't been so rash. *If only* he'd thought about the consequences of his actions before tackling the gunman. *If only* he had let them take the money. *If only* Andreas had stayed in the car. Again, the recriminations. Again, the culpability. A never-ending cycle. Would it ever end?

'You wanted to see me?'

Kessler looked up at Novak, who was standing in the doorway, his hand resting lightly on the handle. 'Come in,' he said, and waved to the chair opposite. 'I want to speak to Jago in front of you. That way he's less likely to lie, having already told you about his reasons for being here in Zürich.'

'All I know about the Cabal is what he told Beth and me at the club.'

'Why did he tell you?' Kessler asked as Novak sat down.

'He needed Beth to help him recover the disk.' Novak avoided any reference to Amy Michaels. He couldn't be sure how Kessler would react. And, anyway, he owed Amy for keeping quiet in front of Jago when she could have sold him out to save her own skin. 'By that time I was also involved and the only way he could convince us to work with him was to bring us up to speed on Ian Grant's involvement with Interpol and their attempt to bring down the Cabal.'

'What exactly is the Cabal?' Kessler asked.

'I think it would be best if you were to ask Jago that. He's the expert. He's been investigating their activities for the past twelve months.'

There was a knock at the door, which opened, and Jago was ushered into the room. The door closed again behind him. Jago looked at Kessler. Then at Novak. There was no recognition in his eyes. 'Which of you is Inspector Kessler?' he asked.

'I should have thought that was obvious as you already know Novak,' Kessler said scornfully.

'I'm afraid you're mistaken,' Jago observed politely. 'I've never seen this gentleman before in my life.'

'You can cut the act, Jago,' Novak snapped back. 'I didn't mind playing along with your little charade when you first came to the club. But then it all went wrong. Voskov and his cronies have been at my house for the past twelve hours. Only now they've gone on the run and taken my son and Beth Grant with them as hostages. Either you tell Kessler everything you know about the Cabal or I will. This isn't about you and your investigation any more. It's gone way beyond that now. My son's life is in danger. And I'm damned if I'm going to stand by while you play games with us. Just tell Kessler what he wants to know so that they can get out there and find John before it's too late.' He stabbed a finger against Jago's chest. 'If anything happens to John before the cops get to him, I swear I'll kill you. And to hell with the consequences because my life won't be worth a damn without him anyway.'

'I have a witness who's just heard you make a threat on my life,' Jago said. 'I could have you arrested for that.'

'I didn't hear anything.' Kessler stepped between the two men, then took Novak's arm and led him away from Jago. 'I know what you're going through right now,' he said, in a lowered voice.

'Kessler, you don't have the first idea of what I'm going through.'

Kessler took out his wallet, and showed Novak the last

photograph taken of Andreas. 'That's my son. Last year he was killed by a stray bullet during an attempted armed robbery. Believe me, I do know how you must be feeling.'

'I'm sorry, I had no idea.' Novak was contrite, the anger gone.

'How could you know?' Kessler replaced the wallet in his pocket. 'I may not agree with the way you've handled the situation but I promise you this. I'll do everything in my power to find your son. I don't want you to have to go through the same torment I've been through since Andreas died. I wouldn't wish that on anyone.' He turned back to Jago. 'Are you ready to drop the charade now and start co-operating with the investigation?'

Jago removed a cigar from his pocket. 'What do you want to know?'

'Still no sign of the decapitated head or of the missing rug, sir.' Special Agent Jim Ellis stopped at the entrance to the sheriff's office and wiped his muddy shoes on the mat.

'I can't say I'm surprised,' Dawson said, from his chair in front of the sheriff's desk. Olsen sat behind it, sipping coffee. Phyllis Kastner had made a fresh brew before going home. 'As I said earlier, whoever killed her has probably buried the head in another state. And as for the rug, we still don't know whether that's Amy Michaels's body lying in the mortuary. If it's not, the rug won't necessarily be part of the investigation.'

'We'll resume the search at first light,' Ellis said, pouring himself a coffee.

'You know as well as I do that it's Amy Michaels's body,' Olsen said to Dawson. 'Height. Weight. Age. It has to be her.'

'I'll believe it if and when we get a positive match on the fingerprints Jim lifted from the house. Not before.'

'When are you expecting the prints to come back from Washington, sir?' Ellis asked.

'I was hoping they would have been back by now. That's why

the sheriff and I are still here.' Dawson looked at his watch: 7.12 p.m. 'I haven't eaten since breakfast. I just wish they'd fax the results through to us. Then I can get back to the hotel and tuck into the biggest steak they can find in the kitchen.'

'Why don't you go, sir? There's no point in both of us hanging around here. I can wait for the fax. I'll bring it straight across to you.'

'I appreciate the offer, Jim, but I want to be here when it comes through. After all, if the body isn't Amy Michaels it won't be a Federal investigation any more and we can be out of here first thing in the morning.' Dawson glanced at Olsen. 'It's nothing personal against you or your town. I want to get back to Washington as soon as possible to continue the investigation.'

'Incoming fax!' Ellis said, and crossed to the machine, hand extended in anticipation as the paper slowly emerged.

'Well?' Dawson asked, as Ellis stared at it silently.

Ellis looked up. 'You can start packing, sir. We're out of here first thing in the morning.'

'What?' Olsen exclaimed, jumping to his feet and snatching the fax from him.

'The prints don't match,' Ellis said, 'so whoever's lying in the mortuary right now, it's not Amy Michaels.'

ELEVEN

It felt as if a forge full of blacksmiths were pounding incessantly on their anvils inside her head. She felt groggy, nauseous, disorientated. She tried to clear her head. Think logically, she told herself. But even that seemed to hurt. She had no idea where she was. It was this thought that seemed to drag her out of her lethargy and it was with a sense of trepidation that she slowly opened her eyes.

A high ceiling. Solid wooden beams. Unfamiliar. She turned her head and lowered her gaze. The wall was constructed of veneered wooden slats. A window. Plaid curtains drawn. A chest of drawers. Unfamiliar. Further investigation revealed a thick wooden door. Closed. A single bed, similar to the one she was lying on, against the opposite wall. Unfamiliar. There was someone sitting on the bed. A child. Familiar. She opened her mouth to speak but only a hoarse croak escaped her lips. She coughed violently.

'Mrs Grant, are you OK?' John asked.

She managed a weak smile but when she tried to get off the bed she was yanked back on to the mattress. A searing pain shot through her head and she squeezed her eyes shut until it had subsided to the original rhythmic throbbing. Only then did she notice that her left wrist had been manacled to the headboard.

'Me, too.' John rattled his handcuffs.

'Oh, God, what happened?' Beth rubbed her forehead with her free hand.

'All I remember is an injection at home then waking up in here,' John said. 'I guess they must have drugged you too. I felt sick when I came round.'

Beth lay back on the bed, staring up at the ceiling as she struggled to collect her thoughts. She remembered being forced into the back of the van and Kilgarry placing the unconscious John on the floor beside her. Then Kilgarry getting into the back of the van and Voskov closing the door after him. She had bent over John to check his pulse and make sure that he hadn't suffered any adverse reaction to the tranquillizer. Then the pinprick in her arm. She didn't remember anything after that . . .

'Where are we?' she asked. 'Have any of them come into the room since you came round?' He shook his head. 'Then I guess we'd better let them know that we're awake. Now, what can we use to get their attention?'

'How about this?' John pointed to a cheap porcelain water jug, which was standing on the table, with a couple of plastic cups, between the two beds.

'How good are you at throwing?' Beth struggled to sit up. 'Because I'm lousy. I've never been any good at sport.'

'What do you want me to hit?' John asked confidently.

'The door. That should do it.'

He poured the water on to the floor then hurled the jug at the door. It disintegrated into myriad tiny fragments on impact.

'Bullseye!' Beth punched the air with her free hand. She winced as pain shot through her head but she masked it with a grin at John.

Moments later they heard a key inserted in the lock, the click as it was turned. Then the door was thrust open and two of the kidnappers appeared in the doorway. Both were wearing balaclavas but Beth could tell from their build that it was Voskov and Racine. The Frenchman was armed.

'What's going on?' Voskov's boots crunched on the porcelain shards as he entered the room.

'You tell us,' Beth said defiantly. 'Where are we?'

'A chalet in the mountains,' Voskov told her, 'well off the beaten track. So shout all you want, nobody will hear you.'

'What do you want with us?' Beth asked Voskov, ignoring Racine. 'I can't possibly get the disk from Strohmaier now. The police will already know what's happened. Mike will have seen to that.'

'You let me worry about Strohmaier and the disk,' Voskov said. 'You and the boy are an insurance policy in case we need to negotiate a safe passage out of here once we have the disk. Not that I think anything will go wrong. But it's prudent to cover every eventuality. Novak's welcome to tell the police everything he knows, but it really won't be much, will it?'

'You're certainly cool under pressure, I'll give you that,' Beth said. 'We both know that this has gone belly-up for you. You're not going to get anywhere near Strohmaier now, let alone the disk. To be honest, I'm surprised you didn't just cut your losses and bail out while you still had the chance.'

'Oh, I admit the situation's far from ideal. It would have been so much easier if you'd got the disk for us the first time round. But don't make the mistake of underestimating me, Mrs Grant. I'll get to the disk before the police do.'

'And if you don't?' she challenged.

'That's not an option.'

'I thought you said that it was prudent to cover every eventuality.'

Voskov held her stare for several seconds then left the room. Racine watched him go, then said to Beth, 'It's late. You and the boy get some sleep.'

'It would be a lot easier if you took off the handcuffs.'

'The handcuffs stay,' Racine told her.

'We've just been told that we're in the middle of nowhere. It's not as if we can escape. Not in these clothes. We'd die of hypothermia out there.' She waited for a response. None. 'OK, leave me manacled to the bed. But at least take off John's handcuffs. Be reasonable.'

'We are being reasonable. We didn't gag you.' With that he closed the door behind him and a moment later the key was turned in the lock.

Beth banged her free hand angrily against the wall once Racine's footsteps had receded as the realization of her complete helplessness washed over her. Not just for her. For John as well. He was only a child. Without his father. That made her responsible for him. But she was powerless to get them out of their current predicament. And that just added to her mounting frustration. She looked across at John. 'Can you see out of the window?'

John slid the handcuff along the rail of the headboard until it was on the far side of the bed then, kneeling on the mattress, he reached up and pulled back one of the curtains. But his manacled hand prevented him from standing on the bed and looking through the glass. All Beth could see was darkness. And the occasional snowflake landing on the windowpane. John eased the handcuff back to the other side of the bed, stood up, and pushed the bed against the wall. Then he got back on the mattress and stretched as far as the manacle would allow until he was just able to see out.

'What's there?' Beth asked.

'Snow. Some trees. It's dark.

'Sit down, John, before you pull your arm out of its socket.'

'What will happen if they don't get this disk, Mrs Grant? Will they kill us?'

'No, of course not,' Beth said quickly. *Too damn quick*, she chided herself. But the truth was she had no idea what Voskov would do if the authorities got to Strohmaier first. It was a frightening thought, and lingered uncomfortably in her mind. She could see from John's face that he was far from convinced by her answer. Rightly so. 'I'm sorry, John, I didn't mean to patronize you like that. I suppose it's because I'm just not used to being around kids. I've always put my career first.'

'Did your husband want to have children?'

Just like a child to go straight for the jugular. 'Yes, but I was always too busy being a businesswoman first, and a wife second. That's something I'll regret for the rest of my life.'

'My mother was like that too. She never even wanted me.'

'How can you say that?' Beth asked gently.

'I'm sure Dad's already told you about her. That she was a junkie. I bet he didn't tell you that she used to sleep around while he was at work. He doesn't think I know about that. But I know most things about her. Dad's just told me the bits that he thinks I should hear because I'm a kid. I know he means well. He's still in love with her. At least, he is in his own way. But she really hurt him. And I hate her so much for that.'

'Drug dependency is a sickness, John. Whether it's alcohol or cocaine, it's still a sickness. You shouldn't hate her because the more you allow those feelings to eat away inside you, the more bitter you'll get as you grow older. You don't want to burden yourself with that kind of resentment for the rest of your life. That's why your dad only told you what he did. To protect you.'

'But she hurt him so much.' John brushed a tear from the corner of his eye.

'She also gave him a son,' Beth said softly. 'And you can bet that alone outweighs all the hurt. That's why he still loves her – in his own way. Because of you.'

John stared at the floor pensively. 'I never thought of it like that. It kinda makes sense . . . I guess. Thanks, Mrs Grant.'

'Why don't you try to get some sleep? I know it's not going to be easy, but you might be glad of it in the morning. Who knows what they've got lined up for us come daybreak?'

'We're going to be OK. I know we are.' He smiled, then lay back on the bed and closed his eyes.

She stared at him for some time, watching his chest rise and fall with each breath. His words had been delivered with a maturity that belied his age. It also gave a much-needed boost to her own flagging self-confidence, even though she knew it was little more than a false sense of security. But it was welcome all the same. The more she thought about it, the more she realized that it was the first time she had ever been able to relate to a child in that way. Was this some latent maternal instinct? *One step at a time, Beth*, she said to herself, *one step at a time . . .*

Kessler remained seated at the table after Novak and Jago had been escorted from the room. So much information to take in. So little time to act upon it. Jago had, to his credit, answered all the questions candidly and, as far as he was concerned, truthfully. Novak had never once challenged anything Jago had said. Admittedly, he had never found out just how much Novak knew about the Cabal – not that it mattered anyway – but his continued silence had surely been proof enough of Jago's honesty. It had left him with a dilemma, though. Now that he had the names of the three assassins, as well as that of Sammy Kahn, his first instinct had been to release details to the press without mentioning the Cabal, in an attempt to locate the hostages. Yet as he had listened to Jago, he had realized that that was not a good idea. Jago had painted a picture of three professional killers with nothing to lose in their search for the missing disk. The cold-blooded execution of Hans Matzke was proof of that. Releasing their names to the press might panic them – after all, they still believed themselves anonymous. And if backed into a corner, they would use the hostages to regain the advantage. That made Beth Grant and John Novak expendable. He couldn't afford any further loss of innocent life. Yet he also knew that the more exposure the case got to the public, the more likelihood there was of someone coming forward with vital information that might lead to the safe release of the hostages.

There was a knock at the door. It opened fractionally and Sergeant Dannhauser peered tentatively into the room. He had initially been part of the surveillance unit at the house but had since been drafted in as a replacement for Matzke. 'Can I talk to you, sir?' he asked, from the doorway.

'What is it?'

'Word's just come in that Willie Meine's been found murdered in his apartment. His hands had been pinned to the floor with knives and he'd been forced to ingest a bottle of bleach. His eyelids had been cut off and bleach had been poured—'

'OK, OK, I get the picture,' Kessler interrupted.

'That's not all, sir,' Dannhauser went on. 'A mother and daughter were also murdered on the same floor of the apartment block. Both had had their throats cut. The child was six years old. Obviously it's too early to ascertain whether the murders are connected, but it seems too much of a coincidence for them not to be. We also have a potential witness. A vagrant who was beaten unconscious in the foyer of the apartment block. He gave us a description of the man.' Dannhauser held up the sheet of paper in his hand. 'We'll know whether it's one of the kidnappers once Jago forwards us photos of the three men.'

'Let me see that.' Kessler took the paper from him. He read the vagrant's description and snorted. 'Racine. I should have guessed!'

'How do you know it's him, sir?' Dannhauser asked in surprise.

'Jago gave me verbal descriptions of the three men. This fits Racine perfectly. It all begins to make sense now.'

'I don't understand, sir.'

'Matzke obviously followed Racine from the house. He was probably told to tail Racine, but not to approach him. Then he was lured into an ambush and executed, giving Voskov and Kilgarry time to flee the house with the hostages.'

'But that would imply that Racine was tipped off about

Matzke. I thought you were the only person who knew he was watching the house.'

'No, someone else knew too. I'm sure the Chief will be interested to hear about this,' Kessler said, reaching for the telephone. 'Sergeant, the moment you get those photographs from Jago I want them faxed to every newspaper and television station in the country with an appropriate cover story about the kidnapping. Say that the motive for the abduction isn't known as yet, but that it's thought to be linked with the murder of Ian Grant. Circulate photos of Beth Grant and John Novak as well. This has gone far enough. The gloves are off now.' He lifted the receiver then glanced up at Dannhauser. 'If you'll excuse me, I've got to call the Chief.'

'Why didn't you tell me they were at the house?' Jago demanded, as Novak drove them to the club. 'You had ample opportunity when you were away from the house. Just one call, that's all it would have taken.'

'And what good would that have done?' Novak countered.

'If I'd known what was going on, I could have brought in the local authorities and this could have been over by now. Instead we've got three professional killers on the run – with hostages.'

'I could understand that kind of bullshit coming from Kessler because he hasn't had to deal with these men. But not from you. You know them. And I believe that Voskov would have had no hesitation in executing the hostages had I blown the whistle on them. So don't try and lay a guilt trip on me, Jago, because it's not going to work. My only concern from the start has been for John's safety. And if that meant playing by their rules, then I make no apologies for doing that. If I had my way, I'd personally hand them the disk on a silver platter if it meant John and Beth being released unharmed.'

'You can forget about that now,' Jago said.

'What's that supposed to mean?'

'The game will change dramatically the moment their true

identities are made public. And they will be. Kessler will see to that. He's got a dead policeman on his hands. The police will be under intense pressure to track down those responsible and bring them to justice. This is Switzerland, Novak, not America. When was the last time you heard of a policeman being executed here in Switzerland? It just doesn't happen.'

'So what are you saying? That John and Beth aren't part of the police's equation any more? That they're expendable?' Novak cast a sidelong glance at Jago when the German remained silent. 'I don't buy it. There would be an even bigger outcry if a child was killed in the crossfire.'

'Not if the kidnappers were blamed. And if they were already dead, it would be so much easier for the authorities to deny any culpability.'

'Are you saying that the police will adopt a shoot-to-kill policy when they confront the kidnappers?' Novak asked.

'I'm saying that Voskov, Kilgarry and Racine would never stand trial. What they could tell in an open court would potentially bring down governments around the world. Does that answer your question?'

Novak pulled the car violently into the side of the road. The vehicle behind him braked sharply, and the driver jabbed his horn furiously as he drove past. Novak turned to Jago. 'You've known this all along, haven't you?'

'I had my orders,' Jago said. 'Retrieve the disk and identify the location of the three assassins. I've no idea how they would be silenced. Probably made to look like accidents on different sides of the world. That way it wouldn't appear suspicious. Only that doesn't apply any more. Not now that they've taken hostages. Now they're legitimate targets. They can't be allowed to leave the country.'

Novak unclipped his seat-belt then tilted his head back, his hand over his eyes as the truth slowly sank in. John and Beth were expendable, as long as the assassins were never allowed to testify in court. Checkmate, with only a couple of pawns sacrificed. A small price to save the integrity of world governments. Well, maybe it was for the governments concerned. But not for him. His initial feelings of fear and anxiety had now intensified to one of pure anger. 'Get out of the car,' he snarled at Jago.

'I can understand your—'

'Just get the fuck out of my car!' Novak yelled.

'I'm on your side, Novak. Why else do you think I told you this? I don't want anything to happen to the hostages either, and I may well be their one chance of getting out of this alive.' Jago stared at the succession of headlights that flashed past the stationary car. 'As I told you when we first met at the club, one of the assassins had been passing information on to Ian Grant before he died. I need him alive, because right now he's my only link to Sammy Kahn. And I want to nail Kahn more than I do any of the others. But if they were conveniently killed in a shoot-out, Kahn will go to ground until everything's blown over, then surface again and rebuild the Cabal. And Kahn's already got the contacts in all the right places. It wouldn't be difficult.'

'Are you saying that *Kahn* is behind the shoot-to-kill policy?' Novak asked in disbelief.

'What I'm saying is, Kahn has enough friends in high places who have the clout to arrange it for him. Maybe now you understand just how powerful Kahn really is. But a lot of that power comes from fear. From what I understand, every contract the Cabal has ever carried out has been meticulously documented and hidden away in some bank vault so that if anything were ever to happen to Kahn, all that dirty laundry would be splashed across the front pages of every major newspaper in the world. As I said, what Kahn knows could conceivably bring down governments. Or certainly damage their credibility beyond repair. So there are a lot of worried politicians out there right now who have Kahn's best interests at heart.'

'And just what makes you think that they're going to let you talk the assassins into surrendering?' Novak said. 'If there is a shoot-to-kill policy, they'll be taken out at the first opportunity.'

'I'm only interested in the informer. The other two are expendable as far as I'm concerned.'

'And once the informer's told you what you want to know, he'll become expendable as well? Is that it?'

'Not if he cuts a deal with Interpol.' Jago bristled. 'We'll protect him, if necessary. But obviously I need to get to him first. Chances are, they'll be tracked down to their new hideout once their faces appear on news bulletins across the country. That's where I would come in. I'm a trained negotiator. I also know more about the workings of the Cabal than anyone here in Switzerland. That should give me the advantage over the local negotiators when it comes to dealing with them. Once I'm in, it won't take me long to work out which is the informer. Not if I ask the right questions, discreetly, of course.'

'And then what happens?'

'I'll bring him out. Along with the hostages.'

'And just how do you intend to do that?'

'Secrets of the trade.' Jago tapped the side of his nose. 'But first I've got to get Kessler on my side. And I believe I can. He'll want to bring the situation to an end without further bloodshed. You can be sure of that.'

'And what if you can't win him over?'

'Come now, Novak, I'm a trained negotiator. I can win over anyone with the right kind of persuasion. Even you. After all, I'm still sitting in your car, aren't I?'

'You're certainly confident, I'll give you that,' Novak said. 'I just hope you know what you're doing.'

'I know exactly what I'm doing. All I have to do now is convince the local authorities of that.' Jago pointed to the ignition. 'Amy Michaels will probably be climbing the walls by now at the club. The sooner she can be reassured about her situation, the sooner I can get the photos of the three assassins from my hotel room then return to the station and talk to Kessler. Shall we go?'

'Where the hell have you been?' Amy Michaels snapped as she opened the door and found Novak and Jago standing in the hallway.

'I'm sorry, but I've been kinda busy,' Novak said, entering the room.

'Yeah, I heard all the commotion from in here. You'd be surprised how well voices carry in this place.'

'That was only part of it,' Novak said, then glanced at Jago. 'You want to bring her up to date?'

'I'll leave that to you. After all, I'm still taking it all in myself.'

Novak spent the next few minutes briefing her on what had happened since he last spoke to her, culminating in the abduction of Beth and John.

'I'm sorry about your boy,' she said, her eyes going to the framed photograph on the table. 'I know how close you are to him.'

'Yeah, we're pretty close,' Novak replied, tight-lipped.

'Does this mean that I'm no longer a suspect in the Ian Grant homicide?' She directed her question at Jago.

'Obviously I can't speak for Kessler but, under the circumstances, I think he must be pretty well convinced of your innocence by now.'

'Then take her into the station and clear this up,' Novak said. 'Surely you can do that now?'

'No, it's best if she remains here, at least for the time being,' Jago replied.

'Why?' she asked. 'Novak's right. If we go to the station together it's going to add credibility to my story about seeing Kilgarry outside the club the night Ian Grant was murdered.'

'The timing has to be right,' Jago told her. 'We go in now, it's going to look suspicious for both of us in the light of recent events. It would look as if you knew what had happened, and timed your appearance to coincide with these latest developments. As far as the authorities are concerned, you're still on the run. And if that's the case, how could you possibly know about the kidnapping and my subsequent meeting with Kessler? It would be just too convenient. Give it another day, Miss Michaels, then I promise that I'll personally escort you to the station to meet with Kessler. That will also put Novak in the clear with the authorities as well.'

'Twenty-four hours,' she agreed reluctantly. 'I suppose there's no chance of anything to eat? I'm starving.'

'I'll get you a take-out,' Novak said. 'What do you want?'

She shrugged. 'Anything, I'm not bothered.'

'I've got to go as well,' Jago said. 'Novak, I'll walk with you to your car, then get a taxi back to my hotel. I've still got a long night ahead of me.'

'I'll be back shortly,' Novak said to her, then followed Jago from the room and closed the door again behind him.

Beth awoke with a start. She had no idea how long she had been asleep, or what time it was, but at that moment neither seemed significant. A shadowy figure was seated on the bed, a gloved hand over her mouth. The other gloved hand held a silenced automatic lightly to her temple. It was one of the assassins, that much was obvious from the balaclava pulled down over his face, but in the semi-darkness she had no idea which one it was. She cast a quick glance across at John. He appeared to be asleep.

'I'm going to take my hand off your mouth now.' The soft voice was unmistakable. Kilgarry. It added to her mounting terror. 'Scream if you want, but if the boy wakes up I'll kill him. It's your choice.' He lifted his hand away from her mouth. She didn't make a sound. 'Smart,' he whispered, then unlocked her hand from the bed and secured the cuff around her other wrist, effectively pinning her arms behind her back. Only then did he lower the automatic and place it on the dresser.

'Where are you taking me?' she asked, in a trembling voice.

'Nowhere,' he replied.

'Oh, my God.' The realization of what he was planning hit Beth like a vicious slap across her face. How could she have been so stupid not to have guessed earlier? Now she was handcuffed and incapable of fending him off. At his mercy. And she already knew there would be precious little of that. 'No.' She shook her head from side to side. 'No, don't touch me. Don't touch me!'

She had raised her voice without realizing it and John stirred in the other bed. Kilgarry snatched the automatic off the dresser and aimed it at the boy's head. Beth held her breath, willing John not to turn round. She was in no doubt that Kilgarry would carry out his threat if John should wake up. How could she live with herself if that happened? How could she live with herself if she allowed Kilgarry to rape her? There was no way out. She had to make a sacrifice. Yet she already knew that she had to protect John at all costs. After what seemed an eternity, John's breathing fell back into an even, regular pattern.

'Please don't rape me.' Beth felt a tear trickle from the corner of her eye.

'Rape?' Kilgarry replied, affecting surprise. 'Surely if I was going to rape you you'd be screaming for help by now and struggling to keep me away from you. You look pretty relaxed to me.'

'You bastard.' She forced herself to convert her fear into anger. 'If I scream, you'll kill John.'

'If you scream, my colleagues will be up here in an instant. You'd be safe. The boy would be dead, but you'd be safe. As I said, it's your choice.'

'It's no choice,' she replied.

'To be honest, you're not even my type. Not like that French

bitch at the house. I wanted to fuck her. I even asked Vos—'
He stopped abruptly, paused, then continued, 'I even asked my colleague if we could bring her with us. If he'd agreed, I wouldn't be here right now.'

'You're filth. You disgust me,' Beth hissed. 'Do what you want with me but leave John alone. You leave him *alone*.'

'That sounds like consent in my book,' Kilgarry said disparagingly.

Beth squeezed her eyes shut when he pulled her skirt above her waist and she bit down hard on her lower lip when she felt his hand slip under her panties, exploring roughly between her legs. She could taste the blood in her mouth, but this only made her bite harder into her lip. The pain was one way of trying to block out what was happening to her.

His hand froze. A moment later he withdrew it from under her skirt. She opened her eyes fractionally, unsure what kind of twisted psychological game he was playing with her, and saw a second figure in a balaclava standing by the bed. He was holding a switchblade against Kilgarry's neck. It had nicked the skin and a trickle of blood ran down Kilgarry's throat and disappeared under his open-necked shirt.

'Please straighten the lady's skirt. She's not some back-street whore.' The voice was French. Racine.

Kilgarry pulled Beth's skirt down over her legs, his eyes fearful as Racine continued to press the blade against his throat. 'Now, I believe you owe the lady an apology.' Kilgarry remained silent. Racine pressed the tip of the blade further into Kilgarry's skin and the blood ran freely down his throat from the new wound.

'I'm . . . sorry,' Kilgarry said between gritted teeth.

'And it won't happen again, will it?' Racine said in his ear.

'No. Never again. I swear.'

Racine removed the switchblade, retracted it, and slipped it back into his pocket in one fluid movement. Only then did Kilgarry get to his feet and Beth pulled her knee up to her chest then shot her foot into the American's groin. Kilgarry cried out in agony and crumpled to the floor at the side of the bed.

'I think that hit the spot,' Racine said, as Kilgarry lay whimpering to himself as he cradled his genitals in his cupped hands.

'Beth, what happened?' John asked, now sitting bolt upright in bed.

'It's nothing, sweetheart.'

Racine retrieved Kilgarry's automatic from the dresser and slipped it into the belt at the back of his trousers. 'Turn over, Mrs Grant. I'll unlock one of the handcuffs for you. And please don't try anything foolish when your hand is free.'

'What's going on?' Voskov burst into the room. His eyes went to Kilgarry, who was still moaning in agony on the floor.

'It appears that our esteemed colleague lost control,' Racine replied, as he secured Beth's wrist once more to the headboard, 'but Mrs Grant was quick to douse his flame. He'll recover, with only his dignity bruised.'

'Did he hurt you?' Voskov asked Beth, but there was no concern in his voice. It was a question. Nothing more.

'Not as much as I hurt him,' she said coldly. 'He's an animal. I don't know how you can work with something as odious as that.'

'Why don't you take him downstairs?' Racine removed Kilgarry's automatic from the back of his trousers and handed it to Voskov.

Voskov hauled Kilgarry unceremoniously to his feet and, ignoring his groans, led him out.

'I'm sorry I didn't get here earlier,' Racine said to Beth. 'As it was, I only happened to be passing the room when I heard the sound of his voice. He had no reason to be in here. That's why I came in.'

'What do you want?' she retorted scornfully. 'A medal?'

Racine ignored her sarcasm and sat down on the bed beside John. 'How are you doing, *mon ami*?'

'I'm OK.' John drew his head back when Racine tried to ruffle his hair.

'I like the innocence of kids,' Racine said, but he didn't appear to be talking to either of them as he stared at the opposite wall. 'I often wish I'd settled down and had children of my own. Maybe I will, one day. Who knows?' He laughed suddenly. 'There are women in Paris who actually want to have my baby. They've said it in so many words. Isn't that crazy? Where's the romance in that? No dating. No getting to know one another. They just want to jump straight into bed . . .' He grinned at John. 'We'd better not go into that, eh?'

'What – you think I don't know about sex?' John said indignantly, as if he had been insulted.

'Ah, the end of the innocence,' Racine said solemnly, then exhaled and got to his feet. He left the room and locked the door behind him.

'What was all that about?' John asked, perplexed.

'Regrets,' Beth replied softly. 'So many regrets.'

'If I had my way, I'd have cut you loose back at the house,' Voskov roared as he stood over Kilgarry, whose face was creased in pain. Both men had removed their balaclavas. 'It amazes me that Kahn even considered you for the Cabal in the first place, let alone hired you.'

'I'm good at what I do,' Kilgarry rasped.

'And just what would that be?' Racine inquired from the foot of the stairs. 'Handcuffing defenceless women with the intention of raping them? That's certainly some skill you've got there, Kilgarry. And I thought any back-street punk with shit for brains could do that.'

'At least I didn't slit a little girl's throat in front of her mother.' Kilgarry glared at the Frenchman.

Racine pulled off his balaclava and tossed it on to the table. 'The mother died first.'

'Even better.'

'That's enough, both of you,' Voskov snapped before either of them could say any more. 'I don't like what Racine did any more than you do. I've got a daughter about that age back in Moscow. That made it even more uncomfortable for me. But I don't see what other choice he had but to kill them. Both the mother and the daughter had seen his face. And the daughter may have seen him leaving Meine's apartment as well. He couldn't take any chances.'

'At least I wasn't tempted to rape them first.' Racine leaned over the back of Kilgarry's chair.

'I've had just about enough of you,' Kilgarry snarled at Racine and struggled to his feet.

Voskov stepped between them. 'Kilgarry, sit down before you fall down. Racine, likewise.'

'I'm not about to fall down,' Racine said.

'Don't tempt me.' Voskov pressed his finger lightly against Racine's chest.

'OK,' Racine muttered, and slumped down in the second chair beside the fire.

'Is there any booze in this place?' Kilgarry asked. 'I could do with a fucking shot.'

'You're out of luck,' Voskov said, with obvious satisfaction. Kilgarry was about to vent his annoyance when the cellphone on the table began to ring. Voskov answered it.

'It's Kahn. I've got some good news for you.'

'I could certainly do with some right now,' Voskov said, eyeing his colleagues distastefully. 'What have you got for me?'

'Strohmaier.'

'Finally,' Voskov said. 'Where is he?'

'A small ski resort in the Toggenburg valley, close to the border with Liechtenstein. My sources had already canvassed that area yesterday and come up blank. It was only when they rechecked that they found him. He's using a false name, which is why they missed him first time round.'

'Why the deception?' Voskov asked.

'He's sharing a double room, but not with his wife. She's at home in Zürich with the children.'

'Has he been approached about the disk?'

'No. It has to be handled delicately. And there's only one person I know I can trust to do it. You.'

'I'm flattered,' Voskov said.

'Well, don't be, it wasn't meant as a compliment. My main concern right now is the cops. If we've found Strohmaier, they won't be far behind. If they get to him first and recover the disk, we're going to be on the run for the rest of our lives. Or until we're caught and sent down for life.'

'So how do you want me to handle it?' Voskov asked.

'I only received the news a few minutes ago, so I haven't had much chance to think about it. Any ideas?'

'I don't know if it'll work, but it's got to be worth a try,' Kessler said, after Jago had outlined the plan to him should the need arise to negotiate with the kidnappers. They had been sitting opposite each other in one of the interview rooms for the past thirty minutes. 'As you said, you know more about the Cabal than any of us. And as the senior officer on the case, my main objective is still to get the hostages released unharmed. Naturally I want to apprehend the kidnappers too. But I don't buy this shoot-to-kill policy. This is Switzerland. Not some Third World dictatorship. If you can convince the kidnappers to surrender, you have my word that they won't be harmed.'

'That's all I wanted to know.' Jago stubbed out his cigar. 'Thanks for your time. I know you're a busy man right now, so I won't keep you any longer. I'll go back to the hotel and await developments there. After all, I'm not officially part of the investigation.'

'Should we track them down to their hideout, I'll be sure to let you know. Of course, whether my superiors will agree to my bringing you in as a negotiator is another matter altogether.'

'When will you ask them?' Jago queried.

'If, and when, the need arises,' Kessler replied. 'That way they'll be forced to make a snap decision. The worst thing I could do is ask them now and let them mull it over. The less time they have to think about a particular strategy, the better, otherwise they tend to err on the side of caution. That's something I've learned the hard way over the years.'

'I know what you mean,' Jago said, chuckling as he followed Kessler out into the corridor. He shook the policeman's hand and waited until he had disappeared back into the squad room before walking the short distance to the stairs that led down to the lobby. He made his way across the black-and-white tiled floor to the main doors and emerged into the street. The early-morning air was brisk and he pulled up the collar of his overcoat. It would be light soon. He flagged down a passing taxi, which took him back to his hotel, and went to his room. A message from the switchboard operator had been slipped under his door. It read simply *Call home*. There was no name, no number. Not that he needed either. He dialled out on his cellphone.

'It's Jago,' he said, when it was answered.

'We've found Strohmaier,' he was told. 'Voskov's already making the necessary arrangements to intercept him before the authorities can get to him. We should have the disk within the next few hours.'

'That's excellent news.'

'How did your meeting go with Kessler?'

'He bought the whole package. It wasn't difficult to draw him in once I'd told him about the Cabal. So once the authorities have been tipped off as to the whereabouts of Kilgarry and Racine, I'll be able to go into the chalet without alerting suspicion. Taking them out won't be a problem. I assume that the gun with Kilgarry's prints on it has already been taped under the cistern?'

'It's there.'

'Excellent. That way it'll look as if I wrestled the gun from him and shot them both in self-defence. You'll have to call first – once the disk has been recovered – so that they'll let me into the chalet. After all, they trust you implicitly. Remember, the police will already have the place surrounded. It has to appear to them as if I'm acting as a negotiator on their behalf.'

'That won't be a problem.'

'What about the hostages?'

'What about them?'

'They could get caught in the crossfire,' Jago said.

'I want Kilgarry and Racine silenced as a matter of precaution. What happens to the hostages is irrelevant.'

'I'd prefer to get them out alive. One's a kid, for Christ's sake.'

'Somehow I never took you for a sentimentalist. But it's your call, Jago. Save the kid if you want and be a hero, it makes no difference to me. But Kilgarry and Racine leave the chalet in body-bags. Is that understood?'

'You're all heart, Kahn.'

'So I've been told.' There was a moment's pause. 'Just remember, Jago, your loyalty's to the Cabal. It has been from the moment you pocketed your first bribe. I had to call in a lot of favours to make sure that you were assigned to this case. Don't let me down.'

'Just see that you make the call.' Jago struggled to contain his rising anger. 'I don't want any problems when I get there . . .' But the line had already gone dead.

The headlights momentarily illuminated the front of the house as the battered pickup truck swung off the dirt road before coming to a halt in front of it. Two men climbed out and looked around slowly, even though they knew no one would be around at that time of night. The black leather gloves contrasted vividly with the ankle-length white robes they were wearing, with hoods over their heads to conceal their features.

The driver retrieved a crowbar from under his seat then strode across the soft, dew-drenched grass to the front door. Inserting the pronged tip between the door and the frame, close to the lock, he pulled sharply on it. The wood splintered but the door held firm. He took a step back and kicked it savagely. It flew open and hammered against the adjacent wall.

The other man took two gasoline cans from the back of the truck and handed one to the driver. They each pulled out a flashlight from under their robes, switched them on and entered the house. The driver went upstairs. His colleague remained downstairs and went from room to room sprinkling gasoline over any flammable material he could find, then discarded the empty can and returned to the front door. Moments later the driver appeared at the top of the stairs, gave him a thumbs-up, then took a box of matches from his pocket and disappeared again, the beam of his flashlight dissecting the darkness around him. He started a fire in every room then hurried down the stairs and did the same on the ground floor. The house was already filling fast with thick, acrid smoke by the time they emerged into the cool night air. They returned to the van then looked back at the doomed house. An upper-floor window exploded outwards and flames shot out through the jagged aperture. The driver opened the glove compartment, took out a can of spray paint, and daubed some graffiti over the nearest tree before tossing the can into the river and returning to where his colleague was still standing beside the van. They both knew that the old house would be gutted long before the town's lone fire engine reached the scene. Which was exactly what they wanted. The driver chuckled contentedly to himself as he got back behind the wheel. His colleague stared at the flames for another few seconds then climbed in beside him. They drove off in the same direction that they had come.

TWELVE

Saturday

He reached out sleepily to switch off the alarm and tapped the button several times, but still the noise continued. Only then did he realize that it was the telephone ringing at the side of the bed. Opening one eye to get his bearings, he picked up the receiver without lifting his head off the pillow. 'Hello?' he mumbled.

'Is that Dietmar Strohmaier?'

He had checked into the hotel under an assumed name. So had his married mistress, who was asleep beside him. 'I'm – I'm sorry, you must have the wrong room,' he stammered. It was a lame reply, and he knew it, but it had been the best he could come up with while still half asleep.

'Herr Strohmaier, this is Inspector Stefan Kessler, Zürich police. It's imperative that you get dressed now and come down to the lobby.'

'Police?' Strohmaier said.

'This has nothing to do with your being here with your mistress,' came the quick reply. 'We have no interest in your private life. This is a matter of national security. Please, get dressed and come downstairs. And bring your office keys with you. I'll be waiting for you in the lobby.'

'National security?' Strohmaier was bewildered. 'What are you talking about? I don't understand.'

'I'll explain everything when I speak to you in person.'

'I'll be down in a few minutes,' Strohmaier said, then hung up and climbed out of bed. He looked down at the red-haired woman lying on her stomach, her head tilted to one side on the pillow. She looked so peaceful. Going through to the bathroom, he doused his face with cold water then reached for the towel on the rail beside the basin. He caught sight of his reflection in the mirror and as he stared back at himself he thought back to the conversation he had just had. Something was troubling him about it, only he didn't know what it was. If only he'd been more awake. He pulled on a pair of jeans and a white sweatshirt. Then, stepping into his moccasins, he took his keys off the bedside table and left the room. Still he felt a nagging unease as he rode the elevator to the lobby. What if the caller was a private detective, pretending to be a policeman? He hadn't thought his wife suspected anything, but . . . Anyway it was too late to turn back now. He stepped out into the lobby and saw the man standing beside the revolving doors at the front of the hotel. Apart from a receptionist, he was the only other person in the lobby. Which was hardly surprising, considering the time.

'Are you Kessler?' he asked, on reaching the revolving doors.

'Yes. Inspector Stefan Kessler.' He took his warrant card from his pocket and showed it to Strohmaier. 'If you'd care to follow me, sir, I'll explain everything in the car. It's essential that we get back to Zürich.'

'I'm not going anywhere until I know exactly what's going on,' Strohmaier replied.

'As I said to you on the phone, this is a matter of national security. I'm asking you to come with me voluntarily, otherwise I'll have you arrested and taken to Zürich in handcuffs. Believe it.'

'You're not a policeman, are you?' Strohmaier said. 'Something's been bothering me ever since you first rang the room. Now I know what it is. You're speaking German. Not Swiss-German. I lived in Hamburg until I was sixteen. That's why I didn't pick it up straight away. I automatically switched back to German myself without even realizing it. You're a private detective, aren't you? Who sent you?'

'You're right about me not being a policeman,' Voskov replied. 'But I'm not a private detective.'

'Who are you?'

'Who I am is irrelevant. What should worry you, however, is that your wife and two children are being held hostage at your house in Zürich. I assume you do still care about them?'

The blood drained from Strohmaier's face and he stared in disbelief at Voskov. Finally he shook his head and a nervous laugh escaped his pursed lips. 'I don't believe you,' he said.

'Do you really think we'd have taken all this trouble to find you just to call your bluff?' Voskov asked.

Strohmaier swallowed. 'Then let me speak to them.'

'Not until I've got what I want.'

'I want to speak to them now!' Strohmaier's anguish burst to the surface.

Voskov's eyes flickered to the receptionist, who was watching them. 'I really would keep my voice down if I were you because if something should happen to me before I report in again to my colleagues, your family will be executed. I don't think you'd want that on your conscience, would you?'

'What do you want?'

'The disk Ian Grant left with you before he was murdered. Once you've handed it over to me, your family will be released unharmed. Surely that's a small price to pay for their safe return?'

'What disk?' Strohmaier asked.

'Please don't insult me with that tired cliché,' Voskov said.

'Ian Grant gave me a padded envelope for safekeeping last week. He said it contained some documents for his wife and that I should give it to her if she came to my office to collect it. He never said anything about a disk.'

'Then let's go and check the envelope, shall we?' Voskov said.

'You can't force me to go anywhere with you,' Strohmaier said defiantly. 'Not in front of a witness. You can't afford to draw any unnecessary attention on yourself.'

'You've got two beautiful daughters, Herr Strohmaier. Eleven and eight. I could have them executed with a single phone call. And if you don't think that we'd carry out our threat to kill them, feel free to walk away. I won't stop you. As you said, I can't draw any unnecessary attention to myself. But by the time you've contacted the police and they get to your house, all they'll find will be three bodies.'

'I'll give you the goddamn envelope,' Strohmaier muttered, 'but I swear when this is over—'

'Spare me the melodrama. Did you tell your girlfriend you were coming down here to meet with me?'

'No, she was still asleep.'

'Then leave her a message. Say you've been called back unexpectedly to Zürich, and that you'll contact her later this morning. We don't want to alarm her when she wakes up and finds you're not there. Ask the receptionist to have it slipped under the door. That way you don't even have to wake her.' He watched as Strohmaier wrote the message on a sheet of hotel stationery, folded it in half, then took it to the receptionist. When he returned Voskov followed him through the revolving doors and opened the back door of the car parked in front of the hotel. Strohmaier got in then Voskov climbed behind the wheel, started the engine, and drove off. He pulled into the side of the road a couple of hundred yards further on, removed a hypodermic from the glove compartment then got out and opened the back door.

'What the hell's that?' Strohmaier pulled his arm away when Voskov reached for it.

'A sedative that will knock you out for the duration of the trip back to Zürich,' Voskov told him.

'You're not going to stick that thing in me,' Strohmaier said determinedly.

'I can assure you, it's quite harmless.'

'Forget it!'

Voskov took out his cellphone and punched in a number. He put his hand lightly over the mouthpiece. 'I'm calling your house so that you can listen to your youngest daughter having her fingers broken one by one until you agree to let me give you the sedative.' He removed his hand. 'It's me. I've got a bit of a problem here. Bring the youngest one to the phone and start to break her fingers – one at a time – until I tell you to stop.'

'No, please.' Strohmaier pulled back the sleeve of his sweatshirt and extended his bare arm towards Voskov. 'Please, anything. Just don't hurt her.'

'You still there?' Voskov said, into the handset. 'Problem solved. Let the kid be.' He replaced the telephone in his pocket then injected the drug into Strohmaier's bloodstream. He waited until the lawyer had passed out, laid him down on the back seat and placed a blanket over him to conceal him from passing motorists. Then, he got back behind the wheel, slipped the car into gear and pulled away.

'You really should try to get some sleep, Monsieur Novak.'

'I thought that's what you were trying to do?' he replied, with a weary half-smile, as Marie entered the lounge. 'Didn't the doctor give you something to help you sleep?'

'I didn't take it,' she told him. 'Would you like some coffee?'

'No, thanks. It's all I've been drinking since I got back to the house. Come and sit down. To tell you the truth, I could do with the company.'

She sat on the sofa beside him, elbows resting on her knees, hands clasped tightly together. 'I should have insisted on going with them, for John's sake,' she said.

'You've got to stop blaming yourself, Marie. Look what happened to you when you did try to do something,' he said, indicating the bruise under her eye where Kilgarry had hit her with the barrel of his gun.

'That's what I keep telling myself, but it doesn't make it any easier,' she replied.

'I feel exactly the same. What if I'd done this or that differently? I've played every possible scenario over and over in my head. It doesn't help, but I can't stop thinking about it.'

'I am responsible for John when you're not here,' she said, continuing as if she hadn't heard him. 'That's what we agreed when I took the job. I should have done more to try and stop them taking him.'

'And have got yourself killed? Because that's what would have happened, Marie. Those men are assassins. They would have had no qualms about killing you if you'd got in their way. There's nothing more you could have done. Not without endangering your own life.'

Marie turned her head slowly to look at Novak. There were tears in her eyes. 'He's all alone. I know that Mrs Grant is with him, but she isn't very comfortable with children. She will not know how to respond to him if he needs her support.'

'Don't underestimate her,' Novak said firmly. 'She'll be there for him if he needs her.'

'You like her, don't you?'

'You almost make it sound like an accusation. But yeah, I like Beth. She grows on you.'

'So do warts! That's what my father used to say.'

'So you obviously *don't* like her.'

'No . . . I don't know,' Marie said thoughtfully. 'She hardly spoke to me. I got the impression that she's a cold, distant woman. Maybe I'm wrong.'

'I think you are. I thought that too when I first met her but maybe it's her way of keeping people at arm's length until she's had a chance to get to know them better.'

'Do you think you'll . . . well, see more of her after this is over?' Marie asked.

'I hadn't even thought about it,' he replied. 'It would never work, though. We're based in different countries and I'm perfectly happy as I am. I've got John. What more could I want?'

'It was just a thought, that's all,' she said, then got to her feet. 'I am going to make myself some coffee anyway. Are you sure you don't want one?'

'Yeah, why not?' he said, and handed his empty mug to her. 'It's not as if I need to worry about the caffeine keeping me awake. I'm not going to get a wink of sleep until I know that John's safe.'

'Wake up!' Voskov shook Strohmaier's shoulder roughly.

Strohmaier groaned, but didn't open his eyes. Voskov took a bottle of smelling-salts from his pocket, opened it and wafted it under Strohmaier's nose. The reaction was immediate. Strohmaier pulled back his head sharply, his face screwed up in disgust. His eyes opened.

'Come on, wake up!' Voskov slapped his cheek.

'I'm awake, I'm awake,' Strohmaier muttered, but when he tried to sit up a sharp pain shot through his temples. He lowered his head back on to the seat, rubbing his eyes with his thumb and forefinger.

'You want me to use the smelling-salts again?' Voskov threatened.

'No, please.' Strohmaier raised his other hand in front of his face. He sat up slowly, his eyes still closed. 'Where are we?' he asked.

'In the parking bay at the rear of your office block,' Voskov told him. 'Is there any other way into the building other than through the main entrance?'

'What?' Strohmaier asked groggily. He jerked his head back when the smelling-salts were brushed under his nose again. His eyes opened. 'I'm awake. What did you say?'

'Is there another way into the building, other than through the main entrance?'

'Yes, there's a back door.'

'Do you have a key?'

'Yes. But why don't we just use the front door? There's no security guard on duty. It's Saturday.'

'There's a car parked out front. One occupant. It could be a plainclothes cop. I can't afford to take any chances,' Voskov said. Strohmaier patted the pocket of his jeans. 'Looking for these?' Voskov shook the bunch of keys he had taken from Strohmaier while he had been unconscious.

Strohmaier took the keys and selected one. 'That opens the back door.'

'Then let's go.' Voskov pulled him out of the car.

'Take it easy,' Strohmaier complained. 'My head's killing me. Jesus, what was in that sedative you gave me?'

'Just open the door.'

Strohmaier paused when they reached it, the key inches away from the lock. 'When do I get to speak to my wife?'

'When I've got the disk.'

'What's to stop you from killing me once you've got the disk?'

'My word,' Voskov replied.

'And that's supposed to reassure me?'

Voskov took the SIG-Sauer P-225 automatic discreetly from the holster at the back of his trousers and held it against his stomach, on the off-chance that they had been observed from one of the surrounding buildings. 'Open the door, or I'll kill you now.'

'Then you'll never get the disk.'

'You wouldn't have to worry about that, would you?' Voskov said coldly.

Strohmaier unlocked and opened the door. Voskov saw the infrared beam at ankle level after he had shoved Strohmaier inside. It was probably connected to a system either at the nearest police station or at a private security firm that serviced the building. No wonder Strohmaier had been so compliant.

His first thought was to take out his anger on the lawyer, but time was against him and if he let Strohmaier think he hadn't seen it he would be more likely to open the safe, believing help was on the way. He closed the door behind him and followed Strohmaier to the elevator.

'I know exactly where your offices are, so don't bother pushing the wrong button,' Voskov said. 'Just remember, the sooner I get the disk, the sooner you see your family again.' He glanced at his watch as he stepped into the elevator behind Strohmaier. Chances were that the plainclothes policeman out front would have been alerted and sent in to investigate. That didn't bother him unduly. What did was the thought of additional back-up being dispatched to the scene, which would hinder his escape. He had to make what time he had left count to his advantage. The moment the doors parted he pushed Strohmaier into the corridor and marched him to the office that bore his name. Strohmaier used another key to unlock it and the two men went inside.

'The disk,' Voskov said.

Strohmaier's hands were trembling as he struggled to open the safe. It took several attempts before he got the combination right. He removed the padded envelope Ian Grant had given him earlier in the week and Voskov gestured for him to put it on the desk. 'Now let me speak to my wife,' Strohmaier blurted out, hand outstretched for Voskov's cellphone.

'Use your own.' Voskov slit open the envelope and tilted the disk out on to his palm.

Strohmaier snatched up the receiver and punched in the digits of his home number. 'Sweetheart, is that you?'

'Dietmar?' His wife sounded surprised.

'Are you all right? Are the kids safe?'

'Yes, of course. Why do you ask?'

'Have they mistreated you in any way?'

'Dietmar, what are you talking about?'

'Oh, my God.' Strohmaier realized that he had been tricked.

'Dietmar, what's going on?'

Strohmaier didn't reply. Instead he looked round slowly at Voskov, who had already screwed a suppressor on to the end of the automatic, which was now aimed at him. 'You should have called my bluff back at the hotel,' Voskov said, then shot Strohmaier twice through the heart.

'Dietmar? Dietmar?' his wife shouted. 'Dietmar? Are you there?'

Voskov retrieved the handset and dropped it back into its cradle, abruptly cutting her off. He checked Strohmaier's pulse. Satisfied that he was dead, he left the office and closed the door behind him. He knew he didn't have much time now. It was imperative that he get out of the building and away, even if it meant abandoning the car. Ignoring the elevator, he made his way to the stairs and threw open the door. The young policeman who had been in the parked car out front when Voskov had first driven past the building was on the stairs directly below him, automatic in hand. For a split second their eyes met.

'Voskov?' the policeman gasped, recognizing him from the photographs Kessler had given him before he took up his vigil outside the building.

That the man knew his name caught Voskov off-guard. His mind was still reeling when he saw the policeman raising the automatic towards him. With the SIG-Sauer at his side, he knew he would never be able to raise it in time before the policeman got off a shot so he fired twice from the hip. One of the bullets tore through the policeman's leg and he stumbled backwards, grabbing at the rail to steady himself. Voskov's next bullet ripped through the policeman's heart. The Russian was already bounding down the stairs two at a time before his victim's body had hit the ground. Within seconds he had reached the back door. Easing it open, he peered out into the parking bay. It was deserted but as he ran towards the car he could already hear sirens in the distance. And they were getting louder. The car was no longer an option. He climbed the perimeter fence, swung his legs over the top, and was still clambering down the other side when the first of the police cars screeched to a halt in front of the building. He jumped the last few feet to the ground and sprinted through an alleyway. The sirens continued to wail. He ran through a second alleyway. Then a third, and a fourth. Only then did he feel safe and he was able to pause, hands on knees, to catch his breath.

Questions flooded through his mind. How had the policeman known who he was? Did the authorities know their identities? If so, who had sold them out? And why? There was only one person who could answer those questions. The only person, as far as he was aware, who knew their true identities. He felt vulnerable. The sooner he spoke to Sammy Kahn, the sooner he would get those answers . . .

'It was Jago who told Kessler about you.'

'And how did Jago know?'

'He works for the Cabal,' Kahn replied.

'Why wasn't I told about this?'

'You're on a need-to-know basis. Jago's my senior contact at Interpol. The perfect mole. Or so I thought. Now I'm not so sure. I think he could be a double agent. Now I have no idea where his true loyalties lie. But don't worry, I've got the situation in hand. The local authorities have agreed to bring him in should they need to negotiate the release of the hostages. And, as I've already told you, I believe that Grant was getting his inside information either from Kilgarry or Racine. So once the authorities have been tipped off as to their whereabouts, Jago will be sent in to negotiate with them. Except he thinks that I'm going to tell Kilgarry and Racine that he's on our side to lull them into a false sense of security so that he can take them out with a gun that's been hidden in the chalet. What he doesn't know is that I'm going to tell them about the gun so that when he goes for it they'll kill him. And once the shooting starts, the police will storm the chalet. Kilgarry and Racine won't let themselves be taken alive. That way I get rid of Jago and the informer, without making it appear suspicious, and there's no comeback on the Cabal.'

'What happens to me now that the authorities know who I am?' Voskov asked. 'I'm finished, and you know it.'

'On the contrary,' Kahn assured him. 'The Cabal always rewards loyalty. You, of all people, should know that by now.'

'I've always been paid well, if that's what you mean. But what good will I be to the Cabal if my face is known to every police force in the world? I can't even go back to Russia now. I'd be arrested the moment I step off the plane.'

'The Russian authorities won't touch you. You have my word.'

'All you are to me is a voice on the phone. So you'll forgive me if I'm a little sceptical about taking your word at *face* value.'

'OK, tell me what you want, and I'll arrange it for you.'

'Kill me.'

'*What?*' Kahn was amazed.

'Kill Petr Voskov – and make sure it's given added credence by one of your senior contacts in government. That way I'll be left in peace. I want a new identity with all the relevant papers. I also want two million dollars to be deposited in an account to be designated by me.'

'That can be arranged. Where will you go?'

'I haven't decided yet.'

'Do you want to take your family with you?' Kahn asked.

'Petr Voskov's dead. Even they have to believe that for it to work.' A rare, albeit sad smile raised the corners of his mouth. 'My daughter means more to me than anything else in the world. I took this job to secure her future. Which I have, only I won't be around to see it. Somewhat ironic, don't you think?'

'I'll set it up for you. It'll take a bit of time, though. So if you need somewhere to stay—'

'I can take care of myself,' Voskov cut in. 'Once you've set it up, and I'm satisfied with the arrangements, I'll give you the disk.'

'If I didn't know better, I'd almost be inclined to think you were trying to blackmail me.' Kahn chuckled.

'*Quid pro quo*, Sammy, that's all it is.'

'There is one last job I'll need you to handle before you do leave the country. Kill Amy Michaels. I don't know whether she's seen the contents of the disk or not. If she did, that makes her the one person still capable of bringing down the Cabal.'

'That's your problem now, not mine.'

'If I were to go down, you can be sure that I'd be naming names to save my own neck. And guess whose name will be top of the list? *Quid pro quo*, Petr, that's all it is.'

The line went dead.

Oliver Strauss had been an informer for the Cabal since its inception. Not that he knew the organization by name. Nor did he know the name of his contact who only ever spoke to him over the phone. Not that it bothered him. Not for the kind of retainer he was on each month. He always received the same amount, irrespective of whether he was contacted or not. Sometimes he wouldn't hear anything for months, but when he did he made the call his first priority. Everything else was put on hold until he had the information Kahn wanted.

He had already heard about Willie Meine's horrific death, not that it had bothered him unduly. He had never liked Meine. And, after all, he had been the competition. Not very good competition, but he had built up some useful contacts over the years, Kessler being one of them. Which was why Kahn's call to the house that morning couldn't have come at a more fortuitous moment. With Meine dead, Kessler would need a new snitch. There would be a few takers. But he now had a head start over his rivals with the information that Kahn had passed on to him. Information concerning the whereabouts of two of the most wanted men in the country . . .

'Kessler,' a voice said, after a switchboard operator had put Strauss through to his extension.

'My name's Oliver Strauss. I've passed on information to some of your colleagues in the past. You may have heard of me?'

'I've heard of you,' Kessler replied, disdain evident in his voice. 'What do you want?'

'I believe you're looking for Beth Grant and John Novak,' Strauss said. 'I know where they are. And it won't cost you anything. Call it a gesture of goodwill on my part. So the next time you want some information, you'll know who to contact. Are you interested?'

THIRTEEN

'You'll be working with Coy Seventeen,' the Chief of Police told Kessler over the phone, referring to 17 Parachuting Reconnaissance Company, the country's élite Special Forces unit. 'They've had a team on standby ever since the hostage situation first broke.'

'Who's the team leader?' Kessler asked, with some trepidation, as if he already knew the answer.

'Colonel Manfred Lehmann.'

'Why doesn't that surprise me?' he said resignedly.

'Do you have a problem with that, Kessler?' the Chief inquired. 'I was told by Coy Seventeen's commanding officer that you and Lehmann go back a long way. Childhood friends, I believe?'

'Yes, sir, that's right. It's just that . . .' Kessler stared at the framed photograph of his son on the desk in front of him. 'Who will be in charge of the operation, sir? Colonel Lehmann or myself?'

'Colonel Lehmann will be in overall command. I appreciate that this is your case but this will be a skilled military operation and Coy Seventeen have been trained to deal with such situations.'

'Sir, you almost make it sound as if they'll be going in with guns blazing. I thought you'd agreed that we should use Jago to negotiate with the kidnappers?'

'I'm well aware as to what was agreed, Kessler,' the Chief

replied gruffly, 'but you know as well as I do that the final decision rests with the President and the Federal Council. They're in emergency session right now. I'll let you know their ruling just as soon as it's passed on to me. In the meantime, stick to the original plan. Lehmann and his team have been fully briefed. He's expecting you at Kloten Airport within the hour. Freight section. Pick Jago up from his hotel on your way.'

'Yes, sir.'

'And, Kessler, good luck.'

'Thank you, sir.'

Kessler waited until the Chief had hung up before replacing the receiver. His eyes went back to the picture of Andreas, but his thoughts were with his wife. She had been on his mind constantly since she had walked out on him. So many different emotions had filtered through him in that time. Anger that she had left him. Then emptiness, remorse, and, finally, anger again. Only now the anger was aimed at himself for the way he had treated her. She deserved so much better. As he had lain awake the previous night, he had wanted to call her. So many times. Just to hear her voice, to know that she and the baby were safe. Now he must make amends – or at least take the first faltering step in the right direction. Yet he found he couldn't do it. *She deserved so much better.*

He would call her when he got back. That way he would have the chance to speak to Manny first and assess the situation. Yet he knew he was avoiding responsibility for his behaviour. But he had never found it easy to admit that he was wrong. It went with the job. Or so he had always convinced himself in the past. It had always been the easy way out. Only he knew there was no easy way out this time, not if he wanted Marthe back. But making the first move was going to be a lot harder than he had anticipated. First he had to come to terms with his own con-science, and that was going to be the hardest part of all . . .

*

Kessler picked up Jago from his hotel but little was said *en route* to the airport, a thirty-minute drive from the city centre. Shortly before reaching the terminal building, Kessler exited the highway on to a side road marked 'Freight' and continued for another five hundred yards until he reached a boom gate. A security guard emerged from a hut, carrying a clipboard, and approached the driver's window. Kessler held up his warrant card. The security guard checked the clipboard, nodded, then peered into the car at Jago, who pulled out his own ID and proffered it. The security guard checked the name, gave Kessler directions, then reached back into the hut to open the gate. Kessler drove to a white Aérospatiale Puma helicopter, which was standing in front of one of the vast Swissair hangars. A couple of soldiers, clad in camouflage fatigues, were standing by the open cabin door and one, a sergeant, hurried across to the car as it drew to a halt.

'Thank you, sir,' the sergeant said when Kessler showed him his warrant card. 'Colonel Lehmann's in the hangar with the rest of the team, going through a final weapons check. If you'd care to come with me, sir, I'll take you to him.'

'Come on, let's go,' Kessler said to Jago, then opened the driver's door and stepped out.

'Just you, sir,' the sergeant said to Kessler, as Jago got out of the passenger side.

'This is Ralf Jago. From Interpol,' Kessler said. 'It was cleared with the Chief of Police for him to accompany us as a negotiator.'

'I wouldn't know about that, sir. My orders are to admit you to the hangar. Nobody else.'

'Whose orders are they?' Kessler demanded indignantly. 'Colonel Lehmann's?'

'Yes, sir.'

'I'd like to speak to him about that.' The soldier hesitated. 'Now, Sergeant!'

'Sir.' The sergeant crossed to the hangar and disappeared inside.

'What the hell's going on?' Jago asked.

'Looks like the Federal Council's finally reached its decision.' Kessler banged his fist angrily on the roof of the car. 'It doesn't make any sense. Why would they deliberately freeze you out like this?'

Jago knew the answer, although he had no intention of telling Kessler. Outside pressure. And Sammy Kahn would have been involved in the final decision somewhere down the line. Only that's what didn't make any sense to him. Not after all the careful planning to get him into the chalet. No, Kahn was up to something. Of that he was sure. But what? And why?

'Stefan, good to see you,' Manfred Lehmann called as he came out of the hangar, the sergeant following close behind him. Like the others, Lehmann was wearing camouflage fatigues and also had a pair of snow goggles hanging loosely around his neck. He shook Kessler's hand, but Kessler knew the greeting was for the benefit of those around them.

'What the hell's going on, Manny? Why isn't Jago being brought in on this? He's an experienced negotiator. He also knows the Cabal better than any of us.'

'I have my orders, Stefan.' Lehmann nodded acknowledgement to Jago. 'I'm sorry, Mr Jago, but this is as far as you go. I'll see to it that you're taken back to your hotel.'

'And just what are your orders, Manny?' Kessler pressed.

'You'll be briefed before we leave.'

'I know what his orders are,' Jago said. 'Shoot to kill. Am I right, Colonel?'

'Sergeant, would you see that Mr Jago is driven back to his hotel?' Lehmann ignored the question. 'Have one of the back-up team take him.'

'Sir, if you'd care to follow me?' the sergeant said to Jago.

'This is not right.' Jago stood his ground. 'I want to speak to your commanding officer.'

'Mr Jago,' Lehmann said, 'either you leave voluntarily or you will be forcibly removed.'

'There will be no need for violence,' Jago said, and followed the sergeant to a car.

Kessler grabbed Lehmann's arm as he was about to walk back to the hangar. 'I know you're angry with me because of what happened with Marthe. And you've got every right to be. But this isn't the time for recriminations. We've got to work together on this because if anything happens to those hostages we're going to be the ones crucified by the press. And you know it.'

'This has nothing to do with you and Marthe, and I resent the implication that it has. I'm a professional, Stefan.' Lehmann pulled his arm free. 'Come with me.'

'So what exactly were you told by your commanding officer, Manny?' Kessler asked, as they walked away from the hangar.

'That the Federal Council had voted against bringing Jago in on the operation.' Lehmann pushed his hands into his pockets. 'They believe the kidnappers would never surrender voluntarily, and that there was every chance Jago would be taken as an additional hostage. What good would that do us?'

'Is it a shoot-to-kill policy?'

Lehmann stared at the ground then shook his head. 'No,' he said. 'It's not. My orders are to launch a surprise attack on the chalet. It's the only way the Federal Council believe we can release the hostages unharmed. Understandably, that's their main concern right now. What happens to the kidnappers is secondary. But there's no shoot-to-kill policy. You have my word on that.'

'And what exactly does this "surprise attack" entail?' Kessler asked.

'From the reports the advance team have already relayed back to headquarters, it's obvious that there's too much open ground around the chalet for us to approach the area on skis.

Which leaves only an air assault. The advance team will fire stun grenades into the chalet to cause maximum confusion moments before my team abseil from the helicopter. The kidnappers will have been temporarily blinded and deafened by the stun grenades and they'll be in no condition to put up any resistance.'

'*If* the stun grenades are successful,' Kessler countered. 'And what if they're not?'

'As I said, the fate of the kidnappers is secondary. If they resist arrest, we'll take the necessary counter-measures. And if that means having to kill them to protect ourselves, or to ensure the safety of the hostages, so be it.'

'That's exactly what the authorities want to happen. You and your men are being used, Manny, can't you see that?'

'The politics of this don't interest me, Stefan. My only concern is for the safety of the hostages, and if I can get them out safely without losing any of my men in the process then the operation will have been a success.' Lehmann took a packet of cigarettes from his pocket and lit one. 'Why the sudden concern for the welfare of these men? One of them butchered a mother and her six-year-old daughter in cold blood.'

'He also executed an unarmed policeman who happened to be under my command at the time,' Kessler added. 'Another killed a second policeman earlier this morning, along with one of Zürich's most prominent criminal lawyers. I had to break the news of their deaths to the families. So you can drop the sarcasm. The politics don't interest me either. What does is seeing that these men stand trial for what they've done. This isn't about vengeance, Manny, it's about justice. And if you weren't so blinkered in your eagerness to carry out your orders then maybe – just maybe – you would be able to see that.'

'You'd better go and get changed. There's a snowsuit for you in the hangar. You'll be dropped off before we reach the chalet. A member of the advance team will take you to a predesignated area close to the chalet. Once the operation's over, the kidnappers will be officially handed over to you, although my men will accompany them back to Zürich.'

'So I'm not even going to be a part of the assault team?' Kessler said.

'My unit has rehearsed this kind of scenario dozens of times. We work off each other. We trust each other. You're not part of the team, Stefan.' Lehmann wagged a warning finger at Kessler. 'Just remember, this is my operation. I call the shots. If you ever question my authority again, especially in front of my men, you will be left behind. Is that clear?'

'It's your conscience, Manny,' Kessler said icily.

Lehmann ground out his cigarette underfoot then strode back to the hangar.

Jago had waited until the sergeant left, then climbed out of the car and dialled Kahn's number on his cellphone. It was answered after the first ring.

'I thought I told you not to call me on this number again,' Kahn snapped after Jago had identified himself.

'And I thought you'd made all the necessary arrangements with the local authorities to get me into that chalet so that I could take out Kilgarry and Racine.'

'I did. What's happened?'

'The Federal Council voted to send in the Special Forces instead of using me as a negotiator, that's what's happened. I'm not even allowed on the helicopter.' Jago stopped when Kahn started to chuckle softly down the line. 'I don't see anything remotely funny about any of this. What if the Special Forces take Kilgarry and Racine alive? Even if one of them was captured it would be disastrous, especially if it turned out to be the mole who was passing information on to Grant.'

'On the contrary, I think it's turned out for the best. I know that the President consulted several other heads of government to find out how best to handle the situation. They made it perfectly clear that they don't want any survivors, otherwise you would have been sent in as a negotiator. After all, they don't know you're working for the Cabal. So by sending in a Special Forces unit, they're forcing Kilgarry and Racine to take a stand. The moment they open fire, the Special Forces will reply in kind.'

'And what about the hostages?' Jago demanded. 'They could be caught in the crossfire.'

'You're getting tedious, Jago. I've already told you, I don't care about the hostages. All I'm concerned about is protecting the Cabal. You'd do well to start thinking along those lines too. After all, you're still a part of it. And you will be until I say otherwise. Now don't call me again unless it's something important!' The line went dead.

Kessler sat silently in the back of the helicopter. He hadn't said a word since it left the airport twenty minutes earlier. Some of the men around him had been joking with each other in an attempt to ease the tension as they neared the prearranged rendezvous with a second Coy 17 unit, which had been sent ahead to recce the area in anticipation of the proposed strike on the chalet, depending on the outcome of the vote at government level. Now that vote was known, the advance team's report would be vital to the success of the mission. Kessler looked at the faces opposite him and they stared back. He was regarded as an outsider, which was why no one had spoken to him. Even Lehmann, sitting beside him, had joined in the laughter. But this was their operation. He was along for the ride, simply because it had been his case. Professional etiquette. Nothing more.

He knew that the members of the ultra-secretive Coy 17, part of the 4th Air Force Regiment, were unique to the world of the Special Forces in that none were career soldiers. All were reservists and each had to keep up to the physical standards required in his own spare time. He had nothing but respect for these men and their dedication to duty. A typical Swiss trait, he thought proudly.

'You ready?' Lehmann asked, nudging Kessler in the ribs.

'Have we reached the rendezvous already?' Kessler asked. Lehmann nodded.

It turned out to be a rectangular helipad situated close to the summit cable-car station which, when the ski resort was open, was used as a landing site for the air ambulance to transport injured skiers to hospital. The advance team had already cleared the helipad of snow and the Aérospatiale Puma was able to touch down on the large H encircled in the centre of the concrete square. Lehmann tapped Kessler's arm, got to his feet and scrambled out of the helicopter. Kessler went after him, but the rest of the five-man team remained on board.

Lehmann returned the salute of the man in the white ski suit, identical to the one Kessler was wearing, and they spoke briefly together in hushed tones.

Lehmann then brought Kessler into the conversation. 'There've been positive sightings of two of the three kidnappers inside the chalet. Kilgarry and Racine. No sign of Voskov. It doesn't mean that he's not in there, though.'

'What about the hostages?' Kessler asked.

'Nothing so far. But the kidnappers are moving about freely inside the chalet, without balaclavas, which would suggest that the hostages are probably secured in one of the rooms. Racine has been seen going upstairs twice in the last few hours with food – and on both occasions he was wearing his balaclava.'

'So the hostages are almost certainly being held in one of the upstairs rooms,' Kessler concluded.

'Which means they'll be out of the way when we hit the chalet – and that can only work in our favour,' Lehmann said.

'Assuming that one of the kidnappers isn't in the room with the hostages,' Kessler replied. 'What if Voskov's guarding them? It would explain why he hasn't been seen up to now.'

'It's possible,' Lehmann conceded.

'But you don't think so?'

'No. If they're in one of the upstairs rooms, possibly hand-cuffed to a bed or a radiator, why the need for a guard? It's not as if they can go anywhere. That chalet's in the middle of nowhere. It's the perfect hide-out.' Lehmann beckoned the advance team member over to them. 'This is Bauer. He'll take you as close as he can to the chalet. Bauer, this is Inspector Kessler. He's in charge of the criminal investigation into the kidnappings.'

'How do you do, sir?' Bauer said.

'I'll let you know once this is all over,' Kessler replied.

'Don't worry about him, Bauer,' Lehmann said, with a half-smile. 'He's really an optimist at heart. The inspector's skis are in the helicopter. Would you get them for him?'

'Sir.' Bauer crossed to the helicopter.

Lehmann unclipped the holster on his belt, removed his SIG-Sauer P-226 automatic and extended it towards Kessler. 'I know it's strictly against regulations for me to lend my sidearm, but I'd prefer it if you were armed. You never know, you might need it.'

'What about you?' Kessler eyed the weapon in Lehmann's hand.

'Don't worry about me. I'll be going in with our standard SG 550 assault rifle. And, believe me, I'd rather have that in a fire-fight than the automatic. Take it, Stefan.'

Kessler slipped it into the fur-lined pocket of his ski suit. He held out a hand towards Lehmann. 'You take care, Manny.'

'I always do, that's why I'm still around.' Lehmann gripped his friend's hand. 'Aren't you even going to wish me good luck?'

'Since when were you ever superstitious? You make your own luck, you know that.'

'I hope you're right.'

Lehmann ran back to the helicopter, his body doubled over as he neared it to avoid the rotors whirring above him. He looked round at Kessler a last time, then disappeared into the helicopter. Bauer hurried across to Kessler, the skis tucked under one arm, and both men silently watched the helicopter rise into the air. Only when the engine had faded did Bauer hand the skis to Kessler.

'How far is the chalet from here?' Kessler asked, as they walked to the edge of the helipad to allow him to clip on the skis.

'About a mile, sir. The helicopter will fly over the area a couple of times to let the men get accustomed to the layout. After all, it'll be the first time they'll have seen the chalet.'

'And the only time before they go in,' Kessler added.

Bauer put on his skis then slipped on a lightweight communications headset, which consisted of an earpiece attached to one end of a thin strip of metal, which ran down the side of his face to a microphone at the other end. 'I know these men, sir,' he said, casting a sidelong glance at Kessler. 'They'll pull it off. I've no doubt of that.'

'Just as long as they don't underestimate the opposition,' Kessler said to himself, as Bauer set off down the slope. Then, securing the goggles over his eyes, he dug the poles into the soft snow and went after him.

He had always considered himself a good skier, although not in Marthe's league. *How I miss her.* The thought flashed through his mind. Not that it surprised him. He did miss her. He had to see her. Speak to her. Plead with her. Get her back. Yet he knew that might be wishful thinking.

Bauer arced his skis sharply in front of him and halted beside a row of trees, each covered with a delicate umbrella of newly fallen snow. Kessler pulled up beside him and followed his gaze. He had no idea what Bauer was looking at.

'Do you see them, sir?' Bauer asked.

'See what?'

'That's the whole point, sir. You're not supposed to see anything,' Bauer grinned.

'I'm certainly glad we've got that cleared up,' Kessler replied sarcastically.

'Strobel?' Bauer called, and Kessler gasped when what had appeared to be a mound of snow materialized into human form and a thumb was raised to acknowledge its position.

'Can you see Reidweg and Kerzel in there, sir?'

Kessler studied the snowy ground around the foot of the trees but couldn't detect anyone. They responded to their names by raising a thumb towards Bauer. Kessler knew he could have spent another hour scrutinizing the area and still have been no nearer to identifying their positions.

'Coy Seventeen's motto is "seeing without being seen".' Bauer led Kessler into the trees. 'And that is what surveillance is all about, wouldn't you say?'

'Definitely,' Kessler agreed, as he unclipped his skis and crouched beside Bauer, who had positioned himself below the lip of a fresh layer of snow. He had taken a pair of powerful long-range binoculars from Strobel and focused them on the chalet in the distance. 'See anything?' Kessler asked. Bauer handed the binoculars to him. Kessler panned them slowly until the chalet came into view. It appeared deserted. No footprints in the snow around the door. No smoke coming from the chimney. No movement through the windows facing him . . .

Then, suddenly, a figure appeared at a window. Bottom left. Racine. The only other time he had seen him had been in a photograph. He could understand now why Grant had nick-named him Pretty Boy. Racine raised a mug to his lips and took a sip from it. Kessler could even see the steam rising from inside it. Then Racine disappeared.

'Well?' Bauer asked, as Kessler handed back the binoculars.

'I saw Racine at the window.'

'That fucking bastard,' Bauer spat, but before he could say any more he heard Lehmann's voice in his earpiece. 'Yes, sir, we're in position.' Again he listened before answering, 'We're on our way, sir. I'll let you know the moment the stun grenades hit the target.' He turned the swivel head of the small microphone away from his mouth and gave Strobel a thumbs-up. Strobel crawled out of his hiding-place and, once clear of the trees, out of sight of the chalet, he put on his skis. A moment later he had vanished from sight. 'The helicopter's in position,' Bauer told Kessler. 'Strobel and I are the company's marksmen. We've been given the task of firing the stun grenades into the chalet. Five windows. Five stun grenades. I'll be taking the three windows facing us. Strobel will take the ones at the rear.' He chuckled like a mischievous schoolboy. 'Enjoy the show, sir. It's going to be pretty spectacular once the fireworks begin.'

'Be careful, Bauer,' Kessler called softly as he slid silently over the top of the ridge. 'And good luck.'

He didn't know whether Bauer had heard him. Not that it really mattered any more. Operation Cabal had started. There was no turning back.

'How much longer do we have to wait around like this?' Kilgarry snarled. 'Where the fuck's Voskov? Why hasn't he called in to let us know what's happened? Shit, we don't even know whether he's got the disk yet.'

'Christ, will you quit whining.' Racine swung away from the window, coffee mug in hand. He walked to one of the armchairs and sat down. 'He said it might take most of the morning to get it. What do you want, a running commentary? We sit tight and wait. Those were our orders.'

'Kahn's orders,' Kilgarry retorted. 'Always Kahn's orders, aren't they?'

'What the fuck is wrong with you?' Racine put the mug on the table beside his chair. 'First you try to rape the woman. Then you want to pick a fight with me. Then with Voskov. Then you want to argue every point either of us makes. Then, when Voskov leaves, you can't stop complaining about every little thing, from the way I make coffee to the way the snow's falling off the roof. Are you claustrophobic or just a fucking pain in the ass?'

'I'm not claustrophobic,' Kilgarry replied defensively. 'I just don't like the waiting, that's all.'

'You're an ex-Marine. Weren't you ever part of an ambush?' No reply. 'Probably not. You'd have been the bait to lure them into an ambush. You'd certainly have made enough noise to attract their attention.'

'Shut up, will you?' Kilgarry grated. 'I've had just about all I can take from you.'

'The feeling's mutual, believe me,' Racine said, scornfully.

'Then maybe we should do something about it. One on one. What do you say?'

'I don't believe this,' Racine said. 'Are all Marines full of this kind of macho bullshit?'

'At least we're not faggots,' Kilgarry retorted.

'I've been wondering when you'd get round to that. In fact, I'm surprised it's taken you so long. It gets a bit tedious, you know. That's what I told the last guy who called me that. And he did it in a crowded bar as well. All so unnecessary.'

'And what did you do about it?' Kilgarry's interest had been roused.

'I played along. Invited him outside for a freebie. Even got him to drop his pants.' Racine's hand blurred as he drew the switchblade from his pocket, activated it and slashed the air inches from his face. 'You'd be amazed at how much it actually bleeds down there.'

'You cut off his prick?' Kilgarry was ashen-faced.

'Well, I sure as hell wasn't going to suck it.' Racine retracted the blade and slipped it back into his pocket.

At the sound of the alarm both men jumped to their feet, their eyes focused on the red light flashing on the receiver by the window. One of the motion detectors they had hidden around the perimeter of the chalet had been activated. They each grabbed a Heckler & Koch MP5 submachine-gun – which had been left for them at the chalet – and Kilgarry was the first to reach the window. For a moment he saw nothing. Then a movement caught his eye. The figure of Bauer lying in the snow less than a hundred yards away from the chalet. He saw the grenade launcher in Bauer's hands, lined up to fire. It was painted camouflage white and blended in, almost to perfection, with its surroundings. Almost. He smashed one of the window-panes with the barrel of the Heckler and fired a volley at the prone figure. A bullet struck Bauer in the head, killing him instantly. The grenade launcher fell from his hands and sank into the bloodied snow beside him. The alarm shrilled again. Racine was about to rush from the room to investigate when he heard glass breaking in the kitchen. Moments later the floor shuddered as the stun grenade exploded in the adjoining room. Although neither man was affected by the blast, they knew the next one could come through the lounge window and incapacitate them, leaving them incapable of defending themselves from what they already knew was a military-style attack.

Kilgarry saw a figure sprint from the trees towards his fallen comrade but before he could cut him down a scythe of bullets raked across the side of the chalet and he was forced to hurl himself to the floor in the split second before the window shattered, spraying slivers of glass over his back. He stuck the Heckler out of the window and fired blindly then ran doubled over to where Racine was standing in the hallway. The sound of breaking glass came from upstairs and a moment later a second stun grenade exploded in the bathroom. They knew they would be little more than sitting targets if they remained in the chalet. It was time to get out – fast. The snowmobiles were parked in the shed adjacent to the kitchen. They had to get to them.

'Listen!' Racine grabbed Kilgarry's arm. 'Do you hear that?'

'What?' Kilgarry was more concerned about getting the hell out of there than waiting for the next stun grenade to land at his feet. Then he heard it. Faint at first. The sound of an approaching helicopter. 'You take the woman. I'll take the kid.'

'Fuck that. I don't want any extra weight on the snowmobile. It'll only slow me down.'

'Well, I'm taking the kid as insurance.' Kilgarry bounded up the stairs, threw open the bedroom door and rushed over to where John was cowering on the bed.

'What's – going on?' Beth stammered as the sound of the helicopter grew ever nearer.

'The fucking cavalry have arrived.' Kilgarry unfastened the handcuff from the headboard and yanked John to his feet. 'You're coming with me, kid.'

'No!' John screamed, tears streaming down his face.

'You want a hostage, take me!' Beth blurted out, knowing she was disregarding her own personal safety. But it didn't matter. Suddenly nothing mattered. Not with Ian gone. John had his whole life ahead of him. What did she have to look forward to?

'No way!' Kilgarry tried to pull John away from the bed but the boy grabbed one of its legs, dragging it towards the door. Kilgarry swung the gun on Beth, his finger tight on the trigger. 'Let go, kid, or I'll kill the bitch. She's no fucking use to me any more.'

'Do it,' Beth challenged. 'Go on, pull the trigger. Or don't you have the guts.'

Kilgarry hesitated, eyeing her uncertainly, caught off-guard by the sheer venom in her voice. It almost sounded as if she wanted to die. Then the helicopter reached the chalet. The noise of the engine was deafening. Another stun grenade exploded downstairs. The sound of the blast disorientated John who unconsciously loosened his grip on the leg and Kilgarry scooped him up effortlessly, then carried him from the room. Moments later a stun grenade exploded in the bedroom. The stairs shook under Kilgarry and he yelled as he was deafened by the blast. Had he been in the room, he would have been totally disorientated and at the mercy of the assault team. Reaching the bottom of the stairs, he was about to make for the kitchen when the front door swung open, smashed in with a battering ram.

He swung the submachine-gun on two men. Although dressed in combat fatigues, he guessed that they would be well protected underneath with body armour. He lowered his aim and fired at their knees, knowing it would be one of the few unprotected areas. Both men fell under the hail of the bullets and writhed in agony in the snow. He backed into the kitchen, still thick with acrid smoke from an earlier stun grenade, kicked shut the interconnecting door, and carried John down a flight of stairs, which led into the shed. The door was half open. Racine had gone. Kilgarry dumped John on the back of the remaining snowmobile and snapped the handcuff around the rear guard.

'You'd better hang on back there, kid,' Kilgarry shouted. 'If you fall off, I'm not stopping. You'll just get dragged behind like a fucking rag doll. Got it?'

John stared at him in fright, unable to understand a word he was saying because he, too, had been deafened by the blast. Kilgarry started the snowmobile and buffeted open the door to exit the shed. He glanced up at the helicopter, hovering directly above the chalet, and his mouth curled in a sneer when he saw the marksman in the open cabin doorway pull his finger off the trigger of his sniper rifle, not daring to risk a shot in case he hit the boy. Kilgarry grabbed the handlebars tightly as the snowmobile hurtled away from the chalet, following Racine's tracks.

Kilgarry's hearing slowly returned and he became aware of the many different sounds around him. It was as if he were hearing them all for the first time. But the most worrying sound – and the only one that really interested him – was that of the helicopter. He craned his neck to look up into the sky behind him and saw not only the helicopter but three muffled figures in white snowsuits on skis. Two were armed with assault rifles. The third appeared to be unarmed. With one hand he unslung his Heckler & Koch, and fired at the skiers. One was hit and cartwheeled across the snow, one of his skis snapping off and spinning away into the trees. The marksman, harnessed in the doorway of the helicopter, opened fire and a row of bullets peppered the snow a feet feet in front of the snowmobile.

Kilgarry turned the snowmobile into a bend and, as he straightened out, saw Racine less than a hundred yards ahead. The Frenchman's back was flaked with fresh snow, as if he had taken a tumble, which would have accounted for him being that close. Racine glanced over his shoulder. Neither man acknowledged the other. Then Racine faced forward again to negotiate a route through a cluster of trees, which ended with a gentle rise in the gradient of the mountainside. He didn't slow down as he manoeuvred a path through the trees and the snowmobile's pads momentarily lifted off the snow as it skimmed over the crest of the ridge. The machine disappeared from view and Kilgarry heard Racine's scream above the sound of the tracking helicopter. Then nothing. He braked hard and the snowmobile came to a halt at the foot of the ridge. The engine spluttered and died. Using the trees as cover from the helicopter above, he scrambled off the snowmobile and peered cautiously over the ridge. The ground continued for another few feet – then ended abruptly in a sheer drop into a gorge below. Racine wouldn't have stood a chance. Not that the man's death bothered him. What did was that he was trapped. He hurried back to the snowmobile, unlocked the handcuff attached to the guard rail, then grabbed John around the chest and, holding the boy against him with the barrel of the Heckler & Koch pressed into the back of his neck, edged his way up the slope as the two remaining skiers approached the stationary snowmobile. Above the trees, ropes were tossed out through the helicopter's open cabin door and several members of the assault team abseiled to the ground. He knew that the boy was his last chance to extricate himself from a hopeless situation. He knew it might not work, but it was all he had left going for him. And if he was going to die, at least he would take the boy with him . . .

Kessler, with the two remaining members of the back-up team who had been concealed in the trees with him, had broken cover and gone after Kilgarry when they had seen him fleeing the chalet with John handcuffed to the back of the snowmobile. One had been hit when Kilgarry fired at them, but only in the thigh. Kessler and Kerzel had continued after the two snow-mobiles with the helicopter.

Kessler was the first to reach the ridge, the automatic in his hand now aimed at Kilgarry, crouched precariously close to the edge of the precipice, his arm locked around John's throat, the Heckler & Koch pushed hard into his neck.

'John, I'm Inspector Stefan Kessler,' he said, purposely speaking English so as not to provoke Kilgarry further. 'I was at your house yesterday. I spoke to your dad. Do you remember that?'

'Yes,' John croaked, barely audible.

'We're going to resolve this, John, don't worry,' Kessler assured him. 'Trust me, you won't get hurt.' He looked at Lehmann, who was standing behind him. 'Tell your men to lower their weapons and back away. You too,' he said softly. 'We don't want to panic Kilgarry.'

Lehmann nodded and the weapons were placed on the ground. He gestured for his men to retreat to the foot of the ridge.

'It's over, Kilgarry. Let him go,' Kessler said.

'Shoot me, and I'll take the boy over the precipice with me. The press will crucify you. Is that what you want?'

'What I want is for you to let him go. You can't get away, you know that.'

'Tell the helicopter to put down,' Kilgarry replied. Sweat

seeped out from under the hood of his parka and into his eyes. He blinked rapidly but it made no difference.

'Then what?'

'Just do it or I'll kill the kid.' Kilgarry wet his lips nervously.

'You know I can't do that. Put the gun down and let the boy come to me. I promise that you won't be harmed if you surrender to me now.'

'And I promise you I'll kill the kid if you don't get *that fucking helicopter down here now*,' he snarled. 'I'm going to count to five. If you haven't made the call by then, I'm going to take the kid over with me. And if you don't believe me, call my bluff.'

Kessler had no doubt that Kilgarry would kill himself rather than surrender. At least he'd given him the option. Now he had to act before the man carried out his threat.

'One,' Kilgarry bellowed.

An idea struck Kessler. If only he could get it to work. But that would entail getting John to trust him within the next few seconds.

'Two.'

'*John, mach als ob du Omachtig wirsch – wirf din Chopf nach vorna. Glaub mir*.' He had spoken to the boy in Swiss-German, assuming there was little or no chance that Kilgarry would understand what he said. Even if Kilgarry spoke German, which hadn't been mentioned in his dossier, he probably wouldn't have understood that he had said: 'John, pretend to faint – and drop your head forward. Trust me.'

Kilgarry hesitated as he was about to reach three. Yet there was a look of uncertainty in John's eyes, which troubled Kessler even more.

'What the hell did you say?' Kilgarry demanded.

'*Glaub mir, John. Glaub mir*,' Kessler begged.

For a moment he thought the boy wouldn't respond. Then, suddenly, his body went limp and his head lolled forward on to his chest. In that split second Kessler had a perfect shot. He

263

fired. The bullet struck Kilgarry above the right eye, killing him instantly. The Heckler slipped from his lifeless fingers but his arm remained locked around John's throat. John struggled to tear it away as Kilgarry's body began to fall backwards. Kessler, who was already clambering frantically through the snow towards the precipice, hurled himself forward and grabbed John's leg as he was dragged over the edge with Kilgarry. For a horrifying second he thought he had lost him, then his gloved fingers clamped around John's ankle as Kilgarry's body fell away into the abyss.

'I've got you, Andreas!' he shouted, over the sound of the helicopter hovering above them. 'I won't let you go, I promise!'

John was hanging over the edge of the precipice, only Kessler's vice-like grip on his ankle preventing him falling to his death. Then a piece of ice broke underneath his back, and he screamed as he slipped further over the edge. Kessler had no idea where the ground ended – they could both be lying on an overhang of ice for all he knew – and he was well aware that their combined weight could break off another section of ice, plunging them both to their deaths. But there was no way he was going to let go.

Suddenly Kessler felt two hands clamp around his own ankles and turned to see Lehmann lying in the snow behind him, holding on to him. The helicopter descended and a rope was tossed out through the cabin door. Lehmann released his grip on one of Kessler's ankles to grab it, and secured it firmly around Kessler's midriff before giving the pilot a thumbs-up sign. The pilot then held the helicopter steady above them as Kessler edged forward until he could grab John's other leg and drag him to safety. Then eager hands reached out to take the child once Kessler had him clear of the precipice. He was wrapped in a warm blanket but as he was about to be led away towards the helicopter he turned back to Kessler. His cheeks were streaked with tears. 'Who's Andreas?' he asked.

'What?' Kessler replied in surprise.

'You called me Andreas.' John wiped the back of his hand quickly across his cheeks. 'Why did you call me that?'

'Andreas was my son,' Kessler said. He had no recollection of uttering his name. It bewildered and unnerved him. 'He was killed last year. I'm sorry, I guess . . .' he trailed off. At that moment he didn't have an answer. He reached out to tug the edge of the blanket around John's shoulders. 'Go on, there's a medic waiting in the helicopter to take a look at you.' He watched John walk to the helicopter, then untied the rope and scrambled to the ridge.

'You could have got yourself killed, you son of a bitch,' Lehmann said sternly, then broke into a broad grin and clasped Kessler's hand. 'That was some stunt you pulled off there. I'll certainly be recommending you for a commendation after that.'

'I don't want it,' Kessler replied gruffly. 'I didn't do it for a commendation. It's something I had to do, if only to exorcise my own ghosts.'

'Excuse me, Inspector,' Kerzel said behind them. 'The helicopter's ready to take off.'

'I can make my own way back to the chalet,' Kessler told him.

'The boy won't let us take off without you on board,' Kerzel told him.

Kessler looked across at the helicopter and his eyes settled on the shivering figure through the open cabin doorway. As he made his way slowly towards it he realized that for the first time since he had lost Andreas, he was at peace with himself.

The fire had gutted the house. A once proud structure had been reduced to a blackened shell. Wisps of smoke still wafted up almost apologetically from the rubble that crisp Sunday morning on the outskirts of Livingstone Point. A crowd had gathered eagerly at the site after word of the fire had swept through town quicker than the malevolence of the blaze, which had been allowed to burn out of control for most of the night before a passing motorist had spotted smoke in the early hours of the morning and raised the alarm. By the time the town's fire engine had reached the scene there was little for the crew to do except douse down the smouldering remains of the 'old Hemmings place'.

The crowd parted when the car pulled up in the driveway and all eyes turned to look at Special Agents Frank Dawson and Jim Ellis as they got out and surveyed the devastation around them.

Sheriff Olsen used his considerable bulk to push his way through the onlookers towards the two men. 'I thought you'd already left for Jackson to catch your charter flight back to Washington,' he said, on reaching them.

'We almost had,' Dawson replied. 'We were checking out of the hotel when the proprietor told us about the fire. I sent the rest of the team on ahead to Jackson. I thought it best if we came to see for ourselves.'

'Not that there's much to see.' Ellis snorted. 'I take it nothing was saved from the house before the fire started?' He hissed angrily through his teeth when Olsen shook his head disconsolately. 'That means all the information stored on the computers has been lost. That's our whole fucking investigation up in smoke. Congratulations, Sheriff.'

'Ease up, Jim, it's not the sheriff's fault,' Dawson said. 'How did the fire start, Sheriff? Was it deliberate?'

'Sure looks that way.' Olsen put his fingers in his mouth and whistled. 'Lester, come here.' The gangly figure of Lester Burman hurried over to him and nodded a nervous greeting to the two Federal agents. 'Tell them what you told me earlier.'

'I seen the men who started the fire,' Lester said, then glanced down at his scuffed shoes. 'Well, at least, I think it was them.'

'What's that supposed to mean?' Ellis snapped irritably.

'Jim, let him speak,' Dawson said firmly. 'What did you see, Lester?'

'I couldn't sleep much last night, so I went downstairs to get myself a sandwich. I looked out of the kitchen window and I saw a pair of headlights on the approach road. That's kind of weird at that time of night. Nobody comes out here much at the best of times, never mind at two o'clock in the morning. Then I saw the truck. At first I thought my eyes were playing tricks on me. It was Henry Monroe's truck. But Henry's dead. Then I saw the two men inside. At least, I think they were men.'

'I don't follow.' Dawson frowned.

'I couldn't see their faces,' Lester said.

'Were they wearing masks?' Dawson pressed, when Lester fell silent.

'They were wearing white hoods,' Lester said, unwillingly. 'Like they were . . . you know, Klansmen. And then there's that graffiti on the tree down by the river. That's why I think it was them started the fire.'

'What graffiti?' Ellis asked.

Olsen led them to the gnarled oak tree at the edge of the river. The words had been sprayed crudely in white paint on the trunk: *Niger go home.*

'You'd think that if they were going to insult me, they'd at least get the spelling right,' Dawson said, with irony. 'I assume you do have some idea who it was, Sheriff?'

Olsen shifted uncomfortably. 'Not as yet, no. I checked out what Lester said. The truck was parked in the garage at the farm, but the doors were open and the padlock had been cut. I'm inclined to believe that he did see Henry's truck last night.'

'I suppose now you're going to tell us that you don't have any Klan activity around here,' Ellis said scornfully.

'Not that I'm aware of,' Olsen replied, 'but I'm gonna have to look into it real carefully.'

'In other words, there's going to be a whitewash,' Ellis said.

'I told you, I'm gonna investigate this thoroughly,' Olsen shot back defensively. 'And if I find that the fire was started by someone in this town, I'll make sure that they stand trial for what they done. I'm the law here. There will be no whitewash, Mr Ellis. That I can promise you now.'

'Thank you, Sheriff, I appreciate that,' Dawson said.

Ellis was about to say something when the cellphone in his jacket pocket rang. He excused himself and walked back to the car to answer it. 'I hear congratulations are in order,' a familiar voice said.

He moved out of earshot of the crowd before speaking. 'Hey, Sammy, I wasn't expecting you to call this early.'

'Why not? I hear you did a good job last night. Burned the house to the ground and blamed the KKK. I like it.'

'It's got the sheriff in a complete spin right now,' Ellis said, as he looked across at Olsen. 'Serves him right, redneck bastard. And he's got the audacity to say that he's not aware of any Klan activity in the area. Who does he think he's fooling?'

'The main thing is you've destroyed any evidence that could have been used against the Cabal. That's why I had you sent down there in the first place. To cover our tracks.'

'A pleasure, as always,' Ellis said. Then he noticed Dawson walking back towards the car. 'Hang on, I've got company,' he said, and put his hand over the mouthpiece as Dawson came into range.

'Who's on the phone?' Dawson asked. Ellis held his stare then extended the receiver towards him. Dawson took it from him. 'Hello?'

'Special Agent Dawson, good to hear your voice.'

'Sammy!' Dawson exclaimed, then opened the passenger door and got inside the car. 'How are things in Switzerland?'

'Good. You two did a great job last night. I have to admit, though, I'd have loved to have seen you dressed as a Klansman. That would have been one for the scrapbook.'

'I even sprayed some graffiti on a nearby tree – I misspelt it to add a touch of authenticity, as if one of these backwoods bigots had done it. It's got the sheriff real overheated. I doubt he's ever had anything like this to deal with before. First a decapitated body. Then a fire. It's great entertainment, I tell you.'

'I can believe it.' Kahn chuckled. 'Tell me, how did you switch the prints you took off Michaels's body?'

'Jim did that. He lifted a set of prints off the switchboard at the sheriff's office and sent them off to the crime lab in Washington. And now, with the house burned to the ground, that's the only set they've got to work with up there. But we were caught off-guard when the body was found – I thought your man was supposed to dispose of it professionally, not bury it in a shallow grave on the outskirts of town.'

'It was a bit messy, I agree, but at least he had the good sense to remove the head. I believe it's buried somewhere in Kansas. No comebacks. Just the way I like it. Once again, well done, both of you.'

Dawson switched off the cellphone then tapped on the driver's window. Ellis got in beside him. 'Do you want to go anywhere else before we drive down to Jackson?'

'No, I don't think so.' Dawson buckled up. 'I think we've finished everything we came here to do. And I won't be sorry to see the back of this place.'

'Neither will I.' Ellis started the engine.

FOURTEEN

Voskov had already come to accept that his lucrative career as an assassin for the Cabal was at an end. What he couldn't accept – what he would not accept – was that he would never see his daughter again. He would have readily forfeited the two million dollars, as well as the disk, just for one last glimpse of her before starting a new life for himself away from his family. But he knew that wasn't possible, not without putting her life at risk. And that was something he could never do . . .

He had thought of little else since talking to Kahn on the phone that morning, and with the pain that had been steadily building inside him had come an overwhelming sense of injustice and betrayal. He felt angry and bitter towards the Cabal, and towards Kahn in particular. Yet in an ironic twist, which only added to his indignation, he knew that he would have to rely on Kahn to get him out of the country and set him up with a new identity in some foreign land if he was to escape the authorities and the inevitability of spending the rest of his life behind bars. It only added to the mounting frustration he felt at his own apparent helplessness . . .

He was jarred from his reverie by his cellphone.

'Racine and Kilgarry are dead,' Kahn told him dispassionately.

'Congratulations. Now you've got what you wanted.' Voskov made no attempt to hide the contempt in his voice.

'It's not what I wanted, and you know it,' Kahn retorted. 'It was forced on me. I had to protect the future of the Cabal.'

'Have you got my money yet?'

'To the point, as always. I'll have it by this evening – although not in cash. But, then, I assume you'll want it transferred to an account in some tax haven?'

'Yes. I'll give you the details before I leave the country. What about my new passport?'

'Ready and waiting for you. I'll tell you where you can collect it once you've finished your last little bit of business out here.'

'You mean killing Amy Michaels?' Voskov said.

'Correct. Have you got transport?'

'Yes. I took the precaution of hiring an additional back-up car when I first arrived here for an emergency like this. I'm parked in a side-street in the town centre.'

'Always the pragmatist – thinking ahead, eh, Petr?' Kahn said. 'Amy Michaels is at Novak's club, Straight Street. She's been holed up there for the past few days.'

'Will anybody be about?'

'Novak's there. She rang him a short time ago at home – I've had the club's phones tapped ever since Novak got involved. He's on his way over there now to let her out. He'll deactivate the alarm, which saves you the trouble of doing it. A window's been left off the latch at the back of the club. You can get in that way. But you're going to have to move fast before she leaves. Find Novak – he'll know where she is – and kill them both, then get out. Call me once you're clear of the area. We can finalize the details of the money transfer and arrange a dead drop for the disk. Then you'll be free to leave the country.' The connection was cut.

Although most of the shops were closed, the numerous cafeterias and coffee-shops in and around the Niederdorf were open that morning, bringing the usual influx of locals and tourists into the area. Voskov found a parking space a couple of hundred yards from the club but felt a surge of anxiety as he got out of the car – what if he was recognized? He removed a peaked cap from the glove compartment and tugged it firmly over his head. Hardly a disguise, but it made him feel less exposed. Instinctively he touched the automatic holstered at the back of his jeans then got out and locked the driver's door. Head bowed, he dug his hands into his pockets as he strode briskly towards his destination.

He paused on reaching the mouth of the alleyway at the side of the club, glanced around and, satisfied that nobody was taking any notice of him, ducked down the narrow passage and continued until he reached a small courtyard at the back of the building. It was deserted. He pulled on a pair of black leather gloves, then hauled himself up on to an ornamental ledge underneath the row of windows overlooking the courtyard. Using it as a support, he edged his way along, checking each window in turn until he found the one that had been left off the latch. He hooked his fingers under the frame, gently eased it open then climbed inside and closed it behind him. He was in the small kitchen at the back of the club. He jumped nimbly to the floor. Removing the automatic from the holster, he crossed to a pair of white swing doors, which led into a corridor. He used the tips of his gloved fingers to push one open and winced when it squeaked on its hinges.

As he left the kitchen, he noticed two more doors leading off the corridor. The nearest was marked: BACKSTAGE – AUTHORIZED PERSONNEL ONLY. He tried it. It was locked. He assumed that the second door led into the club. He moved cautiously down the corridor and pressed himself up against the wall adjacent to the second door, then peered through the glass panel but pulled his head back sharply on seeing the two men seated at one of the tables near the stage. One was Novak. The other was unknown to him. Taking a deep breath, he peered through the glass again. The men were deep in conversation. He scanned the rest of the room but there was no sign of Amy Michaels. Tightening his grip on the automatic, he pushed open the door . . .

'Voskov!' Jago gasped when the Russian appeared, automatic trained on the two men at the table.

A look of uncertainty flickered across Voskov's face but he quickly regained his composure. 'You have me at a disadvantage. Novak I already know. But I don't believe we've ever met before.'

'Ralf Jago.'

'Ah, so you're Jago,' Voskov said. 'Kahn told me about you. The double agent. Tell me, where do your true loyalties lie? With the Cabal, or with Interpol?'

Jago sensed that Novak was now looking at him, waiting for an explanation. 'It's true, I was working as a double agent,' he admitted. 'It was the only way Interpol could get someone inside the Cabal.'

'That's not the way I heard it, but, then, it's really not important any more.' Voskov's eyes went to Novak. 'Where's Amy Michaels?'

'I'm right here.' She stepped into the doorway at the back of the room.

Novak's initial surprise at hearing her voice was swept aside in an instant when he saw the silenced Beretta in her hand. It was aimed at Voskov, who turned his head slowly towards her, without moving the rest of his body. He was still twisting round to fire when her first shot took him in the ribs, punching him back against the wall. The automatic slipped from his grasp and tumbled across the carpet, coming to rest underneath a table. He knew he could never reach it before she got off another shot. The pain in his side was excruciating, and he could feel the blood seeping through his fingers as he clutched his hand to the wound.

'I'm unarmed,' he said, as she approached him, the Beretta held at arm's length. 'You can see I'm unarmed. I surrender. Jago, I surrender!'

Jago, who had pulled a 9mm Glock from a concealed shoulder holster underneath his loose-fitting jacket the moment she had fired, got to his feet, the weapon trained on her. 'Put the gun down, Amy.' No response. 'I said, put the gun down.' Still no response.

She fired twice in rapid succession. Both bullets struck Voskov in the heart, and there was a look of disbelief in his eyes as his body swayed before he toppled forward on to the carpet. Only then did she look at Jago and a faint smile tugged the corners of her mouth. She swung the Beretta towards him. He fired. She stumbled backwards and collided with a table, which overturned as she fell heavily to the floor. She lay motionless, face down, the Beretta still in her hand.

Jago approached her cautiously and knocked the automatic from her fingers with his foot then kicked it away before crouching down and turning her on to her back. The front of her T-shirt was covered in blood. He checked for a pulse. 'She's still alive,' he shouted to Novak, who was standing in front of the stage, struggling to comprehend what he had just witnessed. 'I'll ring for the paramedics,' Jago said, pulling his cellphone from his jacket pocket. 'Get me some towels to help stem the bleeding.' No response. 'Novak, snap out of it! Get me some towels before she bleeds to death.'

'Yes, of course.' Novak was startled out of his shock by the urgency in Jago's voice. He hurried through to the kitchen and grabbed several clean towels before running back into the club where Jago was still crouched over Amy, his hand pressed tightly over her breastbone.

'An ambulance is on its way but I've still got to call the police,' Jago told him, then took the top towel off the pile Novak had dropped on the floor beside him and placed it on her breastbone. 'Hold the towel firmly over the wound,' he snapped at Novak, 'and, whatever you do, don't release the pressure – it could kill her.'

Novak took Jago's place at her side. Jago wiped his hands on a second towel, which he tossed on to a nearby table, then got to his feet and used his cellphone again to call the police.

'I – I still can't believe any of this,' Novak stammered, after Jago had finished talking on the cellphone and slipped it back into his pocket.

'You're not the only one,' Jago said, beside him again. 'OK, you can let go now. I'll continue applying the pressure until the paramedics arrive.'

Novak sat down at a nearby table. 'The call I got from Kessler earlier to say that John and Beth were both safe and on their way back here was the best news I could have got. And now this happens. None of it makes any sense. I mean ... where did she get the gun from? And why did she shoot him when he was unarmed? His evidence could have cleared her of killing Ian Grant. I don't understand any of this.'

'I'm as much in the dark as you are, Novak. She's the only one who knows why she did it. And we're going to have to wait until she's recovered sufficiently before we get those answers.'

She groaned softly, and a moment later her eyes fluttered open. She tried to speak but no sound came from her mouth. 'Don't try to talk, Amy. Just lie still and conserve your energy,' Jago told her. 'An ambulance is already on its way. You're going to be all right.' He spoke in a lowered tone to Novak. 'Can you unlock the front door and show the paramedics through once they get here? They shouldn't be long now.'

'Of course,' Novak replied, and went to the front door, which he unlocked and opened, grateful to step out into the cobbled street. He sucked in several mouthfuls of air as he looked around in vain for any sign of the paramedics. A couple of tourists approached the club but he told them that it was closed. He remained in the doorway, hands in his pockets, scanning the length of the street, knowing that Amy was fast losing blood and that every minute was crucial to her chances of surviving.

At last he heard the approaching siren in the distance. It grew steadily louder until the ambulance reached the foot of the adjacent street and there were several sharp blasts on the horn to scatter the pedestrians. Moments later it came into view. He beckoned towards it and shouted angrily at a couple who got in its way as it negotiated its way through the tables and chairs outside the surrounding cafeterias before drawing to a halt in front of the club. A crowd had already gathered around it even before the two paramedics got out and retrieved the stretcher from the back of the vehicle. He stepped aside to allow them past then locked the door again and led them through to where Jago was still with Amy, a fresh towel now in place. The paramedics took over from Jago and, after checking under the towel, one set up an intravenous drip, attached it to her arm then, between them, they lifted her carefully on to the stretcher before covering her with a blanket.

'I'll go with her to the hospital,' Jago said to Novak.

'What about Voskov?' Novak asked uncertainly.

'He's dead,' Jago replied.

'I guessed that much,' Novak said. 'Aren't they going to take him too?'

'He can't be moved without authorization from the local police. They should be here any minute now. Tell them I've gone to the hospital and that I'll be back to give them a statement just as soon as I know Amy's condition.'

Novak led the way back to the front door, opened it, and watched as the stretcher was loaded into the back of the ambulance. The doors were closed by the driver, who climbed back behind the wheel, put on the siren, and manoeuvred the vehicle down the same road it had come. Novak watched from the doorway until it had disappeared, then retreated inside and closed the door before any of the morbid bystanders could question him about the incident. He needed a drink. He returned to the club and paused to look down at the lifeless body of Voskov before going behind the counter. He was about to pour himself a shot of bourbon when he checked himself. What if the cops smelt booze on his breath? No, not a good idea. He looked at his watch. Where the hell were the cops anyway? Surely they should have arrived before the ambulance. He returned to the foyer to wait for them and noticed, much to his irritation, that several inquisitive faces were peering through the window at the side of the door. He went to the sanctuary of his office, where he paced the floor for a couple of minutes before sitting down to ring the police and find out what was keeping them.

'Yes, good afternoon,' he replied, when a voice answered his call. 'This is Mike Novak, of Straight Street. I'm still waiting for the police to arrive. How long will they be?'

'I beg your pardon, sir?'

'A call was put through to you some time ago concerning a shooting at the club,' Novak said irritably.

'A shooting, sir?'

'Why am I having to repeat myself? Yes, a shooting. Look, if you didn't take the original call, put me on to the person who did.'

'One moment, sir.'

'I don't fucking believe this,' he snapped, when he was put on hold.

'Hello, are you still there, sir?' the same voice inquired a few moments later.

'Yes, I'm still here.'

'You say you're calling from Straight Street?'

'Not again! Yes, I'm Mike Novak, the owner of the club.'

'No call has been received about a shooting at your club, Mr Novak.'

'What?' Novak struggled to contain his rising anger. 'The call was made by Ralf Jago. He's with Interpol.'

'I'm sorry, sir, but we have no record of any call being made concerning an incident at your club.'

'I don't understand, I heard him make the call,' Novak said, in desperation. 'Maybe he rang the homicide unit directly.'

'Sir, I can assure you that *no* call was made to any unit of the Zürich police concerning an incident at your club.'

Novak slumped back in his chair. What the hell was going on?

'Sir, are you still there?' Silence. 'Sir?'

'Yes, I'm still here,' Novak said, with a resigned sigh.

'If you'll give me the details of the incident I'll have them passed on to a patrol unit right away. They'll be with you shortly.'

Kessler was fully briefed about the double shooting at Straight Street after the military helicopter had touched down at Kloten Airport. A patrol car was waiting on the runway to take him, with John and Beth, to the club. The cobbled streets around it had already been cordoned off by the police, which allowed the patrol car to drive up to the front of the building. John threw open the back door the moment the patrol car came to a halt and tumbled out of the back seat. He was prevented from entering the club by a uniformed officer, who grabbed his arm as he tried to rush past him. Kessler produced his warrant card and gave the order to allow him through.

'Dad? Dad?' John shouted, as he ran towards the open door at the end of the foyer. He pulled up sharply when his father appeared in the doorway. For a moment they just stared at each other, then Novak dropped to his knees and John ran into his waiting arms. Novak held his son tightly to him, unable to control the tears that spilled freely down his cheeks. Tears of joy. Tears of anger. Tears of relief. Tears of gratitude. Then, sensing that someone was watching them, he looked up and saw Beth standing a short distance away from them. She smiled at him through her own tears. Kessler appeared beside her and acknowledged Novak with a cursory nod then entered the club, where a forensics team were already at work. He crossed to where the body lay, shrouded by a bloodstained sheet, and lifted back the edge to satisfy himself that it was Voskov.

'Ah, Kessler, I'm glad you could join us,' a voice said behind him.

He looked round to find the Chief of Police behind him. 'Sir, I didn't expect to see you here.'

'I wanted to let Mrs Grant know that the contract on her business partner's daughter has been lifted.'

'How did you find out, sir?' Kessler asked.

'I have my sources, Kessler. Let's just leave it at that. I assume that you have already been briefed on what happened here today?'

'Yes, sir. At the airport.'

'A few minutes ago the ambulance was found abandoned about a mile from here. Two empty sachets, containing traces of blood, were found in the back – she'd obviously secreted them under her clothes to make it appear that Jago had shot her after she killed Voskov. There was no sign of either of them, or of the bogus paramedics.'

'They can't have got far, sir,' Kessler said.

'Where they've gone doesn't concern us any more,' the Chief replied. 'I'll be making a statement to the press later this afternoon, saying that Amy Michaels was forced to kill Voskov in self-defence, and that she, in turn, was shot by Jago when she refused to surrender her weapon to him. She died on the way to hospital. That is the official version, which was sanctioned personally by the President a short time ago.'

'In other words, the Cabal has to be protected at all costs,' Kessler said.

'I don't like it any more than you do, Kessler, but I have my orders. And so do you. The case is officially closed. That's an end to it.'

'As you wish, sir.'

'You seem to be taking this remarkably well,' the Chief said, amazed at Kessler's apparent *sangfroid*.

'It's obviously a done deal. Nothing I say can change it now.' Kessler looked at his watch. 'If you'll excuse me, sir, I still have something to do. Something I believe I still *can* change.' He left the Chief staring bemusedly after him as he left the room and headed for the exit.

'Kessler?'

He stopped. Novak walked over to him. 'John's just told me what happened this morning. You risked your life to save him. I know I can never thank you enough for that.'

'I was just doing my job,' Kessler said, with a shrug. 'Any of the men there would have done the same, had they been in my position.'

'Maybe so, but you were the one who did – and that's what matters to me.' Novak extended a hand towards him. 'I guess I misjudged you, Kessler. I'm sorry.'

Kessler gripped his hand. 'I'm not so sure you did. Perhaps I misjudged myself.'

'I don't understand,' Novak said.

'I do, and that's all that matters to me.' Kessler looked across at John. 'You do realize that your son's still in shock? I don't think he's even begun to comprehend what happened this morning. But when he does, he's going to need counselling to help him come to terms with it. Give me a call at work later today. I can put you in touch with one of the country's top child psychiatrists. I've worked with her before.'

'I'll do that, thank you.'

'In the meantime, you're going to have to give him a lot of support. But, then, by the looks of it, he's already getting that.'

Novak followed Kessler's eyes. Beth was squatting beside John, holding his hand, talking softly to him. 'Yeah, I guess you're . . .' When he turned back, Kessler had gone.

He walked across to Beth and his son and put his hand lightly on John's head. 'I want a word with Beth. You go on through to the office. I won't be long.' He waited until the boy had left then leaned against the wall, arms folded across his chest. 'I haven't had a chance yet to thank you for taking care of him at the chalet. It means a lot to me.'

'We took care of each other,' Beth corrected him. 'He's a gem. You're very lucky.'

'Yeah, I know.'

'Kessler said that now the case is officially closed I'll be able to take Ian's body back to London some time within the next forty-eight hours.'

'Would you like me to fly back with you?' he asked softly.

'I'm not helpless,' she retorted indignantly.

'I know. It's just that . . . well, I've been through this before. It's a traumatic experience for anyone. You'll have your family to support you once you arrive back in England. But it's going to seem like a very long – and lonely – flight home. It helps to have a friendly face around at a time like that.'

'What about John?' she asked hesitantly.

'I'll take him with me. A change of scenery may well be just what he needs to help him start to come to terms with what happened today.'

Beth nodded. 'You might be right. You'll both be staying with me, of course.'

'We couldn't impose—'

'Impose, please,' she cut in quickly, 'because if you don't, my family most certainly will. They may mean well, but the one thing I don't need right now is to be smothered in sympathy. And that's exactly what they'll do. I'm going to need my own space away from them, and I know you'll give me that at the house. As you said, you've been through this before.'

'I guess I'd better ask John whether he's agreeable to all this,' Novak said with a wry smile.

'I guess you'd better.' She looped her hand under his arm and they walked off in the direction of his office.

*

'Stefan?' Bettina Lehmann exclaimed in surprise when she opened the front door. 'Manny's not here. He's being debriefed by his superiors at headquarters. He rang about an hour ago to say that he wouldn't be back until tonight at the earliest.'

'It's not Manny I came to see.'

Her hand tightened on the edge of the door and for a moment he thought she was going to slam it in his face. 'Marthe doesn't want to see you, and I don't blame her after the way you've treated her. You could have caused her to miscarry if that table had landed on her.'

'I didn't come here for a lecture, Bettina.' Kessler raised his hands in a placatory gesture. 'I'm sorry, I didn't mean to snap at you. I'm still pretty wound up after what happened this morning.'

'Manny said that you had been part of the operation, although he didn't go into details.'

'I need to see Marthe,' Kessler said, breaching the uncomfortable silence between them. 'Please.'

'You're not coming in, Stefan.'

'I can understand your anger. It's natural after the way I've been acting since Andreas died. But that's all in the past now. Marthe means more to me than anything else. She always has – I was just so wrapped up in my own self-pity that I lost sight of that. I want her back, Bettina. The very thought of losing her and our child . . .' He couldn't go on. Then he cleared his throat. 'I know I can't just wave a magic wand and hope that everything will get back to normal between us. It can't. It's going to take a lot of hard work to regain her trust. Having said that, I'm well aware that it may already be too late to salvage our marriage – and if it is, I'll only have myself to blame – but at least let me hear it from her. That's all I ask. Please.'

'Very well, but if she doesn't want to see you, you're to leave. Agreed?'

'Agreed.'

'Wait here, I'll go and find her.'

'No need,' Kessler said, when Marthe emerged from a doorway further down the hall. She was wearing a baggy white T-shirt and a pair of loose-fitting dungarees with her hair loose on her shoulders. No make-up, barefoot. She looked so beautiful to him.

'Marthe, do you want to speak to Stefan?' Bettina asked, standing her ground in case Kessler tried to push past her. Marthe nodded without taking her eyes off her husband.

'I'll leave you to it, then. I'll be in the kitchen if you need me.'

Kessler waited until Bettina had gone before he stepped into the hallway. 'You look . . . good.' He cursed himself for sounding like a nervous teenager on a first date. He had never felt so tongue-tied in his life. 'How's . . . the baby?'

'Our baby's fine,' she said softly, approaching him.

'You mean . . .' She placed a finger lightly against his lips. Then he slipped his arms around her waist and pulled her to him. He could taste the tears on her lips as he kissed her.

'You're late,' Jago said tersely, when she got out of her car at the prearranged meeting-place in a deserted warehouse on the outskirts of Zürich.

'We corpses have no sense of timing.' She grinned.

'So the authorities bought the story about Amy Michaels dying in the back of the ambulance on the way to hospital?'

'It's not as if they had much choice. Not with the kind of incriminating evidence the Cabal have got on them. I received word a short time ago that the police have officially closed the case. Getting out of the country won't be a problem either.'

'Maybe *now* you can tell me where the real Amy Michaels fitted into all this?'

'Amy Michaels worked for the Cabal – on a freelance basis.' She smiled at his startled expression. 'When the Cabal discovered that Ian Grant was threatening to go public with an exposé, she was brought in to monitor the situation and find out what he was being fed from inside the organization.'

'Why was she murdered?'

'So that I could take her place and get the disk from Grant. After all, he'd never actually seen her. Only it didn't work out that way, did it?'

'Did you kill Grant?'

'Uh-huh.' She nodded nonchalantly. 'Look, I don't want to be out here any longer than is absolutely necessary. So let's just get this over with, shall we?'

'Have you brought the money?' Jago said. 'I've kept to my side of the bargain and, in doing so, I've also destroyed any future I may have had with Interpol.'

'It's in the trunk of my car.'

Jago tried to open it but it wouldn't budge. 'You said it was . . .' He saw the SIG-Sauer automatic in her hand. A suppressor was attached to the barrel.

'You should know by now that Sammy Kahn rewards loyalty and punishes treachery. You were the one in collusion with Grant, weren't you?'

'*What?*'

'The Cabal's had you under suspicion for some time. That's why you were purposely fed certain disinformation, which has since been found on the disk you palmed off Voskov's body earlier today. I'd say that was pretty conclusive, wouldn't you? It also proves that Grant wasn't passing the information to you, but the other way round. You were going to expose the Cabal, and what better way than by using a respected human rights lawyer to do it for you? Voskov, Kilgarry and Racine were never suspects. They didn't have the necessary clearance codes to access that kind of sensitive information. But as their identities would have been on the disk, that made them expendable. The Cabal will recruit another three assassins to take their place. That won't be problem. And neither will you any more.'

Jago knew it would be pointless to deny his involvement with Grant. Everything she had said was true. 'I don't regret what I tried to do to bring down the Cabal,' he said, holding her gaze. 'I can't reconcile myself with what the organization's become in the last few years. I know that certain intelligence agencies are now using the Cabal as little more than a vigilante unit to do their dirty work for them. That's not what it was originally set up to achieve. I had to try to stop it before it spiralled out of control. I may not have succeeded, but at least I know that I've certainly damaged its reputation as an international strike force. Who knows? Maybe even terminally.'

'The condemned man's last words. How touching.' She shot him twice through the heart, then opened the driver's door and picked up the cellphone lying on the passenger seat. She called directory inquiries for the number of the Swissair reservations office at the airport, then dialled out. 'Hello,' she said, when her call was answered. 'I'd like to book a seat on the next available flight to New York. First class, of course.'

'One moment, please, while I check availability.' A short time later she was told, 'There's a flight leaving tonight at seven thirty for New York.'

'Perfect.'

'Let me take your details. Your name, please?'

'Samantha Kahn.'

Also by Alastair MacNeill

Double-Blind

The gamble? Outwitting a major drugs cartel.
The prize? Ten million dollars.
The forfeit? Your life.

Melissa Wade, DEA agent, is a legend among her colleagues in the Latin American Bureau.

Except she's dead, and her superior, Tom Kellerman, has only one option if he's ever going to bring down the deadly Salcido cartel. Melissa had been working on a carefully orchestrated plan to entrap James Doyle, the cartel's senior enforcer, but Melissa was essential to the plan if it was to have any chance of success …

The only answer to Kellerman's problem is Melissa's identical twin, Laura. A woman who can easily pass for Melissa in the short time he still needs to ensnare Doyle. But Laura is hiding a very dangerous secret from Kellerman.

The perfect sting is about to go down: question is, who can be trusted?

ISBN 0 575 60255 4

VISTA

Nom de Guerre

JEFF GULVIN

International terrorist Storm Crow – real name Ismael Boese – languishes in jail after the threat to explode a chemical bomb in London. He has received no mail, accepted no visitors until terrorism expert Dr Benjamin Dubin arranges to interview him. Boese abruptly curtails the meeting and smuggles out a message to his partner: 'We have been betrayed.' On his way to trial, in the bloodiest manner imaginable, the Storm Crow breaks free.

Leaving a new trail of death in his wake, Boese announces himself once again on the world stage. SO13 Detective Jack Swann follows him from the UK to the United States, where he teams up with FBI undercover agent Harrison.

Somehow, these two must try to second-guess Boese. Why is he leading them from Georgia to Nevada in an apparently motiveless murder spree? Swann and Harrison pursue him – but as they draw closer, a terrible realization dawns . . .

ISBN 0 75282 736 7

All Orion/Phoenix titles are available at your local bookshop or from the following address:

Littlehampton Book Services
Cash Sales Department L
14 Eldon Way, Lineside Industrial Estate
Littlehampton
West Sussex BN17 7HE

telephone 01903 721596, *facsimile* 01903 730914

Payment can either be made by credit card (Visa and Mastercard accepted) or by sending a cheque or postal order made payable to *Littlehampton Book Services*.
DO NOT SEND CASH·OR CURRENCY.

Please add the following to cover postage and packing

UK and BFPO:
£1.50 for the first book, and 50p for each additional book to a maximum of £3.50

Overseas and Eire:
£2.50 for the first book plus £1.00 for the second book and 50p for each additional book ordered

----

BLOCK CAPITALS PLEASE

name of cardholder ....   *delivery address*
....   *(if different from cardholder)*
address of cardholder ....
....
....
....
postcode ....   *postcode* ....

☐ I enclose my remittance for £...............................

☐ please debit my Mastercard/Visa (delete as appropriate)

card number ☐☐☐☐☐☐☐☐☐☐☐☐☐☐☐☐

expiry date ☐☐☐☐

signature ....

prices and availability are subject to change without notice